A Benbow & Wingate Mystery

MURDER OLÉ!

CORINNE HOLT SAWYER

farrago

This edition published in 2025 by Farrago,
an imprint of Duckworth Books Ltd
1 Golden Court, Richmond, TW9 1EU, United Kingdom

www.farragobooks.com

First published in the United States by Donald I. Fine, 1997

Copyright © Corinne Holt Sawyer, 1997

All rights reserved. No part of this publication may be reproduced, stored in a retrieval system, or transmitted, in any form or by any means, without the prior permission in writing of the publisher.

This book is a work of fiction. Names, characters, businesses, organizations, places and events other than those clearly in the public domain, are either the product of the author's imagination or are used fictitiously. Any resemblance to actual persons, living or dead, events or locales is entirely coincidental.

The authorised representative in the EEA is Easy Access System Europe, Mustamäe tee 50, 10621 Tallinn, Estonia.

Paperback ISBN: 9781788424936
e-ISBN: 9781788424943

Everyone's favourite unlikely female sleuths – praise for the Benbow and Wingate mysteries

'Sawyer's **humorous** yet sympathetic **look at retirement-home life and** her **lovable sleuths** keep the reader's interest' *Publishers Weekly*

'Sawyer **writes with wit**, and her characters are well drawn ... Entertaining' *The Post and Courier*

'Once again, Sawyer **writes with a knowing eye** of the foibles and frailties of retirement home characters ... She catches the ebb and flow of life with humor and poignancy' *The State*

'Fun, light-hearted, cleverly plotted' *Booklist*

'Sawyer's energetic pair of elderly nosey parkers, Angela Benbow and Caledonia Wingate, **will charm** their **fans all the way to the end**' *Publishers Weekly*

'There's no one better at this sort of gentle mystery, heavy on characterizations and light on chase scenes, than Corinne Holt Sawyer' *Anderson Independent-Mail*

'Sawyer writes with **wit and wisdom**, and her plotting is impeccable' *Drood Review of Mystery*

Have you read them all?
Treat yourself again to the first Benbow
and Wingate mysteries –

The J. Alfred Prufrock Murders
Angela Benbow and Caledonia Wingate take
to the investigative trail when one of their own
is found murdered on the beach

Murder in Gray and White
An unpleasant newcomer to Camden-sur-Mer
resort checks out sooner than she intended …

Murder by Owl Light
The murder of the gardener is a break
in routine for Angela Benbow and Caledonia
Wingate's retirement community

Turn to the end of this book
for a full list of the series.

Prologue

All Hallows' Eve, October 31

The horse-drawn cart jolted over the rough ground, led at a steady pace by a bored, silent youngster named Pablo, who wore jeans and a plaid shirt—no fancy uniformed attendants here. The occupants within the cart nodded in time to the bouncing of the wheels, through which every pebble, every rut transmitted its contours to the poorly sprung cart frame. There were whispers and giggles from the passengers as Pablo guided the cart into the narrow, sharply curved track formed by two lines of crude, heavy canvas curtains lashed to poles driven into the ground. The cloth walls muffled sounds from the outside and cut off exterior light so that the occupants bounced and rattled along in near silence and shadowed darkness. Here and there, the dark track opened out slightly and the curtains had been moved to form a three-sided stage. Pablo would stop the horse, lean down to a hidden switch beside the stage, and the scene would be illuminated suddenly by naked sixty-watt bulbs hanging overhead from bare wires. The lights flashed on, the lights flashed off, the lights flashed on again, and then off for the last time. The lights did not last long enough for the audience in the cart to see all the details, and the single bulbs overhead threw heavy shadows. Perhaps that was why the figures seemed so perfect, so real.

The first display took them all by surprise, and they were shocked into yelps, gasps, and exclamations of fright and disgust. The sudden light had revealed an Aztec priest holding high a stone knife in one hand, a bleeding human heart in the other; on the stone altar at his feet lay a young man, his chest and abdomen laid open, his eyes wide with terror and his mouth stretched in a grimace of agony. These were only dummies, mannequins as the audience quickly figured out, and not even an animated display— mere replicas of life frozen in a silent tableau of horror. There were sound effects — turned on by Pablo in the dark, after the lights went out for the last time—some sort of tape of screams and groans, but they were hardly needed to make the audience respond. It was a grisly little show. At last, Pablo turned the tape off, and tugged at the reins of the horse, and the cart jolted into movement again, around another heavily curtained curve toward the next little stage and whatever display it might present.

"I thought it said 'The Mummies of Guanajuato,' on the sign outside," Caledonia Wingate whispered. "This is more like 'Sacrifices of the Yucatan.'"

"Give me a little more room, will you, Caledonia?" Angela Benbow whispered. "Move over a ways! You're taking up the whole seat!" Angela was small, barely five feet tall, and though her age and the force of gravity had turned her into the approximate shape of a barrel, it was still a very *little* barrel, unlike the formidable size and shape of her best friend, Caledonia Wingate. "Maybe the mummies are in the next display," she murmured as she eased herself into the scant two extra inches Caledonia had moved.

But the flash of overhead light in the next display area showed them Joan of Arc, mouth distorted by silent cries of torment as plastic flames consumed clothing and flesh. The light switched off, then on again. There was strong movement in the cart that made it sway sideways almost as much as it had when they turned the last corner.

"Oh, dear! How awful!" Trinita Stainsbury said, wriggling with her distaste in the seat directly in front of Angela and Caledonia.

Her seatmate, Tom Brighton, soothed her quickly. "Just look the other way, dear lady."

"Yech," Mr. Grogan said from just ahead of them in the front-most seat of the cart. "Yech, I say! Disgusting! Move this cart along, burro! Move it!" Grogan had indulged himself in several tequila shooters at dinner; his Spanish might have been inadequate to order in the language of the country, but his English, even though he was already well-oiled, was quite sufficient for his well-trained waiter to understand and minister to his needs.

"Not a burro. A horse. Are you okay?" Grogan's seatmate said. "You hang on tight, man. You'll fall out." Jerry Grunke was a taciturn man, a new resident up at the posh retirement home Camden-sur-Mer, a man already known to his fellow residents as one who never spoke if he didn't have to. Thus he missed out on all the small talk, and apparently nobody had warned him to avoid Grogan, the retirement home's resident inebriate. Everyone else on the trip to Tijuana had managed to steer clear of Grogan and the unmistakable fumes of his booze throughout the chartered bus ride to Tijuana (during which Grogan had occupied the backseat by himself), and throughout the picnic on the way down, the afternoon of shopping, dinner at the hotel, and then finally the carnival. But when they were taking seats in the cart, Grunke had volunteered to sit next to Grogan instead of in the other empty seat at the back of the cart, next to another new resident, Miss Elmira Braintree.

"I expect she's too bossy for the silent Mr. Grunke," Angela had whispered to Caledonia as the cart entered the darkness of the canvas corridor. "She's got a pretty sharp tongue."

"Hush," Caledonia whispered back. "The Braintree is right behind you."

"She won't hear! Her hearing is as bad as everyone else's. Except mine. And yours," Angela added hastily. But she lowered her voice all the same.

Now, as Pablo switched the lights off once more, he treated them to a few screams from the Maid of Orleans on the tape player, then pulled at the horse so that the cart hitched forward again. Angela continued to talk in an undertone. "I hope Grogan doesn't throw up on Mr. Grunke. This cart pitches pretty heavily on the turns. I thought we were going to tip over at that last corner. And Grogan's had an awful lot to ... Oh dear! Now this is just what I was afraid the whole show might be ... It's typical Halloween stuff for kids!"

They had reached the next stage where the sudden light revealed a dangling skeleton swaying in the breeze created by a large electric fan—turned on by the faithful, Pablo. The bones were suspended by the neck in such a way as to suggest that their original owner had been hanged. "Well, it is All Hallows' Eve. Halloween. And they take religious holidays pretty seriously here in Mexico," Caledonia said. "I don't mean they don't have a fiesta, mind you, but they never forget 'the reason for the season.' And Mrs. Wilson told us they make a big thing of their 'Day of the Dead.' You have to expect *memento mori*."

The lights went off a second time, and the tape Pablo turned on was the realistic sound of someone gagging as he was strangled. "Good grief!" Caledonia sighed. "Maybe the skeleton's kid stuff, but that sound effect is a bit much, isn't it?"

On and on the cart rolled. A subsequent stage flashed them images of a pile of skulls with red stains all over them, and the tape gave them hollow groans and ghostly screams. Next, there was a graveyard scene, and they heard the clank of chains and wailing— presumably the wails of tortured spirits. Next, they were back to a scene of violence—the all-too-realistic depiction of a man being attacked and torn by wild dogs. After that, the cart stopped at the effigies of two knights in mortal combat, the one being impaled on his enemy's sword; then at a scene of two women struggling against being crushed by a giant serpent; and finally at a beheading by guillotine. The cart bumped and bounced along from one display to the next and Caledonia Wingate was surprised to find herself becoming hardened to the procession of blood and gore. What had been awful and shocking had quickly become boring. And she could even swear that the horse had begun to sigh deeply as each stop was reached.

"Listen," Caledonia hissed to her tiny friend Angela. "Listen to the poor horse. He's as tired of these displays as I am. And where are those mummies the sign advertised? I thought ... Oh good glory! Look!" The cart had stopped again in front of a larger-than-usual stage that had been sectioned into smaller units, individual display cases rather like a series of coffins standing on end. This time the lights stayed on, the audience apparently being invited to inspect the display in every detail. "Here they are!" Caledonia gasped. "What do you think of these!"

Angela seemed quite beyond words. So, apparently, was everyone else, for there were only muffled gasps from the others. Inside each display case was a figure dressed in ragged, rotting, clay-stained clothing suggestive of the previous century—full skirts and bonnets, frock coats and top hats. But these were not replicas of living people, nor even of the dying like those in the grotesque displays along the route to this point. This was the grand finale. These were replicas of corpses in varying stages of dessication—the mummies advertised on the banner out in front—a graveyard full of the dead who had been accidentally unearthed and were now on display in the small, provincial city of Guanajuato. It didn't matter that the figures in this Tijuana sideshow were merely copies of the real thing; these mummies, real or ersatz, were infinitely more horrible than the Halloween frights or the fanciful sadism in the other displays. The fingernails of each effigy were long and dirt-filled; the hair was clotted with clay. Most of the cavernous eyesockets were empty, though here and there a shrivelled eye survived. The cheeks were deeply sunken, the mouths were rounded and open, all the teeth more prominent than in life. Each of the dead appeared to be frozen in a permanent scream.

"This is terrible! Were these people buried alive?" Angela finally managed to say with a gasp.

"Not according to what I read," Caledonia said. "Well, maybe one or two, but the way I understand it, this is pretty much what we will all look like at some point."

"Oh, surely not!"

"Oh, surely yes! They say our hair and nails seem to grow as flesh dries and retracts, and our mouth opens wide as the lips withdraw from the teeth. As it happens, these people were gradually mummified by something in the water that seeped into their wooden coffins, but they were preserved not as they were buried, but gradually over some time while they were being pickled—so to speak."

Angela groaned. "You didn't have to say all that. I really don't want to know any details at all!"

Tom Brighton shivered hugely. "That's enough, Pablo. You can move on now. Giddyap, horse! Oh, please!" he pleaded, and his voice was tight in his throat. "I'm sorry, Mrs. Stainsbury," he went on apologetically, "but this one really bothers me!"

Trinita Stainsbury's own voice was strained as she responded. "All the same, I think I'd rather see this than the real thing, you know."

"Who on earth would want to go see the real thing, Trinita?" Angela snapped. "This is bad enough."

"Well, I'm told it's a big tourist attraction," Trinita said. "Our guide, Mrs. Wilson, told me that some people go all the way to Guanajuato just to see these ... these ... things."

"Well, one thing about this show—it's helped me make a big decision," Tom Brighton said, and his voice wobbled slightly through the darkness that had mercifully descended on them once more. "I'm going to be cremated. I hadn't really decided what to do about, you know, my leftovers. But now I know. I'm going to donate my organs for transplants, and then have the rest of me turned into nice, clean, unhorrifying ashes to help roses grow better. I think— Whoops! Hang on!"

The cart had started up again with a tug that snapped the necks of the occupants. "Everybody okay?" Brighton called out. "This horse surely doesn't have much regard for the comfort of the paying customers, does he? I say there, Pablo, watch it. I get whiplash easily. Mrs. Wingate? Mrs. Benbow? You all right? Mrs. Stainsbury? Miss Braintree? Everybody still got a head on their shoulders?"

There followed a rustling, a series of murmurs and whispered assurances, and even a laugh from Caledonia as the horse plodded along the last ten yards of the canvas lane, and the cart bounced and swayed its way out of the strait and narrow path and into the open carnival lot, into the lights and the gaiety of a Mexican fiesta. Pablo tied the horse to the hitching rail where it had begun its trip and sat down on a box that had been turned upside-down near the ticket booth, from which the proprietor of the attraction, Dante Ortiz, came rushing out, all smiles, to help his customers alight. Apparently, Pablo's duties did not include the gentlemanly niceties.

First the jovial Ortiz gave his hand to the tiny Angela; then he reached out to Caledonia. Grunke got himself down easily and offered an arm to a weak-kneed Grogan, who groaned as he straightened himself up. "My fanny's bruised," Grogan complained. "Hasn't that cart got any springs at all? I haven't had such a hard ride since the last time I rode my Flexible Flyer."

"Careful, Mr. Ortiz," Caledonia cautioned as she let him brace her weight while she stepped down. "Be careful! You got off easy helping Angela down. I weigh a ton, and you better not let go of me."

"Oopsy-daisy," Mr. Brighton said as he helped Trinita Stainsbury down from the bench they had shared. "You okay there? Good."

"Well, did you have a good time?" It was their tour guide, Maralyn Wilson, coming to the cart to greet them, her arms loaded with a variety of souvenirs. "Speaking for myself," the guide went on, holding up her treasures, "I had nothing but good luck! While you were gone, I managed to add a dish to everything else I've won." She juggled a large, purple teddy bear so she could hold up a butter dish of pink glass, complete with a cover. "Neat stuff, huh?" She grabbed again to keep from dropping a vacuously beaming kewpie doll. "Well, what do you want to do now? The dart game might be fun. I haven't done that yet. Anybody want to try their hand at darts with me? Whoops …" The kewpie doll seemed about to slide out of her arms again.

"Here," Mr. Brighton said, "let me help you. Let me take a couple of things. You can't juggle everything by yourself."

"Oh, thank you. I was sure something was going to fall. I've already dropped these things two or three times."

Laughing and talking at the same time, the group began to move away from the horse carts, several people trying to explain simultaneously the ride and the shows, with special emphasis on the horror of the mummies, Mrs. Wilson still juggling her treasures. But they didn't get far before the voice of Dante Ortiz, in obvious distress, cut through their happy chatter. "*Señoras*! *Señores*! Ladies! Gentlemen! Please! *Muerte*! *Su amiga* ... your friend. She ees ... *muerte*!"

They turned back toward the frantic voice, the widely gesturing arms. "I theenk she has fall asleep, you know? Een the dark, some peoples have ... *sueño,* you understand? So I think she has sleeped also. She sits still and her head is forward, you know? But then I touch her arm and she falls in the seat. And *los ojos* ... how you say ... ? The eyes. Yes. The eyes are open, you know?"

"Are you saying someone is dead?" Maralyn Wilson strode quickly back toward him. The others straggled behind. "I don't believe ... show me," Mrs. Wilson demanded.

The excited Ortiz pulled at her sleeve, dislodging her grip on her treasures, so that the purple teddy bear and a velvet pillow with gold embroidery spelling out "U.S. Navy" across it dropped to the rough ground. The guide left them in the dust where they had fallen. In the last seat, now lying down on her side, was Miss Braintree. And as subsequent examination proved, Mr. Ortiz was quite right. Miss Braintree was distinctly *muerte*. Every bit as dead as the replicas of "The Mummies of Guanajuato."

Chapter I

Earlier, through the month of September

It all began, as Caledonia often said later, with tongue depressors. She and several of her fellow residents had come into the community room across the side street from the main building of their retirement home, Camden-sur-Mer, to find a long table stacked with tongue depressors—and their activities director, the enthusiastic but slightly muddled Carolyn Roberts, waiting impatiently for her charges to arrive for the morning's project. Caledonia's heart sank.

Over the years, the problem had not been with the planned activities themselves. The problem had been their inevitable and wearying repetition. Routine can be very useful in a retirement home, especially for those whose memory is starting to fail. But years of the same activities week in and week out had become tedious to many of the retirees; it was aerobics three mornings a week, bingo every Tuesday night, a tea in the lobby every Wednesday afternoon, a film every Monday and Friday, and on Thursdays, live entertainment. A tiresome cycle, especially when the movie was their third showing of Clark Gable and Spencer Tracy in *Boom Town,* and the live entertainment was "Tick and Tock, Songs and Snappy Patter"—a pair of former vaudevillians, themselves residents of a retirement home down in San Diego, who had performed at Camden-sur-Mer so often the audience could recite the punch lines to all their jokes and sing their songs right along with them. Well, all but Mr. Grogan (who was inevitably tipsy by mid-afternoon when the performers arrived) and Mrs. Slaybough (who could scarcely remember her own name, let alone the jokes of Tick and Tock).

The truth was Carolyn Roberts was just plain run out of new ideas, and in response to the growing complaints from the residents, she tried a whole new tack borrowed from people who seemed to know less than nothing about the elderly. For instance, the first thing Carolyn had tried to interest residents in was a project she called "Plant a Flower and Watch It Grow." She had Camden-sur-Mer's professional gardeners clear a space of well-tilled earth and had furnished seeds to the residents who chose to join her "Plant and Watch" group. The retirees listened with puzzled disbelief to her directions, then obediently planted two seeds each in the cleared row. A wooden stake bearing the name of each planter was driven into the ground beside his own seeds, and at the same time each day, the group met to weed and water their one or two tiny plants—sturdy little marigolds that would put up with neglect or overattention, whichever happened their way.

Within a week the majority of the group had dropped out of the project. After all, most of them had nurtured gardens of their own over the years, or had numerous house plants in their apartments even now. There was no novelty for them in a newborn marigold. But if Carolyn noticed the growing lack of enthusiasm among her charges, it didn't show in her own manner. "This one is yours, Mrs. Stainsbury. My, but it's coming on nicely ... already got four leaves!" she would cry in encouragement. "Oh-oh-oh ... don't overwater yours, Mrs. Armstrong ..." By the time the little marigolds had got big enough to be interesting, the group had dwindled, despite Carolyn's unflagging efforts, to Mr. Brighton (who felt sorry for "the Roberts girl," as he called her) and Mr. Grogan, who couldn't think of any reason *not* to wobble his hungover way into the garden on the morning weed-and-water tour. So the project was called off and the gardeners, told to pull out the plants and reclaim the strip of earth, consulted with each other in their native Spanish and then transplanted the tiny flowers to the front garden as part of Camden-sur-Mer's lovely multicolored display.

"The woman must think we're in kindergarten or something," Caledonia complained, when she and her friends were in the lobby waiting for lunch to be served. Pre-mealtimes at Camden-sur-Mer were happy social occasions when residents gathered to catch up on news, exchange gossip, arrange bridge dates, and even swap political opinions, philosophic observations, or fashion notes. Today the discussion had turned to the gardening project, thanks mainly to Caledonia's monumental disgust.

"I believe," Emma Grant said in a tolerant voice, "that our activities director took a special class from the education department over at Camelot Junior College. Some course in planning and directing recreation activities, she said. Something like that."

"It must have been recreation for grade school kids," Angela Benbow complained. "Youngsters who have never seen a seed germinate and a plant grow. But we have."

"I used to grow prize hollyhocks on one side of my house," Tootsie Armstrong said. "People came for miles to see my ruby-reds, and to beg for seeds."

"We did mostly vegetables," Mary Moffet chimed in. "Asparagus was really hard to grow. But the pepper plants always did well. I remember one year ..."

Carolyn Roberts's next project was one she called "The Camden Olympics." She set up a series of tables and stands around the perimeter of the community room and announced her new activity with big signs on the bulletin boards. When the residents showed up at the appointed hour, they found a series of homemade games of skill that were clearly not designed for them. Most of the games hardly tested their abilities—sailing paper airplanes toward a finish line marked with twine, tossing a bean bag at a target set up inside a hula hoop, flipping poker chips at prizes one could win if the chip should stick on the objects (a soap dish, a packet of purse-sized Kleenex, a tiny syrup pitcher, or a roll of Lifesavers). And some of the games ignored the physical limitations of the elderly. For instance there was a "clothes-pin drop" that required each person to kneel on a pair of chairs a few inches apart, and with forearms braced on the chairs' backs, try to drop a clothes-pin into the neck of a glass bottle set on the floor. Almost none of the retirees could balance on the two chairs, and some could not even kneel long enough to sight toward the bottle. The Camden Olympics lasted only one session. And then came the tongue depressors.

"I don't even want to see what an activity called 'Wood You Glue With Me?' consists of," Angela said tartly, when a new notice appeared on the bulletin boards.

"But she tries so hard," the kindly Mr. Brighton said. "I for one will go over to the community room at ten tomorrow to see what this project is all about."

"Now, Tom," Caledonia said, "you know you've been as annoyed as the rest of us with these juvenile activities. I'd rather go back to the boring round of teas and movies and sewing bees."

Brighton grinned. "I confess I've been thinking longingly of sitting through an hour of the songs and snappy patter of Tick and Tock again. But I want to be supportive. I'll say it again ... she tries so hard!"

A fair number did show up at ten a.m. to find a long table set up in the middle of the community room, with folding chairs placed around the table, and small mountains of sticks dumped here and there down its length. "I'm so glad you've all come," Carolyn Roberts twittered after they had straggled in. "We're going to make gifts for each other with these," she said, raising a tongue depressor high for all to see.

"Gifts!" Angela said sharply. "What kind of gift? A bookmark? A plant stake?"

"No-no-no." Carolyn laughed merrily. "I've got glue here." She hoisted the cardboard box she'd been carrying and tipped it slightly, so everyone could see the tubes of craft glue piled inside. "And we're going to fashion items that ... Well, for instance ..." She reached into the box, shoved aside the tubes of glue, and brought out a gilded picture frame made of sticks glued together and covered with gold paint. "And here ..." She pulled out another object.

"Looks like a tiny little ladder," Mr. Grogan said blearily, trying to focus his bloodshot eyes.

"Exactly," Carolyn chirped delightedly. "A ladder for a parakeet.

I understand a number of you have caged birds. Wouldn't this be a darling little gift? Or how about this?" She held up another object.

"A box?" Emma Grant said wonderingly. "A box made of sticks?"

"Yes, indeed." Carolyn waved it aloft. "A holder for memo pads. For someone's desk. Oh, you'll think of a dozen things to make. A holder for a Kleenex box. A holder for an open recipe book. A holder for a roll of stamps, perhaps, though you'd have to cut the sticks down in length, of course. Just use your imagination!"

Gingerly, a few of the residents seated themselves around the table and reached hesitantly for some of the tongue depressors. "Here's your tube of glue," Carolyn Roberts beamed, passing out the supplies. "And I'll put a clipper here, if anyone needs to trim their sticks for length. Now, how about you two?" She turned to Angela Benbow and Caledonia Wingate, who stood side-by-side just inside the door, wearing identically skeptical expressions and making no move to join the others.

"Tongue depressors?" Caledonia said grumpily. "Tongue depressors? I don't think I know anybody who'd want them as a gift even for their original purpose, let alone made into some artsy-craftsy—"

"Me, too," Angela said quickly. No point in letting Caledonia take off on the subject of crafts. She always complained about them, and she always said the very same things. So Angela moved quickly back on track to her point. "Carolyn, we're going to have to have a little talk about this. Would you come to the meeting of the Residents' Council next week? We really need to discuss the whole concept behind our activities programs!"

Angela Benbow and Caledonia Wingate were much alike despite their disparate size and demeanor. Angela, just under five feet tall, was a bundle of energy; she rose early every morning, anxious to meet the new day, eager for whatever adventure might wait for her.

Caledonia, nearly six feet tall and monumental in size, slept late, moved slowly, ponderously, and seemed altogether more relaxed than the sprightly Angela, but in her own way she was every bit as lively and alive.

Both were widows, and both had been married to admirals in the Navy. In fact, meeting Caledonia was the reason Angela first considered giving up a measure of her ferociously guarded independence to enter the communal-living situation of a retirement home. She met Caledonia at a time when Angela was lonely and discontent—feeling vulnerable; it didn't take her long to realize that Caledonia was a kindred spirit with an amazingly similar background to her own. "My kind of person," Angela had conceded to herself with surprise. "And if she thinks this retirement place is so wonderful, perhaps I should consider ..." She had moved into Camden-sur-Mer a prickly, suspicious, solitary person; she had adapted, mellowed, and under the influence of her friend Caledonia, she had become—much to her own surprise—popular and accepted by the other residents, in fact something of a leader.

Now Angela and Caledonia planned to find a way to avoid any more of Carolyn Roberts's unsuitable projects, while encouraging the activities director to continue her programs and entertainments and teas, many of which were, as they readily admitted, more enjoyable than not. "After all," Caledonia said reasonably, "if we don't take part in the activities and we don't attend the programs, they'll stop having them. Our beloved administrator"—her voice dripped with sarcasm—"would love to have an excuse to cut out Carolyn's job and save a bit of money."

"Would Torgeson really fire Carolyn?" Angela said. She might be scornful of Tick and Tock, she might refuse to touch a tongue depressor, but the possibility that her displeasure might actually mean their activities director's job genuinely alarmed her.

So the two women were on hand at the next meeting of the Residents' Council, and they listened in silence to Carolyn Roberts's protestations, "But they said in the class ... you know, the class I took in recreation direction ... over at Camelot College. Our instructor said that old people like you ... I mean, retirees like you ... would love these things."

"I get so tired of people treating us like we're in our second childhood," Caledonia rumbled. She intended to speak only to Angela, seated beside her, but her voice carried through the whole room, and Carolyn Roberts hesitated, then directed her explanations straight at Caledonia.

"My instructor told us," she insisted, "that the elderly love returning to the simple things they did as children. So I thought ... I mean, they said—"

"Okay, listen up." Caledonia held up a huge hand, and Carolyn Roberts stopped her burbling protests. "Simple things—a picnic, a fair, a day at the beach—maybe. Old movies, big band music — nostalgia—yes. But silly games that require us to take awkward positions—forget it. And crafts projects? Well, I guess I've told everybody several times how I feel about crafts."

Trinita Stainsbury spoke up. "Well, I for one adored making those cute little picture frames from those sticks."

"She would," Angela muttered. "Look at her! She's carrying a purple plastic purse and matching plastic shoes to go with her lavender suit. That ought to show you what her taste is like." Trinita was far from her favorite. But she still muttered her comment, making certain the woman could not hear the uncharitable remark.

"I dare say," Trinita went on stiffly, "that more people agree with me than with you, Caledonia. Everybody knows you hate things like macrame wall hangings and crocheted tea cozies."

"Well, why not take a vote?" Caledonia said. "How many really enjoyed the gardening project?" Two hands went up—the kindly Mr. Brighton and the mildly sozzled Mr. Grogan. "And how many loved throwing beanbags and sailing paper airplanes?" Again, Mr. Grogan raised his hand, a hazy smile on his face that suggested perhaps he wasn't quite sure what he was voting for. Nobody else stirred. "And how many really loved gluing sticks together to make picture frames and tissue holders?" Trinita's hand shot up, Mr. Grogan's stayed waving in the air, and that was it.

Carolyn Roberts looked crushed. "I had no idea," she said mournfully. "Why didn't you say something?"

"Nobody wants to hurt your feelings, Carolyn. But there's a limit, and we're certainly saying something now," Angela answered her. "You've got to start treating us like adults with some sense, if you really want to give us things to do that we'll enjoy."

"How about a computer class?" Tom Brighton suggested. "I know some of you don't have your own computers like I do, but I bet we could rent some."

"A computer class?" Carolyn Roberts was stunned. Obviously she had never even considered that computers might interest her charges. Computers, after all, were a big step up from craft glue and gold paint.

"How about a tax expert to talk to us about exemptions and estate planning?" Emma Grant said. "It's not too early to think about things like that."

"How about inviting a financial advisor type to talk about investments?" Tootsie Armstrong said. "Somebody phoned me the other day offering a mining stock, and—"

"You didn't buy any, did you?" Caledonia interrupted with alarm. "You mustn't buy things like that over the phone."

"Of course not, Caledonia," Tootsie assured her. "I may get confused between puts and calls, but I'm not a complete fool. All the same, an expert would have to start at a pretty elementary level for people like me. But he could work his way up to more complex subjects for those who're ready for them."

"Get a doctor in," Elmira Braintree volunteered briskly. "There's all kinds of new information about things like building up one's immunity. And about possible carcinogens. I'd like to hear about things like that."

"Or how about Spanish lessons?" Angela said suddenly. "I've always wanted to learn, and do you know there are stores you can go into in San Diego where *only* Spanish is spoken?"

"And how many of us can actually talk to the gardeners here?" Mr. Brighton said, nodding his approval of the suggestion. "I feel like such a fool when I have to limit my conversation to 'Hello, Juan,' and 'Nice day, Carlos.' Spanish lessons! What a good idea."

"Why do you want to talk to the gardeners?" Trinita Stainsbury said in bewilderment.

"Well, why not? And some of the maids here talk Spanish, too, at least among themselves. Wouldn't it be fun"—Mary Moffet was becoming quite excited, bouncing up and down in her chair—"to surprise Luisa or Carmen by telling them in Spanish where you want them to dust?"

"Great idea," Caledonia said, her interest in the suggestion making her forget to modulate her tones, her enthusiasm registering in a thunderous roar. "I'm not sure I can learn, at my age, but I'm willing to give it a try. How about it, Carolyn? Spanish lessons. What do you say?"

And thus it was that a Spanish teacher from Camelot College was hired (at a very basic fee, of course, the absolute minimum being all that Camden-sur-Mer's penny-pinching administration would offer) to come in twice a week and conduct classes in conversational Spanish. A large number of residents started the class, and most stuck with it, even if they were obviously not linguists.

To her own annoyance, Angela Benbow proved to be one of the least able students. Despite the tutoring of the patient teacher, despite the language tapes Angela bought, despite hours of study in the privacy of her own apartment, Angela somehow couldn't get the pronunciations, the accent, the rhythms of the language. Vocabulary escaped her, verb declensions eluded her, and noun genders were a continuing mystery.

"Como estar in-stead?" she would say.

Then she would turn on the tape and listen to the smooth voice saying, *"¿Cómo está usted?* How are you? *¿Cómo está usted?* Repeat it, please. *¿Cómo está* ..."

And Angela would try again. *"Como ested you-stah?* No, that's not right. Let me listen to the tape again."

Three weeks into the course, Angela was ready to give up. "I swear, I just don't hear it right somehow. Or if I do, I can't seem to copy it when I say it. And it's so hard to remember."

"What you need," Caledonia said lazily, holding up a tiny glass of pre-dinner sherry, "what you need is to go down to Mexico and hear the language all around you. I bet you'd get the hang of it much better. Want a little refill in your glass?"

The two friends were in Caledonia's cottage apartment. The main U-shaped building of Camden-sur-Mer and its gardens running down toward the sea had been outgrown within the first few years after the retirement home opened for business. A refurbished luxury hotel, Camden-sur-Mer offered studio and two-room apartments to its residents, along with three excellent meals a day in the common dining room, maid service, linens, utilities, and built-in activities. Residents had no worries about security, no worries about household repairs. Medical help was readily at hand, church services right in the building, a hairdresser, barber, and chiropodist took appointments weekly on the premises. It was the ideal situation for a person growing older without (for whatever reason) a family to live with. And with its lovely setting in "The Golden Crescent" just thirty-five miles north of San Diego, where the temperature never varied much from seventy degrees, winter and summer, Camden-sur-Mer was soon full. The management then increased the number of available apartments by building two rows of cottages (each containing three or four apartments), each line of little bungalows extending one arm of the main building and facing inward toward the well-maintained gardens. Angela's apartment was in the main building, Caledonia's in the newer cottages, and they often debated over who had the best situation—a debate that never ended and was neither won nor lost. Almost every late afternoon, the two friends met at Caledonia's place for a ritual thimbleful of sherry and to exchange news and views.

On this particular evening, looking out Caledonia's windows at late September's roses and sipping a tiny glass of amontillado, Angela was in despair. She had practiced her Spanish all afternoon with very little apparent improvement. Even to her own tin ear, her rendition of the useful phrases in Spanish —"Hello, how are you? What is your name? My name is Angela. How much does that cost? Is there a telephone here? Where is the bank?"—sounded like an Inuit trying to speak Ukrainian.

"I don't understand it," she mourned. "I'm usually so good at things!"

"That's because you only do things you already do well, Angela. How long since you've tried to learn something completely new? Give yourself a chance. And like I say," Caledonia soothed her, "what you need is to spend time around native Spanish speakers. Just listen. Feel it. Let it wash over you and surround you. You'll gradually find yourself understanding without trying."

"But I don't want just to understand what people are saying. I want to be able to say something back."

"Of course you do, girl. And you will, once you're thoroughly steeped in the sound and feel of it. I think we should ask Carolyn Roberts about planning a little trip."

And thus it was that Angela and Caledonia began to promote the idea of a trip to Mexico. "Not just for one afternoon, mind you," Caledonia added. "We need to go down at least overnight, and preferably for a couple of days."

"Well," Carolyn had said cautiously, "it's not out of the question, but it would cost each of you, because I don't think Mr. Torgeson would be willing to pay."

Olav Torgeson, the administrator who was charged both with caring for his residents and turning a small but steady profit for Camden-sur-Mer's owners, would have died before trying to find the money for a day trip to Mexico, let alone for an overnight stay. But he had no objections whatsoever to the residents making their own arrangements. After all, they had paid for their meals, although their food need not be prepared and served for those days they'd be gone, and as he saw it, that would provide a modest profit for the days they would be away. So though, as Carolyn Roberts had anticipated, he would not pay for the trip, Torgeson enthusiastically endorsed the idea and promised to help out in any way he could that didn't involve money. He wasn't willing actually to do anything, of course, but he never minded talking. So he got on the phone, and later that week he announced that he'd found the ideal arrangement for the group, and if they'd meet together in the chapel-cum-theatre just off the lobby on the main floor at 2:00 P.M. on Tuesday, they'd hear the proposal.

Eighteen residents gathered in the small auditorium at two and Olav Torgeson, beaming, introduced them to a slim, blonde woman who carried two briefcases brimming with papers. "This," he said, "is Maralyn Wilson. She has a small travel agency here in Camden, and she conducts tours to Mexico. She's more or less between engagements right now, so she has said she'll consider arranging a trip for a group from Camden-sur-Mer. I'll just turn the floor over to her." He stepped aside to take a seat among the residents.

The blonde woman was modestly attractive, wearing a smart business suit, and perfect make-up. She was probably in her late thirties, though with women in Southern California, where there were almost as many plastic surgeons as there were orange groves, it was often hard to pinpoint anyone's age. Perhaps she was even in her late forties, "And I certainly hope she is," Angela whispered to Caledonia. "I'm not sure I trust people who are too young. They may think up things that involve tongue depressors and bean bags!"

"I may look young to you," Maralyn Wilson began, as though she had read Angela's mind, "but I want to assure you I'm an experienced travel agent and guide. I have been arranging trips into Mexico now for ... well, it must be three years this month, ever since my fourth divorce left me without any ready cash and I had to find a way to support myself." She laughed lightly.

"I tried acting—like every blonde in Southern California does, I guess. But I couldn't get a break in the movies, and that last husband of mine was the meanest of them all about giving me a settlement. So I tried the travel business, and I've done pretty well. I mean, I drive a Beamer—700 series—and that's doggoned good going, isn't it? And if I want a diamond ring these days, I buy it for myself." She beamed at them and waved her hand—on which they could see the flash of blue-white stones—while she rattled on, marking time as she sorted through one of her briefcases and laid sheaves of papers out on the table.

She seemed to be quite unaware of the ripple that had passed through her audience at the mention of four divorces and her financial successes. It wasn't that her audience disapproved of divorce, exactly, but they had all grown up in an era when one didn't talk quite so openly about a broken marriage and an ex-husband, let alone several ex-husbands. And when these people were learning their manners, talking about how much money one made was considered to be every bit as vulgar as spitting on the sidewalk. More than one of her listeners shifted uncomfortably in their chairs.

"Here's the trip I'd recommend," Maralyn Wilson went on, raising high a pack of brightly colored brochures, still completely unconscious of her audience's reaction to her personal revelations. "I suggest flying to Mexico City and starting the Colonial Circle Tour, after a day or two to see the Pyramids of the Sun and Moon and the Ballet Folklorico. There are some wonderful Diego Rivera murals in the government buildings on the Xocolo and perhaps we could take in the museum in Chapultupec Palace. Then we'll strike out to the north in a couple of vans. We'll start at Queretero and the gem cutters. You might want to buy some of the beautiful opals for yourselves. And it's very historic. It's where the Emperor Maximilian was executed. From there we'll go to San Miguel Aliende, a charming town with a marvelous aqueduct, still intact. An architectural marvel, and—"

"Excuse me." Tom Brighton waved his hand in the air like a child in grade school trying to attract the teacher's attention. "Excuse me, Miss ... uh, Mrs. ..."

"Mrs. Wilson. That was my last married name. I've never gone back to Schultz, the name I was born with. Can you blame me? There aren't many movie stars named Schultz, and I was trying to be an actress. So every time I got married, I kept the new name, even after I got rid of the husband who gave it to me. But that's all beside the point, isn't it? You wanted to ask a question, sir?"

"Yes, Mrs. uh ... Wilson. How long is this circular tour going to take? It sounds as though you intend for us to spend at least two or three days in Mexico City to start with, and then travel through ... how many more towns? How many days?"

"Well, the Colonial Circle Tour usually takes only five days. But I was thinking you could fill the rest of two weeks by flying from Mexico City over to Oaxaca. The ruins of Monte Alban are fabulous. And then, to get back to your question, we'd fly home after—"

"Two weeks!" Miss Braintree gasped. "Two weeks! I couldn't go on a two-week trip! I have enough trouble when I visit my niece in San Francisco for a long weekend! Packing is a nightmare! My medicines and diet supplements and vitamin pills take up one suitcase; my hair dryer and rollers take up another. I don't want more than three bags, so I cram my clothes into another case, but I barely have room for three days' worth in a single case. Now how on earth could I pack for two weeks in a strange country?"

"Much too long," Caledonia rumbled. She didn't much care for this new resident. Elmira Braintree had an opinion on everything and never minded stating her position. For a new resident, who didn't yet know whose toes she might be treading on, such assertiveness was unusual and not at all attractive. All the same, honesty compelled Caledonia to admit that she agreed, even when it was with someone she didn't care for. "Miss Braintree's right. But it's not because of luggage. That would be silly."

"Caledonia!" Angela said. "It's not silly at all." Angela wasn't any fonder of their new resident than Caledonia was, but Miss Braintree's point had touched a nerve with her. "I was already wondering how on earth I'd pack for the trip. I mean, I'd need a few nice dresses for when we dine out or go to the theatre in Mexico City. I'd need slacks for traveling in those vans. I'd need—"

Caledonia waved a hand for silence. "I'll say it again, it's not the luggage. It's our stamina. Or rather, our lack of stamina. Mrs. Wilson, look at us! At our age, we can't put up with all-day drives. We'd need too many bathroom stops, for one thing. And arthritic joints stiffen up if one sits still for too long, so there'd have to be stops for us to stretch and walk a few steps. What would be a five-day trip for you would probably take us seven or eight days! And as for being away from home for two full weeks, well, I daresay most of us are horrified at the prospect of disrupting our routines for that long. I know I am. Frankly, I think that an overnight, or maybe two, three days at the longest is what most of us had in mind. Isn't that right?" She looked around at the others, and was gratified to see most of them nodding (though Grogan's nod suggested that he was falling asleep in his chair, rather than that he agreed with Caledonia's assessment).

"She's right," Trinita Stainsbury said. "That should be plenty of time to get in some good shopping."

"And listen to the language spoken," Angela said.

"And see the people and maybe learn a little something about their culture. Maybe see one or two tourist attractions," Mr. Brighton said.

"And as for flying, well, we could never fly anywhere," one of the Jackson twins ventured, though whether it was Donna Lee or Dora Dee (or was that Donna Dee and Dora Lee?) nobody could ever tell. "No airplanes for us. We thought we'd be riding in a bus."

"Not all the way to Mexico City," Maralyn Wilson said unhappily. "Oh, dear. I'm not sure this will work out at all. Look, I'll level with you. The fee you pay me as your guide wouldn't keep me in soda crackers, let alone paying my rent. Most of my income from these trips comes from the percentage the airlines and hotels give me. If you're only going to stay overnight, it hardly pays me enough to bother with. And there's no way you could see the Colonial Circle or—"

"Who cares about the Colonial Circle?" Mr. Grogan mumbled. "Let's just go to Tijuana. They got margaritas by the gallon ... they got bullfights ... they got good shopping ..."

"Yes, I think that would be the way to go," Angela said. "Just a night or two away from home."

"But my commissions—"

"Mrs. Wilson," Tom Brighton said, ever the practical man, "how would it be if you booked us on three short trips of a couple of days each? Wouldn't that add up to the same amount of profit for you as the one long trip? And wouldn't a charter bus company pay you a commission, just as the airlines would have? Frankly, I'm in agreement with the Jacksons; I mean, flying is getting less and less comfortable, and more and more dangerous every year."

"Well ..." Maralyn Wilson said doubtfully. "I'll certainly look into it. A trip of a day or two to Tijuana, you say?"

"Sure," Grogan mumbled. "Why not? And then maybe ..." His voice dropped even lower to a mere mutter. "Then maybe to Ensenada." The others waited for him to go on, but Grogan had finished with his suggestions. He had actually fallen sound asleep in the middle of his own little speech, his chin on his chest, his hands relaxed and open in his lap, a soft snore whispering from his nose.

"Well, I could try to make the arrangements. I'll have to see," Mrs. Wilson said uncertainly. "I've never done day trips, but if you'd all sign up for—say three trips, one after the other—"

"With time in between to rest up, of course," Caledonia said quickly.

"Well, maybe," Mrs. Wilson said, obviously thinking quickly while she was talking, "it could be worth my time. And yours, of course. I mean, if you really do want to get a feel for the language—and I understand that's one of your goals—you do need more than just one overnight. I'll have to let you know."

That was Tuesday. On Thursday, there was another notice on the bulletin board summoning the same group to meet once more in the auditorium at two. Maralyn Wilson was there again, and she plunged right in.

"I think I've worked it out," she said. "It took some doing, and you probably won't go for it because it costs a lot. But I can make arrangements for us to go to Tijuana for two days on the 31st of October, to Ensenada on November 11th, and again two weeks after that to Tijuana again. Twice to Tijuana and once to Ensenada, for a total of seven days in three trips. I can get us a bus that will seat as many as twenty, if you want more people along. And we can break the drive as often as you need to."

"I suggest," Carolyn Roberts said officiously from her place in the front row, "I suggest we plan a picnic lunch for that first day." She wasn't going along, and the details of the trip really had nothing to do with her, but she was conditioned to make arrangements for other people. "You could stop at Sea World. There are nice gardens for you to sit in while you eat. People could stretch their legs, and you could see a few things at the park before you drove on. Like maybe the dolphin show."

"A potty stop!" Mr. Grogan called out cheerfully. He was, unfortunately, wide awake for this meeting. "All out to use the johns!"

"Oh, do let's stop at the petting pool!" one of the Jacksons said. "I love the slick feel of those dolphins. And that baby whale was so cute the time we went there. You know, I do believe they love having us scritch them."

"Nonsense," Caledonia said. "What they love is you feeding them those little dead fish you buy from the stand next to the lagoon."

"We're off the topic here." Mrs. Wilson tried to rein in her charges and head them toward the point of the meeting. "The cost is going to be pretty high, especially if we throw in stops like Sea World. Maybe you'll want to think about it. I've figured the cost would be more than $1,000 each, I'm afraid, including three separate bus charters, the driver's salary, and meals and hotels and all."

"Sounds reasonable to me," Angela said. "What about you, Cal?"

"Sure. If we're going to do it, let's do it right. You agree, Tom?" One by one, some with more thought than others, the fifteen agreed. They could and would pay the fee, they could and would take the three short trips. They left the auditorium laughing and chattering with anticipation, even though the first of the trips was some three weeks in the future.

"Frankly," Mrs. Wilson said to Carolyn Roberts and Olav Torgeson as the audience moved away, "I'm a little surprised. I thought the fee was a bit steep for old folks."

Torgeson smirked. "A common misapprehension," he said. "Being old and living in 'a home' equates—to those who don't know better—to being poverty stricken and living at 'the poor farm.' I blame all those Little Rascals comedies people saw years ago, where the elderly were consigned to the care of the county in circumstances that would have daunted Little Orphan Annie. Not all the elderly live in bare, unheated rooms and eat dog food, you know."

"I should say not!" Carolyn Roberts agreed, thinking of the elegant cuisine at Camden-sur-Mer. "These people may be frugal, trying to stretch their resources to last out their lifetimes. But they aren't poor."

"Obviously not," Maralyn Wilson said with some satisfaction. "You know, this may not turn out to be such a bad gig for me after all!"

Chapter 2

Morning, October 31

It had really taken some doing to get the trip underway. To begin with, there were several dropouts, defections for perfectly legitimate reasons. First Emma Grant announced that her hearing aid would have to be taken to the shop for needed repairs ("And what's the use of going down to learn the language when you can't even hear it?" Emma said. "Sorry, but I'll have to stay here. You have fun for me."). Then there was a gall bladder attack that took Janice Felton off the list. Mary Moffet was the next to be scratched, after her niece from Cleveland announced she was coming for a visit. And last, the Winslows were involved in a minor automobile accident that resulted in a twisted knee for him and a black eye for her ("I can't travel looking like this," Mrs. Winslow insisted. "I'm really sorry.").

Four days before they were scheduled to leave, Maralyn Wilson called another meeting of the remaining thirteen would-be travelers. "I'm afraid it's all off. I just won't make a profit on so few people, what with renting the van and hiring the driver—I've got a young fellow named Tony Hanlon, who's taking a semester off from UCLA. He's driven for me before, he speaks pretty fair Spanish, and he knows the whole routine. So he costs more than just any old driver might, but he's worth it. And, of course, I have to pay for the hotel and meals and handle all the tipping. Well, the point is, as my second husband, the one who lived in Las Vegas, used to say, if you can't turn a profit, the thing isn't worth doing at all. He was a mercenary son-of-a-gun, and, of course, he was talking about his own work, gambling. But it applies to this trip too, I'm afraid. I can't work for nothing, and—"

"Oh, please!" Angela pleaded. "We've all been looking forward to the trip so very much! Couldn't you just charge us more? I mean, if each of us paid just a little bit extra, wouldn't that make up the difference?"

Maralyn Wilson worked for a while with a paper and pencil and finally came up with a figure. There was some discussion, of course (and two more defections by people who couldn't afford the new fee), but eventually eleven residents agreed to the increased cost. Checks were written and Maralyn Wilson, all smiles again, warned them to be ready to leave Camden-sur-Mer on the 31st at precisely nine-thirty in the morning. She figured they would need an hour to get to Sea World and claim a picnic spot, another hour to see some of the displays and at least one of the shows, and an hour to eat the picnic. Then they would be underway again, by twelve-thirty—bound for Tijuana. And she left happy, apparently convinced that nothing more could go wrong.

Wrong.

To begin with, at nine-thirty on the appointed morning, Caledonia was in a foul mood. She hated getting up early, and it was taking her a genuine effort even to be polite—and when as commanding a presence as Caledonia was in a bad mood, it spread out from her like a cloud. Only Angela dared to risk a conversation, but not until the cloud had dissipated a bit.

The area in front of Camden-sur-Mer where the bus was parked was a scene of total confusion, a forest of bobbing heads and a babble of voices, the staff helping to stow luggage aboard the bus; gardeners trying to transplant some Lily of the Nile from beside the front walk; residents who were going on the tour; residents who had merely come to say goodbye to their friends; and residents who just happened to be walking past.

In the middle of all the confusion stood Maralyn Wilson, vainly trying to get the attention of her charges as she passed out lengths of braided yarn in bright shades of orange and yellow. "Tie these to your luggage!" she was shouting. "One tie per piece of baggage. That way the bellboys will know it all belongs to our party when they pick it up from the rooms in the morning. Are you listening to me? Tie these to your luggage."

"I don't think I understand," Tootsie Armstrong said helplessly. Tootsie was easily confused, of course, especially when she had to cope with new ideas or new procedures.

"Never mind," the travel agent said desperately. "Just tie the yarn onto your bags. Now let me count noses. One, two, three, four ... no, he doesn't belong. Let me start again. One, two, three, four, five ..." She counted from the left; she counted from the right. But no matter how many times she counted, Maralyn Wilson couldn't total eleven passengers for the small bus that stood waiting, the luggage storage area gaping open, its driver looking bored and checking his watch. "But who is it?" Mrs. Wilson kept saying. "Who is it who's missing? Mrs. Benbow ... no, there you are. Let's see ... is it Mr. ... No, I see Mr. Grogan. He's already on the bus." Grogan, who had boarded early, was stretched out on the backseat, sound asleep.

It wasn't till she lined the residents up and ticked off names on her roster that she realized that both Trinita Stainsbury (who this month had dyed her hair a strange shade of pumpkin orange, perhaps in honor of Halloween), and Elmira Braintree (the new resident who was making no friends with her crisp, assertive manner) had failed to arrive. Some of the staff were dispatched to find the missing sheep. "The rest of you," Mrs. Wilson said sharply, "as soon as you see your luggage safely aboard, you go into the bus and take a seat." Nobody paid the slightest attention, too busy talking to friends or to the staff to listen to instructions.

"Cal, get a load of our bus driver," Angela was whispering to Caledonia, who bent forward to hear her little friend's voice above the hubbub. "If he isn't the handsomest thing!"

Caledonia tried to get a grip on her grumpy mood and be pleasant, so she looked carefully at young Tony Hanlon with his heavy tan and his tight chinos, his well-muscled arms rippling as he helped load luggage into the hatch. "Mmmph. Looks like somebody I know, but I can't think of who. Or maybe he's from around here and I've seen him in the mall or something."

"Oh, Cal, you disappoint me. Don't you recognize who it is that he looks like? He's the living image of Tyrone Power!"

"Goodness but I had a crush on Tyrone Power, back then. But so did every girl my age." Caledonia peered more carefully.

"Don't think of Tyrone Power when he was just starting out and sort of a pretty boy. You know, when he was in all those Sonja Henie movies. Or when he was in *Lloyds of London*."

"Oh, I remember that. With Madeleine Carroll, right? They curled his hair for that one, didn't they? And he had to wear a funny sort of top hat thing."

"Well," Angela went on, "don't think of that picture. I meant Tyrone Power as he looked a little later. After he got back from being in the Marines in World War II. Think of *Captain from Castile*."

Caledonia considered. "Maybe yes, maybe no. But this kid is certainly worth looking at, either way. Oh, look ... here comes one of the missing now."

It was Miss Braintree striding out, followed by one of the Camden-sur-Mer maids struggling under the weight of four pieces of luggage: three large overnight bags in various colors of ripstop nylon and a bright wine-red leather train case. "I warned you," Miss Braintree said to the waiting group, though apparently to no one in particular. "I told you I'd have problems packing. I thought you"— she turned directly toward Mrs. Wilson—"were supposed to give us assistance with our travel problems. Never mind, I made it, though no thanks to you. But I don't want to hear a word about how you"—she turned baleful eyes back at the group in general—"how you had to wait!" And she clambered aboard the bus, looked up and down the aisle, and chose a seat near the front, spreading a large purse, a book of crossword puzzles with a pen clipped to it, and a travel robe over the seat next to her. "Well, it might get chilly at night," she said. "It's October, after all. And who knows whether these foreigners know enough to give you extra covers on the bed or not."

"Notice," Angela whispered to Caledonia, "she didn't bother to count seats and figure whether or not there were sufficient places for the rest of us if she took up one whole seat. She was going to sit alone and she didn't care who else was put out. Honestly!"

A moment later, Trinita Stainsbury showed up, the melon-colored hair disheveled, her blouse and travel slacks slightly awry as though she had pulled them on in a hurry. She was dragging a single large Pullman bag that rumbled along on built-in wheels. "I overslept," she panted. "Oh, dear, I hope I haven't been too much trouble. Here's my suitcase. There's still room for it, isn't there? Oh, dear ... I'm so sorry."

"At least," Caledonia growled to Angela, "she had the grace to apologize for being late. I didn't wear my watch. What time is it now?"

"Nearly ten-fifteen," Angela whispered. "Do you think we'll have time for the dolphin show when we get to Sea World? I really love the dolphins."

The bus lumbered along the freeway, but the ride took only forty-five minutes, Sea World being on their side of San Diego. And because it was midweek, there were fewer visitors to take up potential picnic spots in the surrounding park, so they found a suitable place almost at once. "Now you are free to see some of the shows or not as you choose. But be here by twelve on the dot," Mrs. Wilson warned them. "Mr. Hanlon and I will set up the picnic so it'll be ready by the time you get back. Because we want to catch up on our schedule after"—she glared at Miss Braintree — "our late start."

Some faster and some slower, depending on how steady they were on their feet and how much their joints ached, the group set out toward the heart of Sea World, all but Mr. Grogan, who stayed fast asleep, snoring peacefully in the backseat. "The dolphin show is this way," the Jackson twins chorused. "Come on, come on!" they shouted, heading off on a path that was almost 180 degrees in the wrong direction. Trinita Stainsbury, cantaloupe hair confined under a pink nylon scarf, rushed to join them, and one of the four men in their group, Roger Marx, strolled off after the Jackson twins as well. Marx was a widower who had moved into a cottage directly across the garden from Caledonia six months before. A tall, pleasant-voiced man, he had made himself popular from the first with his easygoing manner and his willingness to join any activity, take part in any project. He was glad to be a fourth for bridge or to join someone for a walk by the sea; he was a cheerful opponent at billiards, a clever planner on the Residents' Council, a sympathetic listener ... in short, a real addition to Camden-sur-Mer and—as Angela once said of him—a particular favorite of hers. But today, to Angela's mild disappointment, he had chosen to follow the Jackson twins. Tom Brighton, Elmira Braintree, and Tootsie Armstrong went along as well. That left only the taciturn Mr. Grunke, who watched the others move off, and then went his own way alone down a side path. And, of course, Angela and Caledonia, who hesitated a moment to get their bearings.

"Tell you what," Caledonia said to Angela. "You and I have been to the shows at least a half-dozen times. Let's not bother today. I'm still not really recovered from this early start."

"Well, all right, if you don't feel like it. How about just going over to the petting pool to feed the dolphins? Because that's always interesting. I don't believe the dolphins are the same ones every time. At least, each time we see them, they act different from the ones we saw the last time."

"How could you tell whether they're the same ones or not? All dolphins look exactly alike to me! All of them have the same hopeful grin on their faces." They strolled a few yards along and then Caledonia stopped short. "You know something, I think we better not, this time."

"Better not what?"

"Stop at the petting pool either. We'll have to go all the way to Tijuana smelling of the dead herring we buy to feed the dolphins."

"I think they're smelt, not herring."

"What does it matter? They both smell perfectly awful. Even after a wash, we'll still have the scent on us. Let's just give it a miss this time, okay?"

Angela was in a good mood, excited about the trip and not inclined to argue, even if Caledonia was being a bit tiresome about not wanting to go to the shows and the petting lagoon. Angela allowed herself a moment's regret about giving up the pleasure of touching the dolphins' rubbery skin as they crowded close to the pool's edge, begging for a treat. Then she capitulated pleasantly. "All right, Cal. Whatever you say. I don't mind. Today, I don't mind anything. It's so exciting to be on a trip. So what do you say we just stroll the gardens? They're really spectacular. I always thought they're worth the price of admission by themselves, and … Oh, look! It's Jerry Grunke."

Ahead of them and partly hidden by a tall stand of crimson cannas was their fellow resident, moving easily along a path that ran parallel to theirs. "What do you think of him?" Angela asked.

"Well, he's really not bad looking," Caledonia began. "Sturdy peasant type, I'd say. Still got most of his hair. Bright enough fellow, I'd guess, though it's hard to tell, really, because he's only lived at our place a few weeks, and he certainly doesn't say much, does he? So it's hard to figure him."

"I tell you what, Cal. He bothers me. I always get the feeling he's sizing us up and he doesn't much like what he sees. I mean, he frowns all the time as though he's disapproving. And he's always … I don't know … always watching and listening. Not watching just us. Watching everything. Look at him … he's doing it now, isn't he?"

Jerry Grunke's white head turned just slightly toward their side, and they caught a glimpse of his sharp blue eyes raking the surroundings and the people going past. Then his head moved slightly the other way, and they knew, even though they could only see the back of his head, that he was sweeping his eyes over the other side of the walk as he moved along. Then he glanced back in their general direction and both women stopped dead in their tracks, to be sure they didn't accidentally walk into his field of vision.

"What do you suppose he's looking for?" Angela said. "He makes me nervous. What's he trying to find? Is he afraid of something? Is he expecting somebody? He's always looking, not just here, but everywhere. All the time."

"Oh, you're imagining things." Caledonia shrugged. "I admit he's a watcher. But lots of people notice their surroundings. The man could be an artist making mental notes for a painting. Maybe a writer who's going to put all this into a book. He could be a retired psychiatrist who's used to sizing people up all the time. He could be—"

"He could be a Mafia hit man," Angela said, "used to looking around for his prey. Or looking out for the police. He could be a professional assassin, like 'The Jackal.' Or ... oh-oh-oh! I know! He's an embezzler on the run."

"Angela," Caledonia said calmly, "give me a break! And give Mr. Grunke a break. Look at all the pretty flowers and forget about the poor man. We may not know much about him, yet, but we will after he's lived at our place a while. We know almost everything about everybody else who lives there, don't we? And I daresay we'll even find out more while we're on this trip. Tell you what—if you get a chance, you sit next to him at lunch. Strike up a conversation and just ask him right out what he used to do for a living. But for the moment, let's just enjoy the park here, okay?"

Jerry Grunke was forgotten as the two strolled along, admiring the way the October sunshine warmed Sea World's gardens.

Promptly at noon Angela and Caledonia arrived back at their bus. The picnic—mainly chicken sandwiches and potato salad, properly carried in coolers so that it was still chilled—was waiting. So were some of their party. Mr. Grogan, slightly misty, had arisen from his nap and was sitting propped against a palm, eating a sandwich and nursing a headache. The silent and glowering Jerry Grunke had already returned as well and had taken a seat on the ground with his back against a large eucalyptus tree, a huge rock near his right arm and one of the lines of shrubs near him on the left—no chance for Angela to take a place nearby and ask him anything.

Tootsie Armstrong limped into sight almost at the same minute Angela and Caledonia arrived. "I turned my ankle," Tootsie explained, "and I couldn't walk fast. So I left before the others. I didn't want to be late. Oh, don't worry. It's not a sprain. But it's sore."

"Tootsie," Angela said with annoyance, "didn't you carry any flat-heeled shoes? It's silly to travel in those pumps. You can't go five steps without your feet hurting or something."

"Well," Tootsie said apologetically, "I have some moccasins— for when we get to Tijuana. But I didn't remember we were going to walk anywhere on the way. And you know I love the way these heels make my legs look." She preened a little, turning a still-shapely leg this way and that for them to admire, and Angela snorted with disgust.

One by one and two by two, the others came straggling back to their chicken sandwiches and potato salad. Elmira Braintree, Roger Marx, the Jackson twins, Trinita Stainsbury, and Tom Brighton—Maralyn Wilson checked them in carefully. "All right, we're all here," she said. "So as soon as you're ready, we'll hit the road." Of course, the picnic things had to be packed away, several of the party wanted to stop at the restrooms again, and there was some pushing and shoving as they tried to avoid sitting anywhere near Grogan. But at last they were on their way.

The bus was waved across the border with a smile and a little bow by the uniformed men on the Mexican side. "They're glad to see us, of course," Maralyn Wilson explained to her charges. "Tourists are the number one industry of Tijuana. Now, I'm going to suggest that we get checked into our hotel first before you hit the shops. Get washed up, change clothes if you need to, and then we'll spend the afternoon shopping, if there are no objections."

The men sighed, but the women laughed their pleasure as young Mr. Hanlon turned the bus off the traffic-choked main street and out of the very center of the downtown. Ahead of them loomed a gleaming white edifice that looked as though the White House had been enlarged to twice its size and transported to Tijuana. Manicured grasses and elaborate flower gardens graced the front lawns, and an illuminated sign over its entrance announced it as the HOTEL TIJUANA.

"Oh look! Our hotel!" Angela said admiringly. But the bus wheeled past the entrance and turned the corner.

"That's for the people on deluxe tours," Mrs. Wilson explained. "Or not on tours at all. Our hotel isn't far, though." Along down the side street another block, Hanlon pulled the vehicle into the driveway of a two-story building of cracked stucco and blackened timbers, a building less than a quarter the size of the facade of the Hotel Tijuana, a building that turned a plain, unassuming face toward the street. It could have been a warehouse with windows, a block of apartments, or a suite of offices, but for a painted sign board announcing it as LA POSADA INGLATERRA.

"Here we are, ladies and gentlemen," Maralyn Wilson called. "I'll go and sign us in and get our room keys, and you identify your luggage for the bellboys so they can get your things up to you."

"Boys" was a strange term to apply to the three aging men who, wearing tan uniforms with the hotel's name embroidered across the breast pocket, tottered out to meet the bus. (Despite the name of the hotel, not one of the bellboys seemed to speak more than a mere smattering of English.) The "boys" began to unload the luggage from the bus, carrying four and five bags each at one time into the lobby, but they worked with difficulty because several of the visitors tried to talk to them all at the same time, speaking loudly in carefully enunciated, one-syllable English words and gesturing broadly as Americans tend to do in a foreign country. Apparently they were under the illusion that if one enunciated clearly, threw in a little pantomime, and increased one's decibel level enough, everyone—even those who spoke no English at all— would understand.

"Do be careful!" Trinita Stainsbury said. "I don't want my Samsonite scuffed."

"That one is mine." Mr. Brighton identified his battered duffle. "That duffle. The *maleta alli*"—he beamed with pleasure at remembering a few of his Spanish lessons—"*alli* on the sidewalk. That one's my *maleta*!"

"You sure that's not mine?" Grogan was leaning perilously over the luggage, trying to focus. "No. 'S okay. I see mine. Over there, still in the bus."

"Three nylon bags and a dark red train case," Elmira Braintree was shouting at one ancient. "Two blue, one green, and one ... No, wait ... Two *azul*, one *verde*, and one *rosado*. That red one, it's a *maleta de* ... *de* train. Oh, you know—kind of a make-up case. Anyhow," she went on firmly, "it's red. *Estoy rosado.*" The old man looked surprised and backed nervously away from her. "What's the matter?" she insisted. "All I want is my suitcase. Suitcase. *Estoy rosado*!"

"I think," the bus driver Hanlon said helpfully, "that you're telling him that you've just blushed. Or developed a rash. Something like that. You said something like, 'At the moment I am rosy.' You should have said *es*—meaning 'it is'—*rosado*. Although I'm not sure *rosado* is the word you wanted anyway, if you're referring to that ..."

As people do when they're embarrassed, Miss Braintree turned on the young bus driver. "Who asked you!" she snapped. "I said *rosado* and I meant *rosado*. As for those stupid verbs ... well, who knows one verb from another? Besides, he understands what I mean. Look, he's picked up my luggage. Well, some of it." Two of the elderly bellboys were already staggering along toward the lobby with several bags tucked under their arms, including one of Miss Braintree's larger cases, her red train case, two well-worn black leatherette carry ons, a pair of matched tapestry bags, a smart cerise nylon overnight case with a torn leather handle, and one of the blue duffles.

The lobby was little more than an entry hallway, made more crowded with an old-fashioned oak desk near to which Mrs. Wilson was standing, scooping up a handful of keys. "You're together, Mrs. Benbow ... Mrs. Wingate ..." she called out, handing Angela and Caledonia two of the keys. "Room 4A on the second floor. Next to them, Mrs. Stainsbury, with Miss Braintree. Oh," she called as the bellboys brought the last of the luggage into the lobby, "just put those two over here ... they're mine. The overnighter there and the tote bag." She switched to rapid Spanish and one of the bellboys waded into the pile of luggage. He stopped abruptly when there was an explosion of anger from Elmira Braintree.

"No, this won't do, Mrs. Wilson! I told you, I want a single," she was saying loudly. "I told you I'd pay a premium, but I insist ..." People shifted their feet and looked away, as people do when they're embarrassed, and the bellboy who had been sorting through the luggage edged nervously off, taking up a station across the lobby till the storm should blow over.

"Why can't people ever remember what you tell them? A single room!"

"Sorry." Mrs. Wilson smoothly retrieved the key Miss Braintree was waving around. "That key should have gone to Mrs. Armstrong. She's the one who's supposed to be in with Mrs. Stainsbury. You're right, of course, Miss Braintree. You're down the hall in 8B. A single. Everyone, go right along up and make sure your rooms are satisfactory. Freshen up, or whatever. I'll check on you before I go to my own room. Now, Mr. Brighton, I was saying you're in 6A with Mr. Marx. And Mr. Grunke ... where are you, Grunke? You have a single, too, as requested, and here's your key. Now Mr. Grogan ... where's Mr. Grogan?"

Angela and Caledonia detached themselves from the group and hauled themselves up a broad oak staircase to the second floor, Angela quite easily, Caledonia with some difficulty. "Oh my! Look at the floor," Angela said with delight, as they achieved the second level. They had emerged into an angular hallway with unexpected turns and corners, and were enchanted to see that it was paved in bright-colored floral-patterned ceramic tiles. And as they moved along, checking numbers and looking for their own place, they realized that all the room doors were of heavy, age-blackened wood, deeply carved in elaborate patterns that matched the tiles.

Their room, however, boasted no such opulence. It had a worn wooden floor and oak furniture in the California mission style. There was a high ceiling with two large fans, but no overhead light. Two curtained alcoves proved to be respectively a small closet and a large bathroom (the latter complete with a cast-iron tub with huge eagle-claw feet). And there were two small windows, one facing a courtyard, the other, oddly enough, facing the hallway from which they'd entered. Two niches near the door held a wooden crucifix in one, and a candle and a religious picture in the other. There were no other pictures on the walls, no television set, no radio. "I suppose we should be happy we have a private bath. What do you suppose this place was?" Angela marveled.

"It was built seventy years ago as a private home for a rich guy who thought he'd found oil down here, from what the sign on the lobby wall said," Caledonia answered. "Didn't you read about it while we were there sorting luggage and getting keys?"

"Well, whoever this fellow was, he had a mighty strange architect working for him. The hallways bend at odd angles, the rooms around the corner are up two steps from this one, and what our closet and bathroom used to be, before there was indoor plumbing and before this was a hotel, I'm darned if I know."

"Well, if the bed is comfortable, who cares?" Caledonia sighed and eased herself down. "Ahhhh ... it's firm, but not too firm. Thank goodness. But I guess I don't really need a nap. I dozed off on the bus coming down. So I think—"

Whatever she thought, she didn't get to say anything about it. There was a knock at the door and one of the antique bellboys came in with Caledonia's one case and Angela's two. *"Gracias,"* Angela said with a smile, and handed him a dollar bill. "I'm sorry I don't have any Mexican money. Will that do?"

"Señora," the ancient said smiling broadly, "American money, ees hokay. *Muchisimas gracias* ..." And he bowed his way out. As he eased the door to their room closed, Angela saw that he had a stack of luggage in the hall, luggage that was yet to be delivered.

"But no luggage cart," Angela said to Caledonia as the heavy door swung shut. "That poor old fellow staggered up the stairs with all those bags. I'd say he really earned his dollar."

"You only gave him a dollar? Angela!"

"Well, Mrs. Wilson is doing the tipping. I just thought he deserved a little extra after all that ... Wow! What on earth is that!"

A door had banged down the hallway, and someone was shouting angrily, "Hey! Come back here, Pancho, or whatever your name is. I told you exactly what my cases looked like, but this battered pink thing isn't mine! I want my train case in my room and I want it right now!"

Angela, who had put her head out into the hall, saw Elmira Braintree holding before her a bright pink nylon overnight case as though it were something disgusting. She was scolding a frightened bellboy, who kept trying to explain something in his own language, an explanation that Miss Braintree was too angry and excited to try to understand. Fortunately, Mrs. Wilson came up the stairs from the lobby just in time to intercede.

"What seems to be the problem, your luggage? He brought you the wrong case? Well, what did you tell him?"

Miss Braintree said something Angela couldn't hear, but she heard Maralyn Wilson's exasperated response. "Miss Braintree, the man brought you the only case that could be called *rosado*. But what you wanted, apparently, was a case that was red, not rose. *Rojo,* not *rosado*. Here. I'll take care of it. I saw yours down in the lobby and he'll bring it up. I'll take this other."

She took the cerise overnight bag out of Miss Braintree's hand and spoke rapidly in Spanish to the bellboy, who hurried down the stairs and almost immediately came back up clutching the dark red train case. *"Aquí, señorita, por favor ..."*

Miss Braintree snatched her little train case from the bellboy's extended hand and without a "thank-you," let alone a tip, ducked back into her room, and slammed the door behind her. Angela couldn't hear the soothing and conciliatory words Mrs. Wilson was crooning to the bellboy, nor figure out exactly what she slipped into the ancient's hand, but his wide smile and sweeping bow suggested that she had apologized and tipped sufficiently to wash away the difficulties.

Angela faithfully reported every word, every gesture to Caledonia, who lay lazily on the bed, despite her assurance that she really wasn't tired at all. "What a pill that Braintree woman is! I believe in being assertive, of course," Angela said self-righteously, "but I don't believe in blaming my own mistakes on others!"

"Oh, I agree. Assertive shouldn't mean rude, should it?" Caledonia said. "But we can't do anything about her, now, so let's go shopping, okay? Now, shall we go on our own or do we wait for all the others?"

Mrs. Wilson told them the arrangements when she stopped by a few minutes later. "Dinner is here at the hotel at seven. Don't worry—it's not what you'd think of as hotel food at home. The kitchen is excellent. You'll love it. Till then, you can head back into the shopping district. It's only about two blocks down the street. At least, that's where it starts. Oh, be sure to hang on tight to your purse. Most of the people here are surprisingly honest, you'll find. But there are still sneak thieves and pickpockets—a lot of them imports from the States. It isn't like it used to be, so just be wary, okay?" She headed for the door. "Well, then, if everything else is satisfactory ..."

"Wait," Angela said. "You were going to explain the yarn braids."

"Oh they're just identification for your bags. In the morning before breakfast on the day we leave, you just put your luggage outside your room door, and the bellboys go through the hall and gather it all up. And the ones with the orange yarn on them will all go to our bus. You understand? Then we don't have to see the bellboys in person to tell them which tour we're with if several groups leave the hotel at the same time."

"Ah, very clever," Caledonia said. She sat up and began to smooth her caftan and her hair. "Well, I guess we should pull ourselves together and get going."

"Enjoy the afternoon," Mrs. Wilson said. "Remember, dinner's at seven. You'll be all right on your own, won't you?" And she was gone to the next room to check on more of her charges.

"Hurry on, Angela," Caledonia said. "Let's not wait to see what the others are going to do. We might get stuck with Grogan if we wait."

"Or with that Mr. Grunke," Angela said. "He makes me so nervous! All right, I'm set. Let's go!" And she charged out, leading the way to one of her favorite hobbies, shopping.

Chapter 3

Later the same day

The first impression both Angela and Caledonia had of the commercial heart of Tijuana was of the noise—deafeningly loud, and absolutely unremitting. It was hard to unscramble, but it consisted of voices talking and laughing, arguing, bargaining, gossiping, and shouting. Shoppers and shopkeepers alike seemed to talk at twice their normal volume. Then there were the horns and engines and squealing brakes of passing cars in the tangle of traffic that inched and surged and inched again along the streets. And everywhere there was music; every shop had a radio or a tape player blaring through loudspeakers positioned near their entrances. There were brassy marching music, *mariachi* bands, and wailing *rancheras*—Mexico's version of female country-western singers. There was a bongo on one tape player, the *clickety-clack* of castanets from another, a rock and roll snare drum from a third— all designed to attract the attention of the potential customer to the merchant. "But if they all play the loud music, how can it benefit any one of them?" Angela shouted.

"Dunno," Caledonia shouted back. "In fact, a few of 'em could afford to knock off the sound effects because you can't even really tell which shop the sound is coming from!"

Throw in the chaos of the constant street traffic—autos and trucks, handcarts and wagons, and everywhere, people—people buying, selling, walking, running. In many places, the sidewalks were an obstacle course, for many shops had put out bins and tables of their goods; one could not walk a straight and uninterrupted course from point A to point B, and with the crooked, erratic path one was forced to take, the chances of bumping into another pedestrian increased a hundredfold, so there were numerous exclamations, apologies, and now and then an argument as well.

It took a while to get over the confusion and actually look at the wonderful profusion of goods for sale: plain silver jewelry, jewelry set with stones, glassware, pottery, carvings in wood and stone, tinware, wrought-iron, leather goods, basketry, embroidery, and lace. Many of the items were repeated from one shop and one stall to the next. If one vendor featured a wooden St. Francis, the next ten woodworkers were showing carved St. Francis statues as well; if there was a cocktail set of bumpy, green blown glass in one stand, a dozen other stores featured green blown-glass cocktail sets. "It's confusing!" Angela complained. "I can't sort it out. Everything blurs together."

But the human being is infinitely adaptable, and the women soon found themselves shutting out the blasting music and the traffic and the voices around them; they could even hear each other talk without shrieking as they walked from one shop to the next, skipping not a single one, at least at first. "I could go on like this forever." Angela sighed happily as she fingered a handsome rock-crystal frog. "Isn't he beautiful? And he comes in a dozen different sizes, too. Wonderful!"

But eventually the repetition in the shops grew tiresome, and the work of shutting out the noise to concentrate on the voice of one's companion or the voice of a merchant—that was hard work. Besides, a couple of hours of walking from store to store, booth to booth, market to market was hard on aching feet and aching backs. So though they had very little in the way of actual purchases, even after all the time spent shopping, Angela and Caledonia headed back to their hotel with more than half the shops still unexamined. "After all, where does a retiree put souvenirs in a small apartment like the ones we have?" Caledonia said practically. "I'm going to send these silver earrings to my niece for Christmas, and this wonderful leather wallet to my nephew."

Wearily, they plodded back to bathe and change before dinner-time. Some of their fellow retirees were already waiting in the lobby for dinner, and Angela was surprised to see that time had flown. "It's six forty-five, for heaven's sake! We're going to have to hurry!"

In the privacy of their room, Angela slipped out of her slack suit into a blouse and skirt, a traveler's substitute for "dressing for dinner." "Aren't you going to change?" she asked Caledonia.

"I'm changed," Caledonia said. "Can't you tell?" She spread out the skirt of the floor-length caftan she was wearing. "I wore a brown one this afternoon, but this one's more a kind of maroon."

"All your caftans look pretty much alike to me," Angela said. "And you never wear anything else. I should think that perhaps you'd change when you dress for dinner."

"No, thank you." Caledonia smoothed the flowing fabric that surrounded her. "I found out years ago that a caftan hides me modestly but lets me stay unencumbered. No belts or tight jackets, no girdles or panty hose. If I wore an ordinary dress, I'd feel as though I were in a straitjacket! No thank you. Come on, if you're ready. We'll just make it in time for dinner."

The hotel dining room was huge, but there was only a handful of other diners. A long table had been set up approximately in the middle of the room, away from the heavy greenery—ferns, ficus, bowls of decorative cactus—that hung from the walls on all sides and stood here and there near windows and entryways. "Thees ees your table," a uniformed waiter said, pointing the way as the Camden-sur-Mer party entered, although he gestured Mrs. Wilson and Tony Hanlon to a small table off to one side.

"Not exactly democratic," Caledonia murmured. "Apparently the hotel management makes a distinction between us as the employers and those two as hired hands."

The group jostled a bit for position at their table—everyone trying to avoid Grogan—and a struggle of sorts broke out between Jerry Grunke and Elmira Braintree, who had both headed for a seat at one end of the table, a seat that faced the entrance to the dining room. Jerry Grunke had already seated himself when Miss Braintree came to the end of the table and faced him. "I like an end position, Mr. Grunke," she said firmly. "Please move down one and let me take that chair."

Grunke shook his head. "Rather have this place myself, ma'am," he said, and opening his napkin into his lap, picked up a spoon and dipped into the little cup of soup that the waiter had put at each place when the party entered.

"See that?" Angela whispered, nudging Caledonia. "I told you there's something odd about the man!"

Miss Braintree, standing and glaring, finally had no option but to settle for a chair a few seats away from the end of the table, but she muttered under her breath as she took her place, "Dreadful, rude man. No idea of how to treat a lady!"

"She may be right," Angela whispered, "but she certainly doesn't seem to care whether he hears her or not. So she's not very polite either, is she? And the way he glared at her ... she's made an enemy there! Oh! Oh my! This soup is wonderful! Cal, wait till you try it!"

In fact, as dinner progressed, the group realized that the meal was every bit as fine as Maralyn Wilson had promised it would be, and she beamed at them from her little side table, as one after another complimented the food. "This is really continental cuisine," Trinita Stainsbury said. "I mean, it's not at all like eating at Taco Bell, is it? More like what you'd find in a fine French restaurant."

"I told you," Mrs. Wilson said happily. "The owner of this hotel really tries very hard, and I'll make sure he hears how much you've enjoyed the meal."

"I wonder if they'd give me a second helping of this dessert," Caledonia said with enthusiasm. "What is it? A sort of custard ..."

"Flan, *señora*," a young waiter said, deftly placing a second dish before her. Unlike the elderly bellboys, he spoke excellent English. "We call it flan. Will the ladies and gentlemen have a coffee after their meal?"

"Don't be silly! I want to get to sleep tonight, thank you," Elmira Braintree snapped. "Coffee would keep me awake till tomorrow."

With varying degrees of regret, but with infinitely more tact, the others agreed.

But even though dessert was done and even though they refused coffee, the group stayed in their places, as though they were reluctant to bring such a good meal to an end. Grogan, of course, managed to order a third tequila—or was it a fourth?—as his personal after-dinner drink. But he drank quietly, and conversation among the others drifted easily in and out of several innocuous topics without anyone's bringing up something dangerous like politics or social reform. After a while, Tootsie Armstrong, gazing idly out of the dining room windows, interrupted a general discussion on the subject of new movies (everyone at the table was agreeing that they no longer knew the young "stars"—or even cared).

"Look!" Tootsie said suddenly. "What are all those lights out there?" A few heads turned. "You know," Tootsie went on, "I do believe it's some sort of little fair!"

"Oh, what fun! I haven't been to a fair in I don't know how long!" Angela, forgetting that she had declared herself exhausted, was all enthusiasm again. "Oh, do let's go, everybody. What do you say?

Oddly, considering she had been the one to discover the existence of the fair, Tootsie was the first to refuse. "My ankle still hurts from turning it at Sea World," she said. "I wore flats to shop in this afternoon, but it only helped a little. I'm going to soak in a hot tub and go to bed."

"I don't think we'll want to go, either," one of the Jackson twins said. "When we were girls back in Anniston, Alabama, our daddy, who used to travel a lot, always warned us that no one should go out of the hotel in a strange city after dark. Besides, all these people talking Spanish ... it makes us nervous."

"Well, for goodness sake," Angela said impatiently. "That's one of the reasons we came in the first place. To hear Spanish spoken and learn by experience. Or I thought it was."

"That's the only complaint I really have," Caledonia chimed in. "Too many people here in Tijuana speak English to us. They seem to know we're tourists just by looking at us, and they don't even bother trying Spanish."

"All the same," the other Jackson supported her sister, "the signs are in Spanish, the newspaper's in Spanish, and it just feels ... I don't know ... foreign. And it makes us nervous. So I think we'll stay here, thank you very much."

The usually agreeable Roger Marx also declined, to Angela's disappointment. "I'll just hang around the lobby and read a while," he said. "No use trying to read in my room, of course. Light's not good enough. You all go ahead, though, and have a good time."

But seven—surprisingly including the dour Jerry Grunke and the easily annoyed Miss Braintree—headed out together for the carnival grounds. As they left the dining room, Maralyn Wilson joined them. "I'm not letting you go out at night without me," she said. "Call me a worrywart if you like, but you are my responsibility, after all."

"Always glad," the gallant Tom Brighton said, extending his arm for her to take, "to have a good-looking woman along. Let's go."

As the group left the hotel, Caledonia grabbed Angela by the arm, so that they dropped back behind the others as she whispered to her friend, "Aren't you surprised Roger Marx isn't coming along?"

Angela stopped in her tracks. "Of course not. He said he wanted to read. Don't you believe him?"

"Well, surely you've noticed—the man can't take his eyes off our Mrs. Wilson. And I was certain he'd want to come along to the carnival to be near her."

"What do you mean, he can't take his eyes off her?" Angela craned her neck to look over at the corner of the lobby where Roger Marx had settled down with a newspaper—in English, as they could see by the headline.

"I mean he's so smitten with our blonde travel agent, he gave up a seat at the picnic so he could be at her side, so to speak. Didn't you notice? She was walking around serving the food and drink, so our Mr. Marx pretended standing was better for his bad knee, and there he was, right at her elbow the whole time. If she offered seconds on potato salad, he raced over and toted the bowl for her. You couldn't have missed it. He hardly ate a bite himself, he was so busy doing whatever she needed. I think our Roger Marx is in love."

"Oh, honestly, Cal. You imagine things," Angela said stiffly. "He's sitting there in the lobby now, isn't he? If he's so crazy about her, why isn't he following her to the carnival?"

"Maybe he really meant it when he said he wanted to read tonight. Anyhow, if you ask me, it'd be a good match. He's a widower and she's a divorcee."

"Several times over." Angela nodded. "So she keeps reminding us. I don't really think there's anything to all that, you know? I don't think he's her type, or that she's his."

Caledonia grinned. "You're not going to give an inch, are you? You'd feel differently if you'd figured this all out, I bet. Well, you watch him, then, and decide if I'm not right. But not now! The others are getting ahead of us. We're going to have to step on it to keep up! Come on."

And so, hurrying over the rough and stony ground, the group descended on what was announced on an overhead banner marking the entrance as *El Carneval para Todos Los Santos*—the All Saints' Carnival.

It was very much a makeshift fairground, and the strings of old Christmas tree lights and the naked bulbs hanging from electric cords woven in and out above the carnival's heart seemed pitiful to the group from Camden-sur-Mer. And yet the sound of the carnival was shrill with real excitement. Children were squealing with high-pitched ecstasy, and their parents were chattering to friends and neighbors, hands waving in extravagant and joyful gestures, while the proprietors of the various booths chanted their elaborate enticements. And, unlike the voices one heard in the tourist-ridden areas of Tijuana, these voices were clamoring in Spanish. There was hardly a word of English spoken anywhere. The babble was accompanied by a riotous obligato of other sounds—the clank and clang of metal tokens pitched at glass ornaments in the coin toss, the banging of popguns in the miniature rifle range, the clatter of wooden pins in the makeshift bowling alley, the music of *mariachis* coming from an antiquated wind-up record player that competed with the wheeze of a small calliope—and everywhere the laughter that testified to pure enjoyment. It was strictly a people's carnival; the paint on the booths was peeling and speckled, the tinsel decorations frayed and turning brownish with accumulated dirt, but it was giving as much pleasure to the working folk of Tijuana as a hundred Deglers or Royal Americans could have provided.

"I was going to say that this is more of a back way than a midway," Caledonia remarked as they caught up with the others and arrived at the first of the carnival booths. "But I don't know ... it's been ages since I've seen so many people having fun. It's wonderful just to watch them. I think I'm going to enjoy this. Look around, Angela—see if you can find a hot dog for sale somewhere."

But there were no hot dogs, no corn dogs, no burgers, not even any popcorn. Instead, to the amazement of the visitors from Camden-sur-Mer, the air was redolent with the scent of meat roasting over open fires, meat that would be put into tacos on order. Big pots of rice simmered on small stoves. And there were at least four carts where the proprietors peeled mangos or cucumbers and placed them on sticks for the customers to carry away and nibble as they strolled along. Apples, half-melons, and pineapple were also available for skewered snacks. There were several small stands labeled *Refrescos* that sold drinks—a few of the well-known bottled variety, but since these were very expensive, most of the sales were of a brightly colored, fruity-smelling concoction dispensed in big plastic cups, filled with ice from battered zinc tubs.

"Don't drink any of that stuff," Angela hissed to Caledonia. "It's the ice. You don't know what water it's been made from."

"Don't worry," Caledonia hissed back. "I never did like Kool-Aid, and if I'm not mistaken, this is the genuine article. Hey, look at the little skulls!" At another booth there was an assortment that looked incredibly morbid, but was proving highly popular with the Mexican patrons; candy had been used to shape tiny skulls, little coffins, miniature skeletons and children were buying the little objects with apparent delight. "What's going on?" Caledonia asked in wonder.

"It's in honor of *El Dia de los Muertes,*" Maralyn Wilson said, joining them. "The Day of the Dead. Halloween—All Saints' Eve—is the big celebration in the States and nobody much pays attention to two days after. But here November second is the really big holiday, even though the celebrating sometimes goes on for a day on either side. Look, everyone! Come and look!" She called the others back to inspect the candy stand. "Here's something you won't see in the United States —Halloween or otherwise."

"Disgusting," Miss Braintree said, blunt as ever. "Horrid!"

"Candy skulls? The Mexicans seem to take death rather casually," Tom Brighton said with wonder.

"Not really," Maralyn Wilson said. "But they aren't as afraid of it as we are. And they don't mind poking fun at it now and then, even though there's a deep religious significance to The Day of the Dead. Visits to cemeteries, churches, and small individual altars are set up to the memory of departed family."

"I want one of those darling little skulls to send to my niece," Trinita Stainsbury said, putting action behind her words. "Wrap it in some paper, will you?" she asked the proprietor of the booth. "So I can carry it in my purse." The cheerful man held out the skull to her, obviously not understanding a word she had said. "Tell him, Mrs. Wilson. I need it wrapped so I can carry it."

"Look, Cal," Angela called out, pointing across the carnival lot from where they stood, "it's our gardener!"

"Where?" Caledonia swiveled around to eye the milling crowds. "I don't see anybody. You're imagining things, Angela."

"No, I swear, it was our head gardener, Juan Saenz. The tall one with the moustache. From Camden-sur-Mer, you know."

"For Pete's sake, I know where we live!" Caledonia said. "And I know what Juan looks like. But I don't see him. I think you're having that delusion everybody has in a strange city—thinking you see people you know. Why don't you ..."

"Oh, look, dear ladies, a merry-go-round!" Tom Brighton cried out with obvious pleasure. "Over there!" It was old and creaky, and the horses seemed to have developed leprosy, but it was a real merry-go-round. "Up at home," Tom Brighton went on with delight, "they've replaced carousels with dodge-em cars and whirling swings and upside-down roller-coasters—and all with names from outer space. I don't believe I've seen a plain, old-fashioned merry-go-round in years!"

"And there's a Ferris wheel!" Angela called out, her quarrel with Caledonia about her sighting of the gardener quite forgotten. "Oh, come along ... do let's ride on the Ferris wheel. We can look down on the whole carnival. It'll be such fun."

"I don't know," Caledonia said skeptically. "It looks pretty rickety, to me. And it isn't very tall, is it? Less than half the size of Ferris wheels at home, so we wouldn't see much, even from the very top. I think I'll pass on riding that thing."

"Oh, dear," Angela sighed. "Well, how about one of you others? Trinita? Tom?" They shook their heads, and she pointedly avoided asking Mr. Grogan, who stood unsteadily against one of the poles set up to support the overhead strings of lights, or the silent Mr. Grunke, who—if the truth were told—frightened her a little with his impassive and glowering stare. "How about you, Miss Braintree?" Angela asked without any real enthusiasm.

"Good heavens, no!" Miss Braintree said—too loudly as usual and much too sure of herself (in Angela's opinion).

"I wouldn't trust my life to that collection of wire and rotting wood. Look at the thing! How those people can bear to be lifted up into the air in seats that may collapse, held in by those frayed straps that may break at any moment, on a structure that may topple. No thank you."

Angela turned her back in the middle of the litany and tried another tack. "How about the games of chance? The wheels of fortune. And the coin toss. And there's a baseball pitch, and—"

"They don't look like much," Miss Braintree interrupted with crisp disapproval. "Not much profit in those."

"Profit's not the point," Tom Brighton said gently. "It's the thrill of the chase. Grabbing for the brass ring. Look at all these people playing for plaster dogs and glass mugs and baseball caps. It's not junk to them, it's the prize. Winning the prize."

"I agree with you, Mr. Brighton," Maralyn Wilson said. "I love the games myself. My second husband was a gambler and we lived in Las Vegas a while, and I really got the fever. Look, let's try this one.

They stopped at a large wooden wheel, covered in silvery paint, with numbers painted on it and nails driven into its perimeter. There were corresponding numbers painted on squares of cardboard that were propped up against prizes displayed on a rack next to the wheel. Maralyn Wilson paid her money and started the wheel going; a short leather strap attached to an adjacent pole flapped against the nails until the wheel came to rest and the strap lodged between two of the nails and directly over one of the numbers.

"Look," Angela whispered. "Almost every other number on the wheel is a two or a three and those are the numbers on the cheapest prizes on the rack." And she was right—a colored pennant, a neon-pink knitted headband, a tiny plastic doll, a wooden bank for coins. "The fancier prizes like that brass clock and that portable radio—I don't think their numbers are even on the wheel!"

Caledonia laughed. "All the same," she said, "look at what's just happened!"

Maralyn Wilson, eyes shining, had won a large purple teddy bear on the rack's top row. Moving with reluctance, but smiling valiantly, the man in charge took the teddy bear down and the people standing nearby laughed and applauded. *"Que suerte, señora,"* someone in the crowd called out, and Maralyn called back, "Oh, yes, I was lucky!" and held the teddy bear high so everyone could see it.

Someone else called out, *"Otra vez, señora. Otra vez!"*

"Oh, all right. One more time," Mrs. Wilson said, laughing with delight and turning back to hand across money for another spin on the wheel. "I seem to be having good luck tonight!" Once more the wheel slowed, stopping on another winning number. This time the proprietor's smile seemed a little less friendly as he reached for a second prize, a black velvet cushion embroidered with a gold anchor and "U.S. Navy" across the front, but the crowd nearby was delighted and the applause even more excited and enthusiastic.

"Don't spin the wheel again, Mrs. Wilson," Elmira Braintree said crossly. "You've won so much you may have bankrupted that poor man. And heaven knows you don't need that junk you've won, do you? I mean, you could buy and sell that little man, couldn't you?"

"What's eating Miss Braintree?" Caledonia muttered as they moved off to the next booth, where two or three of them paid to throw a battered, dirty baseball at a pyramid of wooden Indian clubs. "Or does she just naturally tell everybody how to live their lives? Oh, look, Trinita's won a plastic kewpie doll!"

"And I've won a 'gimme' cap," Mrs. Wilson said with glee, as her Indian clubs scattered and fell under the impact of the baseball. The man in charge reached for a billed cap with LA DODGERS across the front. "My brother used to say girls were no good because they couldn't do things like throw a ball! But he taught me pretty well anyhow, I'd say. Of course he only did it so I could pitch to him for batting practice out in the vacant lot behind our house. Well, what next? How about a horse-cart ride?" She gestured over to two old-fashioned wagons, each fitted with four bench seats, one behind the other. The skinny horses hitched to each carriage looked like victims of chronic fatigue syndrome, but the ride's proprietor had done his best to make the rigs look festive. Bright yarn tassels adorned the bridles, and tinsel was strung along the wagons' sides. Even the huge blinders the horses wore were gilded, and unlike the ticket booth to the ride, the carts had been freshly painted in red and gold.

"Where do the carts go?" Trinita Stainsbury asked.

"Een-to the tunnel, *señora*," a voice said in heavily accented English. "Please to buy the ticket? You choose the gardens of Xochimilco or the All Souls' Day ess-travaganza." The man who had been in the ticket booth stepped out of its shelter and moved closer to his prospective customers. "You visit from Los *Estados Unidos,* yes? We find ourselves honored. I am Dante Ortiz, and I own thees ... *como se dice* ... how you say ... thees ... thees show!" He gestured broadly toward the carts and toward what appeared to be a wall of canvas panels nearly seven feet high, the cloth strung taut to upright poles so that they formed a circular structure rather like a huge circus tent, which filled the whole back of the carnival lot. There were two gaps in the drab canvas, each labelled with an overhead banner hand lettered in primary colors. One said *FLORES ENCANTADA DE XOCHIMILCO,* with a smaller banner suspended beneath that read FLOWER WONDERLAND. The other said THE MUMMIES OF GUANAJUATO in

English on one big banner, with neither Spanish translation nor subtitle.

"How much?" Caledonia said. "How much for each of us?"

"Two pesos, *señora*," Ortiz said, flashing a wide smile. "Jus' for you, only two pesos."

"Too much," Miss Braintree objected crisply. "Much too much!"

"Nonsense," Caledonia said briskly. "After all, two pesos is only ... what is it now, twenty-five cents?"

"And do not worry, *señora*," Ortiz said hopefully. "Only twenty-five American cents, an' ees hokay to pay een American money."

"Sounds perfectly reasonable to me," Caledonia said. "How about it, Angela? Want a cart ride?"

"Oh, I'd love to see the flowers—"

"No-no-no, not the flowers. Not on Halloween, for Pete's sake. Let's go for the mummies. Really pretty scary, the way I hear it. And I don't suppose I'll ever get to Guanajuato for real, so I might as well see 'em here. Besides ... flowers? How dull! They've got real flowers everywhere in Mexico. Why pay to see more? Especially since these are probably fakes. Crepe paper and plastic."

"All right, all right. Makes sense," Angela said. "Everybody coming along with us?"

Laughing and chattering, one by one the group agreed and fished around for coins to pay Ortiz. Only Maralyn Wilson hung back. "I've been on this ride before," she said. "I won't spoil the surprise ... but thank you, I think I'll pass. Maybe I'll go back and try more of the games. I'll meet you here afterwards. Oh, here, Mrs. Stainsbury. That cart bumps along pretty hard and you'll want to hang on to the arm of the seat. So I'll take your kewpie doll for you while you're on the ride."

Mr. Grunke clambered up into the front seat next to Grogan while Mr. Brighton helped Trinita Stainsbury into the second seat and swung himself aboard to sit beside her. Angela and Caledonia got in right behind them with the help of Dante Ortiz, who gave the tiny Angela a lift up the high step and managed to execute a tactful boost for Caledonia, since she was too heavy to hoist herself into the cart without help. "Oh, dear," Maralyn Wilson said, her voice sympathetic with concern. "You'll be sitting all alone, Miss Braintree."

"That's all right," Miss Braintree said firmly. "More than all right. I much prefer to sit alone. I think I told you that when we set out from Camden-sur-Mer. I didn't want a seatmate on the bus coming down here, I didn't want a roommate for the overnight stay, and I don't want someone sitting with me now, thank you." Maralyn Wilson shrugged and stepped back.

A skinny boy of eleven or twelve had been sitting on an upturned box near the hitching rail, and now he rose wearily to his feet. "Thees ees Pablo," Dante Ortiz said, pointing at the boy. "He weell be your guide."

"He's just a kid," Caledonia said. "Isn't he too young to be working at a carnival at night?"

"Lots of children hold jobs in Mexico," Mrs. Wilson said. "You'll see kids working all over this lot. Don't get all bent out of shape about it! It's a way for the kids to help out the family. Okay, all of you. Have fun on the ride if you can. You'll see soon enough!" She waved a hand, the other wrapped firmly around her armload of treasures.

Dante Ortiz went back to his booth, and young Pablo seized the horse's bridle and turned him away from the hitching rail toward the canvas walls and the entrance to the show, whispering something encouraging in Spanish as they moved. The horse glanced reproachfully over its shoulder at the full cart he was expected to tow along, and with a deep, horsey sigh, started the cart jolting along toward the shadows and the silence of the canvas maze—to pictures of death and to death itself.

Chapter 4

November 1, All Saints' Day

Ernesto Garcia Y Lopez was a square, barrel-chested man with copper skin, an aquiline nose, glossy black hair, and obsidian eyes. Despite his very Spanish name, his ancestors would not have been among Cortez's soldiers. Rather, if this man were put into a feathered headdress and a beaded breastplate instead of his neat gray suit and polished loafers, he might have been a nobleman-warrior in Tenochtitlan, watching with stone-faced dismay as the forces of European culture and destruction marched into his city. Now, in the dining room of *La Posada Inglaterra,* seated at a small table on which he had laid out a notebook and a fountain pen, he watched impassively as the visitors from Camden-sur-Mer marched in; but these people were hardly armed invaders like those Spaniards long ago. They crowded together in obvious apprehension, and they hesitated in the middle of the room, uncertain as to what to do. He gave a little bob of his head that might have been interpreted as a bow, and he managed to move one corner of his mouth into what might have been a small smile; it wasn't much, and it didn't exactly make him look like a kindly uncle, but perhaps he seemed a little less of a forbidding figure.

"Do please take seats, ladies and gentlemen," he said in excellent if slightly accented English. "This should not take long. I am *Capitano* Lopez with the Baja, California, police force. And who among you is spokesperson? You are on a tour, is that right? And one of you is a guide?"

"That would be me," Mrs. Wilson said as she took a chair in the front row. "Mrs. Maralyn Wilson." She passed over some papers, presumably identification and permits, which Captain Lopez inspected briefly and returned. "This is my driver, Mr. Hanlon." She indicated the young man sitting off to one side. "And these are my ... my party. All from the retirement home of Camden-sur-Mer. As was Miss Braintree. And Captain Lopez, we're all very upset by this, so the sooner this can be concluded the happier we'll be."

"Naturally, *señora*. That goes without saying." Captain Lopez bowed slightly again. "I have only a few questions, and they won't take long. But the whole interview would have been over already, had I been able to find you here at your hotel this morning. It is now"—he checked his wristwatch—"it is now three-thirty in the afternoon, and my men and I have been waiting since just before noon. But the staff here tells me your whole group left the hotel after a late breakfast. We thought perhaps you might have gone to one of the churches in the area to pray for the soul of your departed companion, the late *señorita* Braintree."

Caledonia noted that Captain Lopez had used the respectful title of "Mrs.," rather than calling Elmira Braintree "Miss." "Probably because of her age," she told Angela later as they talked over the day's happenings. "Growing old is the pits, but once in a while we get a few rewards. Like discount tickets to the San Diego Zoo. Or like a little respect."

Now Captain Lopez was more inclined to remonstrate with this group than to treat them with deference. "Some of my men," he was saying in a reproachful tone, "looked into the churches nearest this hotel, but you were not to be seen. So we could do nothing but wait. And here you are, three hours later! Very odd, for a group so recently bereaved. I'm afraid I must ask where you have been." His tone was mild and his expression had not changed, but the group shifted nervously and more than one of them thought that he glared accusingly at them.

"Well," Maralyn Wilson said defensively, "we had tickets to the bullfights. We even got seats on the shady side! My people here didn't want to let them go to waste."

"You went to the bullfights? With your *señorita* Braintree lying dead on the examining table of the police doctor? For people who claim to be upset at the death of a companion, you seem to behave rather strangely." Captain Lopez's voice had not risen, but the group before him reacted as though he had shouted. Some looked guiltily at the floor; a few twisted unhappily in their seats; and Tootsie Armstrong began to leak tears, which she dabbed away with a lacy handkerchief taken hastily from her handbag.

"Exactly what I thought," Maralyn Wilson said. "I told them it was unusual to say the least. Even unseemly. I said people might not understand. But they insisted."

"Of course, we did," Caledonia Wingate trumpeted. Perhaps she didn't mean her voice to be quite so loud, but obviously she had had enough of the scolding, and she meant to defend herself and the others. "And Miss Braintree would be the first to understand. Captain, look at us. We're old, and we live with other old people."

There was a short silence; it would seem that Caledonia believed she had made her point. "I do not understand," Lopez finally said. "So you are old. And you live with old people. What difference can that possibly make?"

"It means," Angela said, taking over the argument, "that we have to get used to our friends and acquaintances dying. In a retirement home, somebody or other dies almost every other week or so. But life goes on—and that's not a cliche, you know. It does. And we do. Because we have very little time left to do the things we want to do. Don't you see?"

"She means," Caledonia took up the narration again, "that at our age, we've become conscious of how short our own time has become. If we were to put off a walk in the garden today, just because one of us has passed away, we might never get that walk in the garden at all. Because tonight it might be our turn to go. So we don't let the passing of a friend stop us from whatever it is we want to do, nor even slow us down."

"And we had these tickets to the bullfights, and we were all terrifically excited about going. We'd been looking forward to it," Angela said.

Lopez looked at his watch again. "But you must have left before the bullfights were over, to get here by this time."

"Well ... actually ..."

Actually what had happened was that they had arrived at the arena in plenty of time. Hanlon found a lone tree along the edge of the boulevard under which there was enough space that he could park in the shade. He pulled the bus up, swung the door open for his passengers, and announced that he'd seen bullfights before, thank you, and he'd just stay with the bus. Mrs. Wilson exited first and stood by the door, doling out the tickets, one to each—"In case we get separated, we'll just meet inside at our seats!"—as they stepped out of the bus into the noise and color of the street. If the carnival the night before had been festive, the streets around the bullfight arena were positively chaotic. The arena's walls were bright with large, gaudy posters advertising the upcoming fights; the streets were thronged with people, all laughing and shouting and talking;

there were vendors selling souvenirs, vendors selling food, and so many beggars that the group from Camden-sur-Mer were stunned. There was a tired-looking man with one leg, holding a tentative hand up toward them, saying nothing but appealing with his eyes; there was a barefoot Indian woman with her baby held against her back in a slinglike arrangement of woven cloth, also holding out a shy and hopeful hand; and there were three children who skittered boldly after the group till Mrs. Wilson shooed them away. Beggars were everywhere along the avenue, holding out their hands in silent supplication, only a few whining appeals, but so softly that their exact words disappeared in the clamor of sound around them. "At least they don't step into your way," Angela said, "and pull at your clothes, or—"

"There are strict laws in Mexico," Mrs. Wilson told them. "Beggars are tolerated, but not if they touch you or shout at you. Of course, it makes it easier to ignore them. I honestly don't know how they make a living." The group looked around and realized that almost none of the crowd in the street seemed to pay the slightest attention to the begging. "Come along now," Maralyn Wilson urged them. "The show is going to start right at one, and you won't want to miss a minute of it, it's so fascinating. It may be," she added, smiling, "the only thing in this whole country people bother to start exactly on time. Hurry along." The Camden-sur-Mer party moved ahead quickly, ignoring the beggars just as the Mexicans were doing, though they found it very difficult.

Struggling through the jostling crowd, the party finally found its way into the arena. It was a good thing Mrs. Wilson had distributed tickets, for the crowds pulled their group apart rather quickly, and though Angela managed to keep up with Caledonia by reaching out and grabbing a handful of her caftan and keeping a firm grip no matter how hard she was pummeled and pushed by the crowd, they lost sight of the others until, one by one, they found their way to the seats—excellent seats in the first and second rows, shielded from the sun that blazed down on the other side of the arena. "Hey look," Caledonia said, nudging Angela. "We landed in the dress circle!" She pointed to the elegantly dressed men and women seated in the front-most rows to their left and right. "Tijuana's uppercrust, all right."

Music sounded over loudspeakers, and the group from Camden-sur-Mer watched in fascination the entrance of the horses in their brightly colored trappings and heavily padded gear, the procession of the *matadors* in their flashing costumes heavy with spangled embroidery, and a seemingly endless train of what appeared to be attendants and assistants of various descriptions. Then suddenly the first bull appeared, his hooves thundering as he galloped into the arena and stopped, pawing the ground and snorting, glaring left and right for someone, something to attack—a sleek, handsome, coal-black animal. Almost at once a man on horseback, "a *picador,*" as Maralyn Wilson explained to her party, entered and went to work, stabbing at the bull with what looked to the visitors like a lance.

"Whatever is he doing!" one of the Jackson twins squeaked. "He'll kill that poor animal!"

"Goodness no, he won't kill the bull," Mrs. Wilson said pleasantly. "This is really just a kind of practice session. And, of course, it will weaken the bull a bit. Notice that the lance is striking near the animal's hump, where the neck muscles are strong. And look over there ... the *matador* is watching every move from behind the wooden barrier wall. He wants to see how the animal reacts. When the bull fights back, does he attack the horse to the left or the right? Does he lower his head and hook ... Oh dear!" Perhaps no one had explained to the bull that this was merely for practice and wouldn't last long. He had not been amused at all by the pricking lance, and ducking free of his tormenter's weapon, had charged the horse. The bull was strong and the horse was off balance; it went down, legs milling, its rider pinned in the saddle. The bull trampled and used its horns, trying to get through the heavy padding that protected the horse. Finally other men, shouting excitedly and waving capes, came running into the arena and managed both to distract the bull and to pull and push at the downed horse, which struggled up and got himself and his rider out of the danger zone.

The Jackson twins followed the horse's example. They scrambled to their feet, quivering with their haste, and excused themselves. "My daddy always used to say," one of them announced apologetically, "that a horse was a noble animal. And my sister and I ... well, we don't feel we can watch a horse abused in this way."

"The poor thing was hurt!" the other twin said. "I mean, he just lay there. He couldn't get up and they had to help him!"

"He didn't want to get up," Mrs. Wilson corrected her. "Would you get up willingly with a raging bull battering at you? But these horses hardly ever get injured. Look how thick their padding is on that horse-blanket thing they wear."

"Well, maybe," the other Jackson twin said. "All the same, I think we'll just go back to the bus and wait with Mr. Hanlon." And they hurried off as fast as their chubby legs would carry them.

Turning back toward the arena, the others realized that another group of three men had entered and had begun to circle the bull. One at a time they ran back and forth in front of and beside the animal, stabbing at him with their bright, ribbon-bedecked spikes of wood and steel, forcing the iron barbs into the bull's hide and twisting to make the decorated sticks stay in place—and of course to cut into the bull's neck muscles so that he would be less able to hook with his horns. The bull was bellowing with rage and pain, charging again and again at his tormentors, and the crowd was cheering. "They're cheering the skill of the *bandilleros*," Mrs. Wilson explained, "and they're cheering the bull because he's so brave. He doesn't run away, you see? He attacks and tries to drive off his enemies."

Tom Brighton cleared his throat and got to his feet. "But of course," Brighton said, "he doesn't succeed, does he? He never does. You know, I just believe I'll go and see if the Jackson twins got back to the bus safely. If you'll excuse me."

"Perhaps," Tootsie Armstrong said quickly, "I should go along. I seem to have misplaced my handkerchief, and I'm sure I've got a spare back at the bus." The two of them disappeared.

"Now when the *matador* starts his work," Mrs. Wilson told her diminished party, "you'll see some fascinating and graceful moves with his cape. That's one of the reasons people go to the fights—to see the cape work." She needn't have told them that. The young *matador*, glistening in black satin and sequins, twirled and danced and swirled that cape in beautiful patterns, and the bull danced with him—head lowered, partly in preparation for an attack, partly because his neck had been weakened by the picks that hung around him like a necklace, and partly in fatigue. Time and again the dancing man teased the animal into charging, time and again the man stepped aside just at the last minute, tricking the bull into chasing the cape and letting his tormentor escape punishment. Each time the crowd thundered its approval.

"This is terrific," Mrs. Wilson said approvingly. "You don't usually see a young bullfighter who's this skillful. They save the stars till later in the program. Of course, real beginners don't appear on the regular season programs at all. So I'd say they expected this fellow to be just sort of fair-to-middling. But he's wonderful! Watch him."

"I'd rather not, really," Mr. Grunke said abruptly, his voice thick. "Thanks all the same." He jumped to his feet. "I'll see you at the bus." And he left in a hurry.

Angela and Caledonia had automatically turned to watch him go, and they missed the defining moment of the bullfight, but the tremendous roar of the crowd, the loudest cheer yet, made them turn back to the arena. The young *matador* stood over the bull, which was sinking onto its knees, its eyes glazed, its mouth drooling; the young *matador's* sword had sunk its full length into the bull's neck, and the bull was already dying. Its hind legs collapsed when Trinita Stainsbury jumped to her feet, a hand held to watering eyes. "Oh dear, my contact lenses seem to be bothering me. I think perhaps I'll join the others in the bus. See you there." And she was gone.

"Cal," Angela said shakily, "I'm not sure I want to stay here myself. Good heavens! What's he doing?"

"Cutting off the bull's ears," Mrs. Wilson said in a pleased voice. "If he was one of the stars, he might get both ears and the tail, but he's just a youngster. Still, he was magnificent, so they've rewarded him. Oh look, you'll love this tradition. He's going to give his trophies to some lady. It's a great compliment."

While attendants dragged the dead bull away, the young *matador* strode with a ballet dancer's measured grace across the sawdust of the arena till he was just beneath the seats nearest to the party from Camden-sur-Mer, but immediately to their right. There was an exchange of salutations and bows between the bullfighter and the cluster of applauding spectators, and then the *matador* lightly tossed his trophies to a lovely young woman in the center of the group. She had a pleated fan in her hand, and if she had not almost automatically raised it as the dark objects flew through the air in her direction, the bleeding ears of the bull might well have hit her squarely in the face. As it was they splatted against the fan, splashing blood across it and the girl's flowered gown. Angela gasped and got quickly to her feet.

"Cal," she said, "I think the heat has kind of got to me. I wonder if you'd see me to the bus? I'll wait for the rest of you there." Bent over slightly at the waist, she edged out into the aisle.

Caledonia wasn't a bit slow to get to her feet and put an arm around her little friend's shoulders. "Are you feeling faint? Here, just lean on me. We'll make it. We just have to take it slow and easy."

Once into the shelter of the passageways leading out of the arena, Angela straightened up. "You can take your arm away, Cal," she said sharply. "You know I can walk just fine."

"You aren't sick, then?"

"Oh, I'm sick all right. Sick about the blood and the torture of that fine animal. But feeling ill? No. I just didn't want to seem impolite. I'd have insulted those people next to us if I made a fuss. If all the blood in the arena wasn't bad enough, the blood on that girl's dress, that was the last straw!"

They emerged into the sunshine and the dust of the road that circled the stadium, and found that somehow they'd got themselves into a wrong passage and thus out the wrong exit. They would need to circle the structure to the north to find the bus, so they set off. About a quarter of the way along, there was an opening in the arena wall, and glancing idly in as they passed, they were both shocked into stopping in their tracks to stare. The two women were looking into an abattoir.

Busy men in horribly stained work clothes were scurrying everywhere. The floor was awash with blood. The head of the bull that so lately shared the applause inside the arena was lying off to one side in a corner and its body, already roughly skinned, was hanging from a hook in the ceiling. Two men in gore-splashed overalls were hacking at the carcass with huge cleavers—"More like attacking with machetes!" Angela gasped. "Good heavens!" While the women gaped at them, the men cut off a hind leg, delivering it to a butcher's table where it was quickly reduced to small sections and tossed into a huge basket, already partly full of bloody and unidentifiable chunks of meat and bone.

"They were cutting the poor creature up!" Angela gasped to Hanlon, when she was safely aboard the bus. "I mean, one minute he was out there and they were applauding him for being so brave—and a few minutes later, he was being hacked into little bits!"

"They deliver the meat to orphanages here in town," Hanlon explained. "They aren't going to waste good young beef. What did you think they did? Gave the bull a Christian burial? It's natural they have a butcher shop going in the basement, so to speak."

Because they had taken the wrong turn, Angela and Caledonia barely arrived at the bus before the last of their party also arrived: Mrs. Wilson, the faithful and obviously adoring Roger Marx, and a dour Mr. Grogan.

"I watched you, Grogan. You slept through the whole performance. You missed the whole show," Caledonia said to Grogan as he climbed aboard. "And you should be grateful. Frankly, if I'd known what a bullfight was like, I'd have had a few stiff drinks myself before I went."

"I wasn't drunk," Grogan said somberly. "This time. I was just pretending. I closed my eyes because I couldn't stand to look!"

"Frankly, I think we could all use a quiet time to rest and forget about the bullfights," Angela said. "Am I right?" The chorus of agreement was heartfelt.

"You didn't enjoy yourselves?" Maralyn Wilson sounded a bit annoyed. "But I asked you weeks ago, while we were planning what to do on this trip. I asked, and you said you wanted to see a bullfight."

"And we've seen one," Caledonia said. "And one is quite enough, thank you. And now ... well, now I vote with Angela. What's needed now is maybe a nice cup of tea, or better yet, a little sherry."

"Maybe a martini this evening," Grogan said hopefully. "I think a stronger drink is called for."

"For once," Trinita Stainsbury said, "I'll join you."

"Tell you what," Grogan said, "I suggest we have a sort of party when we get back, all right? Maybe it'll help us forget about this afternoon."

But they didn't have a party, nor a quiet time: no tea, no sherry, no martini. Captain Lopez and two of his men were in the lobby when the Camden-sur-Mer group entered, and he got the permission of the hotel to use the dining room for their meeting.

"So here we are," Lopez said in that even tone of voice he had used since the meeting began, "a bit late, because like most tourists, you wanted to see the bullfights, but earlier than you might have returned because you found the exhibition repulsive."

"They don't mean to be rude," Maralyn Wilson said hastily. "It's just that they don't understand the Mexican culture."

"Do not apologize, *señora*," Lopez said. "It is unimportant, in relation to the death we are here to discuss. Besides"—and that small smile came back—"I cannot say that I am totally delighted by the spectacle of bullfighting myself, any more than all of you are fans of boxing or professional football." There was a rustle among his audience, and several of them nodded agreement.

"But back to the point of our discussion," Lopez said. "The *señorita* Braintree. Your companion appears to have died of natural causes. There are no marks on the body such as might have been caused by a weapon. There are none of the symptoms of poisoning, though we have not actually tested the organs, if you understand me. All I want from you is some sort of information that would confirm our guesses. How was the lady's general state of health?"

"Well, of course she was old," Maralyn Wilson began, and then hesitated, aware that several of her party had turned to stare at her. "I mean, things happen to older people, don't they?"

"She hadn't been living at our place very long," Angela volunteered. "So we really didn't know a lot about her health."

"I talked to her a few times." Trinita Stainsbury spoke up. "In the lobby, before lunch and all. She said she had a bad heart. That's why she wanted a place on the second floor so she could take an elevator. To get to the first floor apartments," she explained to Captain Lopez, "you have to come up a small flight of steps from the lobby."

"But there are only four little steps there," Angela said. "It's not exactly a flight of stairs."

"All the same, when I had my heart attack," Trinita said, "the doctor told me to walk every day, but to avoid stairs. So I knew what Miss Braintree was talking about."

Lopez had politely followed the exchange to this point, but it was obviously getting off the track again. He held up his hand and such was his commanding presence that he achieved immediate silence from the group. "You say she may have had a bad heart. That confirms our guess. You see, we found medication in her handbag—the usual aspirin and antacids, but also nitroglycerine tablets, often prescribed I am told for heart trouble. Very well. Now, how did she react to the displays at the show of the mummies? Was she upset or badly shocked by what she saw?"

There was a moment's pause, and at last Caledonia spoke up with a shrug. "I'm sure she was shocked. We all were. But how badly she reacted, I can't say. She was sitting by herself, after all."

"We all reacted badly to that first display," Angela said. "I don't know about Miss Braintree, but it made me jump with fright." There was a murmur of agreement from those who had been at the carnival together. "Really nasty," she went on with a shudder.

"Of course," Caledonia said, "I have to say that it all got a bit boring after a while. I mean, we got so we expected to see something unpleasant when each light went on, so it wasn't such a shock after the first one. Except for that last—the replicas of the mummies. Now that was really gruesome."

"You know," Angela said, "we really didn't hear a sound the whole way. I mean, of course we were all gasping and carrying on at the first couple of displays. And then last at the mummies. Even the horse was sighing by that time."

"The horse?" Lopez sounded surprised.

"Of course," Angela said. "Objecting to having to pull such a load, I suppose. The poor thing was as skinny as Rosinante. Don Quixote's horse, you know. And there were seven of us, after all, in that heavy wooden wagon. Who could blame him if he sighed? But Miss Braintree? Nothing. I mean, we didn't hear a sound out of her. Nothing."

"The only unusual thing I can think of," Caledonia said, "was just after we left the first display, when the cart swayed heavily as we turned the corner. I mean, it swayed all the time, but I thought we might tip over as we turned that one corner. Could that have been something?"

Lopez wrote briefly in his notebook. "Well, that might have been when your *señorita* Braintree was dying. Perhaps struggling to catch her breath, you understand? Let us suppose that she was indeed taken by surprise by the first display—and it is shocking. I have seen the show myself and I agree with you."

"You went to that horror show, Captain?" Tom Brighton asked with amusement.

Lopez shrugged. "I have," he explained, "two sons in their teen years. Like most young people of that age, they are fascinated by the bizarre. They begged to see 'The Mummies of Guanajuato,' and I would not let them attend alone. They found the show almost boring. I found my stomach churning."

He shrugged again and spread his hands in that universal gesture that says plainly, "Oh well, what can I do?" Then he went on. "So what I imagine is that perhaps, shocked by that first display, *señorita* Braintree with her weak heart suffered a severe attack. It would not be at all surprising. She struggled briefly to catch her breath—and this is when you felt the cart swaying. Then she died without being able to reach her medication or to call out for help."

Angela shivered. "Oh dear! Poor Miss Braintree! All alone in the dark and nobody even noticed. How sad."

There was a momentary pause in the discussion while Lopez scribbled in his notebook. Then he put the pen and the notebook into his pocket and got to his feet. "It is, of course, futile to guess more than one must. But all you have said confirms my opinion. So I see no reason at all to doubt that the *señorita's* death was natural. Now I shall go back and complete my report. The hotel people tell me you wish to depart tomorrow. Well, I see no reason you cannot leave on schedule, and the poor *señorita* Braintree can take her last journey home as well."

"Whoa!" Grogan, sitting at the back of the group, spoke up for the first time, and the others turned to see that somehow, somewhere, he had found a bottle of tequila, a bottle of what purported to be mixed citrus juice, and a glass. The tequila bottle was half empty, but very little juice was gone, and though it was impossible to guess exactly how much of the potent mixture had gone into Grogan, it was certain that the fog had descended on him once more. "Whoa! You aren't going to put a dead woman into the bus, are you?"

"Don't be such a fool, Grogan!" Every one of his fellows looked at the usually silent Jerry Grunke, seated near the wall against which he had leaned the back of his chair. Grunke had obviously lost his patience and spoke scathingly. "The lady would be in a coffin, of course."

"Packed into the luggage compartment?" Grogan said.

"Of course not," Grunke snapped. "Don't be any sillier than you have to be, man."

Angela turned back toward the front of the room and was just in time to see a peculiar expression appear fleetingly on the face of Captain Lopez. It was, Angela thought, almost a smile. "And when that man smiles, it's something to notice," she told Caledonia later. "I believe that policeman recognized our Mr. Grunke. As if he'd seen that face on a 'Wanted' poster somewhere, you know? And when he left us, Captain Lopez caught Grunke's eye and I'll swear Grunke knew him, too. At least, a look passed back and forth between them."

"What kind of look?"

"You know. A look. A look of significance!" Angela said. Caledonia just snorted.

And she snorted now. "For Pete's sake, Grogan, don't be so silly," she bellowed. "They'll send Miss Braintree home in a hearse, of course. She isn't going to ride with us. Isn't that true, Captain Lopez?"

"Oh, certainly," Lopez agreed. "We intend to make arrangements for a mortuary here to bring your late companion to a mortuary in your city. I believe we will be ready to release the ..."—he hesitated—"the remains by tomorrow morning, when I understand you are scheduled to leave for your home. Will that be satisfactory, *señora?*" He addressed Maralyn Wilson, as spokesperson for the whole group.

"Oh, perfectly," she said, and her voice reflected her relief. She might be an independent woman of the nineties as she said later to her group, but she was happy to admit that she preferred a man to take charge, at moments like this. "If," she added with a sigh, "there are any other moments in my life like this, which God forbid!"

"Amen," Mr. Grogan said, toasting the Lord with his tequila mixture. "Amen to that!"

Chapter 5

November 2-11

"There've been a lot of strange things about this trip," Angela said softly to Caledonia as the bus joggled and groaned its way back along I-5 northward to Camden. "For instance, don't you think it's peculiar that, close as we live to the border, none of us has been to Tijuana before? At least, that seems to be the case. I mean, you and I haven't, and the rest of our bunch, well, they'd have said something if they had, wouldn't they? And I think that's peculiar, considering Tijuana is right here ... right where we could drive over the border easily and all."

"Oh, that's not so strange," Caledonia said. "How many New Yorkers visit the Statue of Liberty or go to the top of the Empire State Building? I expect the Tijuana trip is something lots of tourists would do, but I bet there are scads of people living right in San Diego who've never gone, even if Tijuana is practically one of their suburbs."

"And another thing that's peculiar. I've always heard going through customs was difficult, but they waved us right through at the border," Angela went on. "I mean, they did peek into the luggage compartment. Though what they thought they could see with that quick a look ..."

"Illegal aliens, I suppose," Caledonia said. "They've stowed away in trucks and busses before, you know."

"Well, I don't know about you, but I was relieved when we were waved through so quickly."

"Why? Do you have a guilty conscience? Have you done something you haven't told me about?"

"Of course not. It's just that dozens of men in uniform standing around staring always make me nervous. And heaven knows there were a lot of soldiers and police at the border. But the thing that really surprised me—nobody asked to look at the things we'd bought."

"That's the influence of NAFTA," Caledonia said. "They'd only care if we were bringing in cocaine. Or assault rifles. But we aren't, and we don't look particularly suspicious, I guess. Did you ever think about that? You and I know from our own experience that getting old and infirm is no guarantee of good behavior. But everybody expects old people to be kindly and sweet. People with white hair and glasses are never suspected of anything worse than moving so slow they tie up traffic."

"Well, they may have a point," Angela said. "This group can certainly be hard to move. I mean, I didn't think we were ever going to get on the road this morning."

If there had been confusion when the group arrived at the hotel, there was total chaos as they prepared to leave. Mrs. Wilson counted heads over and over, and finally ordered everybody to get on the bus and stay put till she could be sure the whole party was present and accounted for. Luggage became a problem, too. Tootsie Armstrong simply hadn't understood about the yarn markers on the bags and had used the bright braids to tie her two cases together. Jerry Grunke was already on the bus when he spotted his suitcase sitting with a group of others, apparently destined to go along with another small tour bus that was also loading on the sidewalk in front of the hotel.

"Whoa nelly!" he shouted to the driver. "My bag ... you didn't load my bag aboard!"

Hanlon got out and fetched the case that Mr. Grunke indicated, but he made Grunke check to be sure it was indeed his bag. It was a very ordinary suitcase, and it did not have the bright orange yarn tie on its handle. "The problem is, you've lost your marker," Hanlon said, after he'd stowed the bag in the luggage compartment. "When the bellboys collected the luggage this morning, they naturally thought this bag went with the other group's stuff."

"I didn't lose the marker," Grunke said shortly. "I put it on there. The marker was stolen."

"Oh, that isn't very likely, is it?" Mrs. Wilson said. "Who'd want a length of orange yarn, anyhow?"

"Don't know," Grunke snapped. "Kids maybe. People are pretty honest here, like you said yesterday. Surprising. Don't have much, but most of 'em wouldn't steal. All the same, the yarn tie's gone, isn't it?"

"Where is Mrs. Stainsbury?" the travel agent interrupted, craning her neck to glare around among her charges. "Anybody seen Mrs. Stainsbury?" She turned back to Jerry Grunke. "I think maybe you just didn't tie the yarn very tightly and it slipped off or something. It could happen easily if you were in a hurry."

"No," Grunke said. "I know I tied it on tight. Somebody took it."

Mrs. Wilson sighed. "If you say so. Anyhow the important thing is, we found the bag before we drove away. Oh, there you are, Mrs. Stainsbury. Come along, please, you're the last one. Better hurry."

"I found my own bag," Jerry Grunke said crossly. "No *'we* found it' about it." But Mrs. Wilson had gone on to other things, so he gave up protesting and found himself a seat—alone and near the back of the bus from where he could watch his fellow passengers.

It was a relatively somber trip. There had been plenty of chatter and laughter on the way down, but there was almost none on the way back. "I suppose," Caledonia said to Angela, "we all feel a little down. Because of Elmira Braintree. Nobody liked her, and goodness knows we get used to people we know dying. It happens, when you get to be our age. All the same, it's perfectly natural for our spirits to be a little dampened. Dying on a buggy ride through a wax museum wouldn't be my favorite way to go. Well, anyhow, I think we're just naturally a little subdued. We'll get over it."

They would indeed get over it, but not before they left the bus at Camden-sur-Mer. As they clambered down the steps and claimed their luggage, most barely spoke except for the bare civility of a "Thank you—see you later," called out to Maralyn Wilson and Tony Hanlon. True to her nature, Angela did stop to make one suggestion.

"I don't know why you've planned the next trip for the eleventh," she said to the travel agent. "We don't need that many days between. Speaking for myself, I'll be ready to go in three or four days. Just time to do my laundry, deal with whatever mail has accumulated, pay my bills, that kind of thing. So I don't see why we have to wait so long before we start the second trip."

"Our arrangements are all made," Mrs. Wilson said hastily. "I purposely left that interval between trips because your own Mr. Torgeson said travel would tire everyone out and you'd need time to rest. And after what happened this time, I don't want to take chances on putting a strain on anyone physically. No, Mrs. Benbow. We'll stick to the schedule. See you on the eleventh. Oh, and everybody"—she raised her voice, lofting it to reach the ears of her retreating charges—"remember to keep your little orange luggage tags on your bags. I'll bring another for you, Mr. Grunke, but I don't want to have to replace everybody's ..."

But most of the group had retreated into the cavernous darkness of the retirement home's lobby, dragging along their luggage and heading for the privacy of their own apartments. They were more tired out by the excursion than they would have liked to admit, and feeling in need of their familiar surroundings—and of a nap. Even later, at supper, when other residents asked how the trip had gone, each of the travelers said about the same thing. "Not bad. Interesting. Sad about Miss Braintree, of course." By the next day they had been swallowed by the familiar routines of the retirement home: scheduled mealtimes, the round of activities including the Spanish lessons, Angela and Caledonia meeting to review their day in private during the hour just before dinner, early to bed for Angela, late, late movies on television for Caledonia. Memories of the journey began to recede, and the trip gradually became more comfortable at a distance than it had been first-hand.

Another day later, however, Angela and Caledonia were surprised to find their favorite policeman standing beside their table just as they were finishing lunch. Lieutenant Martinez accepted their offer to join them for a coffee with a sigh. "Very welcome, thank you. I've had a long morning." He pulled over a spare chair and settled into it.

"What're you doing here?" Angela started things off with a challenge. "Not that we're not glad to see you, of course. We're always glad to see you. But you're usually too busy to come just for a visit. So I assume you had a purpose in mind besides just asking after our health."

The lieutenant smiled at her fondly. "You're right; Gilbert and Sullivan said it—'A policeman's lot is not an 'appy one'—and one of the saddest truths of my profession is that our work is never done. The bad guys don't rest—so neither can we. I was in town to look into a break-in down at the Camden Drug Company."

"Our little local drugstore? Did somebody run out of toothpaste and Band-Aids?" Caledonia grinned. "Here's the cream and sugar. I remember you take 'em."

"Both, thank you," he said with a little nod of his head. "You can't pretend to be so innocent, Mrs. Wingate. I know you read the paper and watch television. You know that these days addicts break into doctors' offices, dentists' offices, drugstores, veterinarians' offices, anywhere they might find a supply of—"

"Veterinarians' offices?" Caledonia asked. "They're addicted to worming pills and mange medicine?"

"Of course not," he said. "Vets stock sedatives and painkillers, not to mention stimulants, and if the thieves don't happen to find a drug they can use themselves, they'll sell on the street what they do find and use the proceeds to buy whatever it is they'd prefer to have." He stopped. "But you must know this. Forgive me for belaboring the obvious."

"So, what brings you here?" Caledonia asked. "You don't suspect one of us of being involved in the break-in at the drugstore, do you?"

"Not at all. It's really a kind of courtesy call. Your front desk—in the person of your Miss Clara—has already given me some information that changes my purpose here. I've been talking to an acquaintance of yours, a Captain Lopez of the Baja, California, police. And he asked me to follow up on the death of your companion, Miss Braintree. So I left a team in charge of the drugstore break-in and came over here, intending to initiate an investigation, but I find—"

"Investigation? About Miss Braintree?" Angela said excitedly. "Do you mean you suspect that she might have been murdered?"

Martinez smiled. "Anyone who didn't know you would think you have a morbid mind, Mrs. Benbow. Positively ghoulish."

"Oh, but ..."

"Not I, of course. I understand that you regard crime—and specifically the crime of murder—as an intellectual puzzle. Something with which to while away the idle hours of your retirement."

"Oh, that's not exactly the way it is," Caledonia corrected him. "Our involvement in murder cases from time to time has been almost accidental. It's just that we have special knowledge of our people here that you might not have. That's the only reason we like to take a hand. Well, perhaps not the only reason. I mean, we have enjoyed being useful, and I confess it has been absorbing to ... to ..."

"Take a hand?" Martinez lifted his coffee again to sip, or perhaps he was hiding a smile behind the cup. "It's not so much your hands you insert into police business as it is your noses. Both of you." The words might scold, but his voice was gentle with affectionate amusement. "How many times have I had to ask you to stand aside? To be circumspect? To avoid putting yourselves into danger? The point is, this time I have no need for your special powers of observation, for there will be no investigation. More specifically, I am told I cannot initiate the particular investigation that Captain Lopez thought might be helpful."

The women were flatteringly attentive. "And what would that be?" Angela asked brightly.

"Well ..." He hesitated. "Lopez thought perhaps an autopsy should be done after all. But your helpful receptionist, Miss Clara, has told me that it is too late for that. She says your Miss Braintree had made arrangements with a local funeral home and the body has already been cremated and the ashes shipped to a cousin for interment in the family plot in North Dakota." He paused again, looking at them. "That doesn't seem to surprise you. But even with the death certificate from Mexico being perfectly in order, as it was, don't you think cremation the same day the deceased arrived back here is unusually fast action?"

"Not really, Lieutenant," Caledonia said. "The management of this place requires us to make arrangements for ourselves as soon as we move in. Because we've got to a point in our lives, you see, where we're closer than the average person is to using a funeral parlor's services."

"Or closer than the average person *thinks* he is," Angela corrected her. "Some people live for twenty, thirty years or more after they move in here."

"The point is," Caledonia went on, ignoring her friend, "that it saves Torgeson worrying about what to do with us when we keel over dead in the middle of the lobby some day. He just looks up our file and calls the funeral home where we've made arrangements and they do all the rest. No waiting to contact a relative, no having to get the city morgue to put us in cold storage till some distant cousin tries to figure out what should be done. It's not a pleasant subject, I suppose, but it's completely practical."

"And I suppose"—Angela could only stay out of the narrative for a short time—"I suppose Miss Braintree had prepaid for cremation. So that's what they did. And why not? We all thought she'd simply had a heart attack. She had nitroglycerine tablets in her purse. She had mentioned to Trinita, I think, that she had a weak heart. And she was with us on that frightful carnival ride and must have got as much of a shock as we did from the displays. Captain Lopez thought it was a heart attack, too. But now he's apparently changed his mind. Is that right?"

"Oh, not at all," Martinez said smoothly. "But he wants to be cautious. You see, their doctor who examined the poor lady is an elderly man retired from private practice and perhaps he is not quite as quick as he once was. Anyway, knowing the circumstances, and being asked to make a determination with dispatch, he merely confirmed what everybody thought was true and certified the death to be from natural causes. Then yesterday, in conversation with Captain Lopez, the old gentleman mentioned certain indications that might have been considered suspicious: tiny blood vessels in the eye that appeared to have burst. Of course, these signs don't necessarily mean foul play. They could have resulted from her taking aspirin, and there was aspirin in her purse, or so Captain Lopez reports. But then, as I say, that doctor finally mentioned these things to Captain Lopez, and the captain thought it best to make sure."

The women were staring at him with total fascination, but Martinez merely shrugged. "Well, it is clearly impossible now to do an autopsy. Incidentally, I hope you were flattered to have Captain Lopez take charge personally. The captain is an officer of some importance whose jurisdiction involves the entire area. The local Tijuana police called his office because the deceased was a citizen of the United States. The captain and I have met several times in the past on matters of business so he phoned me when he wanted to check on your group and I told him you were friends of mine. He did me the courtesy of taking charge personally instead of sending a subordinate."

"Very kind of you, Lieutenant," Angela said, "and he was the soul of tact. Very nice. But let's get back to the point. You're saying he phoned you twice—once checking on us, and once again after we'd come back home, when he began to have doubts about—"

"Not doubts," Martinez said. "Just a nagging question in the back of his mind. If he'd had genuine doubt, he'd have insisted on an autopsy right then and there, instead of asking us later to do it up here."

"How could he think you might still be in time?" Caledonia said curiously. "It's been two days since Miss Braintree died. Well, three altogether."

"You are not a Catholic, Mrs. Wingate?" Martinez asked politely.

"Well, no, but what difference—"

"Captain Lopez is. And he is a Mexican citizen. Not only would a Catholic service in Mexico be at least a day or two after the death, but there would be a body present, not merely an urn full of ashes. The captain thought, perhaps hoped, that matters might be handled similarly for Miss Braintree here. And if they had, his request would indeed have come to us in time. Or, if she hadn't arranged for a cremation, we might even have obtained permission to disinter the body for examination. But as it is ..." Once more he shrugged eloquently.

"But cremation's the body-disposal method, of choice here in Southern California, isn't it?" Caledonia said. Then she grinned. "I suppose that's thanks to the tremendous population growth out here. If we were all buried in the traditional way, we'd be using up a lot of pretty high-priced real estate—real estate where nobody could build a new condo or even raise the rent."

"I was certainly surprised when I moved to California," Angela chimed in, "about how many people were opting for cremation. It just isn't that common in the rest of the country. At least not yet."

"Cremation is certainly not all that usual in Mexico," Martinez said, and he sighed. "Well, never mind. Very likely the autopsy would have shown nothing useful anyway. After all, those of you who knew her best believe that she died of her weak heart, don't you?"

"Of course," Caledonia began, but Angela interrupted eagerly.

"Now wait a minute. Elmira Braintree was massively unpopular and it seems to me she went out of her way to antagonize people. She insisted on having a seat to herself on the bus. And she insisted on a single room. As though the rest of us weren't good enough to share with her or something. And come to think of it, she seemed to annoy Jerry Grunke every time she turned around. I remember that when we went into the dining room for dinner, she tried to grab the seat he liked and they practically had an argument about it. In fact, the more I think of it, the more suspicious Jerry Grunke looks, don't you agree, Lieutenant?"

"I'm sorry, but I don't," Martinez said, but he spoke with a smile again, as he finished his coffee and put the cup down. "It would appear," he said, rising to his feet in that graceful manner he had, "that my trip here has won me only one thing—a cup of coffee. Well, except of course that it gave me a few moments to visit with you." Both women beamed. "Unfortunately, my brief time for a rest and a friendly conversation is used up. I need to get back on the job. So I will thank you for your warm welcome and I will say goodbye for the present. It is always a pleasure to reassure myself that you two are well and I have been able to give you in person my affectionate greetings."

Angela sighed her delight as he bowed over her hand, and Caledonia smiled fondly at his gallantries. "Isn't he just the handsomest thing?" Angela said watching the lieutenant's slim back and square shoulders as he left the dining room. "So like the late Gilbert Roland when he was at his very best."

Two more days passed, and then Maralyn Wilson appeared at Camden-sur-Mer in mid-morning and the tour group was hastily rounded up by Torgeson and his staff and summoned to an emergency meeting in the little auditorium off the lobby. Torgeson puffed importantly as he introduced Mrs. Wilson "... for a matter of some urgency. I shall certainly sit here with you, just in case. In case"—he glared at Mrs. Wilson—"there's some question about a trip we have contracted for and paid for in advance."

"You'd think," Caledonia rumbled behind her hand to Angela, "that he helped pay for the tour. I'm perfectly capable of defending myself if I need a defense. I don't need him to argue my case."

Mrs. Wilson, who had moved a chair around to face the group, pulled out a sheaf of papers that appeared to be the contract forms she had insisted each of them sign, settled herself, and plunged into her discussion. "I have to find out if you want to back out of our remaining two trips," she said. "If you do, I'll need to make cancellations quickly. The local Mexican travel agencies would just love it if I didn't give sufficient notice to our hotels. They'd love to see me have to pay a late-cancellation fee and watch me get a reputation for being unreliable. I don't need that. I have enough trouble with those agencies."

"You're having trouble with the Mexican travel agents?" Torgeson asked quickly. Torgeson kept a weather eye out for trouble of any kind that might reflect on Camden-sur-Mer and its people, and most especially anything involving contracts and the exchange of money. "What kind of difficulty are you talking about?" he asked anxiously.

"It's because of NAFTA," Maralyn Wilson said breezily. Torgeson glared; the only trouble he approved of taking lightly was that which happened to the rival retirement home on the other side of town. This had the potential of coming too close to home. "Travel agents here in the U.S.A. used to have to make bookings through Mexican agencies," Mrs. Wilson went on. "We had to hire their guides and their drivers for down there. Now we can take our own busses straight across the border, complete with our own staff, and we don't have to make our arrangements through a Mexican agency. It's a big saving to us, but it's cost Mexican travel agents a bundle. So they make trouble for us at every chance they get."

"I repeat, what kind of trouble?" Torgeson persisted anxiously.

"Well, they say nasty things behind my back. They jaw back and forth with me and my driver whenever we cross paths. And they sometimes play dirty tricks. Like they'll call the hotel and tell them we're going to check in early, and then when we finally get there at the originally scheduled time, the hotel's pretty annoyed with us. They'll make phoney reservations in my name for my tour party ... like, for instance, at a local restaurant. Of course, we don't know about it so we never show up, and then months from now when I do try to make reservations, the restaurant won't play ball because they think I've been responsible for a no-show. Things like that. Nothing I could ever prove, mind you, but things that make trouble all the same. Believe me, I stay out of their way. And I'm always careful to cancel out in plenty of time. So I want to know if you"—she turned away from Torgeson and faced her group again—"if you are going through with our next trip. Mind you, I wouldn't blame you, if you said no. I know you didn't have a lot of fun, what with the death of your companion. And I gather you didn't much enjoy the bullfights, and —"

"Mercy! I should say not!" one of the Jackson twins murmured.

"Anyway, it seemed to me that even though you said you were looking forward to the trip to Ensenada, you might have thought differently after you'd had time to consider. So, are you still going to Ensenada as originally planned?"

"Well, I don't know about the others, but I certainly am," Trinita Stainsbury said emphatically. "I bought some beautiful silver pieces while we were shopping last time, but someone told me the prices were even better in Ensenada than they are in Tijuana."

"That's true," Maralyn Wilson said. "Not surprising, I suppose, because Ensenada is farther down the peninsula, not as easy to get to, and they have to do something to attract tourists now that gambling's illegal."

"Gambling's illegal?" Mr. Grunke said, his ears pricking up. Angela watched him with some speculation. "Weren't we gambling when we played those games of chance at the carnival?"

"Well, technically, I suppose," Maralyn Wilson said. "But I'm talking about big casinos. Really big. The Las Vegas type of thing. The word was that our stateside mobs—Al Capone, that kind of mob thing—they used to have big investments in places like Aguas Calientes and the Rosarita Beach Hotel, back in the thirties. But in 1935 the Mexican government outlawed the casinos, mainly because of the other kinds of crime that grew up around them, or so they said. The point is, prices are better in Ensenada, if you're really interested in the shopping."

"Oh, very much so," Tootsie Armstrong said with enthusiasm. "I should be able to get all my Christmas presents, and here it is only the first part of November. I'm usually so late I have to send things to my niece and nephew back in Iowa by express delivery and that gets terribly expensive!"

"Count me in for Ensenada," Tom Brighton said. "I'm interested in shopping myself. I need a new wallet. So I say, let's go exactly as scheduled."

"Absolutely! I still need a lot of practice on my Spanish," Angela said. "I was telling Cal that too many people spoke English to us in Tijuana and it'll take more than one trip for me to get my verbs straight."

"Me too," Caledonia said. "I vote to go ahead as planned." Jerry Grunke and the Jackson twins signified their agreement, and even Grogan nodded, although he might just be nodding off to sleep, since he appeared to be mildly intoxicated—as usual—even though it was barely ten in the morning.

"Mrs. Benbow may not have improved her Spanish," Roger Marx said shyly, "but I feel as though I'm doing better at the lessons after hearing the language. I wouldn't miss the trip to Ensenada for anything, Mrs. Wilson. I mean, I genuinely enjoyed our first expedition, in spite of everything."

"He would." Caledonia nudged Angela and spoke in a whisper. "I wonder if Lover Boy will ever get up the nerve to actually ask her on a date?" Angela glared, shook her head, and gestured, her movements saying clearly, "Shhh, he'll hear you!" Caledonia just grinned.

"I take it, Mrs. Wilson," Torgeson was rumbling, "I take it the matter is settled then. I'm very pleased." He levered his bulk upward from his chair and started for the exit, as did all the others except for Grogan, who was now snoring slightly with his chair tipped back against the wall, his head still bobbing agreeably up and down to the rhythm of his steady, deep breathing.

"Don't forget," Maralyn Wilson called after them. "We start at the same early hour. Don't be late this time. We want to leave plenty of time for a picnic on the way again. I haven't decided quite where yet, but we'll stop somewhere."

And so at nine a.m. on November 11th, the travelers were once more milling about on the walk in front of Camden-sur-Mer, handing luggage to Tony Hanlon, greeting Maralyn Wilson, and preparing to board the familiar bus. And once more, Caledonia was grumpy because of the hour and was turning her annoyance against anyone within earshot. "Have you noticed," she was saying crossly, "that nobody calls this Armistice Day any more? They call it Veterans' Day. Hah! A wimpy name! It's all this trying to be politically correct. They think they've got to include everybody from all the wars, Revolution through Vietnam, or somebody'll get their feelings hurt. I'll bet nobody even remembers which armistice we're celebrating—and why on November eleventh."

"World War I," Trinita Stainsbury said, overhearing Caledonia's grumbling. "The armistice that ended World War I."

"It took effect," Tom Brighton said gently, "at eleven in the morning on the eleventh day of the eleventh month. And everybody used to wear a poppy in their lapel."

"For the poppies in Flanders—in the big military cemetery where so many of the Allied soldiers were buried," Tootsie Armstrong said. "Though I haven't seen people wearing poppies on November eleventh for years! Remember how wounded veterans used to make the poppies out of crepe paper and sell them on street corners?"

"Well ..." The wind had been taken out of Caledonia's sails by the accuracy of their responses and she had to make a giant effort to control her irritability by changing the subject. "When are we going to get our coffee? These others have had breakfast. I haven't."

"I've decided we're going to stop in Balboa Park," Maralyn Wilson told her.

"Oh! Balboa Park?" Tootsie Armstrong was rapturous. "The San Diego Zoo! How wonderful. I want to go into their rain forest exhibit. They say that first thing in the morning, you sometimes see the tigers roaming around. We take our trips from here in the afternoon, and they snooze in the heat of the day, so I never get to see them."

"You won't get to see them this time, either," Mrs. Wilson said. "I'm not budgeting time for the zoo. I wouldn't even stop in Balboa Park, either, but I figured we'd have trouble making it all the way to Ensenada without at least one rest stop."

"Obviously she's getting so she knows us—she's making allowances for the aging of the bladder. A potty stop about every hour should do it, all right," Caledonia muttered, her cranky mood lifting at last, dissipated by amusement.

The loading aboard of the luggage went smoother than it had for the first trip. Everyone had remembered their orange yarn braid and had dutifully tied one around the handle of each bag. Even Tootsie Armstrong had worked out the purpose of the braids, rather than using them to rope her two bags together. And Maralyn Wilson had brought along several extra ties, just in case, so even Jerry Grunke's bag now sported a bright, identifying braid.

Once more Grunke seated himself near the back of the bus ("He's looking at everybody again," Angela whispered, nudging Caledonia) though not too close to Mr. Grogran, who spread himself out on the backseat and promptly fell asleep. In fact, the departure went smoothly except for one minor emergency. As Tootsie Armstrong hoisted herself aboard, the strap of her large handbag caught on the railing and tore itself free from the bag at one end.

"What will I do?" she wailed. "I can't carry my purse this way. It's too big and heavy to lug around without a handle. Oh, Mrs. Wilson, please make the bus wait. I'll just run back to my room and change handbags."

"There's really no time," Maralyn Wilson said briskly. "Just do as well as you can. Carry the purse under your arm or something." She turned away to help Trinita Stainsbury struggle with her multiple bags.

"Why can't Trinita be satisfied with three suitcases, like me?" Angela whispered to Caledonia self-righteously.

"Or one, like me?" Caledonia whispered back, drawing a glare from Angela.

"Oh dear, oh dear, oh dear ..." Tootsie, still mourning the torn strap, was perched in a front seat, the large purse on the seat beside her. "Look at this thing! I really need to get myself one with a whole handle so I can carry it over my arm. Oh, dear, if only there were time."

Tony Hanlon took pity on her. "Look, ma'am," he said, "there are real fine leather workers down in Mexico. They can mend that strap so you'd never know it'd been torn. Just look for a leather goods shop that has people making bags in the back room. Lots of 'em do that. They'll do that mending better than most places here in the States would do. In fact, why not let me find you a good place?"

"Well." Tootsie hesitated. "Are you sure it wouldn't be too much trouble?"

Hanlon grinned. "Naaa, just the opposite. I'll tell you the truth, some of the merchants are real grateful if I steer customers to them. So I'd be happy to help."

Maralyn Wilson, who was just boarding, having helped Trinita Stainsbury up the steps ahead of her, glared at Hanlon. "Tony, I've spoken to you about this before. I don't approve." There was warning in her voice. She turned back to Tootsie Armstrong. "I'll find you almost anything you want to buy. I know most of these merchants personally, after three solid years of tours. I'll find you the very best Tasco silver, black Oaxaca pottery—you name it."

"She doesn't want pottery," Tony Hanlon said sullenly. "She wants a leather place to get her purse repaired. Like you got your suitcase repaired in Tijuana."

"Well, I know all the best places—in Ensenada just like in Tijuana. So don't you worry for a minute, Mrs. Armstrong. We'll get it taken care of, all right?"

Only somewhat comforted, Tootsie Armstrong agreed. "Oh dear ... it'll be clumsy handling the purse till then ... but I suppose ..." Almost before Tootsie finished speaking, Hanlon had thrown the bus into gear and it jerked forward on its way to Mexico once again.

Chapter 6

November 11

The whole group was brighter after their picnic lunch, not to mention their rest stop, and they chattered like schoolchildren while their bus rattled its way through San Diego, joggled across the border, inched along—starting and stopping, starting and stopping—through the swarming traffic in downtown Tijuana, rolled past the new bullring and past the toll booth that marked the start of the new highway to Ensenada, and finally picked up speed along the wide road, two lanes on either side of a median strip with only a very few cars moving in either direction. "I must remember to tell Emma Grant about this when we get back," Caledonia said. "She'd love a big freeway-type highway with so little traffic around to bother her."

Angela laughed. "Emma's a terrible driver in traffic, all right. But don't tease her with visions of a road that hasn't got any other cars on it. You know she'd never make it this far—she couldn't even get through Tijuana! You saw the traffic. You saw all those intersections without stop signs or lights. I wonder how people survive even one day of driving there!"

"Probably because Mexicans are so polite," Caledonia said. "The drivers on our freeways would simply slam right through the intersections and kill each other on the spot."

"Our poor Emma"—Angela laughed —"would get one look at the streets of Tijuana and just park the car and walk the rest of the way."

The bus passed the old Rosarita Beach Hotel and was sailing along easily as it got to open country, rattling on at a respectable rate for most of the sixty miles between Tijuana and Ensenada. Off and on the sea was within view through quite a lot of the trip, and at one point, Angela gasped when she saw that there was no barrier of any kind between the road and a drop-off down to the beach below. But as Caledonia pointed out, the road wasn't really all that near to the edge of the cliff. "Besides," she said, "you can say a prayer for divine protection. At least, there are a lot of little shrines set up along the highway, just in case you need one. Although I expect they're memorials to people who got killed at that point in the road."

"Thanks a lot, Cal. That's no comfort at all!" Angela shivered. "Boy, but I hate highways that don't have guard rails where there's a cliff or something."

The hotel into which the tour had booked, *El Palacio,* was situated well outside of Ensenada beyond the northern edge of town, "... and well out of the sight, sound, and smell of the big cannery," Maralyn Wilson assured them. "Ensenada used to be little more than a fishing village, and fish are still a big part of the economics here. So you're never far away from fish. Fortunately, you'll never know it while you're at *El Palacio.*"

Their bus swung right off the dual highway to a wide road that headed toward the sea through a small village. "The cannery workers live down there," Mrs. Wilson said waving to the south. "But the rest of this village grew up to serve the hotel. You'll find some really nice shops here." But from the bus the passengers could see very little except for wooden and adobe walls, a number of which were shops and some of which were houses, although the only establishments that were identifiable as they rode along were a couple of taco and fish stands, a small grocery store, and a gas station. The eateries at the roadside were roughly cobbled and shabby looking, and Angela's heart sank as their bus began to slow. What was this hotel going to be like?

The bus turned right again, away from the village, and there was their hotel—not in the least makeshift or shabby. It was surrounded by extensive, gently rolling lawns bordered by beautifully kept shrubs and carefully trimmed trees, with masses of brilliant flowers banked everywhere in the well-tended beds. Beyond the gated entrance and partly hidden by the trees was the hotel itself, a white stucco, two-story building with a red-tile roof, nearly a city block in circumference, with ells, covered walkways, extensions, and additions that stretched out in several directions like the tentacles of a hungry octopus. There were wrought-iron bars on the windows, there were porticos, porches, patios, gleaming tile floors in brilliant colors—it was all very much in the old Spanish style.

"Wow!" Tom Brighton whistled softly. "The name doesn't lie. This place really is a palace!"

"I thought you'd be impressed," Maralyn Wilson said in a satisfied voice. "This hotel is relatively new. A combine has put it together in the hope that the casinos will come back, just the way I told you. Of course, the casinos aren't here yet, and right now it's out of season—there just aren't all that many tourists in Ensenada in November. So we got really reasonable rates and there won't be many other guests here. I think you'll find that the staff will knock themselves out to serve you."

"The grounds remind me of the Hearst Castle up the coast," Tootsie Armstrong said, craning her neck to see everything as the bus wound through manicured lawns, carefully tended gardens, and rare plants. "Except I think these grounds are even larger than San Simeon's."

"Hey look! You won't find *that* at the Hearst Castle," Mr. Grogan said blearily, pointing out the nearest window. "Unless I'm seeing something nobody else sees." He peered earnestly through the glass. "Funny kind of hallucination to have, though. What I think I see is three men with great big scythes, like Father Time, and they're using the scythes to mow the lawn! Tell me, does anybody else see it, too?"

"Mr. Grogan," Maralyn Wilson said, "motorized lawn mowers cost a great deal of money to buy and to maintain, at least a lot of money by Mexican standards. On the other hand, human labor here is cheap, and the old-fashioned methods are highly effective—just slow. But slow doesn't matter—the one thing people here have plenty of is time. Yes, we all see the men cutting the grass with scythes. It's not a hallucination."

"Glad to hear that," Grogan mumbled, still staring at the groundskeepers busy at their work.

The bellboys here were young and strong and spoke excellent English, so the debarking procedure was easier than it had been in Tijuana. Once again, Maralyn Wilson checked them in and got their keys for them. "You'll have an hour to settle in," she told them, "unpack all that stuff, and then there'll be a bus tour into the main part of town. Ensenada has a lovely church and some very nice, very large houses, not to mention all the shops."

"How about the traffic? It took so long for the bus to get just a few blocks in Tijuana," Caledonia said.

"Oh, no," Mrs. Wilson said, "this is nothing like Tijuana. I wouldn't want to try a bus tour around the downtown there. But here I think you'll enjoy this. One hour now."

Angela and Caledonia were delighted with their own room, which was a spacious, airy double dressed in spring colors, with comfortable furniture, a large private bathroom, and a balcony wide enough to accommodate two white wicker easy chairs and a little coffee table. "This isn't exactly Motel Six, is it?" Caledonia said in a pleased voice. "Plenty of space for me to dance the fandango if I have a mind to."

"Don't dance, Cal. Just gaze. I mean, the view of the sea is spectacular!" Angela said happily. "Look across those bright green lawns! Look at all the flowers. And then there's that little drop-off to the beach and, my goodness, look, they've got overhead lights set up down there. We could go for a walk."

"Anybody game to go for a swim tonight?" Roger Marx asked as the group assembled back in the lobby an hour later. "I see the beach is lit up for nighttime use."

"You must be joshing!" one of the Jackson twins said with a gasp. "Surely to goodness nobody even packed a bathing suit!" "I'm not about to go swimming," the other twin squeaked nervously. "I saw a movie about all the sharks there are in these warm waters."

"Well, you can certainly count me out," Trinita Stainsbury said haughtily. "That's not why I came on this trip. Going swimming? Why, I'd get my hair all wet and goodness knows if I'd find a hairdresser here who could ..." She ran a hand self-consciously over her carefully set coppery curls.

"Hey, I was halfway kidding," Marx said. "But maybe somebody will want to go for a walk, at least. It's a gorgeous beach down there. I walked along it for a minute or two after I got unpacked. The only thing ... Why don't they clean up that end of the beach where all the rocks are?"

"That's Pet Rock Beach, Mr. Marx," Tony Hanlon said, as he joined them. "You know the craze a few years ago for what they called pet rocks? Well, most of them came from right here. The locals still snicker over *los gringos muy locos* who used to come down with trucks and big gunny sacks and cart away load after load of the little round stones. Of course, the crazy gringos made a bundle and the locals got nothing at all out of the deal."

"Nobody wants to stroll across those rocks," Marx said. "That was my only point. You'd sprain your ankle for sure. And it wouldn't be very nice to go swimming and have to come ashore in that part of the cove. The sand beach is terrific, but if they were to expand it by bulldozing those rocks away ..." He looked around a minute and then blurted out, "Where's our guide?"

"Mrs. Wilson's not coming," Tony Hanlon said. "Says she's got errands to run. So I'll be your guide for the sightseeing this afternoon. And I suggest we get on our way, because we'll make a few stops down in the town, and we want to be back in plenty of time for you to get dressed for dinner. This is one of those places you don't want to come to dinner in blue jeans, know what I mean? Come on now, let's get on the bus. It's right out in front."

Most of the party obediently headed for the hotel's front doors, which a beaming bellboy held open for them, but Roger Marx hesitated. "You know," he said, "I believe I'll just stay here, after all. I'm not much for the shopping, really. And one of the bellboys told me the shops right here are as well stocked as the shops in town, and the prices are probably lower out here, too. So maybe I'll stroll the gardens here and go down to the beach again. You have a good time and I'll see you back here for dinner."

"Suit yourself." Tony Hanlon shrugged and followed the rest of the party out to the bus.

"Did you get all that?" Caledonia whispered to Angela. "He was all for the trip till he found out Maralyn Wilson wasn't coming."

"Yes, I heard him," Angela whispered back. "You know, maybe you're right about that romance, after all. He shows all the signs, doesn't he?"

The bus wound up and down through the Ensenada streets, past a few large homes in the hills and a handsome old church, then back into town where Tony Hanlon drove slowly along *Avenida Lopez Mateos* where most of the shops were lined up to sell Mexican crafts to United States buyers. Then Hanlon pulled the bus over into a shady spot and swung its door open. "We'll let you go into the famous Hussong's—that's just around the corner there— and you can take a look, maybe have yourselves a drink so you can say you've done it." Grogan's face lit up, but Hanlon wasn't looking his way as he went on, "And then you'll have a half hour in the shops before we head back, okay? Plenty more shopping time tomorrow." The group began to clamber down from the bus, but Hanlon stopped Tootsie Armstrong before she could walk away with the others.

"Say, Mrs. Armstrong, I see you brought that torn bag with you. Tell you what, if you want to come along with me, I'll take you to a place where they'll mend the strap for you."

"Oh! Oh yes." Tootsie beamed. "Thank you! I'd love to!" So Hanlon helped her down the steps, closed the bus door behind them, and led her off to the right. The others turned left in the direction Hanlon had indicated and quickly found the door marked HUSSONG'S in big letters. In fact, you couldn't miss it—the name was everywhere—on the door, across the front of the building, in the windows, and on a temporary sign set just outside the entrance. But once inside that entrance, the group stopped, irresolute. They were in a modest commercial barroom, one that could be called faintly sleazy. Its gray wooden floors were speckled with ground-out cigarette butts. Its heavily stained table tops and chairs alike were damp from being hastily swiped across with a bar rag. "Oh dear," Caledonia said. "Oh dear!"

"Does anybody," Angela said tartly, "know why we were supposed to come here and look at this place?"

"Because, like our driver said, it's famous," Mr. Brighton said. "In the sixties and seventies, California flower children used to swarm down to Ensenada and they all ended up here in Hussong's. Doesn't anybody remember? Every time you turned around, there was a VW bus with a bumper stick advertising Hussong's. Or there was some kid with long hair and an earring wearing a T-shirt with the name big across the chest—Hussong's. They must have had the world's greatest P.R. man working for this place. Even people who'd never been to Mexico in their lives, but just wanted to pretend they were cool, were wearing Hussong's shirts."

"I remember," one of the Jacksons said in a wondering voice. "There was a boy"—her soft Southern accent made the word into a long, three-syllable word—"a boy we knew back in Anniston who went out to California to be a hippie. And he came home at Christmas and he had one of those shirts on."

"Oh yes," the other twin chirped. "I remember, too. Bob Joe Carroll it was!"

"And they've still got the shirts for sale, look." Tom Brighton pointed to a display of the T-shirts pinned on a wall behind the cashier's counter. It seemed to Caledonia that the shirts were perhaps a bit faded from long exposure to the sun that streamed through the grimy windows; they were colored in strangely subdued shades of puce, khaki, and faded-jeans blue.

"Well-well-well! I see they still sell booze as well as shirts," Mr. Grogan said, happily inspecting the display of bottles behind the bar.

"Tell you what, Grogan," Caledonia said. "You can have a drink here if you want to. But speaking for myself, I think I'm going back outside and use my time at a few of the shops up and down the main street here. You can catch up with us later."

She headed for the door, and Angela came pattering along behind. "I think I'll go with you, Cal," she said. "Anybody else want to come along?" The others murmured various forms of agreement and headed out the door behind her.

"Well," Grogan said, "you know, somehow I think I'll just have myself a cold bottle of *Dos Equis* at that nice hotel bar on the main street. Wait up." And he hurried himself out into the open air as well.

"Amazing how clean a city street smells, by contrast," Trinita Stainsbury said, pressing her lips together in a thin line that registered disapproval. "That was a loathsome place."

"Oh, it wasn't all that bad," Mr. Grunke said. "You were just comparing it to our hotel. Totally different thing. Totally different. There's lots of places worse than this. This is just a saloon, that's really all it is. A saloon with a famous name. Maybe you expected too much."

More or less together, moving from one shop to the next, the group strolled the main street inspecting fantasy masks made of shiny snipped tin and set with imitation precious stones, wrought-iron candelabra and bird cages, blown glass and molded glass, tooled-leather belts with silver buckles, tooled-leather appointment books, tooled-leather purses, tooled-leather wallets, tooled-leather briefcases ... "A lot of these leather goods are wonderful," Angela said, "but I'd prefer it if they didn't put the Aztec calendar on every one of them."

"What's wrong with the Aztec calendar?" Mr. Grunke asked. Angela was startled to find that he had silently walked up behind them and was now standing directly at their shoulders as they gazed into a window displaying a mountain of purses, the surface of each intricately incised in the complex circular pattern.

"Goodness, you gave me a start," Caledonia said bluntly. "You must have sneaked up on us."

"Didn't mean to. Sorry," he said, although as an apology, it was perhaps too abrupt to be taken as sincere. "I want to know what's wrong with the Aztec calendar? I kind of like it. Was thinking of buying one to hang on my wall. Just a small one. Like these here." He pointed at the next window where there were a dozen or more replicas of the famous Aztec calendar, ranging from a huge wheel the size of a kiddies' wading pool through dinner-plate-sized plaques to a tiny calendar no larger than a pocket watch ... all of them beautifully carved.

"There's nothing wrong with them," Caledonia said. "In fact, they're quite lovely. Angela only meant that plain leather without a pattern would be nice, too, once in a while."

"You like that big one?" Grunke asked. He seemed completely unconscious of the fact that Angela was still staring wordlessly at him, seemingly too awed by his presence to make small talk.

"Sure," Caledonia said. "But where would you put it? Oh, I guess you could put legs on it and make it into a cocktail table. In fact, that might be very handsome. But how would you get it home? I don't think you could even lift that thing. It's honest-to-goodness stone, you know. Better settle for something a little smaller, Grunke."

Grunke shook his head in silence and didn't answer. If he had been trying to strike up a friendly conversation, he had somehow changed his mind. Or perhaps, as Angela said to Caledonia after they had moved along, out of earshot, he had simply run out of things to say. "He doesn't seem to talk much, does he? I'm still curious about that man."

Back at the bus, they found Tony Hanlon already waiting with a delighted Tootsie Armstrong. "Look," she twittered holding up her huge handbag so they could all admire the strap, now properly in place again. "Isn't it wonderful? You'd never guess for a minute anything had ever been wrong with it. Didn't they do a wonderful job? And look at all these other things I found!" Two colorful woven baskets occupied the seat next to her, filled to overflowing with objects of various shapes and sizes, most wrapped in newspaper, a few in brown butcher's paper. "All my Christmas gifts. When we left the leather shop, Mr. Hanlon showed me the most wonderful market where they have all different kinds of things, all under one roof. If you want a St. Francis for your garden, they have it. If you want a framed velvet painting of four dogs playing poker, they have it. If you want amber jewelry, they have it. You just walk from one aisle to another, and when you're through, you take everything to a counter up front where the cashier stands, and you pay for it all at once."

"You certainly bought a load of stuff, Tootsie," Tom Brighton said cheerfully. "How'd you ever make it back to the bus?"

"Well, Mr. Hanlon was waiting at the cashier's desk and he suggested that I buy these baskets. Then he carried everything back here to the bus for me. Wasn't that nice? And I'm sure he'll show you all where the market is, too, if you like. Maybe tomorrow. It's really fascinating, and it's so convenient with everything under one roof, and ..." And she kept right on babbling as the others filed onto the bus and took their seats, and as Hanlon settled himself quickly behind the wheel and started them on the way back to *El Palacio*.

"Listen, don't you think our driver is acting mighty funny?" Angela whispered to Caledonia. "Tootsie was paying him a compliment and saying he'd guide us to this market—and you'd think the natural thing would be to say that he certainly would. But he ducked his head and turned his back to us and just started driving. And his neck was dark red like he was angry. Or embarrassed. What do you think the problem is?"

"I think," Caledonia whispered back, "our Tony did something he wasn't supposed to do. Didn't you hear him say he had places where the proprietor would be grateful if he brought in new customers? And didn't yon realize what he meant by 'grateful'? And, of course, you heard Maralyn Wilson jump down his throat about that. I bet you the reason he was so johnny-on-the-spot to help Tootsie with her packages was that he'd been checking on the amount of the bill so he could demand his fee later from the cashier. I bet he gets a percentage of the take from each customer he brings in."

"Oh. Oh dear. That sounds a little greedy. I mean, how can we be sure we're buying at the market that really has the best prices? All we'd know is we're buying at the market that offers him the biggest bribe."

"He'd say it's not a bribe, it's just a cut of the profits. I bet he'd tell you lots of guides and drivers do the same thing. But the fact is, our Tyrone Power lookalike was told not to do that. It's no wonder if he's a little sheepish. He might lose his job if Mrs. Wilson found out."

"Are you going to tell her, Caledonia?"

"Not me. Unlike you, I don't enjoy making trouble." Angela started to protest, but Caledonia ignored her and went on, "I mean, I don't know if the fellow is trying to make extra money, but that by itself isn't necessarily something shameful. And I'd sure feel guilty if he lost his job. There are a lot worse things he could be doing, you know, than taking a percentage from the local merchants. In fact, how is that any different from the way Visa and MasterCard do it?"

Angela thought about that all the way back to *El Palacio* without coming up with an answer.

Dinner was served at eight, an early hour for Mexico. Perhaps a dozen waiters stood around between the potted plants in the large hotel dining room with as little to do as the plants, since the meal was a buffet. Again, the party was seated at one long table, except for Tony Hanlon and Maralyn Wilson, but Roger Marx suggested that two extra places be put at the main table, and the waiters, as though anxious to get a little exercise, leaped to oblige. Caledonia grinned and nudged Angela as Marx moved obviously aside to make room next to his place and gestured the blonde travel agent to take that chair.

The dinner was an adventure—not because of the food, though it was superb in the continental manner. It was the waiters who furnished the element of surprise. As each diner finished loading his plate at the buffet, one of the waiters sprinted over to carry his plate to the table for him, to bring something to drink, and to go back to the buffet to rearrange the slices of fresh fruit that garnished each platter so that no one could guess where a pork medallion had been removed or a chicken breast had been taken away. Trinita Stainsbury dropped her napkin, and two young men appeared on either side of her as if by magic, each bearing fresh linen. Mr. Grogan had carried what was left of a glass of beer to the table with him, and to his delight, it was replaced with a fresh glass, filled to the brim. "Hey!" he shouted with glee. "Fresh *cerveza*, did everybody see that? What a great trick! And did you notice I remembered the word for beer? Hot-diggety-dog, it's going to be a good evening!"

Grogan might have been well along into his program of drink, but he was absolutely right. It was a good evening. Dinner was followed by a performance on a platformed area at one end of the room—a local high school group doing a creditable imitation of the famous Ballet Folklorico, presenting spirited regional dances. Caledonia groaned when they first appeared. "More amateur hour stuff! Don't we get enough of school groups at home, for Pete's sake?" But the dancers were very good, even though their costumes were somewhat less spectacular than professionals' would have been and were obviously homemade. The diners clapped in time and applauded enthusiastically, and the youngsters blushed and bowed for several minutes until they gave the stage over to a group of *mariachis*. Only three other smaller tables were occupied, and the group from Camden-sur-Mer was by far the largest party, so as the *mariachis* strolled through the dining room, it seemed to Angela that the musicians spent a great deal of time right next to her, playing directly into her ear.

"I only wish they'd move a little farther away," she said, trying to whisper to Caledonia to avoid being overheard by the performers. A whisper proved to be impractical, however, and she finally raised her voice to a near-shout. "The music is really awfully good, but it's simply deafening so close up. Especially the trumpets. They hurt my ears!" She cupped a hand over the ear closest to the musicians, trying not to be too obvious about shutting away the sound, and gritted her teeth with the effort to keep smiling pleasantly while her eardrums were blasted.

Caledonia didn't worry about being subtle. She raised both hands to muffle her ears and shouted back, "Yeah, there's only one advantage modern rock bands have over *mariachis* ... rock musicians don't stroll out into the audience and toot right into your ear this way. This is as bad as those terrible loudspeakers kids have in their cars these days, the ones that practically blast you out of your shoes as they drive past. And even those aren't quite as painful. They may have a bass that vibrates right in your rib cage, but they don't stick a brass instrument against your head and blare like to break your eardrums."

The musicians kept right on playing, broad professional smiles on their faces, obviously unable to overhear the women's comments. At last, mercifully, the musicians strolled off to serenade a table of four across the room and the women were able to relax. "Thank heavens," Angela sighed. "They're so much better at a little distance. I couldn't appreciate the number they played here at our table, but I love the song they're playing now."

"It is called 'A*delita*,' and it is a song from Mexico's revolution, *señora*," one of the young waiters volunteered in excellent English, so close to Angela that she jumped. ("We're going to have to tie bells on the waiters, to warn us when they're hovering," she told Caledonia later. "They come popping up to be helpful, and they scare me half to death!")

This particular waiter had come to set a frosty pitcher of chartreuse-colored liquid onto the table along with several glasses that had been dusted with salt around their edges. "Margaritas, *señioras y señores,* compliments of the management," he announced to the group. "And when the *mariachis* are through, there will be dance music, and it is hoped you will stay here and enjoy the evening," he added, pouring the mixture out into four or five of the glasses before he tactfully withdrew to a respectful distance.

"Oh sure!" Caledonia said with deep skepticism. "They want us to stay here and buy ourselves another drink and spend more money, so they prime the pump with a little drinkie to start with. Very clever!"

But she seemed to be the only person who was suspicious of *El Palacios* motives. "How nice!" Trinita Stainsbury said, reaching for one of the drinks. "A little after-dinner refreshment!"

"Oooh, but it looks cool and nice," Tootsie Armstrong bubbled. "I'll try it. Can I hand you one, too, Mr. Brighton?"

Tom Brighton smiled and nodded. "But there's a sort of half one at the end of the line. Make it that one, please."

"None for me," Angela said. "Douglas—that's my late husband—got me to try tequila once and I wasn't too fond of it. I'll pass, thank you."

"I've never tasted a margarita before," one of the Jackson twins said, taking a tentative sip from her glass. The second twin just shook her head and pinched her lips together. "You're making a mistake, sister," the first Jackson said taking another sip ... and then another. "It's kind of like the lime slush we used to get at the 7-Eleven back home. A lime slurpee ... remember those?" She took another happy sip.

Grogan took a gulp of his glass. "Pretty weak, but it's free, so we can't complain, I guess. Say, does anybody know how tequila mixes with beer?"

"Not too well, Grogan," Mr. Grunke said with a grimace. "I'd go easy if I were you. This stuff can sneak up on you."

"Mrs. Wilson, when the dancing starts, I wonder if you'd do me the honor ..." Roger Marx was saying shyly. "I mean, would you give me the first dance?" Caledonia gave Angela another hard nudge under the table to be sure her little friend had noticed. She needn't have bothered. Angela looked the other way, so her eavesdropping wouldn't be apparent, but her ears seemed to have swiveled on her head to turn directly toward Marx and Mrs. Wilson, and her eyes were narrowed in concentration as she strained to pick up their every word.

"Oh, I don't think ..." Maralyn Wilson smiled and shook her head. "It's been a long, busy day, and we have a bit of a drive tomorrow to see *La Bufadora*."

"Please, Mrs. Wilson. Or I suppose I should say Maralyn. I won't keep you dancing all night, you know. Just one dance won't hurt you." Roger Marx smiled hopefully. "Please? I'd be so grateful. I haven't been dancing in ages, and I used to be pretty good."

Angela had to make a real effort not to speak up, not to scold him and say something like "Don't plead. It doesn't work." She clenched her teeth together tightly and deliberately stared across the room as the *mariachis* finished a rendition of *"La Paloma,"* acknowledged the applause of their audience, and bowed their way out.

"Well, all right. But just one," Maralyn Wilson was saying. "And provided they play something slow. I'm not much on the modern stuff where everybody dances by himself. I like dancing with somebody, not at somebody."

Caledonia nudged Angela again, grinning widely. Angela glared and shook her head, clearly signifying "Don't do that!" All the same, as she admitted to Caledonia later, the nudge was justified. "I'd have been furious," she said when they'd reached the privacy of their own room, "if you'd heard all that and hadn't called my attention to it. It was remarkable. In my day, that approach would have got our Mr. Marx exactly nowhere! I was astounded when she agreed. I'd have thought a modern young woman would like a man to be more ... well, more masterful."

"Maralyn Wilson is no spring chicken, Angela. Maybe she's more like us than like the girls of today. Besides, do women's libbers really like their men to be what you and I would call masterful? Don't they prefer a man to be gentler? More—what's the word they always say on TV—more sensitive?"

Angela just shook her head. "I only know the approach wouldn't work for me."

"Anyhow," Caledonia went on, "she has to be nice to him, just like she has to be nice to all of us. We're her customers, aren't we? And the customer is always right, right?"

Whatever her reasons, Maralyn Wilson allowed Roger Marx to lead her to the dance floor as the first number filtered through the loudspeaker system—*Blue Moon*, played by one of the old big bands apparently translated to tape.

"I think I'll have me another of those weak little drinks there," Grogan crooned, pouring himself a second glass of the greenish liquid. "Weak is okay, when it's free."

"Pour me another, too, please, Mr. Grogan," Trinita Stainsbury said archly. "Oh look ... I've sucked the salt off the rim of this one! Give me a fresh glass, too, will you?" Grogan obliged, wielding the pitcher with a remarkably steady hand.

"I believe," a Jackson twin chirped, holding out her glass, "I do believe I'll just have me another little ol' sip of that, as well. These really are quite tasty."

"Oh, sister," the other twin said, "are you sure that's wise? They're saying there's tequila in the drink, and I do believe that's some kind of alcohol."

"It sure is," Grunke said. "Miss Jackson, a ladylike serving of this ... this lime slush of yours is probably just one glass full. Especially when a lady hasn't had ... I mean, with a lady who's unaccustomed to ... or who hasn't indulged in ... That is, you might possibly feel the effects if you aren't used to ..." Grunke abruptly ran out of polite ways to say the Jacksons had been alcoholically deprived in their lives prior to that point in time and therefore might get smashed. He fell silent.

The Jackson twin with the glass in her hand took one more long sip and said reluctantly, "Well, I suppose it might be wise." She set the glass down and got unsteadily to her feet. "Dear me! I seem to have turned my ankle there for a minute, or something. I wobbled. Yes, I surely did. I wobbled when I stood up."

The other Jackson rose hastily and seized her sister firmly around the waist. "Probably wise, dear, to go on up to bed. Especially since we have a full day scheduled for tomorrow." With the one Jackson bumping into a chair as she passed and giggling happily, the other Jackson holding on and guiding, the two left the dining room.

"We've got the same problem," Caledonia said, taking hold of Angela's elbow and lifting. "Early to bed, if we're to get up early, I mean. That kind of problem. Not a tequila problem."

"This stuff's no problem. It's really pretty weak," Grogan said again. "And we've drunk up everything they gave us. They only furnished one per person, I think. I believe I'll switch to something a little more ... a little more emphatic, anyway. Waiter!" He flung his arm high as he called. "Waiter!"

Angela found herself first standing up from her chair, then walking rapidly toward the exit, propelled by Caledonia. "Hey! I want to stay and watch the dancing for a while!" Angela protested.

"Oh, come on ... what do you care whether they waltz or two-step? The point is he asked her, and that confirms what I said—that he's sweet on her." And Caledonia walked herself and her friend out of the dining room and straight to their room, a luxurious hot bath, and a comfortable night of sleep with the sound and scent of the sea wafting gently through their balcony's French doors.

Chapter 7

November 12

Breakfast was served buffet fashion, the only difference from the supper service being that there were fewer waiters on duty in the dining room. The menu was fairly standard breakfast fare, except for the dazzling variety of fresh fruit available and the spectacular assortment of sweet rolls, heaped high on platters at each end of the buffet table. *"Pan dulce,"* Angela murmured as she caught sight of the sweet rolls, and then clapped her hands with delight, realizing that this was very nearly the first time since she began her Spanish lessons that she had been able to recall without prompting one of the terms she'd learned. She wondered if she had it right— and then she thought, "I don't care if it's exactly right or not. The main thing is, I thought of it all by myself!" She decided that calories were immaterial this morning, and she rewarded herself with a roll that had more of the sugar frosting than any of the others did.

One by one, the tour group from Camden-sur-Mer straggled in to breakfast, and there was almost no conversation. Caledonia, of course, seldom spoke civilly before she'd had her coffee, and Angela kept silent out of respect for her friend's pre-breakfast mood. Mr. Grogan seemed chipper enough, but it was apparent that he had already been sampling the hotel's bar. He carried a glass of something brown and wicked looking with him to the breakfast table and busied himself sipping at it while he nibbled fruit and a sweet muffin. Tom Brighton came in, his white hair gleaming like a halo around his head in the morning sun, and greeted the others amiably, but he assailed a generous plateful of food with such enthusiasm that he had no time for friendly small talk. Jerry Grunke managed a little smile to the others as he entered and loaded up a plate for himself, but as usual he had little to say.

But if those five were much the same as usual, though relatively silent, most of the others in their party seemed to be slightly the worse for wear. One of the Jacksons, for instance, had on sunglasses and was holding a wet handkerchief against a throbbing temple. Since nobody could ever tell them apart, it was impossible to say whether it was Dora Lee or Donna Dee Jackson who from time to time dipped that hanky into her glass of ice water to refresh the damp cool she held to her forehead, but whichever it was, she announced in a wobbly voice that she was sorry if she seemed unsociable, but she had a little sinus headache. Her traveling companions just nodded without comment—except for Angela, who whispered piercingly to Caledonia, "Sinus my Aunt Tilly! That's a hangover if I ever saw one!"

Trinita Stainsbury came in and promptly stumbled against a vacant chair. "I think my new glasses must have been made up in the wrong prescription," she said. "I'm having such trouble focusing this morning."

"Does this coffee taste funny to you?" Tootsie Armstrong asked. "Kind of metallic? Maybe it's all the salt with those drinks last night, do you suppose?"

Roger Marx, on the other hand, seemed sober and free of hangover, but he also seemed disinclined to start a conversation, remaining wrapped in his own thoughts, smiling a lot and humming constantly under his breath. When Maralyn Wilson arrived to join them for breakfast and urge them to "Hurry please, the bus is waiting, and it's quite a little drive," Marx's smile widened into a foolish grin.

"I can't hurry," Caledonia warned the guide. "I've got to have at least two cups of coffee."

"Well, please finish breakfast as fast as you can," Maralyn said.

Then Roger Marx waved a hopeful hand to her and indicated an empty chair next to his, but Maralyn Wilson bustled off toward the lobby, giving every indication that she wanted to talk to somebody about something-or-other. As usual, Caledonia was observing closely, and she nudged Angela, who simply nudged back and glared. Later that afternoon Caledonia asked her, "Why did you give me that dig in the ribs at breakfast?"

"Because you keep doing the same thing to me! I was trying to tell you to stop."

"But I wanted to be sure you noticed that our Mrs. Wilson isn't nearly as wrapped up in Roger Marx as he is in her. I thought she was faking that 'I'm too busy for conversation' pose, and I wanted to know if you thought so, too."

"Well, of course, I did, Cal. It was painfully apparent, wasn't it? That's very much a one-way obsession, that is. I don't know why she encouraged him by giving him a dance last night, since she obviously isn't interested. But you can just quit giving me a push every time one of them makes a move in regard to the other. I don't appreciate being pummeled that way. Sometimes you don't know your own strength."

Now, of course, breakfast was their main concern. And though Angela fussed and fumed, eager as usual to start her day, the others took their time. She nearly exploded when Caledonia made a second trip to the buffet table. "You've already had muffins and fruit," she said. "Now you're getting some kind of an omelet and some kind of corn meal mush and ... Cal, that looks like salsa!"

"I think it is," Caledonia said serenely. It would take more than Angela to hurry her. "At least I propose to find out. Call the waiter over and ask for more coffee, will you?"

And, of course, after the breakfast was finally over and done with, everybody had to go back to their rooms. "A last little potty stop," Grogan chortled loudly. Everybody else hurried through the lobby and up the wide staircase to their rooms with their heads down, pretending to ignore him and pretending they had quite different errands in mind. But eventually the party assembled in front of the hotel, climbed aboard the bus, and sorted themselves into their seats. And so the trip began.

The bus cleared Ensenada and headed south on Highway One. *"La Bufadora,"* Mrs. Wilson told them as the bus rattled along, "means 'the buffalo.' But I couldn't tell you why it's called that. All I know is it's a favorite thing for visitors and locals both to go and see. It's a blowhole. A geyser created by the sea and the rocky cliffs that make up the shore in that area."

She stood as she spoke, facing backward toward her charges and bracing herself with one hand on the back of the seat she had just vacated.

"Travel agents," Angela whispered to Caledonia, "apparently don't get nauseated if they ride facing backward. I do, but if they did, they'd have to find another profession."

"We'll be standing on a cliff at the end of the peninsula called *Punta Banda*," Mrs. Wilson went on, raising her voice above the steady growling of the engine. "Or as we'd say, Point Banda. And you'll find it's pretty spectacular when the water comes spouting up above this cut in the cliff. Sometimes you just see the top of the foam, but more often the water bounces high ... way high. It depends on the tides and the winds, I suppose, but it's always exciting to watch."

"We got up this early," Caledonia groaned, "just to see some water bouncing into the air? Good night nurse! I could still be asleep!"

"If you've never seen olive groves," Maralyn Wilson went on, "we'll be passing some soon. Lovely, gnarled trees with a kind of grayish bark. When we get to *Punta Banda*, after we leave the bus and pass a bunch of souvenir stands, we'll be walking up a slight grade." The commentary droned on while the bus made steady progress, passing cultivated farm lands and the promised olive groves, until Tony Hanlon swung the wheel and sent them bucking along on a smaller road, somewhat less well kept, that led first west, then northwest onto the rocky peninsula, out along its length nearly to the end, and finally cutting across the point to terminate in an unpaved parking lot. There Hanlon paid a fee to the attendant before easing the bus to a stop and letting the group out to follow Mrs. Wilson to *La Bufadora* itself.

It was a bit of a walk, and the State of Baja California had tried to make the way easier with a little rock work and some concrete. But it was still a dusty path with ruts and rocks and holes strewn along the way, all quite suitable for stumbling on. The tour party picked its way with care to a large concrete slab that had been laid down near a V-shaped cleft in the rocky cliff.

Just as they approached, there was a distant, deep, low-pitched thrumming under their feet. "Hey! I think I felt something through the soles of my shoes!" Grogan marveled, but nobody else claimed to have felt a thing, and with their questionable hearing, the group could not pick up the sound. Then there was a kind of squeaking groan, loud enough that they could all hear it, and suddenly a spout of water slammed into the air from the V-cleft, perhaps thirty or forty feet straight up. Spray splattered the edges of the low rock retaining wall and the platform, and the Camden-sur-Mer party leaped backward as one.

"Gracious!" Trinita Stainsbury gasped.

"Look at that!" Tootsie Armstrong squealed. "Oh, look-look-look ..."

"Amazing," one of the Jackson twins murmured. "We don't have anything like that back home in Alabama."

"That's nothing," Maralyn Wilson said, pleased at their reaction. "If the tide and the winds are right, that spout goes maybe seventy-five feet into the air. I've seen it go at least that high myself."

"When does it do it again?" Grogan asked.

"Well, the water has to build up in the caves underneath," their guide said. "Or so they tell me. The timing seems very irregular. Sometimes it happens sooner than other times, and ... all right, folks, here it comes again."

There had been another almost undetectable grumble of low sound under their feet, and they heard the eerie groan-and-whistle noise as the waves were forced forward through narrow stone passageways deep inside the cliff, and then with a booming *whoooosh,* the water leaped straight upward once more. This time, prepared for the spray, the party stepped backward in plenty of time to avoid being splashed.

"That beats Old Faithful, I'd say," Tom Brighton said. "They make you stand quite a ways back from Old Faithful, you know. And it just spouts and then stops. For a long time. Tell you the truth, I wasn't all that impressed. But this is like ... well, like an explosion from a water cannon. I've never seen anything like it! Anybody seen anything like this?"

"Can I go over there and look down into the water?" Grogan asked.

"I'd rather you didn't," Mrs. Wilson said. "It's not really fenced in, and the ground is slippery with moisture. You could fall."

"I'll stand back. I just want to look down there," he protested, moving forward. She reached out a restraining hand and then thought better of it, shrugging in a way that signified her resignation—but Roger Marx moved quickly to her side, whispered something to her, and then hurried along to follow Grogan. Grogan flinched slightly, but didn't protest as Marx, to the surprise of the others, threw an apparently friendly arm across Grogan's shoulder. But Caledonia thought it was more to get himself in position to execute a grab-and-save should Grogan begin to teeter, than to indicate a newfound sense of fellowship, for when Grogan leaned forward, Marx's hand clamped down firmly around Grogan's shoulder.

"Say," Grogan said in a wondering voice, "that's a steep drop. Straight sides. If you fell down there, you wouldn't get back up soon, would you? I wonder why somebody didn't push that kid over the edge, though? He must've been standing just about here." He leaned over again to peer into the depths of the cleft.

"What kid?" Marx said, gripping Grogan's shoulder even tighter.

"Had to be a kid," Grogan said. "You see that paper Pepsi cup floating down there? Now who but a nasty little kid would throw something like that into a clean, natural ... Whoooooooa!" He started backward convulsively, half on his own, half pulled by Roger Marx. While Grogan was talking, the distant drumming sound had begun to whisper under their feet, followed by the eerie groaning noise, and suddenly the water spout had come blasting upward, even higher than before. Grogan and Marx both were thoroughly sprayed before they could retreat to safety.

"Are you all right?" Mrs. Wilson asked them with concern.

"No harm done." Marx smiled reassurance and moved back onto the solid platform, brushing moisture from his clothing.

"I spend my life wet, one way or another," Grogan said cheerfully. His words were intelligible, but the tongue that formed them was slightly thick. "Mostly I'm soaked from the inside out, of course, so I don't think my system is going to notice the difference if I get a little soaked on the outside. Anyhow ... my own fault. I wanted to get close and see ... and I saw. Don't fuss at me."

"He's drunk!" Angela hissed to Caledonia. "Already! Why, it isn't even lunch-time yet."

"Oh, absolutely," Caledonia whispered back. "He's really irritable when he's sober. But look how chipper and cheerful he is. Even about getting all wet."

"So sorry to trouble you, ladies and gentlemen." A man's voice behind the group drew their attention away from Grogan and the blowhole. Craning her neck to see over the others of her party, Angela caught sight of a middle-aged man with coal-black hair and dark eyes. He was wearing a lightweight cotton blazer of bright yellow that had *Excursiones—Primera Clase,* or First Class Tours, embroidered in black on the breast pocket.

"My people," the man in the yellow jacket continued in smooth, nearly unaccented English, "would like to have their turn here close to *La Bufadora*. You have been here for several minutes now, and we would be obliged if you would move aside." Behind him, waiting along the pathway, Angela could see a small group of perhaps seven adults and two children.

The Camden-sur-Mer tour group began to shuffle obediently back down the walkway, but Maralyn Wilson stepped in front, between them and the guide. "Hey, wait a minute!" Her voice was sharp with annoyance. "Enrique, you can't just move my folks off. It's a free country, more or less. And they may not be finished yet. Let your people wait a minute! We'll be done and then—"

The guide from First Class Tours drew himself up and his eyes narrowed. "You *gringos* believe you can come down here and demand to have things your way without respect to the local people and the local customs." He spoke loudly and enunciated clearly, and Angela decided he was trying to be sure that his own tour group could hear and understand what he was saying. Perhaps he intended the group from Camden-sur-Mer to hear and understand, as well. "In Mexico, *señora* Wilson, it is customary to be polite and to share. Even if you have more money than we Mexicans, and you think you're so much better than—"

"All right, all right, take it easy." Maralyn Wilson had tried to defend her group's rights, but she was obviously unwilling to have a confrontation involving national pride. "Has everybody here," she said, turning back to her own tour group, "seen enough? All right then, I suggest we eat lunch at one of the little cafes right here." And she began to move forward, directing her group around the First Class Tours group, who stood very still, in total silence, perhaps embarrassed by the exchange between the guides. Or perhaps they had not understood the words, no matter how carefully enunciated. Indeed several of them smiled rather shyly and nodded politely as the group from Camden-sur-Mer passed.

"Did you say cafes?" Angela asked when they had moved clear of the other tourists. "What cafes? I didn't see any restaurants."

"Of course, you did. Those shed places near the parking lot, right at the end of this path," Mrs. Wilson said. "Sorry about the argument back there," she went on, "but that's typical. We used to hire First Class Tours and Enrique was one of our guides. He isn't at all happy that we do the guiding ourselves now. Come on now. Stop at the first one, the biggest one. They have a table that will hold all of us."

"That grungy little shack?" Trinita Stainsbury said, drawing her skirt close to her side as though to protect her clothing from brushing against something dirty. "Those places are just ... just shanties! Lean-tos! Sheds! Surely you don't mean for us to eat there."

"Sheds or not, they're fish restaurants," their guide said. "And you'll be in for a pleasant surprise."

With some reluctance, particularly from Trinita, the group sat down at a rough board table in one of the shacks—under the shelter of the roof, but without walls to shield them—and watched as their plates were heaped with yellow rice ("Seasoned with Mexican saffron," their guide explained), beans, a fresh salsa ("Don't be afraid, it's very mild," Mrs. Wilson said), a piece of unidentifiable grilled fish, and one of those hard-crusted, fluffy white rolls that seem to come with most meals in Baja, California.

Angela watched through narrowed eyes as the plates were prepared. "For once in my life," she said, "I agree with Trinita. What a place! Look at that grill! Look at that stove!"

"Oh, don't be such a priss," Caledonia said cheerfully. "Dog-goned ingenious, I'd say. A perfect way to recycle!" The "stove" was a rusty oil drum that held hot coals; the "grill" was just a piece of bent iron, wide enough to hold several pieces of fish and long enough to catch against the sides of the oil drum partway down, so that the fish was suspended over the fire at a good height to be thoroughly cooked.

"But ... but ... rusty iron? An old oil drum? Won't the fish be ..." Angela hesitated. "Won't the fish be dirty?"

Caledonia's laughter seemed to shake the open rafters, from which dusty strings of peppers and grimy braids of onions were hanging. "You're a hoot, you are, my girl! Any dirt that gets on the food is going to sterilize itself immediately in that red-hot fire! There won't be a germ alive inside that makeshift stove over there, if that's what you mean by 'dirt.' And if by chance you mean real grit and sand and other crunchy things ... well, it'll not only be sterilized, but you should remember the old saying—we have to eat a peck of dirt before we die anyhow."

Angela glared, but when her plate was served, she put a tentative fork into first the fish, then after a surprised "Say, Cal ... wait till you try this. It's not half bad. In fact, it's good," she went at the rice and the salsa with some enthusiasm and her face lit up again. "Oh, Cal, I take back everything. This is a terrific lunch!"

So the meal was a success, but the shopping was not. There were at least a dozen vendors gathered along the wire fence that separated the parking area from the path leading up the hill to the blowhole. Some had crude board tables on which to display their pottery, their woven serapes, their tin candle holders, and crude wood carvings. But the majority of these enterprising peasants had laid their goods on blankets or directly on the ground, and had hung various mosaic masks and velvet paintings behind them on the wire fence. And these vendors were more silent than the merchants in town. They neither played music to attract buyers' attention nor sang out appeals to come and look at their wares. "They remind me of the American Indians I saw in Santa Fe, selling their goods from blankets spread out on the sidewalks," Tom Brighton said. "Sort of stoic and resigned, as if to say, 'Buy if you want to, or just walk past if you want to'—as though it were all the same to them."

"Well," their driver, Tony Hanlon, said, strolling over to join them as they moved toward the bus, "that's because these folks *are* American Indians, mostly. Mexico's America, too, you know."

"Oh, I know," Tom Brighton said apologetically, running a hand through his crest of white hair. "I just say it wrong. Like I always say they're Mexicans and we're Americans. But I should say we're ... well, how would you say it? United States-ians?"

Hanlon grinned at him. "That's one I never solved myself. You people ready to head for home, I take it? Well, you better wait here while I de-park. That First Class Tours driver got his bus in at an angle so that I'll have to back and turn a few times to get out. We've already yelled at each other back and forth about it. Didn't do me a bit of good. So it'll take some doing for me to get our bus out."

Maralyn Wilson sighed deeply. "Anything to make life difficult for us. I told you. Well, we'll take our time getting to the bus, Tony. Just get us out as best you can. We'll kill a few minutes looking at the things for sale here."

The group walked slowly along the line of vendors, stopping from time to time to glance at a silver bangle bracelet or a *mantilla* comb of fake tortoiseshell. But mainly, having discovered that the prices were higher than prices in town, the group just kept on walking without bothering to examine the goods more closely.

"I suppose," Tootsie Armstrong said tentatively, "we should have asked if they would come down any in the prices. But bargaining makes me nervous, and I was awfully glad to let Mr. Hanlon do it all for me yesterday when we went to the market in town." Angela raised her eyebrows meaningfully in Caledonia's direction and got a nod in return that acknowledged the subject matter to be something they'd covered before.

"We're supposed to bargain?" one of the Jacksons said. "I didn't know ... I mean, I heard Mexicans did that, but I didn't realize we were supposed to do it, too. We never bargained back in Alabama."

"I've heard," Trinita Stainsbury said, happy to seem to know more than some of her fellows, "that if you don't bargain, they'll think you're foolish, because they expect to come down on almost every price."

"Really? But I wouldn't even know how to begin!" Tootsie Armstrong said plaintively. "Angela, would you know what to say?"

"No," Angela said, "I wouldn't. But then, when Douglas was alive, he was very good at striking bargains and he used to do all that kind of thing for the two of us. I remember once I went to join him for a leave and we were in a market in Morocco ..." Angela's rambling story lasted all the way back to the bus, and once they were aboard, she kept right on, filling in details that only she could possibly have cared about ("I remember what a bright, warm day it was. And the sky was so blue ...") until at last the bus turned back onto Highway One. The others had long since lost interest when she wound to the climax of her tale—that after nearly a half hour of bargaining, her husband had finally acquired at a reasonable price a huge brass tray she had coveted. When Angela finally paused for breath, happy in her memories, Tom Brighton—far too polite to interrupt earlier—had his chance to ask about the remainder of the day's agenda.

"Well," Maralyn Wilson said, rising in her seat and facing backward again, "I thought you might be interested in the San Tomas wine tasting rooms south of town."

"Wine tasting?" Grogan, who had been alternately drowsing and dozing, roused himself. "Wine tasting?"

"The San Tomas vineyards here produce several decent wines," Mrs. Wilson said. "And we might spend a little time there, if you're not worn out after our morning's excursion. What do we say?"

"Is it any different from wine tasting in the Napa Valley?" Trinita Stainsbury said. "I've done that, and after a while, one vineyard gets to be very much like another. And one wine, too. At least, to me. Though I'm sure a real connoisseur could tell the difference." Trinita's words were modest, but her tone implied that it would take some kind of expert to do better than she could.

"Well, I'm certain you've been to grander places, if you've done a tour of the Napa Valley," Mrs. Wilson said tactfully. "And we can surely put the wine tasting off till tomorrow morning."

"Oh, please do. I'm so exhausted," the Jackson twin with the dark glasses, which had never left her face the whole day, said wearily. "Can't we just go back to the hotel?"

"I vote for the hotel, too," Tootsie Armstrong said. "I'm sorry, but that thick feeling I had at breakfast hasn't really left. I need my nap."

"I wouldn't mind going back myself," Tom Brighton said. "I had a hip operation this last year and it aches if I don't rest it from time to time."

"Any objections then if we go straight on to the hotel?" the guide asked the group.

"Hey! What's wrong with just stopping for just a little while?" Grogan said, his voice rising in protest. "A wee taste of the grape—"

"Would kill me," the Jackson twin said sharply. "Please! Home. And a nap."

Maralyn Wilson nodded to Tony Hanlon, who guided the bus straight on into town instead of following the SAN TOMAS signs. "It's fine with me. As I said, we can always do the wine tasting tomorrow morning. I had planned a morning of shopping, but there's really plenty of time to go shopping today, after you nap and before dinner. Oh, and don't forget, the shops at the pueblo will be open after dinner as well."

"What pueblo? There's a pueblo near the hotel?" one of the Jacksons said to her sister, but loud enough that all the others could hear her. There was a little pause before she added, "That *is* one of those Indian houses built in layers, like they have out in Arizona and New Mexico, isn't it?"

Mrs. Wilson laughed. "Goodness, no, Miss Jackson. The word *pueblo* only means 'village.' And that's what the people at the hotel call that village near them—*El Pueblo.* I think it'd be worth your trying the shops there. You were talking about the prices being high out at *La Bufadora*? Well, you'll find the prices much more attractive there."

"I'd be happy to take 'em back into town instead, if they want to go," Tony Hanlon volunteered, throwing the words over his shoulder, but watching the road, for they were still on Ensenada's main street, and the shoppers up and down the avenue had a tendency to dart across whenever they saw something interesting in a shop on the other side. "Tourists!" Hanlon said with disgust as he braked yet again for a stout redhead with sunburned skin, who carried in one hand an uncapped bottle of Coca Cola, and in the other a basket packed with items covered in the familiar newspaper wrappings. "Tourists!" He threw an apologetic glance back over his shoulder. "Not you folks, of course. I just mean these idiots who don't watch where ... anyhow, I'd be glad to help you people and show you that market where Mrs. Armstrong bought—"

"I don't think much of that idea, Tony." Mrs. Wilson's voice wasn't unpleasant, but it was—to say the least—firm. She turned and leaned down, so that she was speaking directly into his ear, but her voice was loud enough that Angela could hear her plainly. "They've been shopping in town once already. So I suggest that this time they look through the shops at the pueblo. And they don't need your help. Clear? Thank you. Well then," she said, facing her group again, "first we'll head for the hotel—to give you a chance for a siesta. Very much in keeping with the Mexican culture, people. You're getting into the rhythm of the place. It's considered very smart here to rest after lunch so you can stay up late at night. Things really get moving around Mexico after dark. Let's see now"—she glanced at her watch, "it's only two-thirty. So there's plenty of time to nap and shop before dinner."

Up in their room, Angela denied that she needed to lie down, but Caledonia was emphatic. "I won't make it through supper without my nap! Especially after I got up so early. And don't forget we've kept going without even pausing for breath, right the way through lunch hour. Siesta, that's the ticket. Darned sensible, these Mexicans." And she threw herself heavily onto her bed, pulling the spread over her to ward off the breeze from the sea, which stirred gently through their window.

"I'm not even drowsy," Angela grumbled. "But if you insist, I'll try. The problem is, I'll probably have trouble getting to sleep tonight, too, if I nap, and I ... Cal, are you listening? Cal?" From the next bed she heard a loud, throaty snore. Caledonia had already dropped off. "Really," Angela said crossly. "She might have waited till I finished talking. I know I'm never going to be able to fall asleep now myself. What a nuisance to have to lie here and rest and lose shopping time."

She pulled the spread over her, as Caledonia had done, and closed her eyes—and the next thing she knew the sun was streaming through the window, straight into her face. She sat up and shook her head. "I thought it was early afternoon," she muttered. "But the sun's in the west already." She picked up the alarm clock next to her and was amazed to find it was already four-thirty. "Good heavens! Cal! Cal, wake up! We've slept the afternoon away, and if we don't hurry, we won't get any shopping in at all."

Caledonia was slow to rouse, and Angela was pacing impatiently by the time her friend had splashed some water on her face, combed her hair, and changed into an unrumpled caftan. "Tell you what," Caledonia said. "I saw something in the hotel boutique that I'm interested in—a glorious lace caftan that appeared, remarkable as that may seem, to be my size, or close to it. I haven't bought clothes off the rack for three decades! Imagine if I came to Mexico and found something I could wear in the ready-mades. Want to come with me and look it over?"

With some reluctance, Angela agreed that they could stop in the hotel's own shops before crossing the road to *El Pueblo* and the larger selection offered there. "So long as I get to look over there later," she said.

But Caledonia did indeed find a caftan that was supposed to he her size, and it was natural she would want to try it on. "Oh, yes, *señora*," the clerk said happily. "We understand about large sizes here in Mexico."

"Where on earth did this exquisite lace come from?"

"Oh, it is our own," the clerk replied. "Handmade in Morelia, as it happens, one of our larger and more cosmopolitan provincial cities." She pulled and patted and adjusted a few minutes, frowning in concentration as she regarded Caledonia's gigantic image in the triple glass. "I believe this will fit better if it is taken up at the shoulder, *señora*. When will you be leaving us to go home? Not till tomorrow perhaps?"

"Yes, sometime in the late morning, I think. Isn't that right, Angela?"

Angela turned from the pile of shawls she was inspecting and nodded. There was simply no use getting cross with Caledonia when she was in the middle of a fitting. Angela took a great deal more time with her own clothes than Caledonia did, and getting a fitting was something she understood completely. Besides, the fabrics of the shawls and the fine hand embroidery that decorated each one had absorbed her attention completely. "Take your time, Cal," she called across the room.

"Well, there will be plenty of time to do your alterations," the clerk said. A seamstress had come out from the workshop behind the little boutique in response to the clerk's summons and moved quickly around Caledonia, deftly pinning the shoulder seam of the caftan, taking a small tuck in the sleeve. "We will have the gown ready," the clerk went on, "by mid-morning."

The caftan was paid for and handed over to the seamstress, and Caledonia put her own clothes back on. She and Angela looked at a selection of handsome sterling silver hairpins, and Angela treated herself to a small bottle of imported French perfume which, as she told Caledonia, was selling here for less than half what it would have cost back in San Diego.

They were amazed to spot a clock and see that it had reached six-fifteen. They had spent nearly two hours eyeing, trying, and buying, and they would have to hurry if they meant to change for dinner.

Chapter 8

Evening, November 12

"Well, what'll we do this evening?" Caledonia stretched her massive arms and yawned with contentment. Dinner had been excellent again—"I can't fault our Mrs. Wilson on her choice of eating places!" Caledonia had said happily—and after a nap and a full meal, the entire group had been quietly convivial, appreciative of the food and service, pleased with each other's conversation. Mr. Grogan had, of course, been drinking heavily to the point of drowsy numbness, but those of the party whose margarita indulgence was excessive on the night before had by this time fully recovered. And when a solicitous waiter asked if anyone would care for an after-dinner drink, the chorus of refusals was unanimous, even including Mr. Grogan, though he had declined because he already had his third large glass of something golden-tan that had been poured over ice cubes.

Maralyn Wilson had refused an invitation (issued, of course, by Roger Marx) to join the group at the big table and dined quickly at a small side table. She and Tony Hanlon seemed to have forgotten their brief confrontation on the trip home or else they had made their peace, for they conversed quietly throughout the meal until Maralyn Wilson excused herself and left the dining room. At the main table, Roger Marx watched her go, and then apparently made a decision. With a quick "Excuse me, folks," he flung his napkin down and hurried after her.

Hanlon smiled wryly as he watched Marx go, then strolled to the buffet to get another helping of the flan. If he'd been upset by his boss's scolding in the afternoon, he was certainly not upset now.

Rather, he seemed particularly relaxed and pleased with life, eating the caramel-covered flan with slow enjoyment.

The Jackson twins had been very interested in Caledonia's story of her new lace caftan. "We can't hardly find clothes for ourselves off the rack either," one Jackson twin said, running her hands over her ample curves to illustrate the reason why. "It would really be something if they could fit us right here in the hotel, wouldn't it?"

"You say they'll do alterations overnight?" the other twin said. "Now that would be worth investigating. What do you say, sister, that we stop at the hotel boutique before we go up to bed?" And the twins jiggled and giggled their way out of dining room, arm in arm.

"I promised all the girls back home—Mary Moffet and Emma Grant and Janice Felton—I promised them picture postcards. But somehow, I haven't found the time to write a single card," Tootsie Armstrong said. "I s'pose I better do that, but I haven't got any postcards, and—"

"Why not buy some at the magazine stand in the lobby?" Angela suggested. "I'm sure they'll have pictures of *La Bufadora*, and—"

"And of the fish cannery," Jerry Grunke said. Angela was startled at his interjection, though whether she was more taken aback by his joining the conversation or by the bizarre suggestion of a scenic photograph, it was hard to say. "That's maybe the most interesting thing in Ensenada," he went on, "and nobody arranged a visit for us. So I thought maybe tomorrow we could stop there before we go to the wine tasting."

"A fish cannery?" Trinita Stainsbury said with fine distaste. "All smelly and slimy and all? What could possibly be interesting about that?"

"Well, it's a big local industry," Grunke said. "And I've never seen a cannery and maybe I won't ever get another chance. Don't you want to see it?"

"Good heavens no," Trinita said haughtily. "And if you people will excuse me ..." and she pushed away from the table and stalked out.

Grunke smiled. "Upset her, didn't I? Oh, well ..." and he, too, shoved his chair back. " 'Night, everybody."

He left the dining room, followed immediately by Tootsie Armstrong, who was in a state of mild befuddlement about her postcards. "I'd better start on them," she said. "But pictures of the cannery? Do you suppose the girls would really like those? I suppose I ought to see what they have for sale. Pictures of the cannery? I'd thought perhaps pictures of that lovely old church." She toddled off toward the lobby on her little high heels, still murmuring her confusion.

"Anything to suggest for activities this evening, Tom?" Caledonia asked Tom Brighton.

He grinned and ran a hand through his crest of white hair. "Well, actually, I was thinking of looking over the grounds. We've got so many lights around here, you can see the flowers and shrubs almost as well as in daylight. And though I don't garden any longer myself, I'm still interested in plants. There are things down here we don't have even in Southern California. So I thought I'd do a botanical tour before I turned in. You ladies"—he made a gesture that included both Caledonia and tiny Angela—"you interested in joining me?"

"Oh, I don't think so, Tom," Caledonia said. "Moving around the country the way Herman and I did all those years he was in the Navy, we never had much chance to cultivate a garden. I mean, we didn't know whether we'd be in our quarters three months or three years, so there was no point in trying to grow roses or something like that. Marigolds, maybe. A few tomato plants maybe. But I just never got into that. I appreciate having flowers in the garden, but I don't give a rip how they got there."

"That," Angela said, "is pretty much my story as well. Cal hit the nail on the head. A lot of Navy wives don't do gardening because of the feeling that they're only passing through wherever it is they're living at the moment. I think I'll just say no to that garden tour, but thanks for the thought."

When only Grogan, nodding over his glass of unidentifiable liquid, and the two of them remained at their table, Angela and Caledonia finally rose from their places and strolled toward the lobby. "Tell you what," Caledonia said. "I can't think of anything I'd rather do myself than read a while in a warm, scented tub. I'll just throw in some bath salts and relax in water right up to my neck. After an hour of that, maybe I'll sit on the balcony and soak up the sight of the ocean and the sound of the waves for a few minutes. And then I think I'll go to bed and sleep like a rock."

"Cal, that isn't like you," Angela said. "You're the one who stays up till all hours watching television when we're at home."

"Ah, but there I can sleep late. I've been getting up with the chickens here."

"Oh, hardly that early, Cal."

"Well, it seems like the crack of dawn. Furthermore, I lead a kind of sedentary life at home, but here I'm tramping dusty trails looking at natural wonders, wearing myself out traipsing through the shops ..."

"Oh Cal, don't exaggerate. We haven't had that hard a day." Caledonia eyed her little friend shrewdly. "Okay, 'Fess up, Angela. You had something specific in mind, didn't you? Something you wanted me to come along for, right? What was it you wanted to do?"

"Go shopping," Angela said. "Don't you remember? We were going into *El Pueblo* this afternoon, but we got sidetracked by the shop here in the hotel. Well, we can go over to the village right now; Mrs. Wilson said the shops would be open tonight."

Caledonia stretched lazily again. "More shopping? Don't you ever get enough? We'll get in some shopping tomorrow morning before we head home, so I don't see why we have to—"

"There's another reason to go over there," Angela said.

"There always is." Caledonia grinned. "Another reason, I mean. The minute you make up your mind to do something, you think of at least four reasons why it's a good idea. In case I object. You spend more time thinking up reasons for your decisions after the fact than you do making the decisions in the first place. Why don't you just tell the truth? You want to go and the reason doesn't matter a bit."

"No, seriously, there is a reason. A good one. We haven't had nearly enough exposure to Spanish on these trips. And I thought—"

"Not enough exposure? Good heavens, girl, the language is all around you. The people are talking Spanish, the newspapers are printed in Spanish, and the signs ... even the signs for the ladies' room are in Spanish! What do you mean you don't get enough Spanish?"

"Well, I mean I don't hear enough of it. Because these people talk Spanish to each other, of course, but they make the effort to speak English to us. The waiters and bellboys, the clerks in the shops we visit, they all do it. And those times when somebody can't understand English, like the fellow at that fish stand where we had lunch today, then Mrs. Wilson steps in and does all the talking for us. And anyhow, when I do hear Spanish spoken, they go so fast I can't make out the separate words. I need somebody to talk to me slowly, pronouncing each word separately—like the man does on the teaching tapes. Then I think I can understand. I keep telling myself it can't be that difficult to learn. After all, we heard little children all over Ensenada today speaking Spanish! But I need the chance to try for myself."

Caledonia nodded. "I take it back about your thinking up alibis. That makes a strange kind of sense. Well, you go over to the village if you want to. I bought my lace gown and that's quite enough shopping for me for today. And as for the language ... well, let's be honest, you need practice more than I do. I'm catching on just fine. You're the one who can't seem to get the hang of it. So I'm going to do just what I said—relax in a warm tub and then get on to bed. You go ahead and go exploring. Or shopping. Or talking to the natives. Or whatever it is you want to do. You just be careful crossing the road from the hotel to the village, okay?"

"What, no cautions about being careful of strangers?"

"You're old enough to look out for yourself in that way, I hope. My concern is that you're impulsive. When you get excited about something, you just plunge ahead and ignore things around you, even when they're important. If you were to see a pretty necklace in a shop window across the street, you might walk right out in front of an oncoming car without even looking left and right. So just be careful, won't you?"

"Okay, Mom," Angela said with a grin. "I'll be good. And I promise I can take care of myself. All the same, it'd be a lot more fun if you'd come along."

"No, sorry. Not tonight. You go ahead." And the two separated at the foot of the broad stairs at one side of the lobby, Caledonia heading upstairs to their room, Angela heading toward the front of the hotel. The ubiquitous bellboy swung the door wide as she stepped out into the night, and she moved quickly down the walk that traversed the front lawns. Once she got to the road that marked the end of *El Palacio's* property, the lights from the floodlights around the grounds no longer reached her. That seemed eerie to Angela; going out alone after dark was something she never did these days, not with most California towns and cities grown so dangerous. Besides, shopping so late at night for anything but emergency supplies seemed somehow incongruous. Feeling strangely apprehensive, she stopped to look carefully left and right before she crossed the road, just as Caledonia had asked her to, but there was no traffic in sight at all. Still she hesitated. It was very dark, and she was all alone. She took heart, remembering that she had read somewhere that the streets of Mexican towns were much safer, even at night, than those in the United States. She told herself that she'd come this far with no difficulties. Surely nothing bad would happen. So, breathing deeply and telling herself not to be silly, Angela shook off a sudden shiver of nervousness, lifted her head and strode, with steps she hoped looked confident, across the road and into the better-lit area of the village.

One short block into the village lay the town square, a small grassy plot with dozens of trees, a large, wrought-iron gazebo in its center that was probably a bandstand, and a number of benches scattered around, most of them occupied by middle-aged couples or families. Even the little children stayed up late, Angela noted; there were several youngsters playing an impromptu game of tag around a hibiscus bush. Young girls and young men, probably in their teens and twenties, were promenading around the square, eyeing each other with varying degrees of hope, speculation, invitation, or pretended indifference—but unlike boys and girls in San Diego, who would be strolling side-by-side and hand-in-hand, these youngsters walked in opposite directions. That is to say, the girls walking with other girls, circled the square in one direction, while the young men, walking in pairs or in small groups, circled the square in the opposite direction. As they passed, they were able to look directly at each other (or pointedly avoid each other's gaze), and they could be sure that sooner or later in their circuit they would pass any particular person in whom they had an interest.

"I just bet," Angela told her friends later, as she described all she had seen, "I just bet they exchanged notes and flirted and made dates and all that as they passed each other, yet they never seemed to stop walking at all."

"That," Mrs. Wilson explained, "is because they were being chaperoned from a distance. It's the strict upbringing of girls from the middle classes. Yes, and girls from some working-class families, too. Times are changing, even down here, and some girls are less closely supervised than they used to be—especially in Mexico City they behave more like girls from the United States do. But out here in the provinces ... Well, those adults sitting around on the benches were the substitute for the old-fashioned *dueña*. Those adults were almost certainly watching the youngsters like hawks, and they'd have made a real fuss if a boy and girl had paired off and left the square, for instance."

"In this day and age?"

"Sure. Even in our modern world. Remember, this is simply not the United States!"

Now Angela looked around her with interest. Bordering the four sides of the square were an open air restaurant full of cheerful people, laughing and talking—apparently locals,

Angela noted, and not tourists; a bank; an American Express office (the latter two were closed, but *Banco de Ensenada* was easy for Angela to translate, and *American Express* was apparently the same in both languages); a small grocery store; and a number of shops, lights on and doors wide open. In fact, the whole square was so brightly lit, it might as well have been mid-afternoon, rather than nearly ten at night.

The shops were modest in size, but a few of them seemed to be rather upscale. There were a couple whose windows were crowded from top to bottom with tooled leather or Aztec calendars, exactly like the shops in town. But there were a few that seemed infinitely more exclusive—like the leather shop that displayed in its window a single handbag of mottled brown and white, tastefully lit with a small spotlight. A neatly lettered card nearby announced in both Spanish and English that the purse was fashioned of UNBORN CALF.

Angela shook her head and moved on. A jeweler's place was next door, and rather than the jumble of silver objects that crowded the window trays of the shops she'd seen in both Ensenada and Tijuana, three black velvet stands in this window held exquisite jewelry. The first contained a long string of carved silver heads, on a second was a matching bracelet, and on a third a huge silver ring carved to resemble a jaguar mask with inlaid obsidian to simulate the animal's coat, and for the eyes, green stones that might well be tiny emeralds. "Wow," Angela said softly. But she moved along to another shop that displayed handsome wood carvings of angels and saints, perhaps antiques, for the wood seemed weathered.

Angela was thinking perhaps she ought to turn around and start over again, back at the first shop on the corner, stopping in each shop in turn as she progressed around the square. "I should get some organization into this, so I'll know what I've already seen and what I haven't," she muttered to herself. "I'd hate to miss something good. Oh, I wish Cal had come with me. She'd love all these pretty ... *Oof!*"

As she turned back, she had collided with three men moving the other way. She bounced off one of them and into the nearby shop wall.

"*Perdóneme, señora,*" one of them murmured politely.

"*Lo siento,*" said a second as they moved past.

Angela was so startled she wasn't able for a moment to think of even an English word to accept their apologies. Then suddenly, as they moved away from her, the Spanish words popped into her head, and she called out, perhaps too loudly, "*¡No importa! ¡Está bien!*"

She was inordinately pleased with herself. She sounded, she thought, exactly like that fellow on her language learning tapes. She certainly ought to, she thought, for she had played and played them over and over. Oh, maybe her pronunciation wasn't exactly the same ... and then she gasped. One of the men had turned slightly as he raised a hand to his forehead in acknowledgment, and it was someone she knew. Or at least ... it surely looked like ... who? Of course, as she reminded herself in the same moment, she'd only seen him for a moment, and then in a heavily shadowed profile. But surely it was ...

Impulsively, she turned and followed the men. They were moving briskly, but only walking, not running, and she was able to gain a bit on them. And the closer she got, the more she became convinced that she had been right. Two of the men were total strangers—not at all surprising in a strange town in a foreign country in the middle of the night. But the man in the middle, surely he was Juan Saenz, the gardener from Camden-sur-Mer. Dodging the girls who were moving straight at her and ducking around two boys in front of her, Angela quickened her pace until, as the men passed under one of the butter-yellow streetlights, she could see them more clearly.

At the same moment, the tall, spare man in the middle turned his head toward one of his companions to say something and Angela caught sight of his luxuriant black moustache. "Yes," she whispered to herself. "It *is* Juan! I thought so. But what on earth is he doing here?"

At that moment the three men swung around a corner and started down a side street, away from the square. When she reached the corner, Angela too turned into the side street, but she moved much more cautiously than the men had. The new street was far narrower than the streets around the square and there was no sidewalk. Furthermore, the roadway was paved with cobbles and there were streetlights only at the corners. Angela made herself slow down even more. It wouldn't do to wrench an ankle this far away from the hotel. She picked her way along what seemed like a stucco-and-adobe canyon formed by the blank walls of houses, shops, sheds, warehouses—it was hard to tell exactly what the structures on either side of the alleyway really were, since they turned a blind side toward the public, and what doors and windows faced the street were closed, covered with protective wrought-iron bars, and either shuttered or dark.

It was a warm night, but she shivered nervously as the light from the square receded behind her. The three men ahead still had not seemed to notice that she was behind them, and the narrow street, the darkness, and the cobblestones didn't seem to bother them. They walked at a steady, unhurried pace, but the distance between them and Angela gradually increased. They were more than halfway down the narrow street, while she was less than a quarter of the way along.

Angela shivered again. What on earth was she doing anyhow? Who cared if that was Juan ahead of her or not? And suppose it was? What was she going to say to him—"I recognized you and I was curious about what you were doing in Ensenada?" But on the other hand, suppose it wasn't Juan at all, but some complete stranger? What would she say then? And why did it matter whether it was Juan or not? Caledonia would scold her for being impetuous again, for chasing after someone who was practically a stranger, acting without thinking, and when she tried to defend herself, Angela thought, she wouldn't have a leg to stand on! She really had no good reason to be ... *Ouch!* Her toe stubbed against a raised paving block, and she caught herself just before she stumbled and fell. "That does it," she muttered aloud. "That does it. There's no point being an idiot, especially when there's no purpose to it. I'm just going to turn around and ... where did they go?"

While she had been busy catching her balance, her attention momentarily on herself instead of on her quarry, the three men ahead had disappeared. The street stretched out completely empty, dark, and silent. Behind her she could hear the faint sounds that meant activity and people and—she hesitated—and safety. Ahead there was silence, except for the lonely *meow* of a prowling cat. Not a footstep, not the sound of a door opening and closing ... Just nothing!

For a long moment, Angela stood stock-still. And then she shook herself. Why was she following this man anyway? Even if it was the Juan she knew, what did it matter? Wasn't a man entitled to ... But surely he had been in Tijuana when they were there as well. She remembered that moment when she had thought she'd seen him across the carnival grounds behind their hotel. And now he was here in Ensenada, and once again near their hotel.

Taking a deep breath, she made up her mind. Back. Go back to home and safety. Wake Caledonia. Ask her about all this. Caledonia was sensible and she'd know what to do.

"I don't know! I haven't the faintest idea," Caledonia growled, rubbing the sleep in her eyes. "For Pete's sake, Angela, I've just got myself to sleep. Then you wake me up and want me to explain why you think you saw somebody you know."

"Our head gardener. Juan Saenz. Just like I saw him in Tijuana. What do you think?"

"I think you need to simmer down and go to bed. And I think I need to go back to sleep. I can't work it out right now, because nothing you're saying makes the slightest bit of sense. So wait till tomorrow morning after breakfast. And then we can ask the others if they've seen this guy, too, or if you're having some kind of delusion. *Folie de gardener* or something." And Caledonia flopped back down in the bed and pulled the covers up over her head to block out the light.

"Oh, but Cal—"

"No but, no Cal, no talk, no nothing!" Caledonia's muffled voice came from deep inside her pillows. "Sleep! Sleep! Look at the crystal ball and listen to my voice: You are getting sleepy ... very sleepy ..."

"Oh, all right," Angela said reluctantly. She supposed it really wasn't urgent enough to risk Caledonia's having a temper tantrum. She'd seen Caledonia in a real rage only once. They had been down on the beach and some teenaged surfer, a stranger to both of them, had leveled a kick at a stray dog trying to get at a scrap of sandwich the boy had thrown carelessly aside. Caledonia's voice had been a thunder clap of doom and her nearly six feet of height, her more than two hundred pounds of weight, had seemed to grow to the size of the Statue of Liberty. She had marched over to the boy, lifted him up by one scrawny arm, and with the kid practically dangling in mid-air, had delivered a scolding that absolutely flattened his ego.

"And if I ever again see you abuse an animal—even so much as a field mouse—I'm going to wring that pimply neck of yours," Caledonia had roared, shaking the boy. "Is that clear? Do you understand? Well, do you?" The boy had nodded wordlessly, and when she freed him from her grasp, he had scuttled over to his backpack to hunt up another sandwich, which he handed to the scrawny and totally bewildered dog. Then he picked up his pack and his boogie board and raced away from the towering madwoman and her fury. And now, years later and miles farther south from that defining moment in time, Angela found she had no wish to keep on annoying her friend. Caledonia merely irritated was far preferable to Caledonia mortally enraged.

"I guess tomorrow will do as well," Angela said soothingly. "You just go back to sleep." And she tiptoed through the room as she slipped out of her clothing, turning off the bedroom lights when she entered the bathroom; she closed that door tightly and muffled the sound of running water for her bath by holding a towel over the stream of water from the tap. Once bathed, she donned her pajamas, brushed her hair, and creamed her face—all right there in the bathroom rather than in front of the bedroom vanity. By the time she turned off the bathroom light and tiptoed back into the bedroom, a deep snore was coming from Caledonia's direction, and Angela snuggled down into her own bed and promptly fell asleep.

She wasn't certain at what time she began to dream, a dream of being in a Sioux village, watching braves in their buckskins, beaded moccasins, and feathered headdresses dancing around to the beat of a tom-tom. *Boom-Boom-Boom* ... the drum stopped, but the dancers kept circling the fire, toe-heel, toe-heel ... *Boom-Boom-Boom,* the drum sounded again. "Mrs. Benbow! Mrs. Wingate! Get up please." *Boom-Boom-Boom* ...

Why, Angela thought in her dream, were the Indians calling her name?

"Get up, please," the voice came again. "Mrs. Wingate ... Mrs. Benbow ... Answer the door ..." *Knock-knock-knock* ...

The drumbeat disappeared as the sound melted into knuckles against wood, the Indian dancers receded, and Angela blearily fumbled for the switch of the bedside lamp. It was still dark, but now she recognized what was happening. There was someone knocking at the door. Calling her. She shuffled across the room and without removing the guard chain, opened the door a tiny crack. "Who is it? What's the matter? Is it a fire? Who's there?"

"It's Mrs. Wilson," their guide said. "Maralyn Wilson. I'm sorry to wake you, Mrs. Benbow, but the police are here and they want to talk to everyone as soon as possible. I'm waking everybody up. Don't bother to dress all the way. Just put on a robe and slippers."

"What time is it?" Angela said blankly. She could hear Caledonia stirring behind her, getting up out of her bed as well.

"It's five-thirty a.m.," Mrs. Wilson said. "It'll be light soon. The police want to see everybody in the hotel dining room. As soon as you can." And she disappeared from Angela's sight. Then Angela heard knocking at a door nearby, probably next door, and heard Mrs. Wilson calling once more, "Miss Jackson ... Yoo-hoo, Miss Jackson ... can you please get up?"

"What's this all about?" Caledonia said muzzily. "The police? Something about the police?"

"I know exactly as much as you do," Angela said. "But the sooner we get downstairs, the sooner we'll find out. Come on." By the time the two of them were decently covered in cotton housecoats and on their way downstairs, the others had already waked and were heading for the hotel dining room as well. Trinita Stainsbury was wearing a flowing pegnoir of cerise satin with some kind of matching netting tied like a turban over her dyed and carefully set hair. She had taken time, Angela noted sourly, to put on lipstick.

Wearing striped pajamas, leather slippers, and brocade robes tied at the waist with a matching sash apiece, Tom

Brighton and his roommate, Roger Marx, looked as though they probably bought their nightclothes at the same shop, but there the resemblance ended. Brighton looked faintly rumpled, his robe creased, his crest of white hair standing on end. Marx by contrast looked as neat as though he'd just donned his outfit for a session as a photographer's model.

Tootsie Armstrong seemed to have had time to dress, for she was in a slack suit and loafers, with a scarf tied around her hair, but the Jackson twins had rolled out in big fuzzy slippers, floor-length flannel gowns, and woolly robes. ("Wouldn't you think they'd swelter? Those outfits are more suitable for the Arctic Circle than for here!" Angela whispered. Caledonia didn't seem able to comment, though she let out a strangled sound that might or might not have been agreement.)

"Where do you suppose Mr. Grunke is?" Angela said, looking around at their scruffy and ill-assorted group standing huddled together in the middle of the dining room. "And where's Mr. Grogan?"

"Grogan's over there," Tom Brighton whispered. "In the same chair he was in at dinner." He pointed down the length of the dining room into an area that was not now lit. There in the shadows sat Grogan, his eyes at half mast, his chin sunk down onto his chest. Whether he was just now dropping off to sleep after a night of drinking or whether he was just now waking up, hungover and only half conscious, it was impossible to guess. "And I have no idea where Jerry Grunke is," Brighton went on. "Of course, he has a single room. I bunk in with Marx. So I couldn't say."

"I am sorry to wake you, ladies and gentlemen." A man's voice came from the entrance behind them. As one, the group turned toward the speaker who had just entered. A man of medium height with dark, graying hair and hooded eyes stood in the doorway from the lobby. He was flanked on either side by a younger man in uniform, a uniform that looked freshly pressed and frighteningly official. Not working policemen, those two, Angela thought. Their function was more that of escort or bodyguard to this man in his brown civilian suit and his ... good heavens, was the man actually wearing a pink shirt? Yes, Angela told herself, it's pink all right. Well, I like pink and brown together. It's just that on a man ...

"Ladies and gentlemen," the man was speaking again, his voice that of a man used to command, with only the faintest Mexican accent, "please find yourselves places to sit down. I am Colonel Esteban Campo of the Ensenada police, and I have some very sad news for you. One of your group has met with a serious accident. Or rather, not an accident. One of your group has been killed. Down on the beach. And there is no doubt at all that it is murder. I have called you from your beds so that you can talk to me—tell me anything you saw or heard—tell me what you know about this man. Something you know may give us an idea of where to go with our inquiries. Some one of you may in fact be of great help. We need to know everything you can remember about Mr. ..." He searched his memory. "Mr. ... ah, Mr. ..."

"None of us really knew him well," Angela volunteered. She never liked to see people hem and haw any more than necessary. Might as well cut to the chase, as she often told Caledonia. And therefore she now answered Colonel Campo's questions before she was specifically asked. "After all, he only moved in a few months ago and he wasn't really very sociable. Men aren't good at small talk, anyway. All the same, we usually find out something about our residents over a period of time. But about him ... practically nothing. We know he's a widower, and we know he lived in Los Angeles before he came to live with us."

"To live with you?" Colonel Campo said. "He lived with you?"

"Oh, not with me," Angela said hastily. "With all of us. In the retirement home, you see."

"He had retired?" the colonel asked again, and his voice showed even more confusion.

"Well, I suppose so. We do get a few who still have parttime work—but usually as volunteers at the local hospital or something. I don't believe Mr. Grunke worked as a volunteer or had a regular job, either one. But I don't know for sure, because, as I say, we didn't really know him well. Didn't talk to him about personal things. But this is still a shock, even if Mr. Grunke wasn't a close friend."

There was a pause, and then the colonel said, "You speak of a Mr. Grunke. Who is this Mr. Grunke?"

"I'm Grunke." Another man's voice sounded, and Jerry Grunke walked into the dining room from behind the colonel and his men, coming around to join the other members of his tour group. He was fully dressed in slacks, a polo shirt, heavy sneakers—and Angela thought that if these weren't the same clothes he had worn the day before, they were very similar. "You remember me, don't you?" he asked the colonel.

"Oh. But yes, of course, I remember you. You are the man who found the body. Oh, and now I see! And you are the man to whom the lady refers," the colonel said, enlightenment raising his brows and opening his eyes wider. "You are the man who lives with them and is retired. Apparently she thinks you are the man who ... *señora*"—he turned to Angela—"this is obviously not the gentleman who was killed down on the beach. This is the gentleman who found the body. I am sorry, *señor*"—he turned back to Grunke—"that I did not understand at first. I had not learned your name. The initial investigation was over when they called me, and I only arrived just over half an hour ago. Forgive my confusion."

"Oh, don't apologize," Grunke said. "I understand. One of your men—the men who responded to our phone call—he took down my name when he interviewed me, but there's no reason you should have known it."

"But if it wasn't Mr. Grunke who died," Angela impatiently interrupted this exchange of courtesies, "if it wasn't Mr. Grunke, who was it?"

The colonel had located a small notebook in one of his pockets and flipped it open to a page of notes. "I have the name right here. Ah, of course. The dead man is named Tony Hanlon."

His pronunciation of *Hanlon* left a great deal to be desired; he sounded the *H* as a guttural compound sound—very much like the X in *Mexico* when the country's name is pronounced by a native speaker. But there was no mistake that he was talking about their tour driver, the young man who had in life looked so much like Tyrone Power.

Chapter 9

Morning, November 13

"There is a small writing room off the end of the lobby; you know it?" Colonel Campo said to the group, most of whom nodded in response. "We will hold our interviews with you there, one at a time. Mr. Grunke, follow me, please. You will be the first." He turned to leave.

"I'll just go upstairs and get dressed while I wait," Angela said to Caledonia. "I don't like sitting around in my bathrobe. I feel so ... so disheveled. And it's only a thin robe." She shivered. "It's really colder than I thought. Maybe the Jackson twins had the right idea. Anyhow, I'm going upstairs to change."

"I would be obliged," the colonel said, pausing in the doorway, "if none of you would leave the dining room until after you have been interviewed. I do not want my men to have to hunt high and low for one of you when I am ready to hear what you have to say. So please stay. It will not take too long. And I will ask the management to open the kitchen early. Breakfast will help you pass the time and will help you to feel warmer." Without waiting for a response, he turned on his heel again. His smartly uniformed escorts marched out at a respectful step behind him, and Mr. Grunke, who had taken a chair at the edge of the group, rose and walked after them.

"He's got long ears, that fellow," Angela said to Caledonia—though she waited carefully to make her comment until the colonel was truly out of earshot. And then she shivered again.

"The sun'll be up soon," Caledonia said comfortingly. Friendly conversation at six a.m. would ordinarily have been beyond her, but the seriousness of the situation had roused her from her usual early morning torpor. "It's plenty warm once the sun takes over," she went on. "I expect we just didn't realize before now that it would be cold before dawn, because we haven't been up and running around in the middle of the night."

"I'm going to go to the kitchen and try to speed things up," Mrs. Wilson said.

"The colonel said not to leave the room," Roger Marx said, jumping to his feet and taking hold of her arm as though he intended to stop her.

Impatiently, she shook off his restraining hand. "I'm not leaving, for Pete's sake! I'm only going into the kitchen." She gestured across the room at the swinging doors. Behind their small, circular windows, lights had come on and the group could hear faintly the metal-on-metal sounds of pots and pans being activated. As she passed through the swinging door, she called out in rapid Spanish, obviously making requests and giving orders.

The group from Camden-sur-Mer sat in silence for a while, and then one of the Jacksons said impatiently, "The colonel's taking an awfully long time with Mr. Grunke, isn't he? It seems like they've been gone forever. Simply forever! I mean, what is there to ask? Mr. Grunke found poor Mr. Hanlon and what else is there to say?"

"The colonel needs to know what else Mr. Grunke saw on the beach," Angela said briskly. She and Caledonia were the only people in the room, or so she believed, who were genuinely knowledgeable about police procedure, and she was delighted to play the role of expert. "What exactly was he doing on the beach, that's one question the colonel will ask. And what time it was, of course. And was there anybody else there. And did he notice anything unusual."

"Unusual?" Trinita Stainsbury said, adjusting her satin pegnoir in a more attractive drape. "Like what would you call unusual?"

"Oh, for instance, if there'd been a flock of cows down on the beach," Angela said flippantly. Within moments, she wished she had not tried to make a little joke, for the conversation quickly got out of hand.

"I don't think cows come in flocks," Caledonia said. "Herds, is more like it."

"What would cows be doing on the beach anyway?" one of the Jacksons asked. "I've never seen cows on a beach."

"Maybe that's why our young driver was killed!" the other Jackson twin suggested eagerly. "They weren't supposed to be there, of course, and the cowherder was frightened Mr. Hanlon would tell someone and the cowherder would get in trouble."

"Not a cow *herder*," Mr. Brighton said. "Oh, I'm sorry. I shouldn't have corrected you, dear lady. Of course you know that cow*boy* is the term. Not cow*herd*."

"Or *cowhand*. Like in, 'I'm an old cowhand, from the Rio Grand' ..." a voice suggested weakly from the far end of the room. It was Grogan, rousing to join the group. But when he got to his feet and wobbled toward them, he found himself dangerously unsteady and slumped into another chair, resuming his silence.

"You know, that's interesting. Why do we say cow*boys*, Tom?" Trinita Stainsbury asked, ignoring Grogan as his fellow residents often did. "Of course, with sheep it's a herder. Shepherd equals sheep herder, right?"

"And it's a herder for pigs, too." Caledonia nodded. "Although it seems to me the last swineherd I heard about was in a Grimm brothers' fairy tale."

"And of course there are goatherds," the other Jackson twin said. "I read about them in *Heidi* when I was a little girl."

"So, Tom?" Trinita challenged. "Why no cowherds? And why are the ... the attendants to cattle called boys anyway? Why cow*boys* and not *cowmen*? I mean, we never say mailboys, or sales boys, or workboys, or ..."

"We say choir boys," Tootsie Armstrong volunteered.

"That," Trinita said loftily, "is because they *are* boys! But the rest of the—"

"You're all way off the subject," Angela said desperately. Usually, she was the one who muddied the conversational waters with side issues. She was, to say the least, an impulsive conversationalist who often said whatever came into her mind. But on this occasion she had cast herself into the role of expert, and she found it galling that the other members of her group seemed to be more interested in oddities of language than in the information she could offer them. "Don't you want to know what the police will be asking you?"

"Oh, put a sock in it, Angela!" Caledonia said. "Nobody here has anything exciting to say to the police anyway, I expect, so the questions are going to be pretty routine. Why not let them find out for themselves what the colonel is going to ..."

"Good news," Maralyn Wilson said briskly, coming back into the room. "Breakfast is on its way, and as a special treat on this chilly morning, the staff is going to make hot chocolate for you."

"What about coffee?" Caledonia said. "I can't function without coffee."

"Wait till you try hot chocolate before you say that," Maralyn Wilson said. "There's as much stimulant in a cup of hot chocolate as in two cups of coffee."

"And there's something wonderfully comforting about chocolate," Tootsie Armstrong said shyly. "But I'm surprised they had it here. It doesn't sound very Mexican, somehow."

Maralyn Wilson laughed. "Oh, goodness, chocolate originated down in this part of the world. The Mexicans have used it in their cooking for centuries."

"Will they float little marshmallows in it? My mother used to do that for me," Tootsie said hopefully.

"Sorry, but I don't think so," Mrs. Wilson said. "That's not the way it's done down here, and ... well, wait till you see it." She started to pull out a chair near the kitchen doors; Roger Marx came across the room and pulled out another chair next to hers, and then politely held hers, as though to help her into it. "Oh, thank you, but on second thought, I believe I'll sit over there nearer the windows," she said and moved all the way across the room, leaving Marx standing irresolutely. Finally he shrugged and sat quietly down, but his eyes continued to follow her.

There was a momentary lull in the conversation, and Angela was about to fill the gap with more explanation of what the police might or might not ask when Caledonia spoke up. "Mrs. Wilson," she said to the guide, "the police woke you up first, didn't they? I mean, first Grunke called them, right? And when they came, I suppose he showed them the body and told them it was our driver and told them about our tour—and that's when the police went and got you. And then, I guess, they called in the colonel, is that right? And he asked you to wake all of us."

"That's about it," Maralyn Wilson agreed.

"Well, what did you find out about all this?" Caledonia said. "What did they tell you?"

"Yes, Maralyn," Marx said, "fill us in."

"There isn't much so far," she said. "Grunke says he couldn't sleep and about two-thirty this morning he went for a walk down by the water. He says he didn't see Tony at first because it was kind of dark and shadowy over there near Pet Rock Beach."

"That's where the body was? Over near the rocks?" Angela asked.

"Right. Apparently Tony'd been hit on the head with one of the larger rocks, or so Grunke thinks. Of course, Grunke didn't examine the body to be sure. He's got too much sense. He just came up here to the hotel and called the police. They weren't exactly prompt getting here. It took them more than an hour. Of course, they had to come out from town and they didn't really hurry, because it wasn't exactly a crime in progress that they could prevent, was it? But eventually they came, Grunke showed them the body, and then they came and got me."

"What time did he die?" Caledonia asked. "Do they know that yet?"

"Well, not exactly of course," Mrs. Wilson said. "But they're saying maybe ten or eleven. It's chillier down by the water at night, of course, so maybe they're off a little bit."

"I was on my balcony facing the beach at maybe ten," Caledonia said, "and I don't remember hearing a thing. Of course, I'm quite a way from the part of the beach where all the rocks are. And I only stayed there on my porch for maybe fifteen, twenty minutes tops before I went in to bed. But I can't remember seeing or hearing anything out of the ordinary."

"I was out on the grounds myself," Tom Brighton said. "I was strolling around from nine-thirty till after ten—maybe as late as ten-thirty. I wanted to look over the plants, and they have all these bright floodlights turned on around the grounds, just like down on the beach."

"It's so pretty to see the waves in those lights," one of the Jacksons said. "It's like the line of white foam—the line where the waves break, you know?—as though that line of white water actually has a light inside it, have you ever noticed? I walked out to the edge of the cliff for a while and just stood looking at the surf before I went on in to bed."

"You didn't get back to the room until maybe ten-thirty," her sister said reproachfully. "I was starting to worry about you. I'm not used," she said apologetically to the others, "to being by myself. We usually go everywhere together. But we'd had a little argument over whether or not to buy ourselves gowns in the boutique. I wanted to wait till we went shopping today, to compare prices and all. But sister didn't. She wanted to buy right then, right there."

"Because it was such a lovely shade of pink!" The other Jackson gestured at their robes and slippers, which were in their favorite of all colors. The Jacksons seldom appeared in anything that wasn't pink. "But you flounced off to our room," she went on in an accusing voice. "And you just left me! So I bought the dress anyhow and had it fitted and all, and then I went out to look at that pretty water with all the light on it."

"You know," Roger Marx said speculatively, "I remember looking out my windows and thinking there were fewer lights on at the beach than usual."

"Didn't Mr. Grunke tell the police some of the lights were out?" Angela asked Mrs. Wilson. "Isn't that what you just told us?"

"Come to think of it," the one Jackson sister said, "the lights at that far end of the beach were out, I think. At least the surf to the south was brightly lit and the surf up the other way wasn't. I hardly glanced toward my right, because there wasn't anything to see up there, of course, with no lights on."

"Well, be sure you tell the police that," Angela told her. "That's just the kind of thing they'd want to know. That the lights were out at maybe ten or so."

"I missed all of this," Tootsie Armstrong said mournfully. "I was writing postcards in the writing room. They have some good ones for sale here, by the way. No pictures of the cannery.

Just pretty things like the church, and this hotel, and the water spout, and all ..."

"I missed it all, too," Trinita Stainsbury said. "I was in my room reading a book. I never get in on any of the excitement when we're home, and now I'm missing all the—"

"What you're all saying," Angela interrupted Trinita's complaint, "what everybody's saying is that none of us has an alibi for the time of the murder. That's about it, isn't it? One of you Jacksons was in her room in a snit; the other one of you was first in the boutique, and then out looking at the water. Mr. Brighton, you were in the gardens, Caledonia was trying to relax so she could get a sound sleep, I was across the road in the village, Tootsie was writing postcards, Trinita was in her room reading ..."

"And the same for me, really," Roger Marx said. "I was by myself. I went to the hotel gym to use the exercise equipment. I've been doing a lot of sitting around, what with all this bus riding, and I needed a good workout."

"And I was in my room giving myself a shampoo and set," Maralyn Wilson said. "If anybody's interested. My hair got pretty badly blown around when we were out at *La Bufadora,* as I'm sure you all noticed."

"Oh, you always look wonderful," Marx assured her quickly. "Not that the way your hair is now doesn't look great, but it looked just as nice before. Different, of course, but—"

"Be that as it may," Angela said, interrupting, "what we're saying is, nobody noticed anything unusual, nobody heard anything." She hesitated. "That's right, isn't it?"

"Oh look!" Tootsie Armstrong's voice was rapturous. "It's breakfast!" Three waiters, and a chef wearing a still-spotless-white uniform and a traditional chef's hat, were entering the dining room from the kitchen carrying sweet rolls and plates of fruit—and a tray on which there were a dozen blown-glass mugs and a huge, steaming pitcher.

"Oh, is that the hot chocolate in the pitcher?" one of the Jacksons asked excitedly.

"No-no-no," Mrs. Wilson said cheerfully, coming back into the center of the group from her chair by the windows. "That's hot milk. The chocolate is already in the mugs. Look close."

She was right. Each mug contained what appeared to be small chunks and chips of chocolate, all angles and edges, as though they had been broken off from a larger bar. One by one, each of the group was served a mug and one waiter poured in a measure of the scalding milk while another waiter spun a peculiar wooden instrument that looked a little like a baby's rattle with wooden rings hung loosely around the handle.

"A *molinillo,*" Maralyn Wilson explained. "A kind of a chocolate whip." The head of the *molinillo* went deep inside the mug, the handle stuck up between the waiter's palms, and he rubbed his hands together as though in glee, which made the wooden implement whirl. Its little wooden rings were also set whirling, and the milk quickly turned soft brown and began to foam as the chocolate melted and the wooden stirrer aerated the milk.

"Amazing," Caledonia said. "That little wooden thing's really a whisk! Just like a French chef uses, only not made of wire."

"You'll want to add sugar," Maralyn Wilson warned them. "The block of chocolate isn't sweetened."

Angela tasted her drink and made a face. "Oooh, this is terribly bitter! Like medicine!"

"Yup." Mrs. Wilson grinned. "That's the way it comes, all right. That's why you have to add sugar. And if you want it like they drink it here, sprinkle in some cinnamon, too. Would anybody like to try making their own chocolate?" She pronounced it in the Spanish manner, as *shaw-koh-lah-tay.* "How about you, Roger?" she asked Marx. "I'll show you how to spin the *molinillo.*" She brought one of the glass mugs over to him. *"Camarero,"* she called to a waiter, *"leche por aqui, por favor."*

The waiter with the milk pitcher beamed and brought it over. "The gentleman wishes to try to whip the chocolate for himself?" he asked pleasantly.

"Oh, gosh no," Marx said shyly. "You make it for me. You do it so well. I'll just watch." The waiter started the whirling action.

"You want sugar, Roger?" Mrs. Wilson asked.

"Oh, sure, thanks."

Caledonia was not too deep in her own mug of hot chocolate to watch the whole performance, and she caught Angela's eye and nodded in the direction of the two, Maralyn Wilson and Roger Marx. Angela nodded back an acknowledgment that she had noticed, and she whispered, "And thank you for not nudging me again. I can see without being punched in the arm or elbowed in the ribs, thank you."

"Attention, ladies and gentlemen," a voice sounded from the main entrance to the dining room. It was one of the smartly uniformed policemen who had escorted Colonel Campo. The uniformed man spoke excellent English, although more accented than the colonel's. Still, he spoke clearly when he said, "The colonel would like to see a Mr. ..."—he consulted a small notebook—"a Mr. Brighton, please? Right this way," he added, leading the way as Tom Brighton, trying to pat down his cockscomb of white hair with one hand and arrange his robe with the other, got to his feet and headed out.

Breakfast was finished and the waiting dragged on and on. One by one, the tour group was called out of the dining room and was not seen again; presumably, Angela thought with a pang of jealousy, they went to their rooms to bathe and dress in street clothes, and she shifted uneasily and shivered again. A half hour passed, then an hour; finally an hour and a half, and still neither Angela nor Caledonia had been called into the colonel's presence. "I swear I'm going upstairs and change," Angela finally said fretfully, when the Jackson twins left the room together and there was no one at the breakfast table but herself, Caledonia, and Grogan, now fast asleep and snoring, head down on the table.

"What do you suppose the delay is?" Angela said. "Could they have arrested one of us already and just forgot to tell the rest of us?"

"Of course not. Who would they arrest?"

"Jerry Grunke, of course," Angela said promptly.

"Oh, don't be silly. Grunke's the one who found the body and called the police."

"The perfect way," Angela said firmly, "to throw off suspicion."

"Hah!" Caledonia's scorn was withering and Angela sighed and fell silent again.

At one point, well after the sky had turned from black to navy to rosy lavender and finally to light blue, Grogan roused himself again and asked what was going on. "Last thing I remember," he said yawning, "was somebody talking about herding cows. Didn't make a lot of sense. Everybody's gone now, I see, but they were all sitting around in their comfies. Why?"

Quickly, Caledonia filled him in about the murder of their driver, Tony Hanlon, and Grogan sighed. "Ah, the poor fellow. Too young to die. Who killed him?"

"Nobody knows yet, Mr. Grogan," Caledonia said. "We're all called here to wait till the police interview us."

"They think one of us did it?"

"I suppose we're all suspects," Angela said. "But maybe not serious suspects. Well, at least most of us aren't. And at the moment, they're probably just asking mostly where we were at the time of the murder and if any of us saw anything unusual."

"I'm not going to be of much help to them," Grogan said sadly. He was relatively sober, slightly hungover, and still very sleepy, but for a wonder (and far from his usual pattern), he was polite and restrained in manner. Usually when he was sober Grogan was a terror, short on patience and long on invective. Annoying as he could be when drinking, his fellow residents had long since decided that Grogan drunk was preferable to Grogan sober. But this morning, perhaps because he had been truly shocked by the death of Tony Hanlon, he was on his best behavior.

"I'm not going to be of much help to them," he repeated, "because I was right here in the dining room all night. At least, I think I was. Naturally, I wasn't really paying attention to my surroundings. I only know I had a little after-dinner drink when the rest of you left, and then I had a couple more for good measure, and finally I had a tall cool one because it was a warm evening ... and then I don't remember much till your voices woke me up this morning. So I think I was right over there, sleeping in my chair. But even if I wasn't—even if I was out roaming around somewhere—I ended up back here, and I didn't see diddley-squat. I mean, how could I? I could hardly see my own feet for the fog, let alone see a lurking stranger."

"There wasn't any fog last night, Grogan," Caledonia said. "It's just that your eyes weren't working very well."

"Oh. Oh, yes. Probably true." He shrugged. "Oh, well, the point is, I didn't see anything that will help them."

"Saw and heard nothing out of the ordinary at all, right?"

"Oh, I didn't say that. I heard something all right. Something that reminded me of my youth. I grew up in Boston in a pretty tough neighborhood and we kids were holy terrors. We would hang around the street corners on summer nights and throw rocks at the streetlights. Not just because we could get up to more devilment in the dark, but because it was fun.

And that's the sound I thought I heard last night. A kind of *clang* ... and once in a while, a *clang-pop-tinkle*. Like the rocks I used to throw hitting against the shade, and when I was lucky, breaking the bulb on those old streetlights."

"Maybe," Angela said speculatively, "maybe that wasn't your imagination. According to what everybody says, the lights were out down at Pet Rock Beach. Maybe somebody broke them out by throwing rocks. Maybe they were doing something in the dark they didn't want anybody to see."

"And the young man came across them and figured out what was going on and they killed him?" Grogan said. "Ah, the poor young man. What a price to pay for being in the wrong place at the wrong time."

"We don't know that, Mr. Grogan," Caledonia reminded him. "All we know is that—"

"Ladies." The uniformed policeman had appeared at the door once more. "Ladies, if you would follow me."

"Both of us?" Angela said. Her voice rang with disappointment. "Together?"

"You share a room, do you not?" The young policeman consulted his little notebook. "Yes, if my notes are correct. We are trying to speed things up a little and we took the last two ladies together, if you recall."

"But they're sisters," Angela said. "Twins. We're not related."

But the policeman had already stepped outside, impatient for them to follow. "I swear to goodness," Caledonia said with disgust as they moved to obey the summons, "I swear, you're so anxious to be considered important, you'd object if they gave you the third degree—you'd tell 'em you deserved the first degree! You're the one who was itching to get out of here and put on some clothes, so stop griping and let's go do it."

"Please sit down, ladies," Colonel Campo greeted them, "and my apologies for saving the best till last." It was as though he'd overheard Angela's objections and was determined to melt her annoyance. Caledonia was amused, but seated herself and said nothing. "And now, *señoras,* if you please, an account of your evening's activities, complete with times as well as you remember them."

"I'll go first," Caledonia said, "because mine is easy," and she quickly recited her timetable for her bath and the period of relaxation on her little balcony. "And I was in bed by maybe a quarter after ten, and sound asleep by the time Angela got back from her trip. And now, Angela, it's your turn."

Angela took center stage with delight. She embellished her trip to *El Pueblo* with a great deal of detail, and twice the colonel looked as though he might interrupt to ask her to get on with her story, but both times he bit his lip and let Angela tell the story in her own way. Actually it only took her a few minutes to get to the heart of her tale—her pursuit of the man she thought was Juan Saenz, the gardener from Camden-sur-Mer. Her voice rose and fell in dramatic emphasis, and by the time she got at last to the moment when Juan and his two companions had disappeared from the dark, narrow street, she was into her full storytelling mode, complete with grand gestures.

Caledonia was grinning and shaking her head, obviously restraining herself with difficulty from laughing aloud. It wasn't the story that she found so funny; it was Angela's histrionic retelling of it. But Colonel Campo showed no sign of amusement. He nodded seriously and from time to time glanced at the uniformed man who was scribbling furiously in a spiral-bound notebook, noting down every detail as Angela told it.

"Señora," the colonel said, "when you have had time to change clothes, I wonder if you would be so good as to come back down here? It is almost certainly too late to locate the man and discover whether he was indeed the man who works as your

gardener. But we can locate the street in question and perhaps unravel the matter of the mysterious disappearance."

"Oh, there won't be time, Colonel," Angela said. "I'm so sorry, but we're due to leave here at ten or ten-thirty this morning, and what with bathing and changing and getting packed, I'll just barely make it to the bus, let alone—"

"My apologies, but of course your departure will have to be delayed," the colonel said, and he sounded genuinely pleased. Probably, Angela thought, he was one of those men who enjoyed his position of authority a bit too much for other people's comfort. "We want to find out more before we release your party, and there is after all the matter of a new driver for your bus. I have told your lady in charge, the *señora* Wilson, to make arrangements with the management for another night's stay, and she has already started efforts to find another driver. So you have time to come with me to show us the street in *El Pueblo* where your mystery man vanished. Shall we say an hour and a half from now, here in the lobby? I look forward to your accompanying us then. It will be"—he checked a beautiful gold wristwatch—"just about ten by that time."

"Well ... can Caledonia come along?" Angela said.

"To what purpose?" the colonel said.

"Well, there were so many beautiful things in the shops there, I know she'd love the chance to see—"

"This is not a sightseeing tour," the colonel rebuked her stiffly. "This is strictly business, and there will be no time to gaze through the shop windows. Ten, and please don't be late." And he got to his feet in an obvious gesture of dismissal.

Chapter 10

November 13

Colonel Campo, strutting slightly in that self-important manner he affected, his two uniformed men (one of whom acted as chauffeur), and Angela (feeling pretty important herself) drove the short way from the hotel to *El Pueblo* in the colonel's wonderfully menacing-looking black Mercedes. They parked on the square in a place marked by a sign that sported a large black letter *E* in a red circle with a red bar through it—a sign that even Angela could guess meant "No Parking." ("Though what word the *E* actually stands for, I couldn't say," Angela told Caledonia later.) Angela pointed out the side street in which the men had been walking when they disappeared, and the colonel led the way into the narrow avenue, Angela talking and gesturing as they went along.

"Colonel," she was saying, "I swear this is the same street, but in the sunshine now, it doesn't look nearly as forbidding."

"It is a perfectly ordinary residential street, *señora*," he assured her.

"Residential? You say these are private homes? But they look like ... well, like commercial garages or something. Where are all the gardens? Where are the windows?"

The colonel smiled. "Nevertheless, many of the places along this street are private homes, although many indeed are commercial buildings. We do not have the zoning regulations like yours that keep such places apart."

"They still don't look like houses to me. They're just blank walls."

"Ah, but we *Mexicanos* spend very little on the facade. Those of us who can afford to do so build houses facing inward around a little private park for our family and friends to enjoy. Hidden inside some of these walls there are balconies and porticoes and tile-paved patios ... all in the Spanish fashion. So blank walls like these often hide private homes. And that brings me to a point. Are you positive the men disappeared in this street? By that I mean, had they not merely turned the corner and gone into the cross street down there?" He pointed to the intersection ahead of them.

"Well, of course, things look different in the daylight," Angela said, "but I'm sure. I'd got to about"—she looked left and right, estimating—"yes, about here. And they were ahead of me by maybe ... Oh, dear ... I'm not good at distances. Let me think. ... Well, do you see that green door down there? They were about that far away." She gestured some twenty yards ahead, where on the left there was a door painted bright kelly green, protected by the ever-present wrought-iron bars fitted like a second door over it. "Then I stubbed my toe on the paving. Some of the blocks stick up, you see, like this one." She went on, kicking at a protruding cobble as though to prove her point. "And by the time I had recovered my balance and looked up, they were gone! I don't believe they had time to reach the corner. Not unless they broke into a run, and I'd have heard their footsteps if they'd been running, wouldn't I?"

"Ah, in that case," the colonel said rather smugly, "I think I know the answer to your little mystery. Come with me."

And he led the group to the bright green door, swung open the guarding barred gate, and tried the latch. The door was, as Angela had supposed it would be, locked. The colonel wielded the large iron ring that served as a door knocker, and after a few moments, a window in the door was swung open and a man's heavily moustachioed face peered through. *"Ah! Buenos dias, Coronel. Momento, por favor."* The face withdrew, and the little window closed. Then they heard the metallic clank of latches and dead bolts being withdrawn and the green door swung wide. A roly-poly man in casual clothing was revealed, a broad smile on his face.

"Bievenido, Coronel," the moustache said. *"¿Adelante, por favor? ¿No?"* He shrugged. *"Bueno."* He leaned against the door jamb and went on amiably, *"Pues ¿que pasa ahora, Coronel?"*

"Ah, Carlos, por favor ¿puede usted ayudarme?" the colonel began in a smooth, polite voice—and then launched into a stream of rapid Spanish that sounded to Angela like a blur of mere nonsense syllables. Strings of words sailed past her ears, words so tightly connected together that she was unable to separate them one from the other. She recognized *puerta,* which she knew meant *door,* and *tres hombres,* which she knew meant *three men.* But beyond that, she was totally lost among a splatter of consonants, and neither the tone of voice nor the two men's extravagant gestures enlightened her. All the same, she was disappointed when fat Carlos (the moustache), with a little bow of farewell, said, *"Bueno, Coronel. Hasta la vista,"* and retreated inside the door, which he swung shut behind him.

The colonel spoke in Spanish to his men, one of whom started back toward the square, the other heading for the far end of the block. "And now," he said, "we return to the hotel with the mystery solved. Or so I believe it to be." He took Angela's arm in a gentlemanly gesture that turned her around, and they began retracing their way down the little street. "Did you understand all we said, *señora* Benbow?" he asked.

"Well, no, not really. In fact, almost nothing. I'm sorry," she apologized. "I mean, I did all right in my Spanish class when the teacher said the words one at a time. It's when they're all stuck together that I have trouble."

"I think your three men, whoever they were, entered Carlos's establishment last night," the colonel said. "You see, Carlos offers a very special kind of entertainment, one that is very popular with the men of the village. For that matter, they come all the way from Ensenada because of Carlos." Angela held her breath—what was he going to say?

"I think," the colonel went on, "that the men you saw were coming down this way to attend a cockfight."

"A ... a cockfight?"

"That's right. I'm surprised you didn't hear the audience cheering their favorites, even though you were out on the street. But perhaps they were between bouts, or perhaps the fight had not yet begun. At any rate—"

"A cockfight! But I thought ... I mean, isn't cockfighting against the law? Because it's so cruel."

"I believe," the colonel said rather stiffly, "that you feel differently about such things in the United States. Here we are not so soft-hearted about animals doing what nature best equipped them to do. Besides, you are a woman."

"That has nothing to do with it," Angela said coldly.

"Ah, but it has everything to do with the matter," the colonel said smugly. "The good Lord gave women soft hearts so that they could be better mothers. Men He made into sportsmen. I myself attend these little sporting events at Carlos's place, from time to time."

Angela thought about that as she pattered along, trying hard to keep up with the colonel's stride. He had dodged the issue of legality, and there seemed no comment she could make that wouldn't sound unbelievably rude. In fact, she thought, her comments wouldn't just *sound* rude, they'd *be* rude! Nothing that inevitably ends in the death of one of the participants is merely a sport, she was thinking, and what's sporting about standing on the sidelines and watching while blood and gouged flesh fly all over the place? That's what she'd have said if she hadn't been intimidated by the assertive manner of the colonel, and if she hadn't been in a foreign country and trying to be on her best behavior. As it was, however, she bit her tongue and hurried along, watching her feet so as not to trip on the uneven paving.

"Yes, I do believe that your three men were on their way to Carlos's little arena," the colonel was saying. "We will talk to the families living nearby, of course. In fact, one of my men has already begun that task. But the chances are—"

"But how did they get in and disappear from my sight so fast? That door was shut tight and Carlos had to unlock it for you. Wouldn't I have heard them knock?"

"On nights when there are cockfights, Carlos leaves his green door unlocked and patrons simply come in at will. There is no admission fee, you know. Carlos makes his profits handling the wagers."

"I still don't see how they could hold a cockfight in a private home. You did say most of the places along that lane are private homes, didn't you?"

"Many of them are," he said. "But the fact is that the property Carlos owns is not a house at all. That structure was indeed a warehouse at one time. There is even a large loading door opening onto the next street, a door you could not see from your position in the side street. Well, here we are." He opened the door of the Mercedes and helped Angela in. The uniformed man who had gone before them was already in the driver's seat and started the engine at once. Before Angela could think clearly, they were on their way back to the hotel.

"The colonel," Angela told Caledonia, "seemed perfectly satisfied. But I'm not. Suppose the men did go to a cockfight? There was plenty of time to get from there to the beach later and find Tony Hanlon and kill him."

"But why would our gardener Juan want to kill Tony Hanlon?" Caledonia asked.

"I don't have the least idea, of course. I mean, that's what the colonel is supposed to find out, isn't it?"

But the morning passed and there was no announcement that a motive had been discovered, no announcement that there had been an arrest, in fact, no announcement of any kind. The party from Camden-sur-Mer stayed close to the hotel, sitting around the lobby and talking to each other, strolling the grounds, and peering over the edge of the cliff to watch the police still examining, inch by inch, the rocky end of the beach where the body had been found. "Leaving no stone unturned," as Grogan said, chuckling hugely at his own wit.

Caledonia, checking back at the hotel's boutique to see if her lace caftan had been successfully altered, found herself browsing through cloth samples while her garment was carefully wrapped for her. It was with pleasure that she realized the lace she so admired came in several colors and patterns. "How long would it take to get a couple more of these caftans?" she asked the clerk. "A blue one, a lime green ... and yes, how about one in cerise?"

The clerk thought a moment. "We couldn't produce them for you this afternoon, of course," she said pleasantly.

"Naturally."

"But perhaps by tomorrow morning."

"You could make me three dresses overnight?"

"Oh, certainly, *señora*. Provided we begin work immediately. I have two seamstresses in the work room, after all. Just leave the completed gown for them to use as a pattern."

Caledonia ordered the new caftans, and over the next few hours she must have expressed to Angela a dozen times her surprise and pleasure. "Speedy Gonzalez," she said, "eat your heart out! So much for the stereotype of lazy peasants taking siesta through the working day. I know a lot of department stores back home that could take a lesson!"

Lunchtime came and the hotel served a meal more like the food the group had expected when they first entered Mexico—a "peasant buffet" with taco shells, tortillas, and a selection of meats, cheeses, and vegetables arranged down the table's length for diners to create their own luncheon plates. Everybody was present except Roger Marx, who (his roommate, Tom Brighton, said) was not feeling at all well. "I think," Brighton said in an undertone to Angela and Caledonia, "and I don't suppose he'd thank me for advertising the fact, so I won't tell the others. But I think that Roger has contracted a case of Montezuma's revenge, if you know what I mean."

"Oh dear, the poor man! Is there anything we can do?" Angela said.

"I don't suppose so," Tom Brighton said. "He'll just have to stay in his room and let it run its course ... so to speak."

"Bad choice of words there, Tom." Caledonia grinned. "Poor fellow. I wonder what he ate for breakfast that none of us tried?" "More probably," Maralyn Wilson said, "it was something he ate last night. It takes a while for the cramps and all to develop. Sorry, but I couldn't help but overhear. I'd hoped our party would get through our trips without the *turistas* hitting any of us. But I suppose it was inevitable. Well, I'll go upstairs after lunch and check on him. See how he's coming along, and—"

"You're in charge and I expect you to do something!" Trinita Stainsbury interrupted. She had brought a heaping plate from the buffet and positioned herself directly across the table from the travel agent, at whom she was now glaring. "When are we getting out of here? I'm supposed to have my hair done tomorrow afternoon. Up at home, I mean."

"There are good hairdressers down here," Maralyn Wilson said, "and if the police won't let us get back home by then, I'll see that you get an appointment here."

"Oh dear," Trinita said, patting her coppery curls. "But it was the day I refresh the color, and down here would they understand the subtleties ... ?"

"I'm sure we can take care of that, Mrs. Stainsbury," Maralyn Wilson soothed her. "Of course, with any luck, it won't be necessary and we'll be going home."

"We're going home?" Tootsie Armstrong said eagerly, placing her luncheon plate next to Trinita Stainsbury's. "Wonderful! It isn't that I don't like having an extra day here. But I had myself all organized for a two-day stay, and I just don't handle changes in plans very well," she said apologetically.

"I'm sorry, Mrs. Armstrong, but we aren't leaving yet," Mrs. Wilson said. "We're waiting for the police to tell us we can go, and so far I haven't heard a thing from them. All the same, I'm going out this afternoon to hire a new driver. I'm afraid I'll have to go to First Class Tours, the company we used to do business with, even if they're pretty mad at me at the moment." She sighed deeply. "Oh well, they'll get over it, if the price is right. One thing I know for sure, money is the great cure-all."

"What have the police found out so far?" Angela said.

Maralyn Wilson shrugged. "They haven't told me any more than they've told you. In fact, you probably know more than I do. You went somewhere with Colonel Campo this morning, Mrs. Benbow. What did you find out on that trip?"

It was Angela's chance to take center stage again, and she didn't let the opportunity pass her by. She enjoyed retelling her trip to the village the night before, her sighting of the man she thought she'd recognized as their gardener, her following him down the dark side street, and finally the colonel's revelation of the gardener's probable errand—attending the cockfight.

She was afforded flattering attention, no doubt about it, though Trinita in particular expressed skepticism that Angela had indeed spotted a familiar face. "I've seen a dozen people I know," Trinita said with just a hint of scorn in her tone. "And, of course, it's never really them. It happens every time I travel to a strange city. I bet that's what happened to you, too."

"Well, it's possible," Angela conceded. She hated to agree with Trinita, but this time it made sense. "Why would Juan Saenz kill poor Tony Hanlon? He didn't even know him!"

"Oh, you can't be sure of that." Jerry Grunke spoke up from the end of the table where he sat, as usual, facing the entrance to the dining room. "Just because we didn't meet that Hanlon fellow till he showed up as our driver doesn't mean Juan didn't know him. For instance, Juan is a gambler, so it's possible—"

"How do you know that?" Angela challenged. "What makes you think Juan Saenz is a gambler?"

"He went to a cockfight, didn't he?" Grunke said. "Why do you think people go to those things?"

"I thought they called it a sport," Angela said. "Though what's sporting about chickens killing each other ..."

"Why do people go to horse races up at home?" Grunke went on. "Not to see the pretty horses, you can be sure. They go to place a bet. Same with the men who go to a cockfight here. So this Juan Saenz is a gambler. Gamblers usually need money, and once in a while they even have money—lots of it. And where there's money, there's a motive for murder. So what I'm trying to say is, if the late Mr. Hanlon should prove to have been a gambler, perhaps there's a connection. Does anyone know about Mr. Hanlon's activities? Mrs. Wilson?"

"Very interesting," the travel agent said slowly. "I'm not sure, but I believe you're right about that. That Tony gambled, I mean. Of course, I can't be certain how much he won or lost or anything. He was an excellent driver, and that's what I cared most about. What he did in his own time was really none of my business. But I remember seeing him buy lottery tickets more than once. And he mentioned he played poker. He said he really needed the money— to help pay for his education, among other things, he said. And he certainly did a lot of things for money that were not quite right. He used to steer customers to certain markets so he'd get a cut of whatever they spent—the way he did with you, Mrs. Armstrong. And he always had his hand out for tips when our trips were over. Oh, you can be sure he'd have been standing at the door of the bus when we finished our third trip, folks, helping each of you down the steps and ready to pocket a ten or even a twenty, if you were kind enough to offer it. That isn't the way I wanted us to do business. I offer people a firm price for the trips I conduct and that's supposed to include all the fees and all the tips. Everything except the things they buy, like silver and pottery and what not. Anyhow, I had to speak to Tony about it over and over."

"But if he was so greedy," Angela said to her, "why did you hire him?"

"I wouldn't have, if I'd had another driver available. But Jimmy Carlen, the driver I use most often, was hired by another agency to take a party to the Grand Canyon and back. And, of course, Tony spoke Spanish and he knew these routes well, so ..." She sighed. "I hate talking about him this way, with him lying dead and all. And I feel like this has probably spoiled things for all of you. You won't want to take the third trip, what with all that's happened, will you? I mean, we've had such rotten luck.

Who could believe we'd get ourselves involved with the police not once but twice!"

As though on cue, Colonel Campo appeared in the doorway. "Now that your luncheon is over," he said in that self-important voice people assume when they make announcements to a group, "may I have a few moments of your time? I want to report our progress and to find out if anyone here has thought of anything he—or she—wants to add to what you've already told us." He moved into position behind a small table, as though it were a speaker's lectern. "First, however, I have good news for you," he went on, while the group pulled their chairs into a semicircle around him. "We are going to let you depart for home tomorrow morning. On the other hand ..."

"There's good news and there's bad news! At least he didn't use that cliche," Caledonia mouthed to Angela, making sure she spoke softly enough that the colonel could not overhear.

"On the other hand, we still don't know exactly what went on last night. Oh, we have a few theories, but we still have to confirm any one of them. Let's begin with why Mr. Hanlon went down to the beach in the first place." He pulled out of his pocket a small notebook bound in tooled leather and flipped it open, apparently to consult it for details. "Your driver left the hotel last night about nine-thirty saying that he intended to have the bus filled with gasoline for your trip home today. At least, that is what he told the desk clerk in their conversation just before he left. But we have noted that the tank of the bus is less than one-quarter full, and we found the keys to the bus in Mr. Hanlon's room, not in his pocket. So we believe that, despite his stated intentions, he did not drive into town. Instead, he walked down onto the beach. Why? Of course we don't know, but we wonder if he may not have gone to meet someone. Could it have been a lady?" He stopped and looked around the room.

"Not one of us, surely," Caledonia said scornfully. "I mean, he was a handsome young fellow, but the word *young* ought to give you a clue. He wouldn't have looked twice at anybody in this bunch!"

The colonel smiled and held up his hand. "Of course, you are all charming," he began, pausing while the Jackson twins giggled, "but actually I wondered if he had not gone to meet you, Mrs. Wilson."

The blonde travel agent snorted her derision. "Of course not. He wasn't my type at all. And besides, I was hiding in my room. I was ducking ..." She hesitated and looked around at the others and then shrugged. "I might as well say it, I guess. There's a member of this tour group who's been paying me a lot of attention. A Mr. Marx. I don't know if any of you noticed—"

The group was quick to respond with "No, no, not at all!" and "Good heavens, really?"—so quick with those denials, in fact, that Caledonia realized that they were lying. She and Angela were obviously not the only ones who had watched the romance developing.

"After dinner last night, Mr. Marx was after me to walk with him over to the village and window-shop, or maybe to go back into town to a night club, or to go for a moonlight stroll on the beach — something or anything. I didn't want to insult him, of course. I'm in the business of making people happy, after all. That's my job. But I certainly didn't want to encourage him. The man is nice enough, please don't misunderstand. But he's just not my type and he's driving me absolutely batty."

"Uh, which one is he?" Colonel Campo asked. "I recall his name, but putting names and faces together is not my strong point. Which of you ..." He looked over the audience and picked out the white shock of Tom Brighton's hair, the darkly sullen face of Jerry Grunke, and the unfocussed eyes of Mr. Grogan.

"He's not here," Mrs. Wilson said. "He's in his room with a bad case of ... Well, colonel, I suppose you realize that many visitors from the United States have a bad reaction to the water, or the fruit or ... or something. And Mr. Marx is suffering just such a reaction."

"That's true, sir." Tom Brighton spoke up. "Roger hasn't left our room—we're sharing a room, you see—and he hasn't left since mid-morning. He's really bad off. In fact, I'm not sure he can ride back with us tomorrow if his condition doesn't improve."

The colonel shook his head. "Ah, what a pity. I have never understood this susceptibility of your countrymen to maladies of this kind. Well, perhaps we *Mexicanos* are just of sturdier stock, could that be so? At any rate, it is that same Mr. Marx that you were hiding from, *señora* Wilson? You were hiding from one man and therefore could not have been out meeting another, is that the case?"

"You could put it that way," Mrs. Wilson said, rather sulkily. It apparently seemed to her that the colonel disapproved of her behavior, for she responded defensively, "Like I told you, Marx is just not my type. Better to let him down easy now than hurt his feelings later, that's what I think. He's nice, but he's a nuisance."

Whether the colonel approved of her solution to the problem of Roger Marx or not, he said no more about it and went on with his timetable of Hanlon's evening. "So he did not go out to meet a lady. At least, not to meet any of you. Well, perhaps he was the type to enjoy the view. Or to want to dip his feet into the Pacific. At any rate, he did go down there into the dark, where someone had knocked out the lights, and—"

"Knocked them out?" Angela said. "You mean someone threw rocks at the lights to break them?"

"Exactly so," the colonel said. "There are three of them, the bulbs all broken and the metal shades dented. But how did you know that?"

"I didn't," Angela said. "But Mr. Grogan thought that was what had happened. He and his friends used to break streetlights that way when he was a little boy."

"Ah, I see. He mentioned the same thing to us when we interviewed him this morning," Colonel Campo said. "Well, you will be interested that we think he is quite correct. What we believe is, the killer made a few impromptu preparations for this attack— among them, breaking the lights and finding something to use as a weapon. This mysterious killer wanted it dark when he met his victim so he could take the man by surprise and fell him with a blow on the head."

"I don't get it. Why did he have to hunt for a weapon?" Tom Brighton said. "He had a beachful of rocks right there."

"But most of the rocks are too small to do the job. If your hand wrapped around the rock too far," the colonel said, illustrating his point by pulling out his wallet and wrapping his fingers around the width, "you strike with your knuckles, not with the rock at all. And while a hand braced with a rock might strike a good blow, it might not be enough to knock the victim out." The colonel assumed a professorial pose. He was enjoying showing off his expertise.

"A rock," he went on, "big enough to have the needed weight, then. But not too big for him to hold easily. And we have in fact found such a rock. It is being examined now for traces of blood and hair, which we think we have seen on it. But one must be sure the marks are not just seaweed, you see."

"How on earth did you ever find that one rock among so many others?" Tootsie Armstrong twittered.

The colonel spread his hands wide. "Credit my staff with that discovery. Actually, that rock was well away from the body, over on the part of the beach where there is nothing but sand, so we think it was tossed or carried there as someone ran from the murder scene. Actually, we have a theory. We think someone robbed Mr. Hanlon. His wallet had been pulled from his pocket and lay discarded beside the body. And it was empty of cash. So we are now looking for our killer in Ensenada."

"In Ensenada?" Grunke asked. "What'd the killer do, leave a card with his address at the scene or something?"

"Not at all," the colonel said. "We are looking in the town itself because the visitors from the United States most usually stay there. You see, the number of well-to-do tourists coming to Ensenada has increased greatly in recent years, especially after the period of the visiting flower children was finished. Unfortunately, the money these wealthier visitors bring in has attracted an unusual kind of import from the United States— something NAFTA is not responsible for. Muggers and con men and panhandlers and pickpockets."

"Oh, of course!" Angela said brightly. "Mrs. Wilson told us so on our first trip together. But I'm surprised, Colonel, that you let people like that into the country at all."

"We wouldn't, if only we knew who they were, *señora*. Alas, they enter our country as ordinary tourists, and they do not wear signs proclaiming their illegal intentions. I suppose in one sense we are fortunate, because these criminals do not come to prey upon *Mexicanos;* they turn their attentions on their fellow countrymen, real tourists, who come with plenty of money in their pockets. In fact, we had such a crime right here on the beach not two months ago. A dentist from Detroit was knocked down and his wallet taken. That time the thief was tackled by an athletic young groundskeeper from the hotel who heard the dentist cry out. So other than a few bruises and a bad fright, no harm was really done—except to the would-be thief, who sustained a fractured left arm and a deep cut, gained when he was thrown down by the groundskeeper. And, of course, the thief is now serving ten years in one of our prisons and complaining bitterly because, unlike prisons in your country, we do not furnish television and exercise equipment. I believe he will go back home when his sentence is over and he will think twice about committing crime on this side of the border. At least, that is the idea behind our prisons—punishment. But where was I?"

"You were telling us," Angela said, "that you decided the killer could have been an American trying to make a dishonest living off his fellow Americans. And after he knocked out the lights on the beach, he lurked there waiting for a well-heeled victim to show up. When Hanlon came along—for a reason we haven't yet determined—the would-be thief knocked him out and stole the money from Hanlon's wallet. But he seems to have misjudged his strength because he killed Hanlon instead of just knocking him out. Have I got it right?"

"Very good," the colonel said. "A truly cogent summary, *señora*."

"Thank you. It's practice, of course. I analyze all our murders this way," Angela said with pride.

"All your murders?"

"She means all the murders we've heard about. Back home in the States," Caledonia said, "we sort of ... you might say we sort of study murder as a hobby, I guess."

"I see." But it was obvious that the colonel didn't see at all. Nevertheless, he went on gamely. "So anyway, we need to clean up the details and find the killer. Or at least confirm some of our suspicions. And then, ladies and gentlemen, as I say, you will be allowed to go home."

The colonel and his men strode off toward the beach once more, but Mrs. Wilson continued the impromptu meeting for a few moments more to ask if her group wanted to spend the afternoon shopping in town. "I did promise you a half day's shopping," she said.

"Oh, I don't know. Somehow the idea of souvenir shopping just makes me sad," Tootsie Armstrong said. "Does everybody know what I mean? It reminds me of Mr. Hanlon taking me to that market."

"I want to go to the boutique here in the hotel," one of the Jackson twins said. "I want to buy a dress like my sister did. It'll need to be fitted for alterations, you see, and that'll take quite a bit of time, I'm afraid."

"And I have to pack," Trinita said. "I didn't bother this morning, because we were told we'd have to stay. But now ..."

"That'll mean no trip to the winery, then!" Mr. Grogan mourned from the corner where he lounged.

"Oh, just buy yourself a glass of wine at the bar, Grogan," Mr. Grunke said sourly. "You will anyway. Most of us are content to let the wine tasting go. We can do that on another trip someday. Nobody feels much like doing something bright and touristy right now, man."

Mrs. Wilson held up a hand. "All right, no trip to town. Agreed? It's just as well. It'd mean getting that driver from First Class Tours out here to handle the bus for us today, and I'll be paying him plenty to get us home tomorrow, including a bus ticket to get him back to Ensenada from Camden. I don't need to pay him for two days—one is enough. So today's a free afternoon. And now if you'll excuse me, I should go upstairs and check on Roger Marx. Mr. Brighton, if you'll come with me."

And the group went their separate ways—to their rooms, to lounge in the lobby or the writing rooms, to wander the grounds, and generally to spend the afternoon as they had spent the morning, just killing time.

Chapter 11

November 14-21

Coming home from Ensenada was an experience quite unlike the homeward trip from Tijuana. The substitute driver hired from First Class Tours was a cheerful, chubby young man who talked incessantly in a bright, almost shrill voice. "I am neek-named Grillo," he told them, pronouncing it *Gree-yoh,* in the Spanish fashion. "That ees, een djour lan-gwich, a kerr-eek-kut. Be-cuss they say I all the time shurp." It took a few seconds for the group to work out that the young man was trying to say he was nicknamed "Cricket," and that by "shurp" he meant "chirp." He twittered away constantly in his heavily accented English, commenting on the weather, the scenery, the other drivers on the road, his bus and its engine, not to mention the state of modern medicine, international politics, and world trade—all in that boyish tenor, and injecting from time to time, as Angela put it, "Spanish subtitles" for his unceasing monologue.

"Lees-ten to me an' djou weel himp-proof djour Ess-spaneesh," he told them. But they could work out very little of what he said in his own language—or for that matter, what he said in his peculiar English. Thus his constant chatter soon became a mere background noise, tolerable and as easily ignored as a real cricket singing from the hearth.

"Grillo, indeed," Caledonia rumbled and then gasped. The man's driving was on a par with his conversation, which hopped at high speed from subject to subject. He coaxed out every ounce of speed and maneuverability the aging little bus had to give and squeezed the vehicle to perform feats that astonished his passengers. "He's having a sight too much fun, if you ask me," Caledonia growled. "Did you see him cut in front of that white van and then stick in the right-hand lane, so the red sports car would have to stop before it could get onto the freeway? Did you see him bounce out to get around that truck and then duck back into the lane ahead of it so the trucker had to brake? I swear, I'd feel safer driving with our Emma Grant!"

But continual chatter and capricious driving aside, Grillo got them home without serious incident. The ride was not a smooth one, but as Angela said later, if one closed one's eyes and thought of other things, it really wasn't completely awful. "And thank goodness our third trip is just to Tijuana, only an hour and something on the road. Tell you what, Cal, I do believe I'll take a little rest before I unpack."

The others in the party seemed perhaps a bit wobbly as well, though none more than Roger Marx. He had been assisted into the bus in Ensenada by a phalanx of bellboys and—to the annoyance of Mr. Grogan, who thought he had "dibs" on the rear seat—had been stretched out along the backseat, swathed in a blanket, and with pillows propping him up. Even Grogan hushed his complaining, however, as it became apparent that Marx was still too weak to stand alone, or even to sit up. And when they got back to Camden-sur-Mer, Grogan became genuinely helpful, assisting Marx to clamber down from the bus to where Mary Washington, senior nurse at the retirement home, took charge of the ailing Marx, easing him into a wheelchair to get him to his room and then, the others assumed, into his bed.

The next day, both Angela and Caledonia had recovered a bit from what they cheerfully described to their friends as "a really hair-raising ride! It was far scarier," as Angela put it, "than the murder. Well, to be fair about it, we didn't have to see the murder or even look at the poor young man's body. But we had to sit there in the bus and feel it sway as our driver made it duck in and out of traffic, and we had to listen to the gears clash and the engine grind away. It wasn't so bad while we were still south of Tijuana. But when we got to Tijuana itself, it was very ... well, very upsetting. And when we got to I-5 ... all I can say is wow!"

"But it sounds so exciting!" little Mary Moffet said. "Racing up the freeway. And I missed it all."

"Be glad, Mary," Angela said firmly. "And you know the thing that got me? Our Maralyn Wilson didn't say a word! I'd have expected her to yell at him every time he swerved or went too fast or whatever, and she never said a thing!"

"Probably afraid he'd just walk out on the job," Caledonia said, "maybe right in the middle of the freeway."

As they so often did, the residents began to gather in the lobby as early as half an hour before dinner to share news and gossip and to find sympathetic listeners to their comments on the state of their world. In one group was Tom with his shock of white hair and Tootsie Armstrong (happily wearing her favorite high-heeled pumps once more), Angela and Caledonia, and two who had not been on the trips—Emma Grant (whose hearing aid had been mended so that she could join the conversation with ease) and little Mary Moffet, the only person in all of Camden-sur-Mer who was shorter than Angela.

Most of the other members of the tour group were not too far away. Grogan lounged nearby on one of the benches placed on either side of the dining room doors, but didn't join any of the discussion groups scattered around the lobby. The Jackson twins and Trinita Stainsbury were across the room, holding forth to several of their fellow residents. Jerry Grunke was sitting by himself just outside the double doors that led to the gardens. Of the travel group, only Roger Marx was not in evidence.

"I dropped by his apartment to see if he was feeling any better, but he was asleep," Tom Brighton said. "But Mary Washington told me he's recovering, although he's still pretty weak. He won't be up and around till at least tomorrow."

"Such a nice man. A pity he had to be the one to get, well, that disease," Angela said.

"I don't believe it's a disease," Emma Grant corrected her. "An ailment maybe. An illness maybe. But isn't a disease something you can pass along to somebody else?"

Whatever one might call it, Roger Marx was sufficiently recovered by the following day to come to lunch. He looked pale and wan, but he certainly seemed past the worst. When Angela asked him directly if he intended to come with them on their third and last expedition—one more trip to Tijuana—he nodded and smiled. "Oh, yes, of course."

"You're not afraid of getting this ... thing ... again?"

He shook his head. "Lightning doesn't strike twice, does it? Anyway, I should have worked up a little immunity, what with all I've been through. I don't see any reason why I shouldn't come along with the rest of you. At least, I assume you're going again, aren't you?"

"Never occurred to us to stay home!" Caledonia said cheerfully. "We've paid for it, after all. So why not?"

"I'll tell you why not," Lieutenant Martinez said to the two women later that same afternoon. "Because I'm concerned. Nervous. Worried. Apprehensive. I think you would be wise to reconsider." The lieutenant had arrived at Caledonia's apartment just as she was serving her favorite pre-dinner sherry to herself and Angela.

"How wonderful of you to come calling," Angela trilled. "But how did you know"—she looked up at him sideways, the same glance a belle might have given her beaux from behind her fan in the antebellum South—"how did you know I'd be here?"

"I knew you'd be here if you kept to your usual routine," he told her. "Not to say you two are predictable, but you seldom miss the chance to get together in the late afternoon this way."

"Won't you join us?" With one hand, Caledonia hoisted the sherry decanter so he could see the amber fluid reflecting the sunlight; with the other hand she reached for one of the tiny etched sherry glasses she kept ready behind her bar.

"Ah, thank you, but I'm still on duty, so much as I appreciate your offer, and much as I should enjoy it, I won't join you for a drink. Besides, I can really only stay a moment or two before I go inland to Vista to investigate what a survivor reports as a drive-by shooting. Except that we have our doubts—two young men in their late teens walking along a quiet suburban street in broad daylight, one gets shot and killed, and the other says it was a car full of gangbangers shooting at them. But a witness says he heard only one shot, and we can't find any bullet holes around except the one that's square in the center of the victim. Nor can we find any shell casings in the street. Nor anyone who saw a car speeding away from the scene. Furthermore, it's an upper-middle-class neighborhood and not one where gang members usually hunt for each other, and neither young man seems to have been involved in drugs or gangs, at least not that their friends know about. Right now, I'm working on a theory that the survivor is the one who shot his friend. Jealousy over a girl, one of their buddies suggested. But we'll see. Anyhow, since I was driving past your home here on my way, I thought I'd take the chance to stop by and talk to you about your latest trip ... and about your next. Except, of course, that I hope to dissuade you from making a third trip at all."

"Well, I don't understand your asking us not to go," Angela said. "After all, as Caledonia says, we've paid for it already. And goodness knows we haven't had nearly enough contact with spoken Spanish even yet."

"Mrs. Benbow, you're forgetting the unfortunate deaths that occurred. And surely you remember that bad things often happen in threes," Martinez said. "Or haven't you noticed?"

Caledonia snorted. "That's an old superstition, sure, but we're not going to cancel out our trip just because of some superstition."

"Well, think about it," Martinez insisted. "Dear ladies, doesn't it seem to you extraordinarily bad luck that you've had two trips and two deaths? First your fellow resident Miss Braintree—"

"Who died of a heart attack," Caledonia reminded him, "or so Captain Lopez seemed to believe. No, to be more exact, we all believed it. And we believe it still. And when you came to talk to us about it, you finally agreed."

"Oh, indeed. But only because there was no alternative," Martinez said. "We had no chance by that time to have a real autopsy done. It was the petechia the old doctor mentioned that roused our suspicions."

"Petechia?" Angela said. "What on earth is that? It sounds a little like that ballet. Or no, that was *Petrouchka*. The first time I saw it, the Ballet Russe de Monte Carlo was touring in the late 1940s and—"

"Petechia," Martinez interrupted her gently, "is something not nearly so pretty as a ballet. Briefly, petechia means there are a lot of tiny broken blood vessels in the eye. Of course, several perfectly innocent things could cause the condition, including taking aspirin."

"Well, there you are," Angela said. "Naturally Miss Braintree took aspirin. We all do, after all the medical reports about how it prevents strokes and heart attacks. Not that aspirin helped her a bit. She still had a heart attack, didn't she?"

"Go on, Lieutenant," Caledonia said. "Pay no attention to her. You were about to add a *but* to that, weren't you?"

"You know me well." Martinez smiled at her. "Yes, I was going to add, as you put it, a *but*. I was going to say that asphyxiation can cause petechia as well. Of course, it may seem unlikely that someone would smother or strangle your Miss Braintree. Certainly the marks of strangulation would have been obvious on the lady's neck, and the doctor found none. But I'd like to have been able to check the possibility of her having been smothered."

"Look here," Caledonia said, "she was in the seat of the wagon right behind us. There was nobody even close to her. Unless, of course, you suspect us."

Martinez smiled and shook his head. "You know better," he said. "All the same, I'd have checked further except that, as you recall, it was too late when I heard about it to order a real autopsy."

"Well, for goodness sake! You certainly didn't tell us this before," Angela said accusingly "About the pete ... you know, about the broken blood vessels. Why didn't you mention all that stuff before?"

"Oh, but I did," Martinez said. "Well, perhaps I didn't give you all the details. But I surely mentioned it, even if I may have neglected to tell you exactly the name of the condition that ..." He stopped and smiled. "Why am I defending myself? This is all beside the point. The point is that now there's been a second death, one that was surely murder."

"An accidental killing, though," Caledonia reminded him. "Colonel Campo seems to think our driver was mugged, and the mugger just hit him too darned hard. Not that being a kind of accident makes it one bit better. I didn't mean that. But it does mean it's unlikely to have any effect on us. I don't mean we're not sad about it. Of course, we are. But other than that ... Why should we be nervous about our trip? A heart attack and a mugging don't mean we're in any danger, do they?"

"All the same, dear ladies, two trips and two deaths ..."

"Well," Angela said, "what's the connection between the two? Except us, of course."

"If I knew the connection, I might more adequately protect you from the threat."

"What threat?"

"I don't know. I wish I did. As it is, you said it—the only connection I can see is you. All of you. Your tour group, or whatever you call it. And I want you to consider seriously staying at home—not going on the third trip."

"Come to think of it," Caledonia said, "how do you know about our driver's death, anyhow? Don't tell me Colonel Campo phoned you up, the way Captain Lopez did from Tijuana, to ask you to vouch for us."

"Well," Martinez smiled, "not exactly. But close enough. Mrs. Wilson, your travel agent, told the colonel about Miss Braintree's death during your previous trip. If she hadn't, he'd eventually have found out anyway, so perhaps it's as well she told him voluntarily. Anyway, he naturally phoned the Tijuana police for information and they referred him to Captain Lopez, who in turn referred him to me. Within the past three days I have talked to both of them. More than once. And I must tell you that all three of us are very uneasy, even though we have no evidence, nothing to go on other than the coincidence of two deaths in two trips. And being professional policemen, we none of us are happy with coincidences of that magnitude. Actually, it was Captain Lopez who suggested I discuss with you whether or not you might consider canceling your Tijuana journey."

"I liked the captain," Caledonia said. "He seemed to me to be a great deal smarter than Colonel Campo. Oh, the colonel was very definitely a man of high rank, and he was certainly used to being obeyed and deferred to and all that. But I thought Captain Lopez was quick on the uptake and—"

"The gardener!" Angela was tired of waiting to be allowed into the conversation again, so as usual she simply interrupted. "What did Colonel Campo say about the gardener?"

"What gardener?" Martinez said blankly.

"Didn't the colonel tell you?" Angela said impatiently. "I'd have thought, after he helped me hunt for the man ... well, to make sure he hadn't just disappeared in the middle of the street the way he seemed to. And of course it was the place with the green door. Not that he couldn't have killed Tony and seen the chickens, too, I suppose." Lieutenant Martinez was blinking rapidly, a look of utter bewilderment on his face. "It's just that it was so strange, first the carnival and then the village square ..."

"You're blathering again, Angela. Give the lieutenant a break," Caledonia said. "She's trying to say, Lieutenant, that she thought she saw our gardener, Juan Saenz, in Ensenada."

"And not just in Ensenada," Angela said. "I saw him in Tijuana as well. When we were at the carnival. He was right there in the fairgrounds!"

"I see." The clouds were clearing from the lieutenant's brows. "And he was doing something you found suspicious? What would that have been?"

"Well, he wasn't exactly doing something suspicious. In fact, he was just walking along. Both times. But he was there, that's the point. Both times. Surely he must have been up to something."

"And have you asked him directly what he was doing there?" Martinez said. "Knowing you—"

"Oh, goodness no!" Angela said. "I'd have been frightened to do that!"

The lieutenant smiled. "I greatly doubt that. In fact, I wish you were a little more easily frightened, my dear Mrs. Benbow. It would keep you out of danger. But even so, you'd probably have questioned him anyway. With you, curiosity has always gotten the better of fear. So the question remains, why didn't you ask him? What really stopped you?"

Angela smiled at him fondly. "Well, I confess I was going to. I was going to march right up to him the first day we were home again and ask him what he was trying to do, following us that way. But I couldn't. Because he hasn't been at work."

"I see. And have you asked the other gardeners about him?" Martinez asked.

"Well, no," she admitted sheepishly. "The truth is, they speak very little English and my Spanish just isn't up to anything complicated. Oh, I'm learning, truly I am. I could ask for a cup of coffee with my breakfast and I know how to ask the waiter to bring more bread ... rolls, really. *Bolillo,* right? Oh, don't you just love those rolls they serve with everything? I said to Caledonia—"

"Mrs. Benbow," Martinez interrupted gently. "Would you like me to inquire among the gardeners, the next time I'm here, and find out what they know about this Juan Saenz? Well, perhaps I can get his home phone number from your office and give him a call."

"I thought of that myself," Angela said sharply. "I'm not stupid, you know. I went to the office, but they say he doesn't have a phone at all. Or at least, they don't have the number and it's certainly not in the book, because I looked. So I was right back where I started, having to ask the other gardeners, and like I told you, I just don't speak enough Spanish yet!"

Martinez jotted something—presumably the gardener's name — into his notebook and folded it away into his pocket again. "Well, dear lady, that is of course no barrier to me. The gardeners have gone for the day right now, of course. But the next time I'm here during their working hours, I'll make a few inquiries. In the mean time, if this Juan Saenz does come back to work, I suggest you stay away from him, Mrs. Benbow."

"But didn't you say I should question him about—"

"No such thing! I asked if you had already questioned him, but I wasn't suggesting you do so. Far from it. Please leave this to me. If he has been, as you put it, 'up to something,' your asking questions might panic him into running away. Or worse, you might even scare him into attacking you."

"Oh, but—"

"Don't deny it, Mrs. Benbow. It's certainly happened before. Partly because you always seem to give people the impression you know more than you really do, partly because the mere fact that someone is asking questions makes bad people nervous. Please ... I strongly suggest you leave the questioning to me. And now"—he got to his feet—"I really must be on my way. But I want you to consider—you and all the others, of course—not going on this third trip you have scheduled. Stay home and learn Spanish from your language tapes. It'll be much safer."

His advice did no good at all. No one in the group canceled. Of course, neither Angela nor Caledonia thought it prudent to pass along to the others all of the lieutenant's concerns. "Who knows," Angela said, "somebody like that odious Trinita might just talk some of the others into dropping out, and then none of us could go. Because I'm sure Mrs. Wilson would balk at taking a smaller group. You heard what she said about needing to make a profit. So maybe it's selfish of me not to let the others decide for themselves, but I'm sure it's safe enough, provided we don't go strolling alone on a beach at night or anything."

"For once," Caledonia said, "I agree with you. What could go wrong this time? Assuming we just behave ourselves, of course." And so on the morning of the 21st, the group was again assembled in front of the main building, their luggage dragged into an untidy pile, waiting for Grillo to load it one piece at a time into the storage space under the bus. There had been some dismay, some amusement, to find that the happy little Mexican was to be their driver once again, and Mrs. Wilson had shrugged an apology; "The regular driver wasn't back from his trip to the Grand Canyon, so First Class Tours provided"—she jerked her thumb at the cheerful Grillo—"him!" As usual, she was busily checking names on a list on her clipboard and fussing about the fact that she couldn't get an accurate head count.

Part of the difficulty was that every time she turned around, Mr. Grogan was in her line of sight. He was moving from one of his fellow residents to another, noisily staking a claim to the backseat so he could have his usual nap as they drove along. "You don't want me sitting up front talking to you all the way, do you?" he said to Trinita Stainsbury, who didn't bother to answer him, but patted self-consciously at her newly redyed hair, today a soft shade of honey blonde. "You," Grogan went on to Roger Marx, "you don't need to be down again, do you old man? You feel fine now, don't you?"

"Yes, Mr. Marx, are you sure you're up to the trip?" Maralyn Wilson said anxiously. "I want to be certain you're recovered. Because if not, it wouldn't be wise. Are you positive?"

Marx was trying to reassure her, Grogan was continuing his claims to the backseat, Tootsie Armstrong was mourning the fact that her high heels had once more been stored away and she was in flat-heeled loafers, Caledonia was yawning and stretching and complaining about the early hour, the Jackson twins were giggling over some private joke, Trinita Stainsbury was asking everyone who would listen whether they liked her hair in its new shade, and Grillo was shuffling the luggage around, trying to decide which piece should go in first. Into the middle of all the confusion bounded a smallish German shepherd, a beautifully formed dog except for paws so huge that they marked him as having a long way to go to being full-grown. The dog had Charles "Shorty" Swanson attached to the end of its leather leash, and tall as the gangly young policeman was, he was being hauled along at a smart rate by the sturdy animal.

"I'm supposed to bring you two a message from Lieutenant Martinez," Swanson said, making his way with difficulty to stand near Angela and Caledonia. "Down, Arnold. Sit, boy. Sit!" The dog paid no attention, but looked around him happily, apparently excited by all the people, several of whom came closer to look at him or to give him a quick pat on the head. "The lieutenant, he'd have come himself if he'd been able to," Swanson went on. "But since I was coming by here anyhow, he said I should bring his message for him."

"So you were coming here anyway? Uh-huh!" Caledonia said knowingly. "Well, of course we're always glad to see you, whatever the reason. But our dear Conchita ... well, your girlfriend will be absolutely delighted. She's in the kitchen, of course, because she—and all the other waitresses, of course—they've started setting up for lunch. But I'm sure she can take time off to chat. Only one thing—I want to know how come you can get off work in the middle of a day to visit your girlfriend?"

"Oh, I'm not playing hookey," Swanson said, blushing to the roots of his blond hair. "My buddy here is on his way to the vet's to get his shots. You remember I brought that police dog by here last spring, don't you? Well, somehow after that, they always seem to call me to be the escort for their trained dogs. Uh ... careful, boy ..."

The German shepherd was straining against the leash, trying to get his snout closer to Tootsie Armstrong's face.

Tootsie had knelt to pet him—"Oh, isn't he just the sweetest ... Look! He's laughing!"—but she stayed far enough away that though she could ruffle his fur with her fingers, he couldn't give her the big, wet dog-kiss he was obviously hoping to bestow.

"Is that an attack dog?" one of the Jacksons asked nervously. "I'm not very good with any dog, but I've heard attack dogs can be dangerous. If he's a trained attack dog ..."

"He isn't a trained anything yet," Swanson said ruefully. "He's in training, all right, but so far it doesn't seem to have taken."

Tootsie got to her feet and moved away, and the dog began pulling toward another potential admirer, Jerry Grunke, who quietly offered a hand for the dog to inspect. The dog apparently approved of the scent, for he rose on his hind legs and put his giant paws up on Grunke's chest. "Down, boy," Grunke said sharply, stepping abruptly backward, bringing one knee up to bump against the shepherd's sturdy breastbone, so that the dog was pushed away and downward.

"Down, Arnold!" Swanson commanded. "Good boy! Arnold's in training as a drug dog, not an attack dog. You remember that dog I brought last year? Arnold's like that. He won't hurt anybody, but he'll try to smell out ..." The dog was still straining after Grunke, and Swanson yanked once sharply at the leash. "Sit, Arnold. Sit!" Reluctantly, the dog sat. "Well, at least he's learned that much. Geeze, he's a handful!"

Respite from the continual game of tug-of-war didn't last long. Arnold seemed to believe that he had done what was required of him the moment his bottom touched the pavement, for he jumped up again immediately and charged toward a new point of interest, Grillo's shoes, which Arnold inspected with the kind of earnestness that suggested the driver had just been tracking through fresh hamburger.

"Behave, Arnold!" Swanson pulled at the leash again. "Come back here, boy."

"I don't understand how you got the honor of chauffeuring the dogs," Angela said. "I mean, they're nice and all, I suppose, but you may remember I was afraid even of that nice dog you brought here before, and he was awfully gentle, not half as active as... Oooooh!" Arnold had inserted his wet nose into the cup her hand formed around her handbag, and he had swiped a soft, dripping tongue over her finger tips. "That's sweet of him... I guess. But so sloppy!" She pulled a tissue from her purse to wipe her hand.

"To answer your question, I get the honor of being dog escort because they think I do a good job of it, that's why," Swanson said sourly. "Of course, most of the dogs mind me better than this one. But Arnold here, he hasn't got very good manners. I'm sorry, Mrs. Benbow."

"It's okay," she said vaguely, wielding the tissue vigorously to dry off her fingers. "He just makes me a bit nervous. If he were as well behaved as that other dog you showed us last spring... but this dog's so... so impulsive. And he's awfully strong, isn't he?"

Swanson was tugging hard on the leash again, because Arnold had decided to follow Grillo through the front doors, where the driver had gone to help drag out a large suitcase—Trinita Stainsbury's big garment bag, bulging with what might well be a dozen changes of clothing. "Listen," Swanson said apologetically, "this fellow is getting to be a nuisance to everybody. I'd better go on and get him to the vet's. After I take a minute to get my girl away from waitressing long enough to say hello. You know, he'd never admit it, but I sometimes think the lieutenant asks me to go fetch the dogs just because it gives me the chance to stop by here for a minute or two on my way. We're usually too busy. But he likes Chita."

"So do we," Caledonia assured him. "And we like you. In fact, we very much approve of you as a couple."

"Of course, today the lieutenant wanted me to ask you one more time if you wouldn't reconsider this trip. So I'm a messenger for ... Come back here, Arnold!" Swanson pulled back on the leash as Arnold strained forward, trying this time to reach Maralyn Wilson, apparently determined to plant another of his big, wet dog-kisses on her. At least his intentions were friendly, for his tail was wagging furiously. The travel agent glared and sidestepped out of the dog's reach, around to the other side of the pile of luggage. The dog didn't seem to want to give up, however, and kept pulling forward to the limit of the leash.

"Settle down, Arnold! Sit! Please sit!" Swanson pleaded. Arnold ignored him and turned his attention to the orange yarn tag on one of the bag handles, bumping it with his nose and barking as it swung past his face. "I'm really sorry about this. Maybe I should have left him in the car while I talked to you, but I hate to lock a dog in a car in the sun. All the same, I should have known. Arnold's so doggoned young. And his trainers told me they're not sure he'll ever learn right, he's so rambunctious. I mean, he's supposed to know the basics already—like *sit*, and *come*, and *find it!* But he pays absolutely no attention. And boy, oh boy, they aren't going to be happy when I get back and tell 'em how he bothered everybody."

"Oh, he wasn't a bother," Caledonia said.

"But he's not supposed to respond at all to people. I mean, if he ever got to be a real drug dog, he'd be going in among crowds of folks, and he should be able to stay calm and ... Oh, Arnold, for Pete's sake! Cut it out!" The dog had nosed down among the piled-up bags and had begun to paw frantically, as though he were trying to bury a bone. "Look, I'm real sorry, folks," Swanson said again and tugged on the leash. "Once Arnold's made up his mind to go somewhere, it's hard to stop him. He's so doggoned strong he just about pulls my arm out of its socket!"

"You know," Caledonia said, "Arnold's an odd name for a dog. How'd he come by it?"

"Well his full, registered, kennel name is Big Boy Austria's Pride. Some handle, huh? But that's too long and fancy to really call him by. So his trainers, they've given him a new name—he's Arnold Schwarzen-puppy!"

Caledonia yelped out a laugh and Swanson grinned. "Pretty good, huh? Now, Arnold, come! Come here before you scratch somebody's suitcase! Enough already! Stop it! Come!" Tail still wagging, the dog suddenly gave up his game amid the scattered luggage and came to sit beside Swanson, as primly as though he hadn't been misbehaving.

"Well! For once he listened to me!" Swanson said. "He's just too much of a handful. Come on, Arnold, we'll go say hi to Chita and then get you your shots. You haven't been a very good boy, and I'll be glad if they flunk you out of school and give you to somebody as a pet. Then I won't have to haul you around the country like this," Swanson said, but while he was talking, he was giving the dog the kind of scratch-and-ruffle behind the ears that spoke of affection, not of annoyance.

Perhaps Arnold was tired out from his frolic, for he seemed quite content to trot along beside Swanson as they started away toward the back doors that led to Camden-sur-Mer's kitchens. "I don't suppose you're going to cancel your trip, are you?" Swanson asked as he and the dog moved off.

" 'Fraid not," Caledonia said. "The lieutenant will be disappointed, I'm sure."

"Oh, the lieutenant won't be disappointed." Swanson grinned. "It's like I told you, he said he really didn't expect you to cancel out no matter what argument he came up with. So you just have yourselves a good time in Tijuana, okay? Now come on, Arnold, and I'll introduce you to a beautiful girl."

Arnold trotted contentedly along beside Swanson, disappearing with him around the corner, and Maralyn Wilson began to call out directions to her group. "If you'll just climb aboard now and find your seats"—she waved her clipboard for emphasis—"I'll be able to check and be sure everybody's here. That's right ... on the bus. Not back into the building, Miss Jackson, please! Onto the bus!"

"Reminds me of Swanson trying to control that dog." Caledonia grinned. "Except Arnold's a lot easier to control than this bunch!"

"Let's see," Mrs. Wilson was shouting. "Mrs. Armstrong? Yes, you're here. On the bus, please. And Mrs. Stainsbury? Yes, already aboard. Mr. Marx? Yes, you're here. Mr. Grogan ..."

And one at a time, settling into their places, the tour group braced themselves for another patented Grillo ride, and the bus bounded off, heading back southward toward Tijuana.

Chapter 12

November 21

Grillo whipped the bus off I-5 at the first exit marked for downtown San Diego. Mrs. Wilson rose in her forward-most seat, turned back in order to face her charges, and swaying as she tried to remain upright, told the group, "Our scheduled rest stop for this trip is going to be at Horton Plaza. Now, if you were tourists visiting Southern California, I'd describe the unusual architecture of the mall and tell you some of the fine shops that are there. But I'm sure you go there dozens of times, year in and year out. So I'll just say that..."

"Well," Angela said, "speaking for myself, thirty-five miles is a bit too far for me to go just to visit a mall. At my age, I do most of my shopping from catalogues or off the Home Shopping Network."

"Pay no attention to her," Caledonia told the travel agent. "The point is, yes, we've all been shopping in Horton Plaza before. So you just go on with whatever it is you were going to tell us when she interrupted."

"I was going to say," the travel agent went on, "that we'll take about two hours here—plenty of time for you to get a light lunch or a snack, and you can window-shop to your heart's content. Just be back at the bus by twelve-thirty. No later. I hope this meets with everybody's approval?" Since she had to interrupt herself a number of times to grip at the seat back for support as the bus cornered, dodged traffic, and squealed to a stop at red lights, she had hardly completed her announcement when the bus halted abruptly beside a ground-floor access to the shopping mall, an entrance with little tables and chairs scattered around a patio between a grocery store and wide stairs that swept upward to the first shopping level.

"Head for the elevator." Caledonia sighed. "Horton Plaza may be an architect's dream, but it's an overweight woman's nightmare with all the levels and balconies—and all the steps! All those steps!"

"You've got to admit," Angela said, pattering along behind her friend, "this place is interesting. It's all bright colors and angled walkways, and what level is the Nature Company on? That's one place I really love to go through. Oh, and, of course, there's Sharper Image. That's fun, too. Let's try the second level." She pushed a button as the elevator door slid shut.

But the second level proved to be offices around an open quadrangle and more of Horton Plaza's inevitable stairs. Angela and Caledonia ducked quickly back into the elevator before the doors slammed shut again, and Angela thumbed the button marked 3, muttering under her breath, "I always do that. Why don't they put a directory here in the elevator so you can figure out where you're going? Once you're in here you're insulated. I mean, you can't see out because this isn't one of those elevators that has a window. And if you forget to stop and check the printed guide before you get in ..."

The door slid open and the two hurried out onto a wide avenue open to the sky, separating left and right around the top of the broad stairs that rose from the entry area. Up and down the concrete balcony were outdoor vendors with carts of fresh flowers, of flavored ice in paper cups, of monogrammed plastic doodads, of souvenir T-shirts, of sunglasses, of silver neckchains.

For a few minutes the two women enjoyed their window-shopping, but as Caledonia said, "The Mexican markets kind of spoil you for things like flowers. I mean, there are such wonderful fresh flowers there—so many different kinds, and so inexpensive. Well, for that matter"—she fingered a silver chain—"the silver here is pretty expensive, too. Not that I'm not enjoying looking at it, but ... Angela, I'm talking to you!" She might as well have been talking to one of the fat pigeons that waddled among the shoppers, trying to cadge a few Mac crumbs from some of the snacks people were nibbling as they strolled from one store to another. Angela was staring down the length of the balcony to where it angled away and out of sight around another stairway leading upward to a fourth level.

"Look, Cal! It's him! It's Juan Saenz! It's our gardener!"

"Oh, come on, Angela. I don't see anybody who looks even remotely like—"

"Down there!" Angela pointed. "That man who just turned the corner under that next set of steps—the ones that lead up to the next level. Didn't you see him?"

"No. You're imagining things, girl."

"Come on, come on." Angela seized Caledonia's hand and tried to hurry her along toward the bend in the walkway where her quarry had disappeared, but trying to pull Caledonia anywhere was about as effective as trying to tow an elephant leashed to the back of a bicycle. "Cal, can't you get a move on?"

"Yes, I can, but I won't." Caledonia planted her large feet, and what little forward progress they'd made ceased abruptly. "If you want to chase this phantom, you go ahead. I'll just keep window-shopping and eventually I'll meet you back at the bus. But it's a futile pursuit."

"Oh, he wasn't running or anything. I think I can catch him if—"

"No, I meant it was futile because that wasn't our gardener. Angela, this seeing of familiar figures in a strange place is just a form of *déjà vu,* I think. Everybody has it. Didn't Trinita mention—"

Angela was hopping up and down with impatience. "Don't lecture, Cal, please! You're sure you won't come with me? Well then, you go on window-shopping and I'll go hunting!"

"You won't get lost? You can find the bus by yourself?"

"West end of the mall near the grocery store, right? I'll be there!"

Angela's voice was fading away as she skittered off, and though Caledonia called out to her, "Don't you be late, Angela!" Angela either didn't hear or didn't choose to respond. She hurried around the bend in the walkway, leaving Caledonia shaking her head and looking amused.

Once around that angle where she could see down the remaining length of the walkway, Angela hesitated, scanning the people ambling along eating their Baskin-Robbins, sitting on sunny benches while they compared purchases, using the public telephones, and moving in and out of the shops. Nowhere did she see the tall, slender figure of the man with the black hair and dark moustache she had spotted a few minutes before. The most sensible move seemed to be to walk along at a leisurely pace, looking into each store as she passed down one side of the walk; then when she reached the end, to turn back and investigate the shops on the other side. The man, after all, had to be somewhere. "Though not, this time, at a cockfight," she muttered.

"Beg pardon?" A hefty woman in a lavender sundress turned sharply. "You were saying something to me?"

"Oh, no, just thinking out loud. Talking to myself," Angela said sheepishly. How many times she'd promised herself never to do that. At least, not where people could overhear and think she was just a scatty old woman getting soft in the head.

"I do it, too. All the time," the lavender lady assured her. "My husband says they're going to come with the butterfly nets one day and haul me away."

Angela didn't want to get into a discussion that might distract her, so she gave a chilly little smile and moved briskly ahead. The first store around the angle was The Gap, and true to her decision, she glanced inside, but she didn't expect Juan Saenz to be in that teenagers' haven, so the glance was hasty. At Eddie Bauer's, however, she had to take a longer, slower look. "Much more reasonable shopping for an adult working man," she said under her breath, and then looked guiltily around. The lavender lady had moved off, however, out of Angela's line of sight, and nobody else was close enough to have overheard her.

The gardener was not in Eddie Bauer's. Nor in Crate and Barrel, nor in The Knifesmith, nor in Walden Books, nor in The Music Man. The next entrance led to a Nordstrom's branch, and Angela hesitated. Should she go in and look through the departments here? At the other shops she could see almost to the back without even walking inside; but a department store wasn't a place Angela could investigate from outside—too many levels and floors, too many departments. "Well, that's why they call it a department store, you fool," she chided herself. She hesitated again. Go in or go past?

She finally decided that if he had gone into Nordstrom's, she wouldn't be able to find him. But she could at least look around in men's clothing, perhaps. She started toward the door and stopped again. Or of course, he might be in the shoe department, or in home furnishings, or even the subterranean bargain basement. "Anywhere on any of three or four floors!"

she said disgustedly. "It's just too much!" The decision was made. She'd take her chances looking in the other shops.

She swung around and started down the other half of the open-air hall, past The Tobacco Jar, Solomon's Jewelers, Banana Republic, and Williams-Sonoma. Again she hesitated at each doorway and scanned the inside of the shop, but without success.

She passed the entry to a small alcove off the main passage where there were two more elevators, a bank of pay phones, and two doors marked respectively WOMEN and MEN. Again she hesitated. If he were not in one of the shops, and he certainly didn't seem to be, wouldn't it be logical that he might have gone into the men's room? The problem now, of course, was how to continue the quest if what she suspected was true. Should she stop a passing stranger and ask him to go into the men's room and check the present occupants for her? Or should she go up to the door herself, swing it open while looking modestly away, and call out Juan Saenz's name, asking him to step outside? She wondered what the men inside the restroom would do if she just walked right in? She chuckled to herself. This might be the age of sexual equality and of freedoms unknown to a generation once removed, but the men of whatever age who were surprised by her invasion would still be horrified, embarrassed, outraged. For that matter, so would she. "I think we're still more modest than we'd like to admit," she said to Caledonia later. "Or anyhow I am. I talked big to myself about going right in there, but I couldn't have done it."

She looked left and right, and there was a small bench, one of several fitted against the balcony railings up and down the walkways, and for a wonder it was unoccupied. Perhaps, and surely this was the best plan after all, she should just stay right on the bench where she could see each person as he came through the swinging door. Of course, it went against the grain with her to sit and wait for anything when she could be active, but there didn't seem to be much else she could do. So she hurried over to the bench and claimed its entire length as her own by the simple expedient of sitting in the middle, taking off her nylon windbreaker, which she folded and laid on one end of the bench, then sliding off the strap of her shoulder bag and setting the purse down squarely in the middle of the remaining bench space on her other side. It would look, she reasoned correctly, as if two friends had just gone to use the restrooms leaving her to guard their places. Caledonia would have asked her, she knew, why she was being so inconsiderate of other shoppers who might be weary from trudging the miles of concrete, but it didn't really worry her that she might look selfish. What she worried about was that she might find herself sharing the seat with a harried mother and two fussing, crabby children with chocolate-stained hands and runny noses, or with a couple of cigarette-smoking teenagers giggling over private jokes and mocking their elders, or even with a lonely, talkative old man looking for a little friendly conversation. Not that she wasn't sympathetic, she told herself—just that she was on a quest from which she didn't care to be deflected.

"I want to be ready when he comes out of there," she said self-righteously. There was absolutely nobody within earshot at the moment, so she didn't bother to carry on her soliloquy in a whisper. "I don't want to have to jump up and interrupt a conversation and be rude. Because I won't be sitting here very long. After all, how long can the man stay in there? I'll give him five minutes," she said, checking her tiny wristwatch. "Five minutes."

So she waited. And she waited. Time seemed to pass ever so slowly, but she told herself to be patient. She turned slightly to one side, not enough so that she lost sight of the men's room door, but far enough that she could glance up and down the way at the other shoppers and amuse herself by guessing their ages, occupations, and even what they might be at the mall to buy.

"Well, hello there, miss, do you come here often?" a husky voice rasped.

Angela started and turned quickly—and found herself looking up at a multicolored sea of flowing sateen—Caledonia's caftan. "Oh, for heaven's sake, Cal, you frightened me to death!"

"Don't be silly. Nothing frightens you. I was surprised to look over here and see you taking a rest. Did you find the man? Or have you given up the chase?"

"Neither one. Actually, I'm waiting for him to come out of the men's room. Well," Angela went on, "I mean, I didn't see him go in. But I looked in every shop along the way but Nordstrom's, and he wasn't in any of them. So I figured he might have gone in here."

"And you decided to wait rather than barging right in there after him, right? Very decorous of you. How long have you been here?"

"Only a couple of ..." Angela checked her watch again. "Oh, dear. It's been nearly ten minutes! I must have lost track of the time."

"And he hasn't come out in ten minutes? Listen, you better get a grip on reality here. Unless he's gone into the men's room and fainted, he isn't in there at all. You missed him. Of course, I don't know if you noticed, but there are elevators opposite the restroom doors, and he's probably taken one of them to the garage and got his car and driven away. If he was ever here at all, of course."

"Those lead to the garage? Oh dear, I never really thought of that. He might be gone from the Plaza already!"

"He sure might. So, come on, Angela, let's grab ourselves something to eat and get back to the bus. Let's not keep the others waiting. I suggest we stop at the deli counter in the grocery store. They've got good salads and stuff."

Angela sighed and gathered her possessions. "I guess you're right," she said, slipping on the windbreaker and adjusting the strap of the purse over her shoulder. "But I wish I knew why he was following us everywhere."

They walked back along the corridor of shops toward the farthest stairway and the elevator that would deliver them to the ground floor. As they passed by the head of the broad staircase, Angela stopped. "Cal, let's go down the steps. I hate that grubby, crowded little elevator and it's so slow. When I want it here on the third level, it's down on first and somebody's holding the door open for a lady with a stroller or something. When I want it on the ground floor, there are two kids playing games, riding up and down between fourth and ... There he is! Look!" Bouncing with excitement, grabbing Caledonia's hand to be certain she looked where Angela was pointing, Angela indicated a slim man in jeans and a black windbreaker, walking slowly down the steps toward ground level.

"I see the man you're pointing at, Angela, but—"

"Oh for Pete's sake, Cal, come on! Come on!"

"I'm not budging!" Caledonia even took a step backward from the stairs to emphasize the point. "I don't do stairs well, neither up nor down! I couldn't catch that guy unless I just took a flying leap and rolled down the stairs in his direction. And even then he'd probably beat me to the bottom. And anyhow, Angela, look at him. That's not Juan Saenz at all!"

"Yes, it is! It is! That's certainly the man I've been following."

"Well then, you've been following the wrong man. Juan is over six feet tall, and that fellow isn't but maybe five-six, five-eight tops. Look at him compared to the people around him."

The man in the black jacket was moving past two women who were climbing slowly upward, each carrying a pair of big shopping bags, and Angela was crestfallen to notice that both women were as tall as the man in the black jacket. "Well, they could be very tall women," she said.

"But even so they're not six-footers. And look at his face!" The young man turned sideways to look at two small children—over whom he hardly towered as a six-footer might—who were blocking the steps, playing some variation of tag, and Angela realized that, although she couldn't make out his features very clearly, the man certainly had no moustache.

"But I'm sure that's the man I saw walking ahead of us down the mall," she said unhappily. "And I was sure he was our Juan, but ... Oh, I don't know. I just don't know."

"You were chasing an illusion," Caledonia said, moving off toward the elevator, "and I told you so." She pushed the button and to her surprise, the elevator door opened at once. A thin teenager with his boom box perched on his shoulder stood inside already, his head bobbing in rhythm to the thunderous beat of the tape playing at full volume.

Caledonia stepped into the elevator and as the door slid shut, she moved very close to the boy, smiling the whole time. "You'll have to excuse me, young man," she shouted to be heard over the roar of the music, "but I suffer from an unusual form of chronic audiomania. Ever heard of it? As ailments go, it's a pip. Strictly psychosomatic, of course." The boy looked bewildered and distinctly uneasy.

"You see," Caledonia went on pleasantly, "when I hear sounds over a certain decibel level, I go into a fit of uncontrollable rage." She smiled benignly down at the youngster, who was starting to shift nervously from one foot to the other. "Do you understand what that means? Well, of course not, so I'll explain. I'm a strong woman"—she lifted one huge arm and the boy edged backward — "and I could easily do those around me a serious injury. So you see, you'll just have to turn off that infernal machine till you're out of earshot or the most appalling things could happen!"

She beamed again, and the boy, his eyes round and staring, reached quickly to snap the off-switch. The tapeplayer fell silent. "Very wise decision, son," Caledonia said, and she smiled even more broadly as the elevator door slid open and the boy stumbled hurriedly out. He did not, she noticed, turn his tapeplayer on again, at least not while he was in their sight.

Whatever the truth of Angela's quest in the mall, the remainder of the trip to Tijuana was uneventful, and the route was familiar enough to them that, as Angela said later, it almost felt like they were going home as they pulled into the driveway of *La Posada Inglaterra*. The ancient bellhop corps welcomed the party like a group of antiquated uncles welcoming beloved nieces and nephews to a family reunion. They beamed, they gabbled what seemed to be warm and friendly words (words that Angela could not unscramble), they helped each member of the party to alight from the bus, they hovered while waiting for instructions, they seized the luggage as it was unpacked from the bus—in short, it was obvious that they were glad to see the group again. More than glad—ecstatic. "I wonder," Caledonia muttered softly to Angela, "just how much they were overtipped last time? Surely this isn't the way they behave with everybody. And it wasn't the way they greeted us the first time. Not that they weren't nice, mind you, even then."

At last the luggage was, just as on the first trip, piled into the lobby and the travelers had assembled, waiting for their guide to distribute their room keys. Angela was almost the last to join the group, but unfortunately, as she said to Caledonia later, she was in plenty of time to hear Trinita Stainsbury fussing about her large garment bag, which had been dumped on its side with other luggage piled on top of it. "Just look," Trinita fumed.

"My suits and gowns will have slid off the hangers, and with all these bags on top they'll be all crushed." Unhappily she started pulling other bags off hers and in her annoyance, flinging them irritably aside.

"Here, here," Tom Brighton said, grabbing his duffle as it flew past him. "No need to get so testy, Trinita. I mean, other people don't want their bags thrown around any more than you do."

"But I don't want my things ruined," she said crossly. "And the longer they're pressed under the weight of these ..." She hoisted another bag and pitched it aside.

"Hey! Be careful, Trinita," Tom said as she wrenched at yet another case. "Let someone help you. One of the bellboys, maybe. You're going to rip the handle right off one of those. There. Look! I told you so. That's exactly what you've done!"

"Oh, dear!" Trinita was startled. She glared at a cerise nylon overnight bag in her hand, from which the leather handle hung loosely by only one end. "Oh, I'm so sorry. I didn't mean ... Whose case is this?"

"Mine," Maralyn Wilson said, reaching awkwardly to take it from her. One of Mrs. Wilson's hands was full of the room keys, waiting to be distributed, and the other held her ubiquitous clipboard, so though she tried to take hold of the broken handle, it slipped from her fingers and she finally gave up. "Just put it down here by my feet, if you please."

"Oh, Mrs. Wilson." Trinita seemed genuinely stricken. "I'm so sorry. I didn't mean to tear the handle."

"Don't think anything about it," the travel agent said, although she had a bit of acid in her tone. "That handle was torn before. I had it mended last time we were in Tijuana, but obviously the mend didn't hold. I'll just take it out and have it done again, that's all."

"Oh, I'll gladly pay for—"

"Don't be silly!" Mrs. Wilson said sharply. "I said it was faulty mending, didn't I? I'll just take it back to the same leather shop and insist they make good. Just drop the subject! Now listen up, everybody." She turned away from the contrite Mrs. Stainsbury and waved the clipboard high. "Listen, everybody! The routine is going to be very much like the last visit. We're going to allow you a little while to settle in and unpack, wash up, and whatnot."

"Speaking for myself, I really need to whatnot," Grogan said from the edge of the group. "That rest stop in San Diego was a long time ago for us older folks. So get a move on with the instructions, will you?"

"After you've settled into your rooms and whatnot ... I mean, and whatever," Mrs. Wilson said, "you'll have a free afternoon, just like you did on our last visit. Since we're having an evening of nightclubbing, you may want to nap longer than usual. But many of you will want to go shopping, and you'll remember that the shops are just over there to the east of us. But whether you go shopping or take a nap, I'll expect to meet you here at seven for dinner. We're eating early."

"Seven isn't early," one of the Jackson twins protested. "We eat at five when we're home. I swear, I just can't get used to having dinner that late. I'm usually through with supper by the time the evening news comes on TV!"

"Seven is earlier than Mexicans usually eat," Mrs. Wilson said. "Surely you remember from our last two trips." Neither Jackson responded, so she went on. "Now listen, and as I read your name, I'll hand you your room key so you can get started. Mr. Grunke, you get a single again, as you requested. You too, of course, Mr. Grogan."

"Thank the lord Harry," Grogan said, grabbing his key and heading for the stairs. "I'd bust if I had to wait one more minute!"

"Now, Mrs. Wingate, you and Mrs. Benbow are in one room together again, and here are your keys, one for each of you. Mrs. Armstrong..."

When Angela and Caledonia reached their room—the same one they'd had before—they found that the bellboy had already deposited their luggage, and Angela set to work on it at once, while Caledonia flung herself across one of the beds sighing, "Ah... I didn't mention it before, I guess, but this firm mattress suits me to the bones. I'm going to enjoy my nap. I need it, after all that exercise at the mall. Especially, if I'm supposed to stay up late tonight, after I got up so early this morning. What are you planning on doing?"

"Well, first I'll unpack so things don't get all wrinkled up. If we're all going to a nightclub tonight, I want to look decent, don't I?" She bustled to and fro, from the bed where her opened case lay to the closet, where she hung each garment with care. "Maybe this blue silk suit. It always looks nice and the clerk where I bought it said it was suitable for any occasion. If I were to wear a string of pearls... Cal, are you listening to me?"

Caledonia was not exactly snoring, but her deep, regular breathing wheezed earnestly. If she was not asleep, she was giving a good imitation. Angela sighed. Now what? Should she wait till Caledonia woke up so they could go to the shops together? Even shopping was more fun with someone along. On the other hand, Caledonia had a tendency to take over conversations.

"Well, to be perfectly fair," Angela muttered, folding her underwear into one of the bureau drawers, "we both do that, I suppose, don't we? But one thing I've promised myself to do is hear and use more Spanish than I got the chance to in either of the first trips." She carefully placed her cosmetics, toothbrush and paste, comb and brush, shower cap and vitamin pills on the shelf above the washstand. "I don't suppose," she went on,

"I learned a dozen new words in both trips together. I might as well have been at home practicing with flash cards. And if you're along, Cal, you'll just get impatient and take over the conversation and I'll never get the chance to try my Spanish. Are you listening?" The deep, regular breathing wheezed on from the bed nearest the windows. "No, of course you're not. And what if I do wait around for you and you don't want to go shopping at all? I'll have lost an hour or so of my own shopping-and-learning time for nothing."

She snapped her emptied cases shut and stowed them under the bed, out of sight. "There, that's better." She picked up her purse, made sure she had her traveler's checks and her room key, slung the bag's long strap over her shoulder, and set out boldly on her own.

Chapter 13

Afternoon, November 21

Tijuana was alive and well, as noisy and jumbled as ever. One area, devoted to fine shops for monied tourists, had been smartened up and made more organized than the myriad of junky shops that had a few years ago comprised the whole downtown. That profusion of tackiness still existed a couple of blocks away from the nicer shops. But even the high-rent areas of Tijuana were still a far cry from downtown San Diego, or for that matter, even from tiny Camden. The sidewalks were still obstacle courses, the streets were congested, and the noise was deafening.

As it had on Angela's first visit, it took her several minutes to get accustomed to the confusion and the blur of movement and sound. But eventually she adjusted and began to look for some of the items she had seen on her previous trip. The rock-crystal frog, for instance, so stylized in design and so modernistic, drew her back and after a few minutes of arguing with herself about where she would put it if she took it home, she bought it. She also bought a silver brooch that depicted a sleeping cat on a window sill, a tiny silver perfume funnel, and finally, a handsome woven basket to hold her treasures, taking a leaf from Tootsie Armstrong's book. At the same time she thought about poor Tony Hanlon, their driver who had steered Tootsie to a market and bought her the two baskets to carry her purchases.

Then, with her purse over one shoulder and her basket hanging from the other arm, she stopped at a tiny shop to look at a handsome woven shawl, one of several piled on a small stand just outside the door. The shopkeeper came out quickly.

"Good afternoon, *señora*," he greeted her, smiling broadly.

"The shawl," he went on in the oblique fashion of the Mexican shopkeeper who is adept at avoiding direct confrontation with a prospective customer, lest he be challenged on the price, "the shawl was made in Oaxaca. It is Indian weaving. Very handsome work. All done on a hand loom."

"I wish you'd tell me about it in Spanish," Angela said. "I've been into four or five shops and everybody so far has talked nothing but English. I'll never learn the language this way."

"You are trying to learn Spanish, *señora*?" He beamed at her as though she had paid him a compliment. He was a middle-aged man, very thick around the middle, which he partly disguised by wearing his shirt out at the waistline—a handsome embroidered shirt that was doubtless one he had for sale, or so Angela presumed. "How gracious of you. And how unlike most of your countrymen, who seem annoyed to discover that English is not the native language of Mexico. You will find Spanish a beautiful tongue."

"Beautiful, but difficult. At least for me. Perhaps because I'm trying to learn so late in life."

"Nonsense, *señora*. You are hardly yet so advanced in years as to be unable to learn. In fact ... Oh, here, let me bring a mirror." He stepped quickly back into the shop to get a small standing mirror, which he placed on the table beside the pile of weavings. "Try on that lovely shawl and look at yourself."

She put the shawl over one shoulder rather tentatively, and he clasped his hands and sighed in apparent admiration. "Ah, *¡qué linda! ¡Qué hermosa!* It is beautiful on you! A real Spanish lady, no doubt about it!"

"Oh! I understood that! I do wish everybody would do that. Talk Spanish to me, I mean."

"They are just trying to be polite, I think, *señora*. Because they recognize you are from the United States, and of course they cannot know that you are trying to learn our language," he said. "But I will be pleased to play teacher. Are you ready? *¿Habla usted español? ¿Comprende?*" He spoke slowly, enunciating carefully.

"Oh!" Angela beamed her delight. "I did understand that! You asked if I speak Spanish, didn't you? Say something else! Please."

He smiled back and nodded and said carefully, "*¿Puedo enseñarle otro manton?*"

"Oh!" This time Angela's exclamation was in a minor key. "I didn't understand at all. You said 'Can I ... can I ... something,' but I couldn't get the rest. I don't know what all that other stuff means! I know it was a question, but I'm afraid I can't answer you."

"Well," the storekeeper said, "I only asked if I could show you a different shawl. *Manton*—shawl. I think you may know the word *mantilla*, no? That means a little *manton*, you see?"

"Okay," Angela said. "Let's see ... *Quiero uno rebozo.*" She beamed back again. "There. How's that?"

"There is a little difference between this"—the shopkeeper touched the fringes of the shawl Angela still had on her shoulder— "and a *rebozo*. This would be more of a *manton*. A *rebozo* ... well, have you seen peasant women wrapped up in a length of heavy cloth like a small blanket? That is what I think of when one says *rebozo*. More wrapped up. Useful, but not perhaps as decorative."

Angela picked up the shawl. "Oh, dear. Then a *rebozo* isn't what I was thinking of buying at all. This ... this *manton*, this is more what I want." She adjusted the shawl across both shoulders and turned left, then right, looking at herself in the mirror. "Do you really think I look Mexican? Maybe I should wear this while I shop, and then maybe people would talk Spanish to me. Do you think so?"

"Well, uh ..." the shopkeeper said, obviously struggling to find an answer that would please this peculiar customer, "uh, not exactly. I am afraid they would still see that you are from the United States. If you want this merely as a disguise ..."

"Oh, believe me," she assured him, "I'd wear it when I was at home, too. I think it's really beautiful. I was just trying to think of whether it would work today. You said I looked like a Spanish lady in it, and I wondered ..."

"Well, if you want it as a sort of a costume, may I suggest this? Mexican ladies sometimes wrap the shawl high, to cover the head. Perhaps ..."

Angela pulled the shawl higher so that it cupped the back of her white hair. "Like this? Now do I look like a real Mexican? Of course, maybe they'd start talking to me too fast, and I wouldn't understand a thing if they started running their words together like ... Oh-oh!"

Suddenly she interrupted herself. In the mirror she had caught sight of a familiar face in the street behind her—Roger Marx, and there beside him was their travel agent, the object of his affections, Maralyn Wilson. They were moving slowly along the sidewalk, arguing as they went, bumping into and dodging around the other shoppers, and they did not seem to recognize Angela at all as they moved near, then around, and finally past her. Of course, she reminded herself, she had the shawl covering her distinctive snow white hair. Besides, they seemed to be concentrating on each other.

"But I don't want you to come with me," Maralyn Wilson was saying in a petulant voice. "Believe me, I know the town, and I don't need a guide. And before you suggest it, I'm not buying a lot of stuff you could carry for me."

"Well, I could carry that overnight bag of yours. It's too heavy for you. Of course, I told you didn't I, that you should empty it before you brought it along. Who knows but what some of your things will disappear while it's being mended. Anyhow, I'll be glad to carry it. In fact, here ... give it to me now."

"No, Roger! I told you, just stop fussing! As for the bag, I just grabbed it and ran before I emptied it completely, that's all. It's not too heavy for me, and nobody's going to steal anything. You're too untrusting." He moved to take the bag from her and she yanked it out of his hands. "I said no! I don't want you fooling with my stuff. Just leave it alone! Honestly, Roger! I'll move a lot faster and get done in half the time if I'm on my own. Just go back to the hotel!"

"But why can't I tag along?" Marx was insisting. "I'll stay out of your way. If you want to bargain with somebody, I'll step outside and you can argue to your heart's content. But the thing is, when you're done with the shops, then maybe we can stop for a margarita or something. I'll let you pick the place."

"Roger, please! Just go on back!"

They passed down the street out of earshot. Angela turned to look after them and saw them cut across the street at the corner and begin to argue again. Finally Maralyn Wilson went into the corner shop while Marx lingered outside, picking over a tableful of leather wallets, watching the crowds, and apparently whistling happily as he waited. Angela assumed he had finally won his argument, and Mrs. Wilson had given in, allowing him to tag along.

Angela turned back to the merchant. "Look," she said. "Maybe I'll be back for this shawl. I'm not sure. It's very handsome, but it would take up too much space in my basket, and it would be so heavy. Oh, dear, I suppose I should say all this in Spanish, but I don't know how!"

"You did very well, when you tried to speak, *señora*. Your accent is excellent." Angela blushed with pleasure, quite forgetting that she had only spoken a total of four words by which he might judge, and also forgetting that this was a man determined to make a sale. "Shall I wrap the shawl for you and hold it here while you shop?" he suggested. "Then you could pick it up as you come back to your hotel."

In the end, that is exactly what Angela decided to do. Of course, she told herself, she should bargain with him. It was expected, even though the tag on the shawl listed what she thought was a perfectly reasonable price. "Oh, dear," she said, "I suppose I should bargain in Spanish, but it's hard enough for me to do it in English, let alone trying to say it in another ..." She cleared her throat and began bravely, "What will you take for this?" The shopkeeper said nothing and she stammered on, "I mean, can't you come down just a little bit? Not that it's not worth a good deal more, of course. It's really handsome. And beautifully made. But the price ... well, can you possibly take a little off?"

Whether because it had been a slow day and the shopkeeper needed the sale, or because he was so amused at Angela's idea of bargaining it would be impossible to say, but the shopkeeper nodded solemnly and appeared to think the matter over before he said, "Well, *señora,* since you are so charming and since it looks so fine on you—and as a gift because you are learning our language—I can perhaps take two pesos off this price." He held the price tag up before her eyes. "But that is bringing it down almost to what I paid for it, you understand."

"Oh! How wonderful!" Angela said, her voice lyrical with pleasure and relief. "I didn't think you'd agree to lower the price at all. Wait till I tell Caledonia how I bargained!"

"Ah, it is true, you do strike a hard bargain," the shopkeeper agreed. "You break my heart as well as my pocketbook." He did not, however, seem too aggrieved as he took her money and the shawl, which he would, as he had already assured her, hold until she returned on her way back to the hotel.

Putting the material over her head had disarranged a few strands of Angela's hair, and she took a moment to put herself back into good order, using the little standing mirror on the table before she ventured on down the street. But she had only begun to smooth and tuck when once again she saw someone she knew in the glass. It was Jerry Grunke, moving past her quickly, silently, almost she thought as though he were running on tiptoe. *He's following somebody,* she thought, turning to look at him disappear down the block, dodging the other shoppers as he moved. *Now how do I know that? Because,* she answered herself silently, *he's looking straight ahead at something or somebody beyond him. He's not looking at the people around him, or at the things for sale—he's looking right through them, looking at something down the street.*

At the corner, Grunke slowed abruptly and stopped, then turned toward the pottery on display there—whimsical animals fashioned in baked clay, designed to go into and around potted plants and not Grunke's sort of thing at all, Angela told herself. He was only pretending to look at the little figurines, she realized. She followed Grunke's intent gaze with her own eyes and realized she was looking at Roger Marx where he dawdled outside the shop on the corner. Was Grunke actually following Roger Marx? She stopped in her tracks and pretended to be examining a rack of souvenir T-shirts in brilliant colors. She bent slightly at the knees, so that her head did not appear above the top of the rack, and she reached to pull aside the screening garments, peering cautiously from between a bright purple shirt that screamed TIJUANA in scarlet letters and a crimson shirt with a tequila bottle painted on its front in neon colors.

To her dismay, she realized that in the scant moments it had taken her to conceal herself and arrange a peephole, her quarry had disappeared. Grunke was not to be seen. But kitty-corner across the street, Roger Marx had moved along to the table of goods in front of the second shop and appeared to be examining some pieces of wrought iron. Was he leaving without Maralyn Wilson? Or was he actually thinking of buying a holder for paper napkins, Angela wondered. And then her attention was caught by movement far down along the side of the corner building. A small door, perhaps a service entrance, had opened and Maralyn Wilson slipped quickly out. But instead of heading back toward the main street where Roger Marx stood—now apparently contemplating the purchase of a parrot cage—Mrs. Wilson turned away toward the alley behind the shops. Where could she be going? The woman had taken great pains, Angela realized, to duck her ever-present admirer. Without even thinking about it, Angela headed quickly down the street and as soon as she was past the corner so that she would be out of Marx's line of sight, she too cut across kitty-corner, heading hurriedly for that alley.

The alley reminded Angela of the tiny street in *El Pueblo* where the gardener Juan Saenz had apparently disappeared. This alley, too, was narrow, bordered by blank walls of brick and adobe, with only a few doors here and there down its length. One door, about fifty yards down the way, however, was just closing as Angela rounded the corner. She hurried to reach it before it slammed shut and she slipped inside.

The confusion in the Tijuana streets had been duplicated and magnified inside the huge market in which Angela found herself, although it took her several moments to realize that it was a market she'd stumbled into through what was apparently its back door.

The building was at least two stories high and wide enough for several aisles of stalls set up along either side of long, narrow avenues. Each booth was a tiny shop displaying goods exactly the way the merchants on the street showed them—standing in racks around the sides and back of the space, laid out on tables across the front, and often projecting into the aisles. The merchants here, with so little space to expand left, right, and backward, had also taken advantage of the building's height to erect tall display racks—poles supporting panels, arches, and cylinders of chicken wire on which their goods could be pinned or hung, so the general effect as one progressed down the aisles was of picking one's way along a very narrow, cluttered street that was strung overhead with a gala showing of holiday flags and banners.

The market seemed to be a strange combination of a people's market and a market that sold to the tourists. Table linens, woven serapes, lengths of lace and embroidered dress goods, T-shirts, and blue jeans fluttered overhead. As one moved along, one brushed against pillars hung with tooled-leather handbags and passed under bridges made of brightly colored candles hung in pairs by their wicks, through archways of *huaraches* and thong sandals, and into tunnels of carved wooden masks that glared down with sightless eyes. Here and there a vendor displayed canned goods and kitchen products, or piles of fruit and vegetables. The noise of commerce was softened inside the market by the hanging draped goods and unlike the merchants in the open streets, these stall keepers used no tapeplayers to attract buyers. Perhaps that was a mistake in strategy, for there seemed to be many more merchants than customers in the market.

Angela edged cautiously through and around the display tables and the mounds of merchandise, glancing into each booth as she passed, but slowing down at none of them. Every few dozen yards or so there was a side aisle running at right angles to the main aisles so that one could cut across into the next passageway without traveling the length of the building. At each of these Angela, who was in the aisle farthest to the right, paused and peered hesitantly toward her left, but all she saw were more tablecloths, shawls, T-shirts, and plastic dinnerware.

She was startled by a grumbling hiss of sound from a booth just ahead of her and moved forward to find to her surprise that an artisan was fanning his fires to heat glass for blowing; the sound was the bellows he was using and the flames were contained in a brick structure very like a brick barbecue pit found in public picnic grounds. He was not the only artisan creating his own goods for sale right there in his place of business. Several women were plying their needles at the delicate embroidery that would adorn some blouse or party frock; a silversmith was bending and shaping metal into an intricate knot, holding silver wire over a Bunsen burner by means of long, wooden-handled tongs; and one artistic chap was using Day-Glo paint to create a lively likeness of Elvis Presley on black velvet.

Several of the stall holders looked hopefully at Angela as she sidled past, but she avoided their gaze. The few customers were too busy buying, rejecting, or haggling to pay Angela any attention at all. And none of them were people she knew. Seemingly, Maralyn Wilson had vanished completely. Angela hesitated at yet another cross-wise passage leading off her aisle, but saw nothing of interest, at least not to her on her quest. She was not here to buy. She was here to ... well, what on earth was she here for, come to think of it? Caledonia, she realized, would be scornful of Angela's never-ending curiosity. She could hear Caledonia now—"What business is it of yours if Maralyn Wilson wants to go shopping without her loving Roger? What do you care if she wants to buy something without explaining—donuts or handbags or whatever? Suppose she wants to go on a bus ride? Or mail a letter? Why should you get involved?"

But a shopping trip or a bus ride, handbag or donuts, Angela argued to herself, none of those would explain why Maralyn Wilson had left that corner shop so stealthily and abandoned Roger Marx to his solitary vigil in front. And nothing either Marx or Wilson had done would explain Jerry Grunke's interest in them. "So what?" Caledonia would argue. "That still doesn't make it your job to find out what's going on. And what makes you think anybody's up to mischief anyhow?"

"Two trips, two deaths," Angela muttered. "That's what."

"You are eenterested een thees leettle trays, *señora*?" A heavy-set woman with Indian features smiled hopefully at Angela and brandished a small, neat tray, its surface showing a pair of brightly colored birds fashioned from real feathers and protected by glass, the whole framed in wicker. *"Muy raro. Muy precioso.* Very ... rare. For a *coleccionista* ... a cull-lecture, you unnerstan'?" Her English was accented, but Angela could understand easily enough. "They have make thees feather pictures *ilegal,* you know? Against the law. But we steell have in shop here—"

"No, no, thank you," Angela gasped. "I'm ... actually I'm looking for someone. A friend. An ... an *amiga*. An American woman. I mean, like me—from the United States, you know what I mean? A blonde—"

"¿Una rubia? Sí ... en el proximo pasillo. Allí." Her English, which was apparently limited to matters having to do with her

tiny feather-picture trays, had pretty much deserted her, but the woman was willing and waved energetically toward the next aisle. "¡*Allí*! ¡*Allí!*"

"Thank you so much," Angela said. "And they're beautiful trays!" She hurried into the next cross-aisle, the last one before the very end of the building, she thought, for she had traversed nearly the entire length of the market. But as she approached the next main aisle, she slowed down. She could hear a woman's voice — Maralyn Wilson's voice, she thought, from inside that very last booth in the next aisle. The booth seemed to occupy the entire end of the aisle so that it had no nearby neighbors, although it was hard to tell exactly because the very end of the cross-passage through which she was moving had been partly blocked by two heavy blankets or rugs made of thickly matted wool in varying shades of brown and cream. The rugs had been hung for display on a stout clothesline so that they formed a kind of screen through which one would have to pass to get into the main aisle beyond. Angela had actually raised her hand to move aside that heavy barrier when she heard the woman speaking again—almost beside her, right past those blankets and around the corner. And it was certainly Mrs. Wilson's voice, Angela told herself, raised in loud complaint. Angela stopped moving, held her breath, leaned close to the hanging blanket, and listened intently.

"You said there wouldn't be any problems. It'd be easy," Maralyn Wilson was saying. "And so far I've had nothing but problems. This simple system of yours isn't really all that simple." Angela pulled back a step to be sure she was safely in the shelter of the hanging rugs. This didn't sound like the kind of conversation into which her interruption would be welcomed.

A man's voice was murmuring something apparently intended to be soothing that Angela couldn't quite catch, something about not talking so loud, about not being overheard. But Angela could still hear Maralyn Wilson's sharp voice with perfect clarity. "Oh, don't be silly. Half the locals here don't talk good English, and those who do will mind their own business. They don't want trouble, and you look like trouble. We've got to settle this. I say we have to think of some other method because this one isn't working. At least, it isn't inconspicuous any more. Somebody mentioned the ripped handle this very morning. Somebody noticed, and next thing you know, they'll notice some other little difference when we pack for home tomorrow."

"The bags are identical except for that handle," the man said. His voice was smooth and genteel, his English barely but definitely accented. "And Pedro here is mending that now to be ready for next time. Nobody will be any the wiser, believe me. Now, there's your new case on the floor beside his workbench. Take it, and—"

"Wait a minute. That isn't the only problem. There was a drug dog nosing around the bag before we left Camden this morning."

"A drug dog! With a police handler? That kind of drug dog?"

"Yes, of course with a police handler. What'd you think? You think he just wandered over to us with a sign on his collar that said 'HEY, I SMELL OUT DRUGS'? Of course he had a policeman attached to him. Anyhow, he apparently thought he found drugs in our luggage and I near about died! I thought they were going to search through the bags and they'd find the money, and—"

"Maybe," the man said slowly, "he picked up the scent off the bills. They say it clings to things like paper money. But nobody investigated, did they? Of course they didn't. Or you wouldn't be here. But then"—the man laughed softly—"why should they? If he'd smelled drugs when your party was leaving Mexico, the authorities would have torn the bags apart. But nobody in their right mind would smuggle drugs *into* Mexico."

"All the same, it nearly gave me heart failure. You told me this was a simple messenger service and nothing could go wrong. But things have been going wrong and going wrong."

"Look"—the man was soothing again—"the only reason somebody noticed something about the bag was because this is the same group you brought with you last time."

"And the time before," Maralyn Wilson conceded. "That's true."

"Usually you bring a tour in only once, you bring them back home, and then you never see them again. A one-time-only group would never have seen anything unusual about the case."

"I was just lucky nobody caught wise about the yarn tag," she said crossly. Angela took a tiny step forward, straining not to miss a single word. "It's Pedro's fault. He gave me the new case and didn't transfer the tag off the old one, and I had to steal one from one of my people's bags. And that guy made such a fuss you'd have thought the world was coming to an end. I said he probably didn't tie it on right, and he just flipped."

"That was completely stupid of you," the man snapped, his patience obviously exhausted. The genteel voice had grown coarse with annoyance.

"Stupid of me! Why me?"

"Because you should have noticed the tag for yourself. That's not Pedro's job to see things go smoothly, it's yours. Furthermore, you have to keep cool. Don't antagonize your charges. Do what any good travel agent would do. Keep them happy, and don't argue with them! I shouldn't have to tell you that happy clients will rally to your side if anything should go wrong—they'll swear you never left them long enough to ... What time is it?"

"A quarter to four," Maralyn Wilson said sulkily.

"Well, you'd better get back, then," the man said. His manner was more commanding now. He was no longer soothing; he was giving orders. "That man who came with you may be patient, but if you leave him there too long he'll begin to wonder. He might even go into the shop looking for you, and that would never do."

"Oh, all right, give me the bag. The new one, Pedro," she snapped. "And be sure you mend that handle on the old one really well this time. I don't want it to tear again. Well, aren't you going to say thanks or anything?"

"Thanks?" The man's voice was thick with scorn. "Why do I owe you thanks? You get paid handsomely. You are not doing a favor for friends, you know. You are an employee." He laughed, but it was not at all a pleasant laugh. "You *Norde Americanos* are amusing. We Colombians are much more practical."

"I've done a lot for you, a lot more than a mere employee would," Maralyn Wilson said angrily. "I've taken initiative. I've done things I never believed I could, and all to keep things running smooth. First when that dreadful woman got hold of my case, I had to take care of it. Then my very own driver ... And what I thought is, you'd be grateful to me for the way I took care of everything. That's what you're always saying I should do. But things keep going wrong, and that's why"—her voice rose nearly into a whine—"that's why I want to work out a new way of doing business. Because this one—"

"¡*Basta*! ¡*Silencio*! I don't want to hear details." There was a moment of silence, and when the man continued, he had mastered his flash of temper. "If you get yourself into trouble, it's up to you to get yourself out. We've told you that before, and I tell you again now. As for gratitude, quite the contrary. You might have drawn attention to us with your ..." His voice dropped to a hiss, much more frightening to the listening Angela than his roar of anger had been. "You listen to me, woman. Stay out of trouble, stop making mistakes, stop doing things that get the police involved—or this arrangement will be terminated entirely. And you don't want that, do you?"

"Well, no, but ..."

"Then this meeting is at an end. Except ... wait a moment. Did you say your next trip into Mexico will be in the first week of next month?"

"That's right." Maralyn Wilson's voice was thick with resentment. "On the second. A bunch of used-car dealers and their wives. I'm taking them down to Ensenada."

"Good," the man said, and his voice was silky once more with satisfaction. "I prefer Ensenada myself. I do not care to get this close to the border. Too many might recognize me. I have been careful about getting my picture taken, but over the years they probably have managed one or two, and I might be observed."

"The Mexican police are—"

"Are paid off. Or enough of the local police to make me feel safe, at any rate. It's police and government agents from the U.S.A. who concern me. Besides, Ensenada is quieter and the food is excellent. I see no reason not to be comfortable when I have to come up from Mexico City for these exchanges." There was a pause, and Angela leaned farther forward. Were they still talking and she was missing something? But no, the man spoke again, abruptly. "Well," he said, "you were just leaving, were you not?" It was not an inquiry, it was another command, and Angela straightened up and began to back hurriedly away from the hanging rugs. It was definitely time to get out and ... In her haste she stepped on a trailing corner of one of the rugs and her foot caught in the thick material. She half turned, trying to kick her way free, and the basket over her arm snagged some of the rug's fringe. She yanked hard with both her foot and her arm, and the rug, which had been suspended only by old-fashioned wooden pegs rather like clothespins, pulled free of its fasteners, sailing hugely out and down as though it meant to cover her in its length. Angela yelped and threw herself to one side—and at the same moment, Maralyn Wilson came around the corner into the cross-aisle and stopped short.

"Wha ... ! What are you ... Mrs. Benbow! What are you doing here?"

"I tripped," Angela gasped. "I didn't see ... I mean, the rug was in the ..." She gulped and began her usual defense, a strong offense. "What are *you* doing here?" she demanded, and then stopped.

A large male figure had suddenly appeared around the corner behind Mrs. Wilson, but Angela was too startled to take in the details of his dark presence. "This is someone you know, Mrs. Wilson?" The menacing voice was that of the man whose conversation Angela had been eavesdropping on, and she was thrown into the kind of panic she seldom experienced. "May I have the pleasure of this lady's acquaintance?" he said, but Angela knew those words were not what he really meant. In most circumstances, she'd have stood her ground and lied her head off. But something about that tall, looming, dark figure and his smooth, forceful voice terrified her, and she let out a frightened squeak, turned, and fled back along the cross-aisle, heading for the long aisle where she had entered.

She meant, of course, simply to get to the little back door, to get out of the building, and then to run for her life. But baskets of carved wooden figurines and racks of embroidered material, pyramids of briefcases, and tables covered with glassware all seemed to move out to choke the passageway. She dodged and weaved, skittering along as rapidly as she could. It was no real comfort to her to hear things clashing and banging, falling and breaking behind her, which meant that whoever was pursuing was having the same trouble getting through the aisle as she was. She was not making enough progress, in her view, and hearing the man's voice calling for reinforcements, *"¡Pedro! ¡Pedro! ¡Ayúdanos¡"* didn't cheer her up at all. It was like one of those awful dreams where one runs and runs and gets nowhere.

The stall holders and the scattering of customers up and down the aisles were shouting, asking questions and barking out their protests as their goods were knocked over and scattered, and Angela had a fleeting thought that it was a pity there were so many voices—she had even less chance of unscrambling the Spanish her pursuer was speaking. She ducked under an archway of cutwork table linens and speeded up on a short straightaway thinking that it was as though she were two people at once, one frightened and running away for dear life, tripping and bumping and dodging and skittering her way down the crowded aisle—while another Angela inside her head was trying to remember her Spanish vocabulary.

"Ouch!" Both Angelas came together in shock and frustration as she tripped, nearly falling over a serape trailing from one of the stands; squirting tears of frustration, she twisted herself free of the cloth. And suddenly, as she wriggled and started to sprint forward again, she realized that she had reached yet another cross-aisle leading off to her right. Without thinking about it, she plunged down that side way, dashing right on past the next main aisle (since for all she knew she might meet with the advancing Pedro there), and at the third of the main passageways, she turned to her right, heading back the way she had just come—away from that back door and toward the front of the building. Again, she was experiencing that strange sensation of being two people at the same time; half of her was still scared witless, but the other half had decided that there was bound to be a front door to this market as well as that tiny back door, and whether that was true or not, she still might gain on her pursuers by confusing them with her change of direction.

This aisle was no easier to navigate than the one she'd just left, and she tripped and stumbled, weaving her way through, bumping into people and stacks of goods with equal force and no hesitation. Suddenly, from yet another side aisle, a familiar shape appeared in her line of vision—and there, right in her path, was Jerry Grunke. "Mrs. Benbow!" he hissed at her. "Come here." He reached both hands out and grabbed at her, but Angela lowered her head and shoulder and threw a block that would have impressed a professional linebacker, butting Grunke right in his solar plexus. He gasped and fell backward into the corner stall, landing on a pile of what seemed to be multicolored bath mats, and Angela raced on, with only a fleeting thought that she was glad he hadn't been near the glassware displayed in the next booth—and *bang!* The glassware exploded into a thousand clashing, tinkling shards.

Angela ducked automatically and hesitated in midstride for a split second before she realized what it had to be. "They're shooting at me!" she choked out. Her pursuers had found her again and were hot on her heels. "They're shooting! At me!" She bent forward and picked up speed at the same moment she realized that the stall holders and customers she passed were all crouching and cowering. These people apparently knew gunfire when they heard it and had acted accordingly, finding urgent reasons to examine immediately the concrete flooring of the market.

Bang! Metal clanged, and a set of wrought-iron fireplace tools clattered to the ground just ahead of her. She hippety-hopped over them and kept going. She thought suddenly that she should be zigzagging the way commandos did in the movies when somebody shot at them. And in the same moment she realized that she was already zigzagging through the aisles to avoid the obstructions, not the pursuers and their guns. Nevertheless, it was just as effective.

Ahead of her at the far end of the aisle she caught sight of two men, their faces invisible in the shadows cast by the overhead lights. But there was something, she thought, that looked familiar about those two customers, and ... *bang!* Flower pots in a stand on her left exploded. "Get down," she shrieked at the newcomers, and then realized that they were already bending low as they moved, but they neither threw themselves flat nor stopped their forward progress. "Lie down flat! Down!" she shouted to them, as she swung right past a rack of cotton peasant dresses, then ducked left around a stack of brightly painted toy carts. Behind her there was a metallic clanging as her pursuers tripped over the set of andirons their bullet had dislodged. Someone with a gun was behind her, and these two ahead of her were advancing... And then, as though everything had slowed way, way down—like a movie in slow motion—one of the men ahead raised an arm as though he were pointing toward her, and she caught the glint of metal in his hand. He, too, had a gun, and he was pointing it straight at her!

She should, she was thinking, do something—duck into another side aisle or hide under a table. Then without warning, she was pulled, and pulled hard from one side. She found herself swung violently back toward her pursuers, just as the gun ahead of her went off. *Bang!*

She thought she felt the bullet graze her face—thought she felt the breeze as it passed. She thought how lucky she was that all her enemies were such rotten shots! And then she thought that her luck couldn't possibly last. And she thought what a shame it was she was going to die on this grubby concrete floor, because it would get her nice suit all dirty. And then the darkness closed in.

Chapter 14

November 21

Soft hands were touching her; soft voices were rippling around her. She was tucked into a bed with an extra-firm mattress, her head slightly elevated. She was, Angela realized, in a hospital. The lights were turned down in the heavily shadowed room, but there was no mistaking the unrelenting white walls and medical uniforms, the blood pressure machine in one corner, the tank of oxygen in another. And there weren't many beds in the world except in hospitals that had steel railings on the sides. Yes, she was in a hospital all right.

Uniformed nurses came and went, talking Spanish to each other and to a solemn man in a white lab coat who wore a stethoscope like a necklace—the doctor, Angela assumed. The doctor talked to the nurses and to two men wearing business suits, who stood across the room in a darkly shadowed corner. The two shadowy men talked to each other in hushed tones and to the doctor, and finally to Caledonia, who arrived after a time and paused to talk to the men and then to the doctor. Angela couldn't hear what was being said—and probably couldn't understand most of it if she could have heard it. But she still found herself resenting the fact that everybody talked to everybody else, but nobody talked to her. They seemed to be too busy to notice that her eyes had finally opened. "Hey!" she shouted. "Isn't anybody going to let me know what's going on?"

As soon as she called out, the doctor and two of the nurses hurried to her. One nurse shoved a thermometer into Angela's mouth and the doctor placed his stethoscope against her chest, while the other nurse strapped the blood pressure cuff around Angela's arm. The solemn men came from the shadowed corner to stand awkwardly near the foot of Angela's bed, and Caledonia hurried across the room, her caftan flapping in the breeze she created as she waded through the crowd to plant herself in the chair immediately at Angela's left side. "Okay, Angela, don't get excited. Stay calm. We're all here. We'll take care of you."

"I don't want to be taken care of," Angela said as soon as she could get the thermometer out from between her lips. "I want to be talked to. I want to know whether you caught the man who shot me. I want to know how badly I'm hurt. I want to know—"

"You are obviously not badly hurt, Mrs. Benbow," one of the men said, "and nobody shot you." He moved closer toward the head of the bed, after one of the nurses—apparently satisfied that the patient would live — moved away, and as he advanced, stepping into an area where the lighting was better, Angela saw to her surprise that he was her favorite policeman, Lieutenant Martinez of the San Diego County Police.

"Wait a minute," Angela said. "Wait ... am I home in Camden? My head hurts and I can't think, but it seems to me I was in Tijuana."

"You are indeed in Tijuana, *señora*." The other man moved to stand beside Martinez, and Angela recognized him as Captain Garcia y Lopez of the Baja California police force.

"Captain Lopez," Angela said in surprise. "Was it you who shot at me, then? It was somebody ... I even felt the bullet whiz past me."

"Neither of us shot at you, *señora* Benbow. Though I confess I did use my revolver. I was trying to shoot past you at the man behind you. The man who was pursuing you. For one terrible moment, when you fell so hard to the floor, I thought perhaps I had shot you. You had turned around so quickly, I thought you'd gotten into my line of fire."

"I didn't turn, I was pulled," Angela said. "Somebody grabbed hold of me as I was running. They yanked me almost 180 degrees around!"

"Not somebody," Martinez said. "Something. The strap of your purse. When we got to your side, we saw that your purse strap was still caught on a protruding nail in one of the display towers in the aisle. That is why you seemed to duck so suddenly—and nearly got yourself shot."

"But if I wasn't shot, why am I here?"

"You are here," Captain Lopez assured her, "because you hit your head on the concrete floor of *El Mercado Grande* and the doctors fear you might have a *conmóción*." He hesitated. "A ... a ..."

"A concussion," Caledonia filled in, and Lopez accepted her help with a nod of his head. "And you're supposed," Caledonia went on, "to lie still and not wiggle around and ask a lot of questions. At least till they're sure that you don't have such a big crack in your skull that your brains will leak out."

"We will come back later to answer your questions," Martinez said, turning toward the hall door. "Now that we know you will be all right. Captain ..."

Captain Lopez turned to join him, and only Angela's agitated voice kept them from leaving the room altogether. "No, you two. No siree! You come right back here and talk to me.

And you can just stop shushing me, Caledonia. I'm not going to lie down and be still till somebody tells me what exactly happened back there. Who was that man who was chasing me? Why were you there? It's all making my headache worse, and I won't be able to rest until you explain."

Martinez stopped in the doorway to hold a quick conference with Captain Lopez and then with the doctor in Spanish ("Why was I surprised that he spoke fluent Spanish?" Angela said later to Caledonia. "I suppose because I've never heard him speak anything but English before. But I should have guessed he was bilingual."). At last he returned to Angela's side, a rueful smile on his face, and Captain Lopez joined him. "The doctor tells us, Mrs. Benbow, that it will do a lot less harm for us to ease your curiosity than it will for you to bounce around in your bed complaining. So we bow to your request. What exactly do you want to know?"

"First of all, why was Captain Lopez shooting at me? Shooting past me, the way you tell it."

"He was trying to save your life, Mrs. Benbow. The man behind you had already fired at you once, and—"

"More than once, actually. But I guess maybe the other shots were fired before you showed up. It's still all kind of mixed up together in my head, and it happened so fast. Anyhow, what became of that man who was chasing me? Did you hit him, Captain?"

"Fortunately, yes," Lopez said. "Hit him and missed you, though for a moment I thought I'd hit you both with a single bullet."

"Like the little tailor! Seven at a blow!" Angela said.

"I beg your pardon?"

"Ignore her," Caledonia said. "She's babbling. It's a story for little children, Captain. A tailor who kills seven flies with a single swat. Go on about the man. You say your shot hit him?"

"Indeed it did. In the arm. He dropped to the floor himself, bleeding, clutching the injured arm, and cursing eloquently in Spanish with a thick Colombian accent."

"The captain doesn't know you as well as I, Mrs. Benbow," Lieutenant Martinez said. "If he did, he would not be so surprised to find that you have somehow got yourself involved with an incredibly dangerous character. That fellow turned out to be Angel de Santiago, a cousin of one of the biggest drug dealers responsible for shipping drugs from Colombia through Mexico into the United States."

Captain Lopez nodded. "We have been watching him a long time, that Santiago, trying to put together solid proof against him. We know he has been living in Mexico City, and whether we can prove it or not, we know he has been acting as facilitator for his cousin's cartel—arranging the receipt of the goods, their transshipment, and the delivery of payments after the money has been sufficiently laundered so that it cannot be traced in either direction."

"The man apparently had such organizational ability, not to mention such an amazing head for detail," Martinez said, "that had he applied himself to some legitimate enterprise and got a decent education, he might have made millions as the CEO of some large company. What a waste of intelligence and talent."

"He would not agree, Lieutenant," Captain Lopez said softly. "Santiago considers himself a complete success." He paused and smiled broadly. "Except, of course, that he now resides in a jail cell here in Tijuana, while your Bill Gates, to cite one example of a good businessman, is living in a penthouse in Seattle. So perhaps one cannot completely agree with Mr. Santiago's self-assessment."

Martinez took up the discussion again. "He should not have shot at you, of course. That was hardly prudent. But apparently he lost his head because you overheard his conversation with your travel agent, Maralyn Wilson, and that might have meant his having to scrap all his carefully made arrangements and find a new courier. Or so he told us."

"He told you all that?"

Martinez smiled. "Well, not directly. But he shouted a number of things at us before he could control his rage—he has a bad temper, that Santiago—and we were able to figure out what he was saying because we had so much knowledge of him beforehand. In his mind it would have been easier to dispose of you than to make a whole new plan of delivery and find a new courier. Mrs. Wilson would no longer be useful, if you lived to identify her, but he had put a great deal of time into finding just the right person to avoid suspicion."

"Suspicion of what?" Caledonia had been listening closely, shaking her head, and her voice was plaintive. "I can't follow a bit of this. I need more explaining than Angela does because, don't forget, she already knows a lot of this. From her eavesdropping, according to you."

"Mrs. Benbow, this may take a moment ... may we?" Lieutenant Martinez pulled up a chair on the other side of the bed, offered it to Captain Lopez, and then took one for himself. The chairs, Angela noted, were simple wooden chairs of the kind found in old-fashioned kitchens. In fact, everything in the room was bare-bones austere, from the undecorated walls to the bare concrete floor. No luxury suites in this hospital.

"Let me go back to the beginning," Martinez was saying. "Your Mrs. Wilson was apparently being paid handsomely to act as a messenger bringing in drug money that needed laundering."

"I've never understood money laundering anyhow," Angela said, rubbing at her temples. "I mean, money's money, isn't it? How can you tell what's clean money and what's dirty money?"

Martinez cleared his throat, and his voice took on a professorial tone. "Well, you see, at home in the States, huge sums of cash can raise awkward questions. Buy a Cadillac or a diamond ring and pay cash and eyebrows will be raised; try to deposit several hundred thousand in cash in a bank, and the FBI will be alerted. And yet cash is what these people have, because drug dealers don't write checks to their suppliers, do they? So there has to be some way for them to enjoy their profits without arousing suspicion—the cash has to be converted into something that could be sold legitimately and the proceeds from the sale used, instead of the original cash. Do you see?"

"Well, I think so," Caledonia said. "But it seems awfully complicated to me."

"You're right. Money laundering can be a fairly complex process, but to put it simply, the big sums of cash from criminal enterprises in the United States are transported to banks and businesses in places like Mexico and the Caribbean islands where people aren't quite so curious. Eventually, that cash is replaced by investments that can be sold, loans that can be called in, bank deposits that can be withdrawn. Things like that."

"I'm surprised that Mrs. Wilson would get involved with drugs, though," Angela said fretfully. "She seemed like such a nice, ordinary person. And drugs are such a dirty business!"

"She'd have told you," Martinez said, "that she was merely running a messenger service. What she was doing, on each of her trips into Mexico, she would bring a suitcase full of the money—money gathered by the cartel from the sales of their product—and she would exchange her case for a case containing stock certificates, deposit slips, real estate deeds, small business partnerships. I can't tell you exactly till we've done more investigation, but it would be various proofs of all kinds of perfectly legitimate investments Santiago had made for his brothers-in-crime—investments that could be turned into clean cash, once Mrs. Wilson delivered them back in the United States. All she did, she'd tell you, was carry an extra suitcase—and take great care that nobody saw her when she exchanged it for a duplicate."

"You haven't explained, though," Angela said. "How come you were there in the market? What are you doing down in Mexico anyway?"

"I invited him," Captain Lopez said. "After he phoned me to voice his suspicions."

"Suspicions of what?" Caledonia said. "How did you catch on to what Mrs. Wilson was doing?"

"It was Arnold who tipped me off."

"Arnold?"

"You remember ... Arnold Schwarzen-puppy," Martinez said. "Shorty Swanson—he's my partner," he explained to Lopez, "he'd brought a dog-in-training by the retirement home just as these ladies and the rest of the group were packing up the bus to leave for this trip. Well, when Shorty got back to the office, he told me about the dog's behavior—acting as though he'd scented drugs in the luggage. It couldn't be, of course. Who would import drugs into Mexico from the United States? But the idea nagged at me. Why had the dog acted that way?"

"Santiago said something about that in the market," Angela said. "I remember now. He said it was probably their money that the dog smelled. He said the paper money would smell like drugs."

"He's absolutely right. We've often seen a drug dog point us to money. Lots of bills come into contact with drugs, one way or another."

"My money has touched drugs?" Caledonia said in a horrified voice. "Money right in my very own purse?"

"Of course. And bills in bank vaults, bills in handbags and wallets. You don't know where any particular bill has been before you got it, do you? As I say, if the dog had started pawing at some man's pocket, it wouldn't have surprised us in the least. But pawing at the luggage? That made me think. I wouldn't expect any of you to be carrying money in your suitcases. And I could rule out drug smuggling. And yet something in one of those cases smelled of drugs. And after I got to thinking about it, I thought how clever it would be to bring money into Mexico with an otherwise legitimate tour. It would have to be the driver doing it, or the guide, and not the tourists themselves, because it would have to be someone who came down often."

"I see, I see," Angela said excitedly. "But it couldn't be our driver, because our regular driver had been killed and our new driver was only coming on this one trip. It had to be Mrs. Wilson herself."

Martinez nodded. "I did a little fast checking. She's living awfully well to be running a small-time travel agency; she drives a BMW, she owns a condominium in La Jolla, she has an active account with a brokerage firm. It was very suspicious. So I phoned the captain and when we talked ..."

"When we talked," the captain took over the story again, "I put a computer to work comparing the dates of the lady's trips into our country to the travel schedules of known members of the drug cartels who live in Mexico. Oh yes, we keep track of those particular visitors. We are every bit as eager as you are to catch them when they break our laws. And"—he gave a small bow of acknowledgment to Lieutenant Martinez—"we are eager to cooperate with the United States government in its war against drugs. So we keep track. And when the computer matched *señora* Wilson's travel dates to Santiago's many flights to and from Mexico City into Baja California, we realized we had something."

"So the captain was kind enough to invite me to join him here to keep an eye on Mrs. Wilson."

"Of course," Captain Lopez said, "we had someone covering Santiago's movements already. And as it happened, we all met at *El Mercado Grande*—the men following Santiago and those of us following the *señora* Wilson—and we were just in time to find you fleeing and Santiago chasing you. And now, Santiago is in jail," he said happily, "facing charges of attempted murder. I really do owe you a debt of gratitude, *señora* Benbow, for according to our laws, up to the time he took a shot at you, he seemed to be doing nothing illegal. It is not against the law in Mexico to receive a large sum of cash—even if it is delivered in a suitcase—or to deliver a packet of mortgages and promissory notes."

"How about Mrs. Wilson?" Caledonia asked. "Are you charging her, too?"

"Well, to tell you the truth," the captain said, a bit less expansively, "we do not have Mrs. Wilson in custody as yet."

"We have her duplicate suitcases," Martinez said. "One of them contained what the captain just told you—deeds and evidence of loans. And an envelope with her name on it—an envelope containing her paycheck."

"Paycheck?"

"Well, not exactly a check, of course. A stack of twenty-dollar bills, actually. Five thousand worth. I must remember to ask her whether that was her fee for a single trip or for several trips. Not that it matters. The other suitcase contained bills—lots and lots of bills. We're having them counted, but I'd say easily over a hundred thousand."

"That would be the suitcase with the broken handle," Angela said. "She was bringing that to be mended, she said. But of course she was really bringing it to deliver it to that Mr. Santiago. Right?"

"Right."

"But you don't have her in custody?" Caledonia said. "Why not?"

"Because she was too clever to chase along behind Santiago," Lopez said. "Intelligent woman. Apparently, from what we've been able to put together from witnesses, she followed only until you cut across the building on that crosswalk with Santiago chasing along after you. At that point, she abandoned the parade and headed straight on out the back door."

"My men at the back of the building," Lopez said, "were among those assigned to watch Santiago, so they hadn't been alerted to look for the *señora* Wilson. And they didn't care if a tourist—that's what they thought she was—left the market. They let her go."

"But she'll get away!" Angela was outraged. "And she's a criminal!"

"No, she won't," Captain Lopez corrected her. "The border patrol has been alerted, so she can't get back home. And she can't escape us for long if she stays here. A blonde from the United States—even one who speaks excellent Spanish—is not going to move about Baja California unnoticed. Someone will tell us where she is."

"Now," Lieutenant Martinez said, "I think we've answered most of the questions you had. And we should go about our business and let you rest."

"Oh, but you haven't told me where Jerry Grunke fits in!" Angela said.

"What's Grunke got to do with all this?" Caledonia asked.

"I don't know," Angela said, "but he was there in the market, too. And he was chasing me, just like that Santiago. Grunke came right out of a side aisle and grabbed me. But I got loose, and ... and surely you got Grunke, didn't you? I hit him pretty hard and I may actually have injured him."

Lopez and Martinez exchanged a smile and Martinez said, "Mrs. Benbow, Jerry Grunke was not trying to hurt you. Or to hold you for Santiago. He was trying to pull you to safety.

He arrived at the market before we did, and when Santiago chased off after you, you made so much noise bumping into things and knocking things over with the vendors all yelling at you—there was so much noise that Grunke could follow the pursuit by ear as easily as though he could see the whole thing. So he cut across the building on that cross-aisle deliberately. When he reached out to you, he was trying to save you—perhaps to help you hide. Except you misunderstood, so his attempted heroism was effectively neutralized by your butting him right in the midsection. He didn't even get his breath back, let alone get back into action, till after we'd shot Santiago and you'd knocked yourself unconscious."

"But why? Why would Mr. Grunke try to help me? And why was he following Mrs. Wilson anyway? I thought he was one of them."

"Oh no, Mrs. Benbow," Martinez said. "He's not one of them. On the contrary, he's one of us. Your Jerry Grunke is a retired Los Angeles policeman."

"A policeman!"

"Detective, actually. But a policeman from the top of his thinning hair to the soles of his big, flat feet." Martinez grinned.

"Well," Caledonia said slowly, "somebody once said that when trouble starts, and everybody else ducks or tries to run away, only one kind of man stands upright and starts toward the trouble instead of going in the opposite direction, and that's a policeman. And maybe that explains why Grunke's such a watcher. We noticed that he sits with his back to a wall whenever he can and his eyes move all the time. He could tell you where everybody is in the room at any given minute."

"He's a watcher, all right," Martinez said. "He tells us he's been watching Mrs. Wilson ever since an identifying tag was taken from his suitcase on your first trip, and she tried to tell him he'd tied it carelessly. But he knew better because he'd been very careful to do it right in the first place, and her accusation got under his skin. So maybe because he was annoyed, he's been watching her ever since. And he was following her when he entered the market. He was positive she was up to something, even though he wasn't sure exactly what. Actually, he was one aisle over from you, listening to the same conversation you overheard, but standing on the other side."

"Incredibly careless of them," Lopez said, shaking his head, "to discuss their private business so freely in such a public place."

"She said," Angela explained, "Mrs. Wilson, that is, she said nobody would pay any attention and everybody would mind their own business."

"They didn't know you very well, Angela, did they?" Caledonia said with amusement. "And not only did you listen to every word they said, but when Grunke tried to save you, you knocked him down. Do I understand that you butted him right in the gut?"

"Well, how did I know he was one of the good guys?" Angela said sulkily. "He came out of nowhere and grabbed at me. It scared me! Besides, I barely had time to recognize him. I even thought for a minute he might have been that Pedro. You know, the henchman. The other guy that was with Santiago."

"Don't worry about Pedro," Captain Lopez said. "We have him in custody as well as Santiago. Pedro was trotting along waving a pistol, but he apparently didn't have the desire to fire it at anyone, because when he saw us—and he recognized us at once, which shows you the kind of company Pedro's been keeping—he threw the pistol at us as hard as he could while throwing his hands in the air and shouting out that he surrendered. Not a very determined or dangerous villain, that one."

Caledonia got to her feet. "I think," she said, "that Angela should probably take the doctor's advice at this point and rest, instead of talking and asking questions."

The two policemen got quickly to their feet as well. "Do forgive us for taking so much of your time," Lieutenant Martinez said, "but you did ask us about these things."

"We are delighted that you are on your way to recovering, señora," Captain Lopez said. "But of course your friend is quite correct. We have overstayed our welcome." And in a flurry of goodbyes and good wishes and promises to return, the two men left.

"I'm on my way too, Angela," Caledonia said. "Our bunch will be wondering what's happened and I can't wait to tell them." "Except for Roger Marx," Angela said. "I forgot to tell you. He was downtown shopping with Maralyn Wilson and she went off and left him standing outside a store. I guess she told him she'd be right back ... but she cut out a side door and snuck off to her meeting with Santiago in the big market. Poor old Roger Marx may still be standing there waiting, for all I know."

"Oh, dear, and I'll have to tell him his lady love's involved with drug dealers and money laundering."

"I wish you'd hold off," Angela said. "I know more about it than you do, and it was my adventure, after all. I want the chance to tell everybody about it myself."

"Oh no! For once, I'm going to be the center of attention at dinner." Caledonia grinned. "I wouldn't wish you confined to a hospital, mind you, but as long as you are ..." and she swept out, leaving Angela alone in the shadowy room.

There was no television set to watch, no magazines to read, and very little traffic back and forth in the hall outside her open door. She was still suffering from a headache, so Angela was more than uncomfortable and not a little fretful by the time two nurses came into her room. One of them flipped on the overhead light and pulled the bedclothes aside while the other readied a hypodermic needle large enough, Angela thought, eyeing it with suspicion, that it could have served as a turkey baster.

"Here! Hold on. What do you think you're going to do?"

"Eet ees the doctor's orders," the nurse with the hypodermic said. If the other spoke English, Angela never discovered it, since she never spoke aloud. "Eet weel make djou ess-leep," the be-needled nurse added.

"I sleep just fine. I won't need that thing. You tell the doctor I don't want a shot."

Angela might as well have argued with the chair in the corner. The silent nurse firmly rolled Angela onto her side and pushed away her flimsy hospital nightgown while the other jabbed the needle into Angela's behind.

"Ouch! You stuck me!"

"Eet deed not hort djou," the nurse said. "Don' make a fuss. Now. Ees water here." The silent nurse fetched a plain metal pitcher which she set on the bedside table with a glass. "Djou ess-leep, hokay?"

"I'm not sleepy yet," Angela protested. "And my head aches."

"Ess-leep," the nurse commanded as she and her fellow headed out of the room. "Chust ess-leep." The silent nurse flipped the overhead light off again and the room descended into shadowy silence.

"Hospitals here," Angela muttered crossly, "aren't one bit better than at home in the States. They still do whatever they please and they don't ask you what you want. Natural, I suppose, since obviously they don't *care* what you want. So why should they ask? Mmmmmph ..." The last sound was a cross between a sigh and a groan. Or perhaps it was a yawn. "Maybe I am a little sleepy after all," Angela said. Or she thought she said it. Perhaps she only thought it. Whichever, it was the last thing of which she was conscious for some time—she had no idea how long. All she knew was that it was sometime later when two more nurses returned to the room and she was pulled forward to sit up in bed and urged to get onto her feet.

"Djou are to have hex-uh-rays," one of the nurses said. She was a beefy female with huge, muscular arms. "Can djou ess-eet in the share, or shall I leeft djou?"

"Oh, I can get up," Angela said as she put tentative bare feet on the concrete floor and tried without success to stand. She was surprised how fuzzy her head was, how lightheaded she felt. She sat back down on the bed again. "Perhaps I could use a hand. It's that shot those other nurses gave me," she said. "I can walk as far as the wheelchair, but perhaps a little help ..." The large nurse obliged, and Angela eased herself gratefully in the wheelchair and pulled her feet onto the rests. "Oooh ... that seat is terribly cold," she said, and she shivered. "These hospital gowns aren't really good enough."

The nurses held a whispered conference there in the dark; then one of them went to the little closet in the corner and brought back Angela's nylon windbreaker jacket. "Poot thees on, plees," the sturdy nurse said.

"How about my shoes? Or do you have bedroom slippers?"

"Djou are not to go for *uno paseo*," the woman said. "No walk in a park, no. Now, moof back. So the ess-trops will reach."

"Strops?" Angela was having a hard time with the woman's accent.

"Djou mus' be ess-trop in the share," the nurse continued. Angela still did not understand until the nurse and her helper, a slighter woman wearing a heavy white cardigan over her uniform, began to fiddle with the two sturdy leather restraints attached to the chair.

"Oh, please don't do that. I'm not going to fall out!" Angela protested, wriggling in discomfort.

"Hospital regulations," the nurse in the cardigan said and kept right on working the buckles. "There, that does it. Let's go."

Angela noted idly that this second woman had only the merest trace of an accent, unlike the other nurse. A better-educated woman, perhaps, Angela thought. Angela sighed. Educated or not, that nurse was every bit as bossy as her muscular colleague. Give some women a starched white uniform and they believe they've got the right to give orders, Angela was thinking. So much for nurses as angels of mercy!

She started to turn, trying to look at the second nurse, but she found her head swimming. Her eyes didn't seem to want to focus. "Why am I so dizzy?" she asked the nurses. "And everything looks so fuzzy. What was in that shot?" Neither nurse answered. "Well, don't pay any attention to me," Angela said grumpily. "I'm just the patient!" Her voice was surprisingly husky, she realized. Maybe they couldn't hear her. "What was in the shot?" she asked again. Again nobody answered, and Angela realized that her croaky voice had been only a kind of whisper. Oh well. She'd sleep this off and feel better in the morning.

She yawned deeply and let her mind drift away into a gentle fog as the nurses maneuvered the chair out of the door and pushed it smoothly down the silent corridor, past a desk—the only brightly lit area in the hallway—where three more nurses were working busily over charts and records, through a little waiting area empty of visitors at this hour, and onto an elevator. Nobody spoke and the wheels of her chair made no noise. It was like moving through a dream. It was probably night, Angela told herself. Things always quieted down around a hospital at night. She'd apparently been asleep for at least a couple of hours. "Nobody told me it was night," she said to the nurses in that strange, husky voice she seemed to have acquired. "What time is it?" Neither answered her. "What time is it?" she demanded again.

The elevator arrived and the one nurse, the one Angela knew mostly as a sweater-covered arm, pushed the wheelchair into the elevator and turned Angela to face forward. The other nurse was still standing outside in the hallway, and it was she who finally answered Angela, gesturing back at a clock on the wall behind the nurses' station. *"Ocho y media, señora,"* the nurse said. *"Más o menos ..."* Angela thought she understood at least part of the statement, probably because the hands on the clock showed a few minutes past eight-thirty. So she was right, it was night.

The elevator doors slid shut, and the last she saw of the burly nurse was the woman turning toward the desk, presumably to go back on station. "I suppose an X ray makes sense," Angela said. "I did hit my head, after all."

"You're not going to X ray," the nurse behind her chair said.

"But that other nurse told me—"

"She was wrong, that's all. You're being discharged and sent home."

"Home? You mean I'm going to my hotel? Wonderful. But ... but in my nightgown?" Angela felt confused and anxious. "Well, it's not *my* nightgown, of course. It's this little hospital pinafore thing ... And bare feet! Oh, why didn't you let me at least put my shoes on?" She was pleased to note that her thoughts might be spinning, but her voice seemed to be a little stronger. "And that was a nice pair of slacks. I don't want to lose them."

"Relax. I have your things right here," the nurse said, bringing a hand around Angela's shoulder so that Angela could see that the nurse was holding a plastic bag from the top of which protruded a corner of black cotton and a red-and-white-striped sleeve—Angela's slacks and shirt, of course.

"Oh, that's good," Angela said. "So, if you'll just give me a minute so I can change—"

"No time."

"Listen! I'm certainly not going to walk home in my bare feet," Angela said with as much emphasis as she could muster—which really wasn't much, since the dreamlike haze kept threatening to take over. "And where's home from here anyway? I wouldn't know what direction to start walking in. That means I'll have to get a taxi, I suppose, so I'll *have* time to change, won't I, before it arrives?"

"No-no-no, a ride has been arranged," the nurse said, as the elevator bumped to a stop and the door slid open to reveal a small lobby. The nurse pushed Angela's wheelchair in the direction of the hospital's large double doors, outside of which, Angela could see, it was indeed night. "A van is there in front waiting now."

"Well, I still want to change. I don't feel comfortable."

"No time now. You can change later. Let's put this across you." The nurse grabbed up a lightweight blanket that had been folded carelessly across one of the lobby chairs and threw the coverlet over Angela's knees, but she kept the wheelchair moving, out through the entry doors into the dark and chilly night. Angela yawned and shook her head. The feeling that she was wrapped in cotton balls, insulated from the real world, persisted, surrounding her—making it hard for her to think clearly.

The van was one of those with a wheelchair lift, and a steel platform had been lowered to street level from the van's open side door. The nurse rolled Angela's chair straight onto the platform, pushed a button inside the van's door, and the lift groaned its way upward to the level of the van's floor. The nurse rolled Angela forward so that the wheelchair was beside the driver's seat, where a passenger's seat might ordinarily have been. She maneuvered the chair into position, then bent down to secure its large wheels with metal clamps of some kind. Angela craned her neck, but she couldn't quite see the clamps, although she could hear the metal snap down into place and feel her chair sway slightly at each snap, so it was easy to work out what was happening.

"Thank goodness this van is closed in," she said dreamily. "I mean, it's really chilly outside." She pushed rather feebly against the restraints, twisting this way and that, but turning her head made her dizzy again, and she stopped, yawning heavily once more. "That's odd. I seem to be nodding off again. Maybe because it's dark out here," she said sleepily. "Now if you'll please take these straps off me ..."

"The straps have to stay in place, Mrs. Benbow," the nurse said. "Like seat belts." She flung the plastic sack of Angela's clothing into the back of the van and slid herself into the driver's seat.

"You're much safer strapped in as you are. And so am I." She started up the van, then pushed another button and the van's big side door slid shut. Then she put the van into gear and they began to move off, away from the hospital's front door.

"It's a good thing you know the way," Angela said, the words coming slowly. "I'd get lost right away." There was a pause in the conversation. "That shot," she said finally. "Powerful stuff, I guess. I don't seem to be able to keep my eyes open. Can you believe I'm falling back asleep?" She tried to watch the van moving along, watch the way they were going, but she felt her head nod forward and her eyes slide shut. "I guess you were right," she murmured. "It's a good thing I'm held in with these straps. I'd slide right out of the chair without them."

There was a long pause. Angela knew she was dozing, but it was only a kind of half-sleep. She was aware that the van was easing along, she was aware of traffic in the streets around her and of the bright lights. From time to time she raised her head to look blearily at the shops they were passing, at the people thronging the streets, at the cars and the motorcycles and scooters. "There are a lot of people out in the middle of the night, aren't there? Why don't they go home to bed? Like I'm going to." She yawned and her head nodded forward.

A few minutes later—she wasn't sure how much later—she roused again. The van was still inching through downtown traffic. "How long till we get to the hotel?" she said. "I hate sleeping in cars, and I really need to be in my own bed. I'm chilly, and these straps hurt, and—"

"Oh shut up," the nurse said crossly.

With the tiny portion of her mind that was wide awake, Angela noted that the woman seemed to have lost even the tiny trace of accent she'd once displayed.

"Behave yourself," the woman went on. "Go back to sleep."

"Don't talk to me that way!" Angela's protest was muffled by layers of mental fog. The acid she would ordinarily have allowed to etch her voice didn't seem available through the narcotic haze.

"Maybe this was a lousy idea," the nurse was saying crossly. "I thought you'd be my ticket out of Mexico. My insurance policy. Now I'm not so sure. You just go back to sleep and let me do all the talking when we get to the border."

"What ... what's ..." Angela struggled to focus on the profile next to her. For the first time she took in clearly the crisp white uniform, the glossy black hair, the familiar profile. "Wait a minute! I know you."

The van stopped under a streetlight, held up by a car trying to pull into a parking place ahead while traffic waited impatiently to pass. "I know you," Angela said again, looking at her companion through bleary eyes. "Don't I know you?"

"This black wig must disguise me better than I thought it would," the nurse said.

Angela looked at the woman's face again and gasped. "Wilson! Maralyn Wilson! But the hair ... the nurse's uniform ..."

"Theatrical costume. No big deal. I told you I know my way around this town. Now settle down. I've got a gun." She took one hand off the steering wheel and slid her fingers into her cardigan pocket. Angela, still trying desperately to focus her eyes, thought she detected the outlines of a small pistol showing through the heavy knit. But she didn't feel like asking for proof. She didn't feel, in fact, like saying much of anything, because for one of the few times in her life, she was absolutely speechless.

Chapter 15

November 21

"You brought this on yourself, you know," Maralyn Wilson said, inching the van forward through the heavy traffic. "It'd never have occurred to me to go get you from the hospital if you hadn't got yourself involved with your snooping. I'd have picked some old lady off the street to be my grandmother."

"Grandmother?" Angela's confusion was total.

"Yes, my grandmother. I figure they'll be watching the border, but they'll be looking for a blonde by herself. They won't be looking for a brunette and her sweet old granny."

Angela's brain, usually so busy and so agile, was in slow motion. "But ... but why me?"

"I said it was all your own fault, and it is. You heard us talking in the market, me and Santiago. But you're the only one who knows about the money and my involvement. And if you aren't available to give testimony, they haven't got a thing on me. I'm killing two birds with one stone, so to speak."

Foggy as she was, Angela still registered the word "killing," and began to wriggle in the chair, pulling against the restraints.

"Oh, sit still," Maralyn Wilson said crossly. "If you make trouble, I'll get rid of you right now."

"But you're going to get rid of me anyway, aren't you?" Angela said.

"Of course not. What makes you think so?"

"You just said that only my evidence—"

"Well, the truth is"—Mrs. Wilson maneuvered the van closer to the car that was creeping along in front of her—"the truth is I haven't made up my mind yet." Angela shivered, but not just from the chill of evening. She could tell a bald-faced lie when she heard it, even if it was presented in a coaxing tone of voice. "If you're very good and you help me," Mrs. Wilson was saying, "maybe I'll reward you by letting you go."

"Anyhow, you're wrong. I'm not the only one with evidence against you." Angela was fighting to clear her head—to be able to think in a connected line. She might feel detached, as though she were floating through the things that were happening, but her instincts for self-preservation had been aroused, and she knew she had to do something. A lamb to the slaughter had never been her favorite pose. Now she struggled to get herself out of the spotlight. "There are others besides me who know about you. Jerry Grunke was in the market this afternoon too, and he was listening to you. So even if I weren't around, he'd give evidence. And the police have your fingerprints on the suitcase with the money. Oh, they're on to you, all right. They don't need my testimony."

She waited, but Mrs. Wilson said nothing, and the van continued to inch its way forward. "Did you hear me?" Angela insisted. "You really have no reason to get rid of me." There was no comment, and Angela tried again. "Did you hear me?"

"Oh, I heard you. I'm just trying to take it in. To decide what I should do—what it all means," Mrs. Wilson said. "Things have got so complicated." She sighed deeply. "I thought the last problem I'd have was Tony Hanlon," she said. "And I thought, once I took care of him, it'd be smooth sailing."

"What do you mean 'took care of him'?" Angela said. "Are you saying—"

"Watch out!" Mrs. Wilson jammed on the van's brakes so hard Angela was scrunched against the restraints that held her in the wheelchair.

Two couples clutching bulging shopping bags had dodged between the slow-moving cars to cross the street directly in front of the van. "Boy, do I hate driving through this district! Stupid tourists! But it's the shortest way to the border. Now do you see why you're strapped in? It's really for your own safety."

"You can't fool me," Angela said crossly. "It's to keep me from running away." Her annoyance was helping to wake her up a little, and though she still felt groggy, she realized that the hypnotic effect of the drug was wearing off, at least a little bit.

"Well, yes, that too. I want you to stay put. I didn't pay out all this money just to have my escape plans fall apart because you slipped away."

"Money?"

"The van rental, this costume, and the bribe to that nurse to help me get you out of bed and strapped into the wheelchair."

"But you don't need the straps. I mean, you have a gun, right? And I'm barefoot and in this see-through nightie thing with not even a bathrobe, for pity's sake! Why not at least loosen these straps a little bit?"

"No! The straps stay on!"

"But it's cold out there and except for my jacket and this blanket, I'm dressed like—well, Gypsy Rose Lee wore more clothes than this for her grand finale! So I'm not likely to make a break for it, am I?"

"I knew your bare feet and having a bare tushy would be a deterrent, all right," Maralyn Wilson said smugly. "But the straps stay on, all the same. For insurance," she added, and she inched the van forward with the traffic again.

"Oh, at first I thought about trying to get away, all right," Angela said. "I'll admit it. But I decided against it when you showed me the gun. Besides, I'm so sleepy I can hardly sit up straight, never mind running away. And I'm too old to run anywhere, anyhow."

"You weren't too old to run at the market." Mrs. Wilson sounded amused. "Santiago was really panting as he chased after you."

"Speed's relative I guess," Angela said, a bit sulkily. "I was trying to run, but I was mostly dodging and ducking around mountains of stuff—baskets and belts and bags and pottery. So I wasn't really going very fast. More skittering than really running."

"Well, just you remember that I have the gun." Mrs. Wilson patted the cardigan pocket. "And you can't outrun a bullet, let alone outskitter it. So don't try anything funny. Besides, you don't have to. I've made up my mind. If you behave yourself and if you help me—play along when we get to the border—I'll let you go as soon as we're safely across, okay? So settle down now. It won't be much longer."

Angela subsided into silence. She didn't believe a word the woman was saying, and the thought of doing nothing to help herself was not natural to Angela. Very quietly, moving a centimeter at a time, her hands hidden from view under the blanket, she inched her fingers toward the buckle of the first strap of the two restraints that bound her into her wheelchair, and began very gingerly, very quietly to feel around for the buckle's release. If she could just ease the straps free without their falling all the way off, perhaps Mrs. Wilson wouldn't notice. There was still the gun, and there were her bare feet and lightly clothed body to worry about, but ...

"I'll tell you again, you brought this on yourself," Mrs. Wilson was saying as the van finally cleared the last of the shops and rolled into the stretch of road that broadened almost at once into several lanes, the lanes to the left lightly traveled at this hour with cars coming from the United States into Mexico, the lanes to the right choked with cars full of people, most of whom were heading home to the States. Traffic on the left moved smoothly along, but the cars in the right-hand lanes moved a few inches, then stopped—eight feet, stop again—a few feet more, stop again.

"This is moving too slow! The border patrol must be asking a lot of questions tonight," Mrs. Wilson said tensely. "Listen, you don't need any more trouble, do you, Mrs. Benbow? So you be sure to keep quiet and leave the talking to me when we get up there. I know that'll be hard for you; nosey people just naturally get into trouble. Like Tony did." The van moved forward again, one more car length, and stopped. "If Tony had minded his own business, he'd still be alive. But no. He had to follow me till he found out about the visits to the leather shops and discovered what I was doing with the duplicate suitcases. Then what did he do about it? He came to me and asked for money. Boy, I hated to have to get rid of him. He was a good tour driver. But he said he'd let the police know about my arrangement with Santiago if I didn't pay him."

"So it was you who killed him? Not some stranger—some mugger? That's what you're saying?"

"Certainly. But it wasn't my fault. It was his. For being so greedy. To be fair, he seemed to be in a real bind—behind on his car payments and owing money on tuition. I told you he was a graduate student, didn't I? Anyhow, he said he didn't want a lot. Just enough to pay off his debts. But I knew that that wouldn't be the end of it. People like that"—her voice was rich with scorn — "people like that have no conscience! I don't know what the world's coming to. You can't trust anybody to just do what they say they'll do. Well, I can't work with a threat hanging over my head that way. That's why I divorced my second husband, you know. Because he was too demanding. I don't operate well under pressure. So I told Tony to meet me at the beach, I pegged rocks till I broke the overhead lights, and I waited in the shadows so he wouldn't see me coming at him. He was pretty strong, you know, so I had to sneak up on him like that."

"Then it really wasn't a mugger and it wasn't gamblers."

"Gamblers?"

"You told that colonel fellow in Ensenada that Hanlon was involved with gamblers."

"Pretty good story, I thought."

"It wasn't true?"

"I don't have any idea. Mrs. Benbow, I heard you were a pretty sharp old lady, but you're acting like you haven't got all your wits tonight. You're going over and over the same things. Try to concentrate."

Angela shifted angrily in her seat. Calling her old always got that reaction from her. But she swallowed her resentment and kept working quietly, using only a single, surreptitious finger to pluck at the release on the buckle. If she could just get the first strap loose ...

"Stop wriggling around like that!" Mrs. Wilson said suddenly. "You trying to get loose?"

"No-no," Angela said. "Just trying to get comfortable. I told you these straps don't feel good." Perhaps it was the adrenaline coursing through her system; Angela realized that her head was getting clearer by the minute and her voice was returning to normal.

"Maybe I'll loosen the straps for you. Even take them off. But after we get through the border here," Mrs. Wilson said, moving the van forward again. "I'm not any more comfortable than you are," she went on, "having to inch along this way, wondering what they're going to ask us when we get there—wondering if they'll see through this disguise of mine." She sighed again. "It's like I said, I just don't do well under pressure. Damn, but things have got complicated. I did just fine before you and your group came into my life, and nobody even suspected. Santiago was right—if the police were to look for a courier, they'd look for somebody who takes regular trips every week or every month. Maybe a truck driver, and like that. All I had to do was bring that extra bag along with my luggage whenever I brought a group to Mexico. It worked perfectly—till you people came along. And that's so funny, because I thought you would be so perfect, you old people. Because you wanted three little short trips close together."

"You said," Angela accused, "that you didn't like short trips like ours, because you couldn't make any money on them! You almost wouldn't take us!"

"That was just for show. Don't you get it yet? I wasn't really unhappy about those short hauls. Just the opposite." Again the van moved forward one more car length. "Don't you see it? The money I make off you people is small change compared to what I get making these deliveries. I was actually pleased as punch to make three trips in one month. But you'd have thought it was strange if I didn't object—so I objected."

She drummed her fingers impatiently on the steering wheel. "Why won't this traffic move? Get going? What's the big holdup? I hate this! This traffic, this dumb van, this whole mess! That stupid Santiago, shooting up the market that way! This is all his fault! He could have taken care of you quietly. There weren't all that many customers around and the stall holders would have ignored us— minded their own business.

It would have been easy to drag you into that end booth of ours where nobody could see."

"What would you have done then?" Angela scoffed. "Tied me up and gagged me? I'd have been out of there in five minutes, and—"

"Oh, I think we'd probably have had to dispose of you. Quietly, of course. Pedro carries a knife—I've seen him use it on the leather he works with. And if that was too messy, we could just have choked you, couldn't we? That's a quiet way to do it, there's no mess, and it wouldn't take very long. Especially with an old woman like you."

"Oh, puh-lease! You're a rank amateur. You don't know the least thing about killing people and whether it's hard or easy to get rid of an old lady."

To Angela's shocked surprise, Maralyn Wilson giggled. Giggled! "Miss Braintree wouldn't agree with you," she said. "I planned an absolutely perfect way to get rid of her, didn't I? Of course, I didn't know she had a weak heart, but that made things go even easier. I think she had a heart attack while she was struggling against the pillow."

Angela caught her breath. "The black velvet U.S. Navy pillow!"

"You remembered!" Mrs. Wilson actually sounded pleased. "I didn't think anyone would remember that pillow!"

"You smothered Miss Braintree! But why?"

"Because she got my bag by accident—you know, the one with the money in it. There was a mix-up and the bellboy brought her my case instead of hers when we first arrived—before I'd had a chance to make my delivery. She saw all that money. At least, I think she did. She didn't say so exactly, mind you, and she returned the case with no problem. But she started making little remarks about how rich I really was ... things like that. And that could mean trouble."

"Miss Braintree would never have worked out what you were up to. She wasn't a very pleasant person, but she wasn't very worldly either."

"Maybe. Maybe. But if she kept on dropping hints the way she was doing, saying things about me having such a lot of money, and saying why would anybody carry that much cash?—things like that—well, sooner or later somebody else would have figured out what was going on. So she had to go. And after all, nobody really cared about her, did they? She was a nasty, demanding woman, wasn't she?"

"But you don't just remove a fellow human being because she's inconvenient to you—like brushing off a piece of lint."

"Hey! That's good. A piece of lint. That's it exactly."

Angela sighed. "Well, I don't believe you anyway. You weren't with us on the cart ride. You were outside waiting for us when we came out. How could you have—"

"Oh, that was so easy. Didn't you notice that I was the one who maneuvered all of you onto the horse carts? I'd seen that ride before, so I knew how they did it, and even though you had someone to lead the horse through your half, it was different for the cart going into *The Flowers of Xochimilco* side. They didn't send anybody to lead the horse along in that half. I guess the horse knew the way for himself and ordinarily he'd just plod along on his own. So as soon as your cart was out of sight, I got myself a ticket and went into the flower thing—all on my own, you know, just me and the horse and the wagon— Hey! You can't cut into line that way! Wait your turn!"

Mrs. Wilson's anger was turned toward the driver of a battered Volkswagen Beetle who had tried to edge into line ahead of the van. Whether the driver heard her shout or whether he simply spotted a better opportunity up ahead, the Beetle pulled sharply back and wheezed its way two cars farther forward in the queue, where a large white Chrysler braked hard to let the little Beetle duck in ahead. "People are so inconsiderate!" Mrs. Wilson said in a peevish voice. "Wait your turn!" she shouted through the closed window. Then she turned back to Angela. "Where was I?"

Angela had found the release button on one of the buckles and had taken the opportunity during the Beetle diversion to ease the buckle open, so that one of the two straps around her now actually hung free. "Oh look! We're moving again," she said quickly, and as she'd hoped, Mrs. Wilson turned her eyes toward the road as she let the van inch forward once more. Very slowly, very quietly, Angela edged the first strap off her, sliding it silently to the floor beside the wheelchair. "Go on," she said, trying to keep the excitement and hope out of her voice. "You were telling me about how you'd gone in your horse-drawn cart into the—"

"Oh, I remember," Mrs. Wilson said, her eyes still on the traffic. "I wasn't in the same passageway as you people were, of course, but I could hear you whispering and laughing in the passageway that ran parallel to mine. The walls were only made of canvas, after all. So, I stopped my horse and tied him to a pole, I unlaced the canvas from the support, and I slipped through into your corridor. Your cart was stopped right ahead of me as I entered, and you were all goggling at that first display."

"I never saw you at all. I never even heard you!"

"It was pretty dark most of the time, and I came from behind you. As for hearing me, you were making so much noise, all of you gasping and shrieking and carrying on after you saw that first display—I could have sung the national anthem and you might not have noticed. All I did, as soon as the lights flipped off—you know how they went on and off, on and off—well, I just eased up into the seat beside Miss Braintree in the dark and put that pillow over her mouth and nose. And she went limp right away! Then the cart started moving again, so I slid off and went back to my own cart in *The Flowers of Xochimilco*. I even thought to lace the canvas wall back together again the way it had been. Well, maybe not perfectly, but nobody noticed. And then I made my horse really trot through the rest of the flower show, so I was outside before your wagon got maybe halfway through. I even had time to go back into the midway and pitch a few pennies at one of the games before you arrived."

"But the man who sold you the ticket knew you'd been in there. He never said—"

"Oh, for heaven's sake, he didn't care where I went or what I did as long as I paid full price. The point is, I got away with it. Or I thought I did. You say the police know about me. What tipped them off? Or maybe they figured out about Tony. Which one? You've talked to them. What did they tell you?"

"Oh, you're so wrong!" Angela said. "They don't even want you for murder. They just want you for this money-laundering thing. They don't know anything about the murders."

"You're kidding!"

"No, I'm not. Nobody knows about the murders."

There was a long pause while Mrs. Wilson looked straight out into the night. "Nobody," she said softly, "but you."

Maybe Angela still wasn't thinking too quickly yet, what with the drugs in her system. But it wasn't until that moment that she realized she had made a mistake. A *big* mistake. "Well," she said hastily, "Lieutenant Martinez certainly has his suspicions. The only problem was he couldn't do an autopsy."

"Why not? I was sure they'd—"

"Oh, they couldn't, because she was cremated right away when the body got back home. Didn't you know?"

"No! I never asked. How wonderful!"

Mrs. Wilson giggled again and Angela was suddenly chilled with fear. The woman was demented, Angela told herself, and this situation was definitely getting more dangerous by the minute. After these confessions, there was no way the woman would release her after they crossed the border and ... "Oh!" she suddenly said aloud. "Oh wait! I see! You never did mean to let me go, did you? Or you wouldn't have talked so freely about the murders." She wriggled around so that her right hand was in contact with the buckle of the remaining strap that held her into the wheelchair. "You were lying, weren't you, when you said you'd let me go if I cooperated?"

"Well, sort of," Mrs. Wilson said, and her voice was as relaxed and pleasant as though she were talking about the weather. "I mean, first I thought maybe the police didn't know I was involved at all. I heard they'd got Santiago, but he wouldn't tell them anything about me."

"Pedro—"

"Pedro's an idiot! No, you were the only one who might say anything to tie me into the money delivery. So you had to be taken care of. I found out you were in the hospital, and first I thought I'd just slip in and silence you, just like I did Miss Braintree. But then—and here's the clever part, although maybe you probably can't appreciate it—I thought I could turn the whole thing to my advantage in another way. You could be part of my disguise while we crossed the border. You'd do double duty for me, do you see? You'd help me escape, and that would get you out of the way before you had a chance to tell the police about me."

She passed a hand across her forehead and sighed deeply. "Except I guess I shouldn't have told you about the murders, right? Well, don't worry about it. You have nothing to be afraid of as long as I need you. And I need you to be my little granny, just the way I said. Oh, here we go again." The van jerked forward once more in its lane.

"Listen, we're getting close now," she went on. "In a few minutes it'll all be over. So you just remember, when we get up to the guard, you sit there and say nothing. Because I have the gun, and if you don't back me up, or if you try to call for help, I'll shoot, I swear I will. And with all the noise and confusion around here, nobody'd hear the sound of a shot from this tiny gun."

"But then I wouldn't be of any help to you, and—"

"Oh sure you could. I'd say Grandma was taking a nap. Oh," she cooed in a high-pitched, make-believe kind of voice, "don't wake her up. She's so fragile. It'll be nice if she can sleep for the drive home." Her voice changed back into her normal register. "They'd fall for that, I think. It wouldn't be as effective as having you sitting up and looking alive, but I won't hesitate to shoot if you say a word or give any sign, I promise you. So if you want to live to get even as far as the border, you behave. As for what I'll do about you afterward—well, while there's life there's hope, isn't there?"

Angela pinched her mouth together tightly and said absolutely nothing. They were finally at the checkpoint for their lane, and a fresh-faced, youthful redhead in a khaki uniform stepped forward to the driver's side window. He paused beside the van and let his eyes run over its length, from hood to back bumper, before he spoke. "Evening, ladies," he said. No mistaking that they were back in the United States, with that flat, nasal accent. "Anything to declare?"

"Nothing," Maralyn Wilson said. "Not a thing." She let her left hand rest on the wheel, but she put her right hand into her cardigan pocket again, and the outline of the automatic was clear to Angela.

"You didn't buy anything in the shops?" the boy said. "Silver or pottery or anything?" He looked the van over again, and Angela wondered what the problem was. Could there be a big scratch down the side or something?

"My grandmother here is visiting from Kansas," Mrs. Wilson said in a chatty tone, "and she wanted to see

Tijuana. Never been here before. I mean, Kansas is a long ways, isn't it? So we did the shops, but Granny didn't buy anything because she'd have to pack it, you know, and there's only so much you can carry on an airplane, isn't there?"

"I see." The officer's boyish face puckered into a halfway frown. "Where you from in Kansas, ma'am? Ma'am?"

Angela jumped. The young man was looking across the van at her, obviously waiting for her to answer. "I-I-I-uh ..."

"She's from Wichita," Maralyn Wilson said quickly, tapping a forefinger to her temple, then whirling it around her ear, obviously indicating that Granny wasn't running on all cylinders. "Do you know Wichita yourself, officer?"

"Actually fairly well," the officer said pleasantly. He was looking across at Angela again. "You like living there?"

"Oh ... oh, yes," she said shortly.

"What about the wind?" the boy persisted.

"What wind?" Angela said blankly. She moved her right hand to work harder on the remaining buckle, the one that held the last strap in place.

"Well, I remember Wichita as being windy all the time. Not something you could forget about." The boy looked quickly over one shoulder and made some sort of gesture to another of the uniformed men nearby. The second officer was older, heavier set, and he walked as though his feet hurt as he moved around the van to Angela's window.

"Is there some problem, officer?" Maralyn Wilson said.

"Not really," the boy answered. "Ma'am," he was looking at the van again, "how long were you in Tijuana?"

"Oh, just since three. Long enough to visit a few of the shops and have dinner. Granny really liked the meal. Good Tex-Mex, peasant style with tamales and frijoles and everything. She didn't like the guacamole, mind you, but she had at least a taste of everything else on the plate, didn't you, Gran?"

"What?"

"I said, you liked the food, didn't you?"

"Oh. Oh, yes." Angela had found the release on the first buckle easily enough; but this buckle seemed to be a different kind with a different clasp. It didn't want to come loose. And yet, there was a chance, she thought. *These officers being so close on either side of the car ... would Maralyn Wilson dare to pull out that tiny gun and fire with the two men right here? And she'd shoot me first, you can bet. Or no, maybe not. Maybe she'd go for one of the officers first. But if I got them shot, that would be just awful!* Her mind was spinning, but the circles weren't productive of anything except more circles. She became aware that there was a pause in the conversation. Both officers were looking at her.

"Ma'am?" the young redhead was saying. "Can you tell us where you and your granddaughter got hold of this vehicle?"

Maralyn Wilson started to answer. "She wouldn't know, because I—"

"I'm not talking to you," the young officer interrupted her. "Please, ma'am, let your grandmother answer. Where did your granddaughter get this van?" Mrs. Wilson glared and opened her mouth again, but the young officer raised a hand—"Please ..."—and she fell silent once more.

"She ... she bought it in San Diego," Angela said vaguely. "I think ..." She hesitated and realized they were all looking at her intently, the two officers and Maralyn Wilson and for all Angela could tell, several other uniformed customs officers and policemen. What on earth was the problem?

"I wonder if you'd step out of the vehicle, ma'am?" the young officer was saying to Mrs. Wilson. He swung open the driver's door. "Just for a moment."

Maralyn Wilson hesitated, and Angela could read her mind as plainly as though she'd spoken aloud. The woman was wondering whether she should do exactly as she was told and keep up the lies, whether she should just hit the accelerator and try to blast out of there in the van, or whether she should slip out of the van, shoot the officer, and run back toward the Mexican side where they would have trouble pursuing her through the crowd. For a moment, she sat there—working her way through the alternatives, Angela thought. Finally, she appeared to make up her mind. She shrugged and slid tamely out of the door with a smile on her face. To Angela it was clear that the woman had decided on deception; since it had worked well for her up to this point, she would try it again. "Is there some problem?" Mrs. Wilson said sweetly.

Two more officers had approached the van, one beside the young man who seemed to be in charge, another on Angela's side. "Your grandmother is wrong about this vehicle," the boy was saying. "It's a rental with Mexican plates, so you certainly didn't buy it in San Diego. In fact, I'm wondering why you're driving a Mexican rental if you're on your way home. How did you get down here in the first place?"

"Oh. We took the streetcar over," Mrs. Wilson said smoothly. "You know, the red tram. But Granny's tired and I thought this would be easier for her for the trip back."

"And how come," the boy said, "how come you came on a shopping trip wearing your work clothes? Why are you in uniform?"

"Oh! That! Well, I just got off work and I didn't have time to change."

Suddenly and without warning, Angela lost her temper. This ... this veritable child in the khaki uniform just kept standing there asking those stupid, pointless questions, and worse,

Maralyn Wilson seemed to be able to invent an answer for everything he asked. If he didn't wake up, if he didn't get a whole lot smarter in a big hurry, he was going to let them go—let them drive right over into the United States and the Wilson woman would literally get away with murder.

And just at that moment, the buckle holding that last strap let go. The unlatched restraint dropped to the van floor and then everything happened at once: Angela wriggled hastily out of the wheelchair, threw herself across and into the driver's seat, and flung out an impatient hand to yank hard on Maralyn Wilson's black wig. The glossy brunette pageboy went flying off, and Mrs. Wilson's dyed blonde hair, rumpled and mashed from being pushed up under the wig, tumbled messily free.

"Oh! Oh!" One of Mrs. Wilson's hands flew to her head, as though to try to replace the wig; the other flew to her sweater pocket. "You ... you ..."

"I'm not her grandmother!" Angela shrieked at the same minute. "I'm not anybody's grandmother. And the police are looking for her!"

Mrs. Wilson's hand came quickly up out of the pocket and into view—but without the gun. She might be completely mad, but her madness did not include a suicidal streak. Angela's shout, the falling wig, and the presence of four officers standing close to the van had drawn attention from all over the immediate area, and at least a dozen other men—police, border patrol, and customs—had begun to move toward them. Nobody was running, but they were definitely converging. Angela was about to be rescued.

"Well!" she said with deep satisfaction. "It's about time!"

Chapter 16

Thanksgiving Day, November 26

"We have a great deal to be thankful for," Caledonia said, "not the least of which is Mrs. Schmitt! How Camden-sur-Mer was ever lucky enough to attract a chef of her skill ... Angela, have you tried the crab pate?"

"No," Angela shouted from the area of Caledonia's kitchen, "and don't you either. That's for our guests. If you start nibbling early, you'll spoil the arrangement on the plates. Did you say we could use these little glasses with the etched pattern on the side?"

"Sure. Use any glasses you want to. That's what glasses are for. I didn't get them so they'd look pretty on the kitchen shelves, you know."

Angela came into the living room with a tray of glassware that she off-loaded onto Caledonia's dining room table next to a sherry decanter and four plates of hors d'oeuvres. "Light things," Mrs. Schmitt had suggested when Caledonia arranged with her to create a few odds and ends of what Caledonia called "munchies" for a Thanksgiving cocktail party that would precede dinner. And Mrs. Schmitt, who genuinely loved her job, threw herself into planning a menu of finger sandwiches filled with walnuts in cream cheese, a platter of fresh fruits with a sweet-sour dip, tiny meatballs in a mysterious tomato puree with spices that teased the palate and, of course, the wonderful crab pate, surrounded by toast points.

When one is having Thanksgiving dinner at one's home, the turkey and cranberries would probably be served in mid-afternoon, later than lunchtime to allow time for the extra cooking, but early enough that guests would have recovered from overeating before the long trip home began. At a retirement home, where as a rule the big meal of each day is served in the evening, feast days are no exception. Camden-sur-Mer's turkey dinner was scheduled for six, the usual dinner hour, so there was plenty of time beforehand for Angela and Caledonia to meet for their accustomed session of sherry and conversation. But on this occasion, and in celebration of Angela's escape from danger and the threat of death, Caledonia had expanded her usual cocktail hour to include guests. She and Angela had spent nearly two days making their plans, ever since Angela was released from a San Diego hospital, where she'd been taken for examination after her ordeal. It took over a full day of testing before the doctors pronounced her remarkably healthy and concussion free and sent her home, where Caledonia greeted her with the suggestion of the Thanksgiving party.

"Lieutenant Martinez, of course," she started the guest list. "And his partner, Shorty Swanson."

"Oh, and please ask Jerry Grunke," Angela suggested. "That poor man! Imagine my knocking him down when he was only trying to help me!"

"Grunke it is, then. And Tom Brighton, naturally ... he's such a dear."

"Yes, and how about Roger Marx? I feel so sorry for him, having to be told that the woman he's been so crazy about is a common criminal!"

"Not really very common, but that's debatable I suppose. How about Tootsie Armstrong?" Caledonia asked. "She'd be hurt if we had any kind of party and didn't invite her. Besides, we're inviting five men for just the two of us and that seems a little greedy, especially at our ages."

Angela registered surprise. As far as she was concerned, five men—perhaps even six or seven—to every two women was just about the right proportion for a good party. She had grown up in an age of dance cards and stag lines and coming-out parties, and always the fear of being a wallflower. But she agreed that perhaps they should ask Tootsie after all.

"That's almost the whole tour group," Caledonia said after a moment's thought. "You know, I believe I should just bite the bullet and invite the others, too—make it a kind of reunion. Trinita, much as we both dislike her, and the Jackson twins. And Grogan, of course. After all, it would be too much of an insult to invite everybody else and leave those four out. Maybe the Jacksons won't giggle, and maybe Grogan will be sober for a change."

"Bite the bullet? Hah! That's an awfully big bullet to bite," Angela said. "Are you absolutely sure we should?"

In the end, of course, kindness and courtesy won out and all eight of their fellows from the tour were invited to join them at four for a little finger food and a glass of sherry before the big Thanksgiving dinner. They were delighted that when they caught up with him by telephone, Lieutenant Martinez accepted not only that invitation, but their invitation to join them afterward for the holiday meal, although he declined on behalf of his partner, Swanson. "He's having Thanksgiving dinner with the Cassidys. You know—Conchita's family. It's nice that he's fond of his future in-laws."

"But Chita will be busy waitressing here. The entire dining room staff is on duty to serve our Thanksgiving dinner."

"Ah, but they thought of that," Martinez said pleasantly. "I'm told that the Cassidy turkey is being served at one in the afternoon especially so that Chita can be finished with her own dinner in time to help with yours. Swanson has already told Chita that while she's working, he will be resting up from gluttony and enjoying the company of the whole Cassidy family—waiting for her to get back so they can go roller skating. Roller skating! When I was his age, a date meant dancing or the movies. You can't get romantic on skates. Anyway, count him out, though I'll pass the invitation on, and I know he'll be grateful that you thought of him. But for me— I will be your guest with pleasure."

And so promptly at four on Thanksgiving afternoon, Martinez presented himself at the door to Caledonia's cottage apartment in the gardens behind Camden-sur-Mer. One by one the other guests arrived until the room was full of people and it seemed as though not one more could have been worked in. Anybody could have identified this as a festive occasion, even if they could not hear the laughter and the happy voices. The hostesses were dressed to the nines—Angela in a wool crepe suit of pale lavender, Caledonia in a caftan of heavy satin in the bright, jewel tones one associates with stained glass. The male guests were dressed for a party in jackets and ties—most unusual for a California afternoon—and Grogan was relatively sober for a change and even relatively sociable. Tootsie Armstrong's little high heels seemed higher than ever; Trinita Stainsbury was resplendent in pale blue, her hair tinted to match; and the Jackson twins wore identical dresses—the kind of dresses their mother would have identified as "frocks"—of droopy rayon, sporting a lot of ruffles, and from collar to hemline vibrant with their favorite color, pink.

The group was a cheerful kaleidoscope of color and shifting motion, as well as a jumble of noise.

But after several minutes of greeting and small talk, the conversation turned to the subject they were all interested in, and the clamor of voices grew still as they crowded close to listen to Lieutenant Martinez. "Yes," he was saying, "it was a money-laundering scheme and your travel agent ... your tour guide, Maralyn Wilson, was the courier. Unfortunately for your fellow resident Miss Braintree and for the young driver Tony Hanlon, she was also a violent and unstable person who wanted to protect the very good living she was making delivering money for the drug syndicate. She nearly got you, too, Mrs. Benbow, and I am grateful things worked out as they did."

"She said she'd let me go as soon as I helped her get safely across the border," Angela told the assembled group, "but I knew she wouldn't. Because she'd told me all about the murders, you know. So she couldn't afford to let me go. But I believe she was awfully confused. If she'd been thinking straight, she'd never have come near me at all. Why take the additional risk of going to the hospital in disguise? It seems to me that every minute she spent in Mexico exposed her to additional danger of being caught."

"It was a strange thing to do, all right, but with her mentality, it's possible," Martinez said, "that she felt the need to talk to someone who would understand."

"Oh, she talked, all right," Angela said sourly. "She talked from the minute she got me into the van and she never stopped the whole way to the border. I still can't think why, though. It seemed to me such an odd thing to do."

"Well, perhaps since you already knew part of the story from your eavesdr—" He bit his lip and changed the word to something less insulting. "Your overhearing of her conversation, you were in her view an ideal listener. I think I've told you before that many of the people we arrest are desperate to explain themselves to us. Thank goodness that is so, of course. It makes our work much easier."

"What actually happened, Angela?" Trinita asked. "We've never heard it all. The police arranged for Grillo to drive us in the bus, you know, that very night—got us right out of our beds, told us to dress and pack, and sent us on home. But they wouldn't tell us anything about where you were or anything. And Caledonia wasn't with us either. And, of course, you haven't told us anything since you got back Tuesday."

"I was over at the border with Angela, as it happens," Caledonia said. "The police got me out of my bed, too, to take me to Angela. And when I got there, she was talking a mile a minute to a couple of nice young border patrol fellows. Or are they customs officers? I never am quite sure. Anyhow, I could hear her babbling away the minute I got out of the police car."

"I wasn't babbling," Angela protested. "I was trying to explain what had happened. What I'd found out."

"Well, you kept talking about how 'she came right through the wall to get Miss Braintree' and you said 'but I pulled her hair right off her head! I scalped her!'—none of which made an awful lot of sense at the time. It took nearly an hour," Caledonia went on to the others, who had settled into chairs and onto sofas around the room, listening intently, "before I got the straight story myself."

"But the point Trinita was making," Tom Brighton said, running a hand through his snow white hair so that it stood erect like a cockscomb, "her point was that even though Caledonia told us that night at dinner at the hotel that you'd been injured, and that Mrs. Wilson was somehow involved, she didn't fill us in on the details."

"I saved the full story for you to tell," Caledonia said to Angela, who flashed an affectionate smile at her friend.

"So," Tom Brighton went on, "none of us has heard the ins and outs and we really don't know what you're talking about. We've tried to be patient, not wanting to bother you, Angela, especially after they told us you'd been in the hospital in San Diego. But here you are now, and you're obviously perfectly healthy, so can't you give us the story?"

It took a minute to sort out who would narrate what, but finally it was agreed on, and Lieutenant Martinez retold the story of Maralyn Wilson's moonlighting and murdering. Then Angela took over at the point where she followed Maralyn Wilson into *El Mercado Grande,* overheard the tour guide's conversation with Santiago, and finally fled for her life through the jumble of goods piled in the market's aisles.

"And then," Jerry Grunke suddenly spoke up, "I tried to save you. I tried to pull you out of the aisle you were in, away from that fellow who was chasing you, and I got knocked onto the floor for my pains. Mrs. Benbow," he explained to the others, "thought I was working with the bad guys and she rammed me—got me right in the ribs with her head. Knocked the breath out of me and took me right out of the action."

"I really have to apologize," Angela said contritely. "I couldn't see who you were there in the shadows," she lied. She didn't want to admit that she had suspected him all along of being some sort of gangster. "I'm glad I didn't hurt you."

"No, I was lucky. I fell into a pile of serapes in one of those booths. So except for my ... my middle, Mrs. Benbow, you didn't damage me very much."

"Well, I wasn't grateful at the time," Angela said, "just scared. But I want you to know that was really terribly brave of you, and I appreciate it." Jerry Grunke looked at the floor and actually blushed.

"Jerry's not going to tell you people," Martinez said, "that he was decorated for bravery several times while he was a policeman in Los Angeles. And he's not going to tell you he was suspicious of Maralyn Wilson before anybody else was."

"Except for poor Miss Braintree," Trinita Stainsbury said, patting her pale blue hair self-consciously, as though hoping someone would notice the new shade and comment on it. But no one did and she went on, "Of course, Elmira shouldn't have hinted that she knew Mrs. Wilson was up to something odd. That was incredibly foolhardy. You never said anything about thinking that she wasn't on the up and up, did you, Roger?"

"Of course not. I never even suspected her of any wrongdoing," Roger Marx said sadly. "In fact, I don't know if anybody noticed, but I was quite taken with the lady."

The others tactfully said nothing, and most of them tried to look in any direction but his. Caledonia got to her feet, taking advantage of the lull in conversation to pass around the sherry once more. "These little thimbles hardly hold a swallow," she said. "Do allow yourself a second glass, just this once."

"Well, just this once then," Grogan said solemnly, but he gave her a broad wink as she refilled his sherry glass.

Lieutenant Martinez, meanwhile, was staring at Marx with lively curiosity in his glance. "Well, well ... you must be the one, then," he said. "She didn't give us the name, but she told us about you along with everything else she was talking about. She went on and on about how she was forced to commit murder, so it really didn't count—about how she wasn't really involved with drugs, she was just helping out a group of businessmen by carrying all that money, so we shouldn't really look at it as a crime at all—about how she'd really done Mrs. Benbow a big favor by driving her to the border. Nothing she'd done was really a crime and none of it was her fault. Not even your ailment."

"My ailment?"

"Mr. Marx, do you remember the day you became very ill? When you had a case of what you identified as 'Montezuma's revenge'?"

"Why, yes. Did Mrs. Wilson mention that? I was pretty bad off for a while. In fact, I was so weak they thought I might have to return home here by ambulance, but I was finally able to take the bus back with the others, even though I was laid up for two full days, weak and dehydrated. But no permanent harm was done. I'm gratified that Maralyn ... uh, Mrs. Wilson ... was concerned enough to discuss it with you. Although, I suppose I shouldn't be pleased. I mean, considering what she's done and all."

"And considering that she caused your problems," Martinez said.

"Oh, no! That's impossible. The doctor told me it's caused by germs ... microbes ... bacteria ... like that."

"Maybe so, but not this time. You see, Mrs. Wilson had decided you were getting more and more interested in her, sticking closer and closer to her during the first two trips. She was afraid that by the time of the third trip, you might hang around so closely she couldn't get to her appointment with Santiago. So she created your ... your ailment in the hope that it would discourage you from taking that third trip."

"But how?"

"Didn't she arrange for everyone to have hot chocolate for breakfast one morning? She says she sat next to you, and when you weren't watching, she dropped Ex-Lax into your hot chocolate," the lieutenant said, and glared at Caledonia when she first snorted with laughter, then hastily turned her laugh into a cough. The others' reactions ranged from outrage by Trinita Stainsbury to total confusion by Tootsie Armstrong, but most expressed sympathy in one way or another.

"Man, but you were really sick," Tom Brighton said, shaking his head. "I thought you were gonna die. And I was certain you wouldn't want to come with us again on our third trip."

"That was the response Mrs. Wilson hoped to achieve," Martinez said. "But Mr. Marx proved to be stronger physically than she had anticipated. As he says, he recovered in only a couple of days."

"And I thought she was so wonderful," Marx said bitterly, "that I pushed myself to go on that third trip so I could be near her. Believe me, I didn't feel much like risking it, after I was so sick. But I'd have done anything ..." He stopped nervously. "Well, not anything, you understand. I'd never do the kinds of things she did—kill people, and work with the drug syndicate, and—"

"And poison people with laxatives. Listen, I'm sorry I laughed, Roger," Caledonia said. "It's just, that's the kind of thing that happens to little kids who mistake Ex-Lax for candy. I never heard of an adult who ... well, she overdid it, of course. You were awfully sick and awfully weak."

"Mr. Marx," Lieutenant Martinez said, "you mustn't waste your time feeling sorry for her, you know. She is a sociopath."

"I said she was absolutely crazy, didn't I?" Angela crowed. Then, after a pause, "What's a sociopath?"

"One who doesn't care about anyone but herself," Martinez said. "Total selfishness to the point where other people and their lives and welfare have absolutely no meaning at all. Lying, cheating, stealing, murder—none of these matter except as tools to get the sociopath what he wants."

There was another pause, and then Angela said, "The one thing I can't work out at all is how Juan Saenz fits into things."

"Who's Juan Saenz?" one of the Jacksons said.

"Our gardener. The head gardener, actually," Mr. Brighton said. "But what's he got to do with this?"

"Angela kept thinking she saw him all over Mexico," Caledonia said scornfully. "She thought he was following us. I told her she was full of prunes, but—"

"But I did see him," Angela protested. "He was at the carnival in Tijuana. And I followed him down an alley in Ensenada. Of course, he was just going to a cockfight, mind you, but I didn't know that." The others were listening in fascination. "And then I thought I saw him in San Diego, but of course it wasn't him at all, really, was it, Cal?"

"It sure wasn't. And I'm not that certain about the other sightings, either."

"Oh, it was Juan Saenz she saw, all right," Lieutenant Martinez said. "I promised I'd check into him and I have. Mrs. Benbow, when you first caught sight of him, your head gardener was enjoying a month-long vacation. He'd gone for a visit to his boyhood home, Tijuana. He'd taken a niece and nephew to the carnival. Later on in his holiday, he went to Ensenada with two longtime friends to see the cockfights. And then he came back here to San Diego and spent the rest of his well-earned vacation swimming and surfing off Pacific Beach. And as of next Monday, he'll be back here on the job again. You saw him, all right, but he had absolutely no involvement in the drugs or the money laundering, either one. I hope you're not too disappointed."

"Not really," Angela said. "I kind of like Juan. And he's an awfully good gardener. I'm glad he wasn't involved with that awful woman. Well, what now? She goes to prison for murder and kidnapping, right?"

"I'm afraid not, Mrs. Benbow," Martinez said sadly. "At least, not yet. Those murders were committed on Mexican soil, even though she was arrested here in the United States. You two had crossed over the border when she was taken into custody. So she is waiting arraignment now, but on a charge of money laundering. There's plenty of evidence that should convince a jury, and we're looking into other possible charges."

"But she confessed to murder. Something has to be done about that! And she's a kidnapper. Of me. Of course, I guess technically that happened in Mexico, too, didn't it? Oh, dear ..."

"Look," Martinez went on, "here's how it is, even though it may not make much sense to you. If she's convicted as we expect, she'll go to prison for at least three years."

"Three years?"

"Three years is what the federal guidelines say should be the sentence for money laundering. But as I told you, we're going to throw in everything else we can think of, so who knows how long she'll serve? And that's just here, on the charges we can bring. The murder charges in Mexico will still be pending when she gets out. Captain Lopez has agreed that he'll ask for extradition after we're done with her. So don't worry. It isn't as though she'll go free without paying for her crimes, you know."

"But after several years ..."

"There's no statute of limitations on murder, and the evidence against her will be as clear then as it is now. She will not go free." There was another pause in the conversation, broken finally when Angela sighed softly. "And to think I did it all!"

"You did all what?" Caledonia said.

"I got her arrested. When she stepped out of the van, I pulled her wig off so they could see her blonde hair, so they arrested her!"

Martinez smiled at her fondly. "Mrs. Benbow, it's not a crime to wear a wig. A lot of women do it. Frankly, your calling out at the same time, saying the police wanted her, that did almost as much to get their attention, though your de-wigging her certainly helped. It frightened her and made her believe she'd been recognized, so she didn't resist arrest—she just gave up. But let's give credit where credit is due. The truth is that young fellow Callahan was already suspicious of her. That is one sharp youngster."

"Callahan? That was the redheaded kid at the border—the kid in the khaki uniform?" Angela said.

"That's right. By the time he asked her to step out of the van, he had a whole list of things he'd got suspicious of. Her driving a Mexican rental, her going for a day of shopping wearing a nurse's uniform. But mainly it was that she gave him too many details. Every time he asked a question, he didn't get just an answer, he got a three-page essay! That's one of the things guilty people do. Smugglers for instance."

"Smugglers talk too much?" Caledonia was amused. "I'd think it would be quite the opposite. That they'd try to avoid giving full answers and—"

"Apparently, or so the customs people tell me, a guilty conscience makes people struggle to sound normal and ordinary, and a lot of them think that everyday details—what color things are, what they ate for lunch, that kind of thing—those details will sound innocent. Customs folks always watch out for the incoming traveler who tells them a lot of things they don't really need to know."

"Yes, it's true," Angela said, "Maralyn Wilson certainly did that. She talked about what we'd had for supper and how I tried the guacamole. Oh, and I remember she told the young man that I was from Wichita. Wichita!" Angela was indignant. "I ask you, do I look like somebody from Wichita who eats guacamole, for heaven's sake? Of course the boy would be suspicious."

"Well, I don't know about that," Martinez said with a smile, "but Callahan certainly knew something was wrong. He just didn't know what. Then after you shouted out she was wanted by the police, they arrested her and they found the gun in her pocket. You can bet they knew for sure then that this was serious business. All the same, they still weren't sure just exactly what they had. She, on the other hand, thought the same as you did—she was convinced that they'd recognized her. So she just started talking away a mile a minute, trying to get everybody to see her as a victim, explaining that she'd been pushed into what she did—pushed by her need for money, pushed by pressure from Santiago, pushed by your interference. It was everybody's fault but hers. Yes, they warned her not to incriminate herself. So did we, when we finally arrived. But she kept right on—and she may still be rattling away, for all I know, explaining herself to everybody who'll listen."

"Will anybody have another sherry?" Caledonia got to her feet. "There may just be time for one more little taste—"

"Oh, my goodness, look at the hour," Trinita Stainsbury said, rising quickly and moving toward the door. "We've clean forgot we have to go up to the dining room for dinner. So nice to have seen you, Lieutenant, and to hear the details of the story at last. Well, I hate to run ..."

There was a flurry of activity as guests emptied glasses and took their leave, heading up the walk to the main building toward the dining room. Martinez, ever gallant, gave an arm to each of his hostesses, Angela on one side and Caledonia on another, to escort them to their table, now set for three. They beamed as Martinez first held Angela's chair, then moved to help Caledonia settle. It was so nice, the women were both thinking, to have a man with them for a change. Throughout the dining room the staff began to serve plates of turkey and dressing, bowls of mashed potatoes, glass dishes of cranberry sauce.

"There's only one thing about this that's not as good as at home ... they don't show us the whole turkey," Caledonia said. "We get it on our plates already sliced, restaurant style. Not that it isn't good, but I love the look of the bird before it's all cut up— with all that crispy brown, skin and all, and ... Ah, here's our food! Marvelous, Chita. Thank you." Their favorite waitress smiled at them as she delivered each a plate and set the side dishes around on the table.

"Happy Thanksgiving to all of you," Chita said. "Swanson is sorry he couldn't be with you, by the way. He'd have been glad to eat two Thanksgiving dinners, one with my family and one with you. But my brothers had asked him to watch the football games with them while I was working. He says he will write you a note." And she bustled off back to the kitchen to get the next trayful.

"Such a nice girl," Caledonia said.

"I agree, Mrs. Wingate," Martinez said. "Shorty could not do better."

Caledonia picked up her fork in one hand and reached with the other toward the basket of dinner rolls, but Angela stopped her.

"Wait, Cal. We're going to say a Thanksgiving grace together. Do you mind? You know I'm not much for public prayer, but this is a special occasion. I'm safe, we have one of our best friends here with us to share the holiday, you and I are both healthy ... I think we should return thanks."

"Okay," Caledonia said agreeably. "Go ahead. God deserves a good thank-you, now and then."

"Mrs. Benbow," Martinez said gently, "Mrs. Wingate ... may I say the grace? I have much to be thankful for, too, not the least of which is the friendship of you two ladies. And your continued safety." Not waiting for them, he clasped his hands and bowed his head; both of them quickly followed suit. *"Padre nuestro,"* he said softly, *"por comida, por amigos, por salud y por vida, gracias. Para siempre gracias."*

"Amen," Caledonia said.

"Amen," Angela said.

"And by the way," she said happily, I understood everything you said, even if I didn't understand the actual words! Isn't that wonderful? I'm finally learning Spanish! And now ... please pass the cranberry sauce!"

Also Available

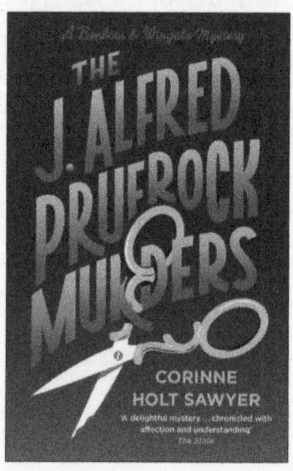

**The J. Alfred Prufrock Murders
(Benbow and Wingate, Book 1)**

Angela Benbow and Caledonia Wingate and two reluctant pals in their retirement community shrug off their infirmities and take to the investigative trail when one of their own, a not-so-sweet busybody named "Sweetie", is found murdered on the beach.

The four not-so-gentle ladies realise what the young investigating officer has trouble accepting – that even the most seemingly docile among them may be provoked into taking a life, even a series of lives, if the pleasure of the time they have left is threatened.

OUT NOW

Also Available

Murder in Gray and White
(Benbow and Wingate, Book 2)

It was the considered view of the elderly residents at the posh retirement community on the California coast that the death by stabbing of Mrs Amy Kinseth (only six weeks after her arrival) occasioned no great loss.

For Angela and Caledonia, live-wire veterans of an earlier murder investigation at Camden-sur-Mer, the case offers a glorious opportunity to have some fun as they help their handsome detective friend, Lieutenant Martinez, with a bit of on-site snooping. It's soon clear that awful Amy had indeed been up to something fishy. And with the killer still on the scene, intrepid Angela may be the next victim …

OUT NOW

About the Benbow and Wingate mysteries

These rousing whodunnits take place in the fictional retirement community of Camden-sur-Mer, in Southern California. In each book, long-term residents Angela Benbow and Caledonia Wingate turn amateur sleuths when one of their fellow oldsters unexpectedly meets an end. And each time Benbow and Wingate realize what the younger police constable fails to realize – that even the seemingly most docile of residents can be provoked to murder when the pleasure of time they have left is threatened.

The full series –

The J. Alfred Prufrock Murders
Murder in Gray and White
Murder by Owl Light
The Peanut Butter Murders
Murder Has No Calories
Ho-Ho Homicide
The Geezer Factory Murders
Murder Olé!

About the author

Corinne Holt Sawyer was born in 1924. She gained a BA in Minnesota in 1945; and later a PhD at the University of Birmingham in the UK, where she lived during 1951–1958. For many years she worked in radio and television, serving as director of broadcasting at WNCT-TV in North Carolina. She also taught English at Clemson University. She is now one of the longest-term residents of a retirement community in Southern California.

Note from the Publisher

To receive background material and updates on further titles in the Benbow and Wingate series, sign up at farragobooks.com/sign-up